Lilamani

A STUDY IN POSSIBILITIES

by

MAUD DIVER

Edited by

RALPH CRANE

OXFORD
UNIVERSITY PRESS

OXFORD
UNIVERSITY PRESS

YMCA Library Building, Jai Singh Road, New Delhi 110 001

Oxford University Press is a department of the University of Oxford. It furthers the
University's objective of excellence in research, scholarship, and education
by publishing worldwide in

Oxford   New York
Auckland   Bangkok   Buenos Aires   Cape Town   Chennai
Dar es Salaam   Delhi   Hong Kong   Istanbul   Karachi   Kolkata
Kuala Lumpur   Madrid   Melbourne   Mexico City   Mumbai
Nairobi   Sao Paulo   Shanghai   Taipei   Tokyo   Toronto

Oxford is a registered trademark of Oxford University Press
in the UK and in certain other countries

Published in India
by Oxford University Press, New Delhi

ISBN 0 19 566622 4

Typeset in Sabon
by Guru Typograph Technology, New Delhi 110 045
Printed by Roopak Printers, Delhi 110 032
Published by Manzar Khan, Oxford University Press
YMCA Library Building, Jai Singh Road, New Delhi 110 001

CONTENTS

ACKNOWLEDGEMENTS

I would like to thank the following for their assistance in the preparation of this edition of Maud Diver's *Lilamani*: the Faculty of Arts and Social Sciences at the University of Waikato for the award of a Research Grant; Ken Arvidson, for re-reading Swinburne, Sarah Shieff, for her useful comments on the Introduction, Joanna Janssen for scanning the text; Betty Ann Kamp, for preparing the map; and Elleke Boehmer, who steered me to the elusive Sorabji references. I am particularly grateful to Radhika Mohanram for agreeing to co-author another Introduction, and to Alexandra Barratt for her invaluable advice on a range of editorial matters.

Thanks, too, and much love to my wife Joy, and my children Callum and Rhiannon, who in various ways live with and support my continuing relationship with India and the Raj.

INTRODUCTION

Maud Diver is best-known as an Anglo-Indian novelist of military life. In works such as the quartet of novels which focus on the Desmond family, *Captain Desmond V.C.* (1907), *The Great Amulet* (1909), *Candles in the Wind* (1909), and *Desmond's Daughter* (1916), Diver draws on her considerable knowledge of the life of Anglo-Indians, particularly in the military stations of the North-West Frontier Province.

Diver's heroes are frequently military men who square with the stereotypes that people imperial adventure fiction—daring soldiers and born leaders like the eponymous hero of *Captain Desmond V.C.*, or Eldred Lenox in *The Great Amulet*. Her plots are usually straightforward, and much of her fiction conforms to the 'skeleton of a typical Anglo-Indian novel'. Bhupal Singh describes in his *Survey of Anglo-Indian Fiction*:

> A typical novel generally begins with a voyage, bringing the hero, more often the heroine, to the shores of India. On her arrival in a Presidency town or a mofussil 'station' she is welcomed by a father, aunt, or some distant relation, and invariably causes a flutter in the small Anglo-Indian colony there. She becomes the belle of the season, is much sought after, and goes through the usual round of Anglo-Indian gaieties. There follow accounts of *burra-khanas*, shooting-parties (generally tiger-hunts), picnics, visits to places of historical interest, balls and dances with their *kala-juggas*, and race-meetings. There are scandals and gossips at the club regarding her 'doings', interlaced with love-rivalries and misunderstandings, and finally everything ends in a happy marriage.[1]

However, in *Lilamani: A Study in Possibilities* (1911), Diver reconstitutes the skeleton in a way many Anglo-Indian readers might have

[1] Bhupal Singh, *A Survey of Anglo-Indian Fiction* (London: Oxford University Press, 1934), p. 2.

thought monstrous. She shifts the site of her romance from India to Europe, supplants the English heroine with an Indian one, and replaces the perfect military heroes of the Anglo-Indian mofussil (rural) stations with a bohemian community of artists.

In *Lilamani* Maud Diver describes the meeting between an English aristocrat, Nevil Sinclair, and a beautiful, high-caste Rajput, Lilamani, and the events that lead up to and immediately follow their interracial marriage. This in itself is not remarkable; there are numerous Anglo-Indian romances that deal with the problems or dangers of cross-cultural love that lead to near marriage or, in a minority of cases, marriage itself. Many of them, including J.W. Sherer's *A Princess of Islam* (1897), A.E.W. Mason's *The Broken Road* (1907), and Donald Sinderby's *The Jewel of Malabar* (1927),[2] were written in the final decades of the nineteenth century or the early decades of the twentieth century. What makes Diver's novel particularly unusual, then, is less that the marriage takes place, than that the *mésalliance* she describes has a happy conclusion. More commonly in Anglo-Indian fiction such connections are fortuitously averted, or, if they do take place, providentially dissolved, frequently (even ideally) by the timely death of the unfortunate Indian woman, as in Diver's own story 'Sunia: A Himalayan Idyll,'[3] where Phil Brodie is left to contemplate the narrow escape he has had from an 'an act of sentimental folly, which would probably have ruined his career'[4] and isolated him from the company of the men and women of his own race.

In stark contrast, in *Lilamani* a marriage between East and West is seen not only to be possible—hence the subtitle, 'A Study in Possibilities'—but, with its happy conclusion, acceptable or even desirable. For Diver, at least in this novel, Kipling's (in)famous line—'*Oh East*

---

[2] In Sherer's *A Princess of Islam* the marriage of George Wilton and Princess Nooroon-Nissa proves to be a terrible mistake; in Sinderby's *The Jewel of Malabar* Sir John Bennville is saved from a similar fate when Kamayala becomes a Christian and enters a convent; in Mason's *The Broken Road* Violet Oliver realizes herself that marriage to Sher Ali would have 'meant ostracism and social suicide.'

[3] 'Sunia: A Himalayan Idyll,' in *Sunia: and Other Stories* (Edinburgh and London: Blackwood, 1913), pp. 1–27.

[4] Ibid., p. 27.

is East and West is West, and never the twain shall meet[5]—is not to be accepted unconditionally. Instead, in this novel she explores alternative possibilities to those offered by Kipling in his negative interpretation of the relationship between East and West. Indeed, her male hero, Nevil Sinclair, believes that binary opposites can sustain rather than repel each other:

> Mighty opposites were they—irreconcilables? By no means. Six weeks of closest intimacy, of spelling out letter by letter the unknown quantity he has taken to wife, inclined him to believe rather that East and West are not antagonistic, but complementary: heart and head, thought and action, woman and man. Between all these 'pairs of opposites' fusion is rare, difficult, yet eminently possible. Why not, then, between East and West?[6]

Different but complementary. Yet it is worth noting the correspondences in these pairs of complementary opposites: heart, thought, and woman; head, action, and man. Despite the novel's apparent nonconformity, Nevil is nevertheless always cast as the dominant partner, Lilamani as the submissive or dependent one. Thus, despite in many ways going against the grain of Anglo-Indian fiction, *Lilamani* maintains the colonizer–colonized relationship, depicting Britain as the dominant partner and India as the submissive one, and even reinforces it in the marriage it portrays between England and India. If Lilamani is presented as an ideal woman, it is because only an *ideal* Indian woman could possibly be worthy of an English husband.

The consequences of this marriage of East and West are explored further in three later novels that complete a loosely-connected Sinclair family quartet: *Far to Seek: A Romance of England and India* (1921), *The Singer Passes: An Indian Tapestry* (1934), and *The Dream Prevails: A Story of India* (1938). Together, the four Sinclair family novels offer the reader a portrait of Anglo-India that encompasses significant Indian characters and the Eurasian baronet, Sir Roy Sinclair, Sir Nevil and Lilamani's son, as well as the more familiar civil and military representatives of the Raj, who are the usual subjects of these

---

[5] Rudyard Kipling, 'The Ballad of East and West,' in *A Choice of Kipling's Verse*, ed. T.S. Eliot (London: Faber, 1941), pp. 111–16.

[6] See Nancy Paxton, *Writing Under the Raj: Gender, Race, and Rape in the British Colonial Imagination, 1830–1947* (New Brunswick, NJ: Rutgers University Press, 1999), p. 194.

fictions, and who we find, for example, at the heart of Diver's Desmond family saga. (Interestingly, members of the Desmond clan feature prominently in the later Sinclair family novels.)

By focussing in *Lilamani* on the life of an Indian, specifically an Indian woman, in Europe and England, rather than on Anglo-Indian life in India, Diver opens the way for an exploration of female agency and mixed marriage within the contexts of both the British Indian Empire and late-Victorian Britain itself. With the advent of the 'New Woman' and the attendant 'Woman Question' in late-Victorian Britain (which she pointedly introduces into the novel), Diver appears to have consciously depicted Lilamani as an embodiment of 'all the feminine qualities that [were] under threat in England.'[7] It is precisely because the novel deviates in these several ways from the usual pattern of Anglo-Indian fiction (including those which deal with mixed marriage), precisely because it does not unquestioningly parrot nineteenth-century views on miscegenation or unconditionally reproduce nineteenth-century theories of degeneration, that *Lilamani* is of interest to the modern-day reader.

The novel does, of course, inevitably follow many of the conventions of romantic adventure fiction, and the stock characters of the genre can as readily be found in *Lilamani* as elsewhere in Anglo-Indian fiction. Nevil Sinclair's sister, Lady Jane Roscoe's racist views echo those voiced by English memsahibs in numerous Raj novels and stories, while Mrs Despard amply performs the less common role of the more liberal or enlightened memsahib. Similarly, Nevil's brother, George, who has served in India with his regiment, is typical of the boors found in both the Presidency towns and the 'up country' stations. Of more interest, though, and what we will focus on in this Introduction, are Lilamani's relationship with Audrey Hammond, and the trope of miscegenation that brings to the fore some complex issues concerning masculinity, femininity, and sexuality in the Empire context.

The interaction between Lilamani and her mentor, Audrey Hammond, under whose patronage she has travelled with her father to Europe, raises important questions about the relationship between British and Indian women. How does the women's movement of the

[7] Indira Ghose, *Women Travellers in Colonial India* (New Delhi: Oxford University Press, 1998), p. 64.

late-Victorian period inflect their relationship? How do racial hierarchies function in the construction of femininity within imperialism? How does the triangulated relationship between British men, British women, and Indian women function in the production of desire?

Overtly, the text devotes very little space to Lilamani's and Audrey's shared relationship. Audrey seems important to the plot only insofar as she gives Lilamani access to Europe, and Nevil Sinclair access to Lilamani. Once she fulfils these requirements of the narrative she is largely written out of the story, reappearing briefly only at the very end of the novel, where we see her once more at the Cap d'Antibes, waiting to return to India, and to 'take up regular work again.' Audrey is not the Victorian Angel in the house; instead she is carefully positioned as the new woman, influenced by the suffragette movement, aware of her abilities to do medical work (that had traditionally been a male preserve), keen to complete 'an article on nerve crises for a semi-scientific magazine,' and free to travel.

During the course of the novel she is variously described as a 'bachelor-girl,' someone who cultivated her 'brain and ego at the expense of the natural emotions,' and a woman who had 'boyish straightness and suppleness of limb.' In contrast, Lilamani is exoticized throughout the text as a 'pale lotus-bud,' a 'purdah lady,' and someone who combines a 'peculiarly eastern mingling of demure aloofness with a delicately direct appeal to the senses and the heart.' Her clothing is similarly exoticized, and frequently described in detail; at the Cap d'Antibes Hotel, dressed in a sari, Lilamani is represented as an exotic bird, 'an iridescent vision of grey and gold, shot through with mother-o'-pearl tints that shimmered changefully when she moved,' whereas the dull plumage of the 'full evening dress' worn by the white women at the hotel is represented as a norm that warrants no particular description. Notwithstanding this exoticization, and the stereotypical racial remarks directed at Lilamani and her father, it is Audrey—unfeminine, unmarried, intellectual, and independent—who is presented as aberrant to the values of Anglo-India perpetuated in the text. Despite the fact that Lilamani is Indian, her femininity and later her worship of her husband make her more acceptable to Anglo-Indian, and perhaps even late-Victorian values than Audrey, who insists on her independence and pursues a traditionally male career.

Though perhaps of minor interest to the early-twentieth-century reader, it is instructive for the modern reader to consider Audrey's positioning in the text in relation to the changing roles of women within the context of British imperialism. While bourgeois women were frequently located as the Angel in the house in the mid-Victorian period, by the end of the century women's roles had started to change. Alongside the suffragette movement, there was increasing demand for university education for everyone, including women, municipal suffrage, marriage-law reform, and the abolition of the Contagious Diseases Acts. In particular, the struggle for the repeal of the Contagious Diseases Acts, successfully led by the feminist Josephine Butler, galvanized the women's movement within Britain, and, when the repeal movement turned its attention to India, eventually led to its direct involvement with the politics of Empire.

The language of imperialism is present in, and in many ways defines, Audrey's relationship with Lilamani: the parameters of cultural superiority, political trusteeship, and modern English behaviour are all carefully established. As Antoinette Burton points out in *Burdens of History*, '[f]or feminists, the British Empire was evidence of the superiority of British national culture and, most important, of the obligations that British women were obliged to discharge—for the benefit of colonial peoples and, ultimately, for the good of the imperial nation itself.'[8] British feminists saw Indian women as helpless victims who lived lives of backwardness. The practice of sati became a metaphor for Indian women's lives and the zenana, where women and girls were secluded, proof of their imprisonment within Indian culture and patriarchy. According to Florence Nightingale, British feminists had to seriously think about their 'stewardship in India,' while for Josephine Butler it was inevitable that British feminists had to next campaign for the reform of prostitution in India. Most importantly, Mary Carpenter insisted on the educational work that needed to be done in India by professional women teachers from Britain. Thus the plight of Indian women became a rationale for explaining the British presence in India, and the alignment of British feminists with imperialism was a means of demonstrating their attachment to national–imperial culture and therefore that they were worthy of

[8] Antoinette Burton, *Burdens of History: British Feminists, Indian Women, and Imperial Culture, 1865–1915* (Chapel Hill: University of North Carolina Press, 1994), p. 7.

suffrage alongside British men. Indeed, British feminism was able to articulate itself especially within the structure of the racial hierarchies enabled by colonialism.[9]

Audrey's relationship with Lilamani is distinctly inflected with the historical nuances of late-Victorian British feminism as well as the parent–child binary of Empire. She feels charged with the role of educating Lilamani so that she can 'do greater things for her self-restricted sisters in a few years than I could do in a lifetime,' and, along with Sir Lakshman Singh, appears to exercise a parental role over Lilamani. In response to her ministrations, Lilamani acknowledges that Audrey, 'the woman she loved and respected only less than her own mother,' 'stood in the place of Mataji.' Interestingly, Mataji's exclusion from the text and the way Audrey replaces her as the maternal figure introduces a second moment of miscegenation into the text, ostensibly positing the 'family' grouping of Sir Lakshman Singh, Audrey, and Lilamani as an alternative nuclear family.

If Audrey, as a British feminist, or New Woman, can access some control over her own future, can she also access control over Lilamani's future? In other words, is the notion of agency only ever gendered or racialized in the text? It is obvious that the British feminist's work in India was predicated on the Indian woman's lack of rights. In *Mother India*, her enormously popular work on Indian women's rights, Katherine Mayo states, 'A girl child, in the Hindu scheme, is usually [considered] a heavy and unwelcome cash liability. Her birth elicits the formal condolence of family friends.'[10] Mayo, an American, was hardly non-partisan in her approach to the topic. *Mother India* was written in 1927 at the instigation of a British officer, J.H. Adams, whom she met in London, and who worked for the Indian Political Intelligence Department which functioned to counteract the growing Indian nationalist propaganda. Mayo's work suggests that unless Indian women were given more rights, India would continue to remain backward and poor. The issues of Indian nationalism and agency were thus explicitly tied to the condition of its women.

Lilamani must be read within its cultural context. Within the framework of Indian women's rights, Lilamani has no agency. Indeed, first her mother arranges her marriage with a man much older than

[9] See Mary Carpenter, *Six Months in India*, 2 vols (London: Longman, Green, 1868).

[10] Katherine Mayo, *Mother India* (London: Jonathan Cape, 1927), p. 60.

her, and then Audrey determines an alternative future in medicine for her. In his cornerstone article on the construction of the Victorian Indian woman's femininity and her rights, Partha Chatterjee points out that the difference between the colonizer and colonized in India, or western and non-western, materialized in a series of binary opposites, outer/inner, material/spiritual, world/home, male/female, which were all paradigmatically linked. The woman, representing the inner life, was given the task of maintaining greater spirituality and also confined to the home. The Indian male, in contrast, was given access to public spaces, but also ones contaminated by western mores, behaviour, and ideas. Maintaining pure Indianness was thus entrusted to the Indian woman, who, under colonialism, was relocated within a neo-patriarchy both Indian and British.[11]

How is Lilamani located within such a configuration? Does she have any agency? For instance, she is undoubtedly submissive towards Nevil, openly proclaiming that 'the measure for an Eastern woman's submission is the measure of her love,' and that 'For the Indian woman religion is all; and marriage is the chief part of that religion.' She is posited as a 'pure Hindu woman in her capacity for sacrifice of self.' As she tells Nevil: 'In my country—husband of every true woman is even as her God,' a sentiment that may recall Milton's *Paradise Lost*, but which is nevertheless meant to be read as outdated in the West.[12] The way Lilamani is constantly exoticized and subordinated renders her mute, suicidal, ill, and almost anorexic, her physical fading miming the way she is silenced by the text and within British imperial culture.

Lilamani's lack of agency is further emphasized by the fact that Nevil does not intend to expose himself to the stigma that would attach to him if he were to visit India as the husband of an Indian woman, or as a man with an Indian father-in-law. The depth of his feeling about India, and more generally the 'East,' is evident during his brief sojourn in Egypt with Lilamani and Sir Lakshman Singh. He may love Lilamani, but he is not at this stage willing to embrace her country or

[11] See Partha Chatterjee, 'The Nationalist Resolution of the Women's Question' (1990), rpt. in *Postcolonial Discourses: An Anthology*, ed. Gregory Castle (Oxford: Blackwell, 2001), pp. 152–66.

[12] John Milton, *Paradise Lost* (1667), Book 4, line 297: 'He for God only, she for God in him.'

her culture, except insofar as he can exploit it for his own profit, whether that be in terms of his wife's slavish devotion to him, or, more literally, as a subject for his art. In this sense he continues to tread the imperial path that has always marked Britain's relationship with India. Anything else would be interpreted as a form of regression or degeneration. It is Lilamani who must make all the sacrifices, and she must make them in the name of advancement.

Here, again, Diver departs from the stock-in-trade pattern of Anglo-Indian romance. As discussed earlier, in most examples of the genre it is the Englishman (or occasionally the Englishwoman, as in E.W. Savi's *The Daughter-in-Law* [1915][13]) who marries an Indian that makes all the sacrifices, risking his career and his (or her) standing in the community. In this novel, though, Diver insists that Lilamani, rather than Nevil Sinclair, is the one who makes the sacrifices, giving up her home, her religion, and her family, in order to marry an Englishman.

What is of particular interest to the modern reader of this novel, written from an Anglo-Indian view point which predates postcolonial studies, is the issue of agency, which is so central to any consideration of race, gender, and nation. We can see that notwithstanding the dislocation of Lilamani from any sense of power or any ability to control her fate, within the frameworks of imperial British feminism, Indian patriarchy, and British patriarchy, the text does offer her a sense of agency, albeit one so faint that it can only be established, negatively as it were, through moments of refusal. The first of these moments is her refusal to marry her mother's choice of a husband, which, we are told, was supported (and thus made possible) by her father, and led to her embracing the alternative of travel to Europe and training in medicine proposed by Audrey. The second moment of agency is, ironically, her refusal to accept Audrey's prescribed role for her in order to marry the man of her choice. In so doing, she appears to move back

[13] Such marriages are rarely brought about, and are inevitably unhappy. More often, the English woman comes to her senses before the marriage takes place, or is persuaded that such a match would be ruinous. In Diver's novel, *The Dream Prevails*, for example, when it appears that Chrystal Adair is in love with the 'Brindian' (an Indian officer of 'good caste' who has been educated in England) Pathan, Sher Afzul Khan, ironically the mixed-race hero, Sir Roy Sinclair, persuades her that such a marriage could never work.

towards the traditional role of wife initially offered to her by her mother—but with a difference. By exercising choice, by opting for a love-match rather than an arranged marriage, Lilamani appears to be permitted a degree of agency. Yet if the Indian woman's confinement to interior spaces is read as lacking the freedom that her English counterpart enjoys, Lilamani's embracing and creation of 'the Inside', or zenana, and the establishing of her shrine at Sir Nevil's ancestral home, Bramleigh Beeches, suggests that notions of agency should not be read in a literal way, but through the framework of the politics of difference. Rather than signalling a lack of agency this is another moment when Lilamani's agency is predicated on a refusal, this time her rejection of the role of English wife, which highlights the trope of miscegenation.

The trope of miscegenation or race-mixing is, of course, central to the mixed marriage that lies at the heart of this novel. It is important to unpack this trope in the text because the reconfiguration of British and Indian masculinity and femininity, all seem to converge around Lilamani's marriage to Nevil Sinclair. Further, miscegenation functions as a taboo in this text as it does throughout Anglo-Indian fiction. However, as Kenneth Ballhatchet points out in *Race, Sex, and Class under the Raj*, historically this had not always been the case. In the seventeenth century there were many inter-racial sexual liaisons, which were actively encouraged by the East India Company to facilitate British and Indian interactions, and which in time led to an increase in the Eurasian community in India.[14] Nevertheless, by the late-nineteenth century, racial hierarchies strictly underpinned comprehensions of British and Indian interactions. In fact, the so-called Indian Mutiny of 1857 was instrumental in solidifying this taboo as it shifted the meaning of British masculinity by reconfiguring it within a militaristic framework: adventurous, athletic, and with an emphasis on homosocial bonds between men. This reconfiguration, constructed on the terrain of colonialism, also meant that British masculinity appeared to be in a diacritical relationship to Indian masculinity. In other words, both British and Indian forms of masculinity seemed to be constructed in relation to each other rather than in relation to their

[14] Kenneth Ballhatchet, *Race, Sex, and Class under the Raj: Imperial Attitudes and Policies and their Critics 1793–1905* (London: Macmillan, 1980), p. 96.

respective femininities. If British masculinity became more militaristic, then Indian masculinity, following the events of 1857, became more duplicitous and untrustworthy.

Racial hierarchies between white and brown men are articulated in the text through the figures of Nevil Sinclair and Sir Lakshman Singh. Though the latter is older than Nevil, he is frequently (though not quite always) presented as deferential to his white son-in-law. The text posits Sir Lakshman Singh as an acceptable Indian (just as it posits Lilamani as both dutiful and beautiful) in order to make the miscegenation palatable to its readers. Sir Lakshman Singh is positively portrayed as an enlightened Indian primarily because he is so strong a supporter of Empire, and recognizes the superiority of British culture. He is Diver's idea of a perfect Indian precisely because he believes absolutely in British rule in India. Significantly, during a discussion of Indian nationalism, it is Sir Lakshman Singh who urges a strong hand to deal with anti-British agitation in India: 'In my belief . . . no worse harm could befall to India than that Great Britain should cease to be paramount power. But only this—in order for being paramount she must be, in the best sense, a *power*.' Like Rudyard Kipling, Diver has no room for pro-nationalist voices in her fiction. For all its liberal views on inter-racial marriage, *Lilamani* frequently demonstrates what Benita Parry calls Diver's strident 'pride in the British as a master-race.'[15]

The modern reader influenced by the cultural and theoretical discourses within postcolonial studies is struck by the fact that, notwithstanding the text's desire to keep racial differences foregrounded in the story, and to maintain the British as superior within any context of race-mixing, *Lilamani* simultaneously seems to posit that both races are mutually interdependent. The text posits a more syncretic viewpoint. The textual strategy of undercutting that which it appears to valorize and hold dear is present throughout and causes interesting ambivalences in the text. For instance, it attempts to circumvent the horror of miscegenation by positing Audrey as a possible wife for Nevil. However, Lilamani and Nevil's growing intimacies become utterly problematic for Audrey right at the beginning of the narrative.

[15] Benita Parry, *Delusions and Discoveries: Studies on India in the British Imagination 1880–1930* (Berkeley and Los Angeles: University of California Press, 1972), p. 70.

Interestingly, modern readers recognize the ambivalence in the novel as they are never sure whether Audrey is jealous of Lilamani's conquest of Nevil, or of Nevil's conquest of Lilamani. The conflation of Audrey's desire for Lilamani to be remade in her image with that of her desire for Nevil as well as that for Lilamani gives the text an ambiguity which foregrounds the escape of rigid gender and sexual boundaries in the text. Furthermore, the maintenance of rigid boundaries between Britain and India is once again scrambled when Nevil seems to disregard anything that has to do with India with the exception of his wife. However, he is soon dependent on ideas about, and attitudes to, India in his very work. His reputation as a painter and his ideas for painting are predicated on Indian mythology, so much so that the *Ramayana* paintings and Lilamani's shrine room become prominent features of Bramleigh Beeches. This aspect of the novel, which can be read as an invasion of the metropolis by the colonies, points to a wider crisis of Empire rather than a crisis pertaining to the Sinclair family alone. Soon, race-mixing in the novel is overtaken by a mixing of ideas that seem to get away from the social and cultural limitations Diver attempts to place on her novel. If Sir Lakshman Singh is an acceptable Indian because he is almost white, then Nevil establishes his reputation as a painter because of his Indian ideas. And by accepting his wife's husband-worship and the Indianization of Bramleigh Beeches, Sir Nevil himself is relocated as an Indian husband, and effectively feminized. Thus, notwithstanding the valorization of Anglo-Indian values and the superiority of whiteness in the authorial comments in the text, it is precisely the collapse of the boundaries within gender and race hierarchies that renders *Lilamani* fascinating to the modern reader.

University of Waikato   Ralph Crane
Cardiff University   Radhika Mohanram

A NOTE ON THE TEXT

This edition of *Lilamani* is based on the edition published by Hutchinson & Co. in 1911. Typographical conventions of the time have been maintained as modernization is not needed to make the text accessible. Words no longer in current use have been glossed in the Explanatory Notes. Obvious typographical errors have been corrected silently.

As the Explanatory Notes aim to offer geographic and cultural background detail that will be useful to both Indian and non-Indian readers, some annotations will inevitably appear redundant to some readers.

A CHRONOLOGY OF MAUD DRIVER

For this outline I have drawn heavily from *Edwardian Fiction: An Oxford Companion*, ed. Sandra Kemp, Charlotte Mitchell and David Trotter (1997); and *The Oxford Guide to British Women Writers*, ed. Joanne Shattock (1993).

Little information about the life of Maud Diver (1867–1945) has been published. She was born in India, sent to Britain for her education, and returned to India at the age of sixteen. In India, like so many of the heroines of Anglo-Indian fictions, she married a sub-altern. Diver only began to write her stories and novels about Anglo-Indian life after she had left India permanently and moved to England in 1896. Her writing career eventually spanned five decades.

1867	9 September, Katherine Helen Maud Marshall born at Murree, Northern Punjab, India, eldest daughter of Colonel Charles Henry Tilson Marshall (1841–1927) of the Indian Army and Laura Frances Pollock (1846–1912)
1883	returned to India aged 16, after education in England
1890	25 March, married Thomas Diver, subaltern in the Royal Warwickshire Regiment, later Lieutenant-Colonel (d. 1941)
1892	11 April, son Cyril Roper Pollock Diver born
1896	settled in England, began writing short stories for a variety of magazines including the *Pall Mall Gazette*, *Longman's*, *Temple Bar*, *Cornhill Magazine*
1907	first novel, *Captain Desmond V.C.* published
1908	*The Great Amulet* (novel) published

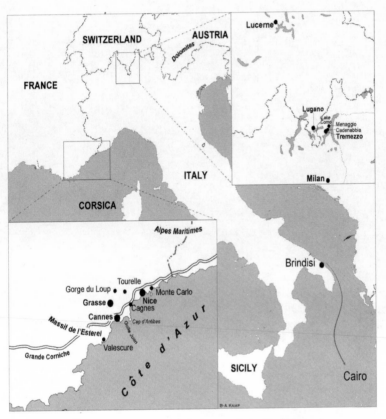

Map showing European places mentioned in *Lilamani*

Lilamani

A STUDY IN POSSIBILITIES

'To hold by leaving; to take by letting go,
Leaving and again leaving, and ever leaving go of the surface of things;
So taking the heart of them along with us—
This is the Law.'

—Edward Carpenter

To You

Who have always sympathized,
. Always believed, always understood,
I dedicate this book.

—M.D.

'There is a collaboration loftier and more real than
that of the pen. It is the collaboration of thought
and example.'

—Maeterlinck

BOOK ONE

The Seed

ONE

'I stay my haste, I make delays,
For what avails the eager pace?
I stand amid eternal ways—
And what is mine shall know my face.'
—Burroughs

'Where on earth did she spring from? And who, in the name of all that's exquisite, can she be?'

Nevil Sinclair asked himself the question, with quite a keen touch of curiosity, as he sat idly smoking under the araucarias that front the Cap d'Antibes Hotel. A slim, clean-cut figure of a man, with long sensitive hands, a mobile face, and thoughtful eyes where a smile lurked always like a beam of light. He looked round in search of information. But no one was at hand to enlighten him, and his gaze reverted to the vision on the corner balcony; a vision unusual as it was arresting to an artist's eye and brain.

The olive skin faintly aglow, the velvet darkness of eyes that brooded upon sky and sea, were framed in a gold-bordered *sari*, pale as an evening primrose, that half veiled without hiding the sweet seriousness of the girl's face. These, and her aloofness from the chattering teadrinkers in the verandah below, conspired to give her an alluring air of unreality; and her purely Eastern stillness, in that temple of unrest, a Riviera hotel, enhanced the effect.

Sinclair had leisure to approve the delicate curves of brow and cheek and nostril, the slender symmetry of the hand and arm resting on the balcony's ledge, the classic poise and outline of the veiled head. For all the gravity of her eyes, a hint of passion in the ripe lower lip, and of wilfulness in the round chin that matched it, promised just those varying elements of light and shade that would some day make her all a woman. At present she seemed little more than a sheaf of possibilities; a bud half open awaiting the strong kiss of the sun. And behind her loomed the wide, white façade of the Hôtel du Cap, uncompromisingly square and solid; as it were the House of Life with its hundred rooms, and hundred complications, old as the sea, yet eternally changeful as the myriad waves thereof.

Sinclair had dallied with love in more than one form, even as he had dallied with art and life; reaching the core of none. But art had lured him farthest; and he saw this child of an alien race rather as a possible picture than a possible woman. Her absorption tempted him: so also did the sketch-book on his knee. He opened it, and paused—looking upward. The thrill of inspiration was on him: a visitation too rare, too imperative to be ignored. There was also the insidious joy of yielding to temptation. Out came the pencil, and he went swiftly and skilfully to work. Naturally she moved the moment stillness was essential. But it was only to set an open book upon the ledge and give him an instant's fuller vision of her face. Then, her cheek lightly resting on her hand, she fell into a pose more lasting, more enchanting than before.

'Ye gods! I'm in luck!' the Englishman muttered; and worked on.

Slowly the sun dipped behind the araucarias and the lofty blue gums, with their slender, listless leaves. Slowly the shadows engulfed the gravel path. The militant snortings and puffings of motors, that bore away chance visitors, sounded faint and fainter in the deepening quiet, and the chatter of tea-drinkers was hushed. Those that were not chance visitors took unto themselves books, work-bags, shawls, and strolled down the wide, tree-bordered road to the coast-line of tumbled rock that gleamed, grey-white, against the blue enchantment of the Mediterranean. The Princess from the Arabian Nights watched them, as they went, with eyes that questioned and wondered and dreamed. Then she reverted to her book; and Sinclair to his sketch.

Slight though it was, instinct told him that—in years of promising and even distinguished amateur work—he had never come so near to 'the real thing.' Be she Princess or Peri, by some means he must get speech of her, and win leave to convert his sketch into the picture—long dreamed of yet never achieved—that should prove him indisputably an artist, and bring home to the father, who would fain have him a politician, the futility of trying to force a square peg into a round hole.

He had left England mainly to escape a political 'gathering,' organized for his benefit at the country house of an elder sister. Lady Roscoe, wife and daughter of politicians, lived and moved and had her
being in the strenuous atmosphere of party politics. 'More party than
politics,' Nevil averred—but not in her hearing. Like her father, she
could appraise pictures, books, music intelligently enough; could
even enjoy them in the rare moments when she was socially and poli-
tically 'off-duty.' And, like her father, she had a tendency to scorn the
creators of these superfluous delights. It was a case of 'music and pictures must needs come. But woe unto him through whom they come.'
Authors she could condone, provided they were not poets and had
achieved material success. Journalists she almost venerated. Without
them where would be the newspapers that were her daily bread? Such
were her views in regard to ordinary mortals. But that a Sinclair, and
an eldest son to boot, should associate himself professionally with
anything of the kind was an innovation against which she set her typi-
cally Sinclair face like a rock.

The Sinclair men—and a distinguished line of them stretched backward through a score of generations—had so far been singularly free
from such vagrant impulses. But family traditions, however sacro-
sanct, are lamentably at the mercy of individual impulse; and a woman of poetic temperament had cast her spell upon Nevil's father, the
present Sir George, luring him from sage consideration of Sinclairs to
come. Such, at least, was Lady Roscoe's version of the matter. Any
other had seemed to impugn the wisdom of the man in whose image
she herself was made. She preferred to shift the burden of responsibility on to Lady Sinclair, who had been gone long enough to be exemp-
ted from the kindly fiction that the dead can do no wrong.

Yet wrong or no, she had seriously inconvenienced the house of
Sinclair by bestowing her own name and nature upon the first man
child she had gotten from the Lord. On him, too, she had expended
her repressed genius for devotion—as little understood of her husband as any other form of genius. For nine years the boy had been
hers, body and soul, and in those years the man was made. Not all the
after influences of school and life could efface the stamp of her personality on the child she had so loved. But Nevil had a streak of Sinclair in him also. Hence complications. Fondness for his father and

dominant elder sister made him shrink from disappointing them; while he shrank, yet more, from the path worked out for him by tradition, and by ambitions that were not his own.

So it came about that Lady Roscoe's letter of a week ago, hinting at a house-party that might prove profitable in view of the General Election looming ahead, had spurred her refractory brother in quite the wrong direction. Scenting fresh schemes for his political salvation, he had wired straightway for his favourite room in the Cap Hotel, and had fled to the South of France, on the wings of an express, to paint Antibes sunsets, and possibly Italian fishermen; and, if the Muse were kind, add a few poems to the small volume he had in hand. The kindness of the Muse had taken a form quite other than he sought; for the which he blessed her fervently, while the sketch grew under his hand and inspiration fluttered nebulous wings in his brain.

'By Gad—it's not half bad!' he muttered, surveying it at length, with a rare glow of satisfaction. 'Martino shall see it—to-morrow.'

Then, from the tail of his eye, he discerned a slim grey figure at the foot of the wide steps; he looked round started, and sprang up, hastily pocketing his treasure. The girl in grey started and quickened her pace. But she was not of the type that scurries. She merely took a longer stride that accentuated her boyish straightness and suppleness of limb.

Sinclair greeted her impulsively. 'Why, Miss Hammond! *You* back again, too, at the dear old "Cap"? What luck!'

She smiled upon him frankly with clear eyes, almost as grey as her dress, and, being observant, he noticed that her hand had grown harder to the touch since he held it last.

'It used not to be "Miss Hammond" in the old days,' she said as they sat down. 'I am still Audrey—to my friends.'

'Audrey, then—by all means! I didn't dare, at first sight. We have grown up so aggressively since then. And you've been doing great things in India, I suppose—doctoring, riding, dancing?'

'Not a great deal of the last,' she answered cheerfully. 'As a rule, I felt too done up by the evening. Hyderabad isn't exactly bracing; and my life out there was a very full one.'

'Ah!'—a shadow of envy lurked in his tone. 'And mine, at home, has been quite the reverse. I often thought of you, and your progressive schemes, and wondered whether doctoring zenana ladies had modified your advanced views on the Woman Question, or whether you had fired them with a craving for the Suffrage—or its Eastern equivalent!'

Audrey Hammond laughed outright. 'How little you know of me or of them, poor dears, to imagine either! My own views have not retreated one inch; and as for them—well, I did more than doctor them. I taught a few, and helped—in other ways, when the chance offered. Rather like trying to alter a coastline by shifting pebbles on the shore. Still—one may have done *some* good; let a little light into their custom-ridden souls. But I won't tax your good-nature by boring you with such things——'

'Which means that they are too sacred to be discussed with a mere man; even an old friend who has come within sight of the thirtieth milestone since we lazed and argued on this enchanted headland four years ago.'

'And has not yet achieved a seat in Parliament, or a picture on the line?' she queried, slipping past the point at issue with the self-possessed ease of her type.

'Neither,' said he, and opened his silver cigarette case as one in search of consolation. 'The good old man at home is still hopeful. Jane, the indefatigable, will not suffer the temples of her head to take any rest till she has cajoled me into swallowing the gilded political pill. But the failure of the family remains where you left him——' He paused to light his cigarette, and the girl scanned his well-remembered face and figure with kindly critical eyes, that, like her hands, were a trifle too hard for her years.

Her silence was more pregnant than speech; and he looked up again quickly with a disarming smile.

'You disapprove, of course. We never did agree about things, did we? Which was just why we couldn't resist discussing them! I'm not "indifferent to my country's welfare," as Jane assures me in her most parliamentary voice. The larger issues interest me enormously. But minor details of legislation weary me to death; and I confess I feel no serious call to take an active part in "the savage wars of peace" that can be waged very effectually without my lukewarm assistance!'

She smiled in spite of disapproval.

'Have you ever in all these years felt a serious call of any kind?'

'Frankly, I can't say I have,' he confessed without shame; the twinkle deepening in his eyes. 'Too many-sided, perhaps; or too little call to exert myself. That's the curse of the ready-made income, plus family records! But I've not been altogether idle while you tried to hustle the East. I've written a fair sheaf of essays and verses; painted a few decent pictures, read widely and knocked round Europe with my eyes open——'

She waved aside his list of mild 'achievements.'

'Mere dilettantism! In a world full of work worth doing, and wrongs crying out to be set right!'

'Hear, hear!' he applauded, with his most imperturbable smile. 'Spoken like the "Minerva" of old times! Study the "Apology for Idlers," Audrey. That's my credo—if I have one. After all, there must be a few of us, if only to keep the balance of things. And since a million or so of women have waxed strenuous or nothing, what can the superfluous male do but sit mutely admiring and look on!'

'A rôle for which he gets finely trained at school—watching cricket and football!' she retorted with a touch of heat.

'Yet even there I seem to remember that now and then he gets out into the field and kicks or slogs the ball to good purpose. Some day, even I may get out into the field too, when I really discover a ball worth kicking, or a game worth playing.'

'You call yourself an artist and talk so——'

'Pardon me. I call myself a double-distilled amateur.'

'Oh—you are as exasperating as ever!—I mean—you care for your art. At least—I thought——'

'So did I, worse luck! But the Fates must have quarrelled badly when I was born, so that all my threads came out tangled. And they had not even the grace to endow me with a gift for unravelling tangles; or with enough selfishness to go my own way in spite of my dear old father's prejudices. For him, my art is "futile piffle"; a decorative hobby that has helped to keep me out of mischief—or so he believes. For me, it is the one thing on earth that might have been worth doing; would have been if—if my mother had lived——'

She turned on him—rebellious and decisive.

'Don't be weak-minded and shift the responsibility. If it would have been, it *is*, still.'

'You forgot the long apprenticeship, the great gulf that divides the artist from the amateur. If my spell in the *Quartier Latin* taught me nothing else, it taught me that.'

'You could go there again—why not?'

'Oh, for a score of reasons. And I'm almost too old for it now. Every idle year that slips by puts achievement farther out of reach. Inspiration grows rarer. Which reminds me—you interrupted one just now.' And he glanced towards the balcony, fearful lest his vision had fled.

No. She had merely deserted her book, and leaned over the parapet watching them with absorbed eyes. Then, as Audrey Hammond looked up also, she smiled and waved her hand.

'You know her?' Nevil cried eagerly, and Miss Hammond's brows went up ever so little.

'Certainly, I know her. I am more than half responsible for her being here. And was she responsible—for the inspiration?'

A faint change of tone checked the artist's impulse to produce his work; and he merely answered: 'Yes. I was trying to make a sketch of her when you came up.'

Miss Hammond frowned. 'That was a mistake. I am glad I interrupted. They would hate the idea.'

'And who are they?'

'She and her father—a high-caste, cultivated Hindu gentleman. I came home with them.'

'But when did you arrive? That should have been my first question! Just like us to plunge headlong into an argument without playing How, When, and Where? I never saw you at dinner last night.'

'No. We are wealthy and exclusive! We have private rooms and feed upstairs. The daughter is the one tangible, practical result of my three years' crusade. She has been plucky enough to break through the hampering laws of purdah and caste; and is still rather shy and bewildered with it all. But at least she is here, studying medicine, under my guidance—for the present.'

'Studying medicine! That beautiful child——'

The masculine implication annoyed her.

'Well, why not? Because she is beautiful, or because she is a child?'

'Oh, a little of both. Of course, I am an ignoramus about such matters, and you're quite the reverse, only——' He glanced again at the embryo student of medicine. His vague recoil from the idea did not readily phrase itself under the quiet challenge of Audrey's grey eyes.

'What is the rest of the programme?' he ended lamely 'The final goal in view?'

'You are really interested?'

'Immensely. Catholic tastes breed catholic interests. Call it dilettantism if you choose. Well?'

'My hope is, of course, that when I have put her in the way of things, she will go to college and take a degree. Then she will go back to India—and move mountains! Her loss of caste can be restored by ceremonies of purification; and she will do greater things for her self-restricted sisters in a few years than I could do in a lifetime. The more one sees of Indian life behind the scenes, the more one realizes that the ideals and aspirations of the West can only be instilled into Easterns *by* Easterns—not by foreigners. One can only hope to make some impression on units, and trust them to carry on the larger work.'

A rare glow of enthusiasm transfigured her face; she looked almost beautiful. Nevil, though still unconvinced felt a sudden pang of envy. This was the quality he lacked; this, and the invisible assurance that vibrated in her voice.

At that moment the Princess, who would be a doctor, left the balcony. Both followed her with their eyes. Then Nevil spoke.

'And has she caught fire from your zeal?' he asked half anxiously.

'Only in part, so far. But once her foot is on the ladder, that will come. It was her own wish, and I believe she will carry it through. They have a fund of character and courage that would surprise you—those gentle, dreamy-looking Indian girls who have seen nothing of life outside their own walls. But I must go up now. Lilimani may be wanting me.'

'Lila—how much?'

'Lee-la-mun-nee,' Audrey said slowly; and he, repeating, it after her: 'Was there ever a more musical name? The lilt and the rhythm of it! I hope it has a meaning to match.'

'I don't know about matching! *Mani* is jewel, and *lila* Sanskrit for delight.'

'Jewel of Delight,' he mused aloud; and she, with her practical briskness:

'Yes. Rather too fanciful, isn't it? Eastern names are apt to be.— Well, good-bye till to-morrow.'

'Why not to-night? Do they never come down?'

'Not in the evening; at least, not as yet. Lilamani is still ridiculously shy. *I* should insist. But her father says "not till she wishes it herself."

He spoils her; idolizes her. When he is gone, I shall have a better chance.'

'Well—introduce me, will you, when they do come down. New types are interesting.'

Thought of his unfinished sketch imparted a veiled eagerness to the casual request; and Audrey, noting it, smiled her inscrutable smile, that too rarely invaded her eyes.

'Sir Lakshman Singh often comes down, and is very well worth talking to,' said she. 'As a young man he spent several years at home; studied at Cambridge, I think. And though he still remains within the pale of Hinduism, his whole view of life is admirably sane and broad. The girl has mainly been taught by him. But with all her free and fearless mental outlook, her actual emancipation is still not much more than skin deep; and being a well-bred Hindu girl she naturally shrinks from promiscuous talk with strangers, especially men——'

'Surely—as an old friend of yours—I might be privileged.'

'Possibly. We'll see. But, Nevil, you must tear up your sketch.'

He started visibly. 'Great Scott—that's a pretty cool request. And why on earth——'

'Oh, for a dozen reasons. I told you they would hate the idea; and "one can't spend the day in explanations,"' she quoted with a little nod of friendly decision. 'It's really very nice to find you here again. *Au revoir.*'

She ran lightly up the steps into the wide hall; and Sinclair stood looking after her in a mixed frame of mind—expectant, interested, yet vaguely annoyed. He liked her greatly; always had done. He had felt a real glow of pleasure in meeting her again. He admired her pluck, her single-mindedness, her unobtrusive strength; all of which had been emphasized by four years at grips with stern realities. In those four years she seemed to have grown older than he; had done so, in fact, since the soul's calendar is measured by acting and doing, rather than by months and days.

Yes. He admired her as much as ever. But he did not approve her scheme for conjuring a lady doctor out of an Arabian Nights Princess; and no word of hers should induce him to destroy his latest-born— his gift flung straight from heaven; earnest of greater things to come.

'The new hath come, and now the old retires:—
And now the soul stands in a vague, intense
Expectancy and anguish of suspense,
On the dim chamber threshold. . . .'

—Sarojini Naidu

'Tired of studying, my pale lotus-bud? No need yet to do too much. We are here for rest!'

Sir Lakshman Singh put out a welcoming hand and drew his daughter towards him. A creature of infinite grace she seemed in her primrose-pale dress and *sari*, that clashed oddly with the setting of a modern hotel sitting-room. Not tall; though her slenderness and up-rightness, as of a young palm, gave an illusion of height, and her movements had the leisured, rhythmic quality that comes to fullest flower in the East.

Now she crouched kneeling, with a small, glad sigh, by the great arm-chair in which her father sat; his own light English suit and jade-green turban aptly symbolic of the dissonance within. At the meeting of their eyes soul spoke plainly to soul: too plainly for the man's peace of mind. He, like Sinclair, had his doubts about the scheme, accepted by him as the one way out of an *impasse*, typical of India as she is to-day.

His wife, orthodox to the bone, had rebelled fiercely against the Anglicizing of even one daughter out of three. But for a time the will of her husband had prevailed. The child had been his own, to make or mar, till the question of betrothal could no longer be deferred. Then did outraged orthodoxy assert itself with power. For there be two autocrats in the Hindu home: the mother and the family Guru; the holy man, who carries good or ill in the hollow of his hand. These, between them, had discovered a bridegroom, elderly and dissolute

but wealthy and of unimpeachable caste; a sinner rigidly conservative, whose eagle-nosed mother might be trusted to reclaim a spoilt
daughter-in-law and cure her of new-fangled follies. Reports of Lilamani's beauty fired the bridegroom to impatience; and the matter was
formally set on foot.

But they reckoned without the daughter of new India, and the
blood of Rajput fighters in her veins. Lilamani—proud, wilful, and
lightly disciplined—would have none of him; and her father, after
heart-searchings and vain pleading with the autocrats, had refused his
consent. Followed a slow, implacable battle of wills, till the girl's
health gave way under the strain, and Lakshman Singh, distraught
with anxiety, had insisted upon calling in Miss Hammond—caste or
no. It was then that Audrey had seen her chance of enlisting an Eastern
recruit. Why should the girl marry at all? Why not complete her unorthodox education by studying medicine at home, and returning, in
due time, to help those who were so pitifully unable to help themselves? It was a daring suggestion: but Sir Lakshman had caught at it,
as a drowning man at a straw. To Lilamani—bruised and broken from
the storm—it seemed as if a gate had been opened into Paradise. And
Audrey Hammond had her way.

Thus it had come about that at last—in the teeth of stormy reproa-
ches and bitter opposition—the three peaceful-looking rebels had set
sail for France and the sun-smitten headland where Audrey herself
had recruited after hospital training. Such heroic snapping of chains
is still comparatively rare among high-caste Hindu women; and
Lakshman Singh—for all his admiration of the best in English thought
and life—felt not a little anxious as to the ultimate fate of this daughter, who was in truth as well as in name his Jewel of Delight. In the beginning it was much that health and gladness once more had their
home in her checks and eyes. For the rest, he was content to wait, and
watch the confluence of her clear spirit with the complex spirit of the
West. And at least they were together without let or hindrance: which
sufficed.

He slipped an arm round her crouching form; and she, with the
light laugh of a child, leaned nearer, one tapering finger at her lips.

'Breathe it not to Audrey, father mine. But all thought of study has
been far from me. The book she lent me had ugly words in it; and in
all this loveliness they seemed to hurt my mind, even as an ink-blot on

my *sari* would hurt my eyes.' Slipping her fingers beneath a gold-flecked corner, she regarded it with grave tenderness, then turned to him again, her sensitive face alight. 'Oh, father—how it is beautiful, the way of the sun upon the sea! As if for very love, he had flung himself into the deep blue heart of it; and the sea godlings had bewitched him into a million golden butterflies with tireless wings that yet cannot bear them aloft——'

'And was that the sum total of your studies, child of learning?' the man asked, smiling at the quaint conceit. 'Was there not a book also? Twice I passed under your balcony. But you never looked up, nor even turned the leaf; and I thought I would speak to Miss Hammond that until you were stronger she should not press you too hard.'

'Kindest! It is true there was a book. But not hers. The way of the brain had wearied me. So I followed instead the way of my own heart—and I was happy.'

'That is always good hearing,' spoke the father, whose idolatry stood in Audrey Hammond's light. 'Yet, remember, Light of my Life, the way of the heart too seldom winds up the hill of achievement.'

'It is the way of all true women, none the less,' answered she of seventeen summers with a low-toned passion of conviction, that was in itself a tragedy, seeing that her own feet were set upon a stonier path.

Words and tone smote the father's heart. Bending his head to hers, he spoke softly in his own tongue. 'Lilamani, dost repent?'

And she, in the same tongue, while sudden tears pricked her eyeballs: 'Nay. I chose the lesser of two evils, and—I look not back. That is for weaklings: not for the daughter of Lakshman Singh. But—if there might have been talk of another bridegroom——'

'Child, child—that I feared. I spoke of it to thy mother. But thou knowest how it is. When a woman and a priest are agreed not even Durga the Ten-handed can prevail against them. Moreover——'

'Yes—I know—I know——' And now it was upon his lips that her light hand was laid. 'Of what avail to speak? There was no help but this; and I have peace and freedom and *thee*. Enough of trouble——' She waved it aside as if an actual presence shadowed her, and her sudden relapse into English had the effect of a snapped thread. 'Better a hundred times to talk of the sun and the sea and of my deep, deep studies! Look!' She drew from under her drapery a small volume bound in fawn and gold. 'What would Audrey say? No dusty book about cobwebs in the House of Life and how to brush them away. But my wonder-woman of India—Cornelia Sorabji! Her words are never ugly. Even upon the hard way of the brains she makes flowers peep between the stones. And why I did not turn the leaf was because I was reading—no, dreaming—over and over, the words of her "Wise Man, Truth-Named," when he tried to make "a clearing in the jungle" where they two might sit and speak of "the big-little things." '

He smiled at her young enthusiasm, her musical flow of speech.

'What words, child? I have forgot. There are too many words in these days, when the wayside fountains run ink; and the mills grind out books for flour, so that a man's brain cannot hold a tithe of all that passes through it. But the big-little things are always good to remember. Show me——'

'No need to show. I have it all here,' touching her forehead, 'in letters of gold upon a scroll of blue.' And closing her eyes, 'the better to read,' she spoke, half in recitative, with the grave simplicity of a child praying at its mother's knee.

'"God! By what sign shall we know him? How conceive? Imagine only light and light and light, everywhere pulsing, throbbing. From the beginning was that and only that; and that was God. But with God exists the power and mercy of God; not separate; but as closely allied as . . . the scent of the rose to the rose, as the colour of a flower to the flower. Men talk of one God, as if there could be two or three. There is just God—the All-pervading, the heart of the heart of Beauty, the great first Flame which lights every flame that leaps into life. . . . Light and light and light; brilliance at the soul of brilliance . . . the God-spark in every soul, in everything created . . . only by recognizing this shall we recognize God. There is no other way!" ' Then, lifting her gaze to his, she added, still softly, but in the tone of every day: 'And the Wise Man says also: if we do not keep our windows clean, and the light cannot get through—is that the fault of the flame? Was he not rightly "Truth-Named"?'

Her father's answer showed in his eyes, while his hand caressed her brow.

'So small a casket to hold such great thoughts,' said he. For being a man—even though of the religion-breathing East—he could not readily speak of such things.

Then they started, almost as if they had been lovers. For there was a hand upon the door.

It proved to be Kali Das—faithful through all vicissitudes, even unto loss of caste; and he brought the Indian mail, the second since their coming. It was a day early, and Lilamani caught her breath at sight of the thin envelopes. A little ache of home-sickness contracted her heart, not for the first time. Lakshman Singh, being a man of note in Hyderabad, had much official correspondence. But there was only one envelope out of half a dozen that really mattered—to them both.

In a silence eager, yet anxious, they explored its contents—a long letter from Ram Singh, eldest son and brother, and a short one in laboured English from fourteen-year-old Vimala, smuggled doubtless without her mother's knowledge. A quaint, childish effusion it was. The small writer hovered incoherently between envy at her sister's daring, a pretty self-importance at her own recent betrothal to an unknown fairy prince; in her case, happily, a young one. Lilamani smiled as she read, and was glad, though a needle-pointed arrow pricked her heart. She also envied. It is the way of life.

Then she glanced at her father, who was scanning his son's letter hungrily, yet with clouded brow. Feeling her gaze upon him, he looked up, and there was a moment of silent communing before the girl said wistfully: 'No message from Mataji—even yet?' For Mataji, obdurate to the last, had refused to bestow her blessing on the impious quest.

'It will come in time, little one—in time—' he answered, enclosing her hand in his. 'Ram Singh writes that she is well. For the rest—quarrels and worries the minute my back is turned.' And he held out the sheet for her to see.

While they pored over it, head close to head, Audrey Hammond softly opened the door; shutting it again yet more softly, even as Lilamani stirred, and her father glanced at the clock.

'Lucky these came so early,' said he. 'By writing tonight, I may just catch the out-going mail. You can send a few words to Vimala also. The child is happy?'

'As a young green parrot in love-time,' Lilamani answered lightly. 'I will speak my few words to her out there on the balcony, that I may watch the great sea fall asleep at the passing of the sun.'

'Little idolator!' he chided, as she went; and she shook her head, smiling back at him over her shoulder.

The sun's passing was near at hand now. Lilamani's 'butterflies' no longer flittered on the waters. The faultlessly-carven coast-line of the Esterelles—so close and varied an hour earlier—seemed to have stepped backward miles upon miles into a wonderland of golden mist, that translated them from solid rock and stone into dream-hills of a strangely thin, clean outline that enhanced their delicacy of shape and hue. At their feet the great sea dozed already. The fine light wind of the Riviera scarce stirred it to a responsive ripple. Truly a sea of seas for colour! It was as if amethyst, jade, and sapphire had been melted in the crucible of some giant alchemyst, now one prevailing, now the other, as the sun slowly gathered up his gift of light. To Lilamani, whose passion for colour made it almost a form of self-expression, the ever-varying beauty of it all seemed each evening fraught with some new meaning; and with an indrawn breath of content she sank into her chair. Her few words must be swiftly writ before the coming of that supreme moment when—in poetic Eastern speech—'the Sun drops into the Sea and splashes up stars for spray,' and silence passes over the earth like a presence, unseen yet piercingly felt.

From the folds of her bodice she drew out her father's latest gift, a gold fountain pen, set with one flashing diamond—her name-stone, the 'jewel of delight'; and for a while it sped over the paper, keeping pace with her thoughts, that transported her, as she wrote, back into the sun-splashed courtyard whose four walls had been, for seventeen years, the boundary lines of her actual world.

So essentially is an Indian woman the product of that hidden sanctuary of home, and all it stands for, that a sudden uprooting involves the snapping of a hundred delicate fibres, the entire readjustment of thought, feeling, and conduct to the complex, unstable elements of the outer world. And at seventeen a child of the fulgent East is already a woman; which complicates matters not a little, in more ways than one. So it was with Lilamani, a creature saturate with the poetic symbolism, the passion and religious fervour of her race, reared on age-old traditions and ideals not to be eradicated by a change of continents and a few years at college. Details, these last, too often overlooked by the fervent progressivist, who 'reforms' in haste and is tripped up by them at leisure.

The first ecstasy of escape, the first bewildering revelation of the fullness and beauty of earth, the marvel of riding upon the limitless ocean, 'as it were upon a horse,' had left no space in the theatre of her sensations for the ache of uprooted fibres, the sense of a familiar foothold gone. Like a child in its first crowd, she clung to the two hands she knew, and at night put herself to sleep with tales of the wonders she would achieve when she fared back as torchbearer to the land she loved. Audrey Hammond had turned her racial idealism to good account.

But now in the quieter life of the hotel, where as yet they kept mainly to themselves, there was leisure to feel the pain of those severed fibres, the vague, insistent yearning for the lost things of home; leisure to wonder if her venture were foredoomed to failure by a mother's blessing withheld. And the beginnings of higher study proved less inspiring than she had hoped. The natural poet in her recoiled from dry facts set forth in Latinized English, with neither glow of colour nor gleam of fancy to lighten the grey page. Studies with her father, who had trained her ear to the music of written speech had set a halo about the mere word. She discovered now how much hung upon the subject—and the teacher. For all her fine qualities, Audrey lacked the peculiar sympathy and insight that can make all learning a delight. For her a fact was a fact. Its utility sufficed. With Lilamani it was otherwise. Hence the beginning of disillusion. But because she had good grit in her, and the Indian woman's heritage of self-repression, she kept silence about these small troubles; nor dreamed that any guessed at their existence.

And while she sat writing, the sun slipped out of sight unheeded. A small shiver, like the breeze of a passing spirit, chilled earth and sea, where amethyst and jade had given place to sapphire, and that in turn to indigo and grey. The girl, who had begun the last page of her letter, looked up expectant. But to-night the sun's passing was a tender thing. No fairy islands in a lake of gold; no 'crimson blaring of his shawms.' The sky, emptied of his presence, flushed delicately, like a maid under her first kiss. A trailing banner of cloud that hovered near, caught the wild rose tint and held it, while light and colour ebbed slowly, till all was grey—sea and sky and the Esterelles between—a cool, delicate grey, as of a dove's wing; not one tone, but a harmony of half-tones, a nocturne in a minor key. In the upper grey a memory of palest blue; in the lower grey shimmerings of jade and indigo, changing near the

skyline to a luminous pallor, neither silver nor white; the hills themselves pearl-grey transparencies, as if washed in by the brush of a
master.

Then, as she sat gazing, her round chin cradled in her hand, behold
a change—an aftermath of life before day's ultimate end. Grey above
and grey below were slowly transfused with rose, so faint, yet all-
pervading that it was as if air and water blushed. No lines of light, no
hint of the sun's presence, only this ghost of a blush that faded softly
as it came, leaving, at last, one grey; and across it the twin islands of
the gulf lay like a smudge of Indian ink.

Lilamani sat on, still as any Yogi of her own land, the gates of her
receptive soul flung wide to the inflowing message of this strange grey
sunset; a message of peace shot through with the rose of hope. Such,
at least, was her fanciful belief; and there is much virtue in belief, however fanciful. In her case, it quieted a new, unreasoning ache that she
had vainly willed to disregard, healed the arrow-pricks dealt her by
Vimala's childish chatter of new bangles and the betrothed. With a
deep breath of relief she looked down at the blank sheet upon her
knee, vaguely wishful to crystallize the music of the spheres into the
halting music of her own verse. But the ancestral spirit of meditation
was still strong upon her. The white emptiness of the paper held her
gaze, shutting out the sense of things actual; and in place of verse living memory-pictures real and clear as crystal visions, moved before
her eyes.

The familiar, white-walled courtyard with its central tank and
deep-pillared verandah glowed beneath its turquoise dome. In the
blue-grey shadow of an arch sat Vimala and little Radha chattering
like a pair of minas, and outside in full sunshine the grey crane walked
delicately, and her own peacock sunned his jewelled tail with the self-
conscious airs and graces that she loved. Along the flagged pathway
by the tank, scarlet of pointsettia, and blood-red hybiscus flowers
made splashes of passionate colour, while over against the house itself
a gold mohur tree flung out cedar-like branches ablaze with orange-
golden bloom. From without came the sound of hoofs and wheels and
the voices of passing men. Then a small shiver ran through her, for to
the ears of her soul came clearly the heart-stirring wail of conches
from the temple hard by; and a figure that she knew for her own, in

its simple home draperies, came out to listen, to bask in the fragrance of champak and neem.

By now all sense of illusion was lost. She was there, feeling, seeing, hearing; all else forgotten as though it were not. Next it was Mataji herself who came forth—plump, practical, and a trifle sharp of tongue; but yet—Mataji, guardian spirit of the home, honoured and beloved by all. She had come out to scold her dreamy daughter—no infrequent happening—for careless rendering of her morning duties, and worse than all, for having insufficiently watered the sacred *tulsi* that languished already from the heat. She felt the compelling hand on her shoulder, felt it so forcibly that she started and turned with an actual shiver, a feeling as of a light blown out.

And lo—it was Audrey's hand that held her shoulder, Audrey's voice that reproved her in kindly practical tones.

'My dear child—are you crazy, sitting out alone in the dark? You know it made you feverish the other night.'

'But I love it so,' the culprit murmured lamely as the other with gentle professional deftness touched her wrist and brow.

'Of course you do, dear. But health must stand first. Besides, it's nearly dinner-time. Come to my room. I'll give you some quinine.'

Lilamani gathered up her unfinished letter and obeyed.

There were moments when Audrey's tone and opinions faintly recalled Mataji herself. Both were capable and decisive; both slaves of a fetish. As the last word of Mataji was *dastur*, so the last word of Audrey was health; and to-night, jerked abruptly out of her vision, only to be confronted with quinine, this gentle-mannered girl (who had bought freedom from *dastur* at a heavier price than she guessed) came near to wondering whether, in truth, she had but exchanged one form of tyranny for another, after all.

THREE

'I find, under the bows of love and hate,
In all poor foolish things that live a day,
Eternal beauty wandering on her way.'

—W.B. Yeats

With engaging docility Lilamani swallowed her quinine, accepting it, without conviction, as an article of Audrey's faith, that must shortly be her own also. But on the suggestion that to-night she should make a fresh advance by dining downstairs, docility vanished. Her small decisive chin asserted itself, the chin that had defied Mataji and *dastur*.

'Eat my food in a crowd of noisy strangers? Audrey, I cannot. At least—not yet.'

She spoke quite gently; but Audrey Hammond knew by this time how delusive was that gentleness.

'Quaint child! I thought you enjoyed seeing new kinds of people and things,' was all she said.

'Oh, I do! They are so astonishing. I love to see them all. But I think—not too close. And not at food-time.'

That last made Audrey smile and shrug her shoulders. It is difficult for the West to understand the Eastern sanctification of such prosaic essentials as bathing and feeding; though in their own Book of Books it is written, 'whether ye eat or drink, ye shall do it unto the Lord.' But that Book came from the East, and even after two thousand years the essentially Eastern spirit of it still remains a stumbling-block to the practical, self-assertive soul of the West. Even Sir Lakshman Singh, whose civilization was more than skin deep, still disliked hotel meals. Hence his reluctance to force them on his daughter. Audrey admired him greatly, though innate self-assurance convinced her that she would have managed her rebel better alone.

'Well, my dear, if you won't, you won't!' she said with a touch of good-humoured irritation, unfastening brooches and buttons as she spoke. 'We might try going down after dinner one evening. You must make a start some day—now you're here.'

'Yes, oh, yes—some day,' the girl answered, catching at the soothing vagueness of the word. 'But you, Audrey, you need not miss what pleases you because—I am shy.'

'No. Of course not,' Audrey agreed; then paused, considering the matter while she tidied her soft, fair hair. Till to-day she had felt no particular wish to join the after-dinner gathering in the central hall, where a local band played twice a week, and people danced, when the spirit moved them. But her meeting with Nevil Sinclair had set the clock back. After years of arduous service to find him just where she had left him—attractive, leisured, and irresponsible—made her feel unaccountably young again. Though full eight-and-twenty, and mature of her age, her pulses had never quickened for any man, nor, in her belief, ever would. But, from the first, this thwarted artist and good comrade had secured a corner of her heart; and on meeting him again, she found that the same corner, not an inch more, belonged to him still. It is even possible that his arrival may have strengthened her conviction that Lilamani's nascent home-sickness should be combated by a fresh step in advance. She would have denied it upon oath, in all sincerity. But that is neither here nor there.

Catching sight of Lilamani's face in the glass, she nodded and smiled. 'Your looks belie your name-stone, child, and your father seems worried since the mail came in; so I won't "dine out" to-night. I may run down afterwards; and I *may* insist on taking you with me. Now—run along.'

So Nevil Sinclair looked in vain for the possible descent of his Peri into the crowded room, where the truly civilized discussed their dinner—in both senses—under conditions that might well seem barbarous to minds not hypnotized by habit. Through an intermittent roar of human tongues and clattering plates, preoccupied waiters scurried to and fro balancing a silver dish on either hand; and one only of the glass doors into the verandah stood open to the cool and quiet of the night.

In the neighbourhood of this friendly door, Sinclair shared a table with another Antibes *habitué*, Cuthbert Broome, novelist and essayist of no small repute; a big, bearded man, nearing fifty, with a thatch of tawny hair, and sailor-blue eyes, that missed no detail of men or things. And there is a sufficiency of both for the born observer at a continental hotel. Behind them two Hebraic Germans, napkins tucked under ponderous chins, fought their business battles over again, with variations, in the intervals of damning cold soup and the monotony of the menus. On one side, a party of Londoners, correct to the last hook and button, had a politely inquiring gaze for Sinclair's well-bred profile. The two girls, in unimpeachable 'restaurant frocks,' had evidently been to Nice studying the momentous hat question, over which they argued like a pair of theologians over a point of evidence. On the other side a French couple, not long married, drank champagne and made love surreptitiously when they imagined no one heeded them. But Cuthbert Broome, listening to Nevil with scrupulous attention, was quite aware of it all. The third chair at their own table remained empty; and when a fresh ebullition of waiters skidded past armed with *noisettes de veau*, Nevil commented on the fact.

'Little Martino's late. Anything wrong?'

'Yes; poor chap. Temperature, with a slight touch of haemorrhage,' the big man answered, and the voice that matched his frame had a sympathetic note in its depths. 'Sat out too late the other night over an after-glow effect. The result's magnificent—on canvas. Quite the reverse on his luckless carcase. But he wouldn't go to bed; though I prevailed on him to dine upstairs. He deserves immortality, does Martino, if ever man did. A born fighter, though his weapons are only a paint-brush and a mahl-stick; and all the odds against him.'

Nevil nodded thoughtfully. Here it was again, the primal quality that makes for achievement.

'"Life but a coin, to be staked in the pastime, whose playing is more than the transfer of being,"' he quoted. 'That's Martino's creed.'

Said Broome: 'A plucky one. And he lives up to it. He'll die for it years before he need. But he will leave his mark. He was alternately choking and holding forth on a new colour-theory all this afternoon. I could only keep him quiet by dosing him with extracts from a purple epic, which my editor friend of the "Book World" is bound over to pat on the back; and I am the chosen instrument, for my sins.'

'A chance to air your gift of subtle irony,' suggested Nevil by way of consolation.

'In which case the great Wigmore would come down on me like a ton of best Wallsend and I might snap a connection I don't want to lose. There's a side-light for you on the ethics of reviewing! But the book has *some* good stuff in it, once you're through with the Epic, which you shall read, my Nevil, if only that you may learn what not to write——'

And, having fallen upon a subject of mutual interest, they clave to it till the doors into the hall were flung wide to admit the spirited strains of 'Serimamide.' For it was band night; and frivolity would be the order of the evening. Frivolity of the mildest, and most innocuous; since Antibes lies a little off the beaten track of the Riviera as it is understanded of Society, and the budding millionaire. Cannes, Nice, and Monte Carlo entangle, in their jewelled meshes, the gambler, the devotee of bridge, restaurant and promenade; the well-bred idler with a taste for forbidden fruit; and restless young America, with a taste for all things costly and effervescent. To the grey, rocky headland of the Cap, with its pinewoods and aromatic cushions of myrtle and lentisk, come rather invalids in search of health, overworked professional men and women in search of rest or renewed inspiration; a fair sprinkling also of those travellers who have enough of resource within to ask no more than large draughts of peace, and light, and colour from the twin goblets of sea and sky; a passing respite from the complex machinery of modern life and work. Folk of this kind do not always look promising at first sight. Such riches as they may possess are not to be vaunted in terms of silk and precious stones, and the last thing in motor-cars. But a little delving under the surface will often reveal an unexpected streak of ore; and those gifted ones, swift to detect the God in the clay, have even been known to dig up diamonds.

Of such was Cuthbert Broome, most sane and human of novelists. The fact that half a dozen critics of note had hailed him as a creative genius—word too lavishly used in this our age of spurious masterpieces—had neither upset his equilibrium, nor engendered the disease of acute self-consciousness that is the bane of modern talent. His bodily strength and power of work were phenomenal; no less so, perhaps, his sympathy for those lacking in both. He turned up at the Cap Hotel every few years; and more often than not lighted on a friend or two worth keeping. In one visit he had discovered Andrea Martino, the consumptive Italian artist with the body of a grasshopper and the soul of a hero. In another he had chanced upon Nevil Sinclair, beneath whose modesty and seeming lightness he discovered a measure of talent and strength as yet unsuspected by the young man himself. There be natures that come late to fruition, and Nevil was one of these; the more so because of the smooth ground under his feet and the curse of the ready-made income.

Cuthbert Broome, kindly yet critical, grieved over him as a victim of the sorrows of happiness, the vital poverty that may result from wealth. But he did not grieve as one without hope. The finer qualities were there; and he awaited with interest the pointed pain or pleasure that should stab them broad awake. For himself, Necessity had belaboured him generously ever since he could remember, with excellent result.

Now, as he passed along with the crowd, that surged out into the great square lounge, his tawny beard wagged and his sailor eyes twinkled in one direction and another. There was the small convex widow, Mrs. Heath, yclept the Hen Sparrow, by reason of a propensity for twittering in and out of season. Beside her sauntered the pretty niece with the 'pompadour coiffeur' and secret hankerings after Mentone and Monte Carlo. Then there was the handsome French woman with lips a little drawn, and a hunted look in her eyes, because the five-year-old son, her light of life, was smitten with the curse of asthma, and her husband, smitten with the curse of a 'system,' was flinging away with both hands the money needed to keep his child alive.

Broome had an almost tender twinkle for her; as also for the eager-faced maiden lady, Miss Swithin, in freckles and spectacles and her best summer dress of the year before last. On the sandy-grey knot of hair half-way up her head sat an irrelevant blue bow, dropped, as it were, by her youth in its passing, though gleams of it still lingered in her inquiring eyes. A lone soul, one of the thousand and one oddments of earth, squandering the savings of years on a lone peep into Paradise. Shy of speaking to strangers without introduction, she played Patience zealously every evening at a lone small table in a corner; and nearly fainted between delight and trepidation, when the big, bearded 'sailor-man' had boldly introduced himself, and talked to her all the evening. She had sat up late that night, in her third-floor bedroom, adding a rather incoherent entry to her neatly-written 'Journal of a Golden Month,' bound in vellum and tied with white strings.

After that, he often joined her when she looked specially forlorn and the blue bow more irrelevant than usual. Sometimes they played double patience; and when she won, enjoyment could scarce go farther. Now when a known writer goes out of his way to make friends with stray humans, there are those who are sure to believe him—not quite without reason—merely in search of 'copy.' But, in the case of Cuthbert Broome, such belief were libel. The man's creative impulse was too spontaneous and exuberant, and he himself too great-hearted to be so tempted, even did he not strongly disapprove.

'If ever I caught myself taking deliberate notes of a fellow-creature,' he had said once to a simpering admirer, who rather hoped he might be taking notes of her, 'I should burn all my skeletons of projected novels, and devote the rest of my life to picking holes in other people's!' But like many of us when we take pains to speak truth, he was not believed.

Be that as it might, he saw in the wearer of the blue bow simply a woman starved of legitimate hopes and emotions; and out of his own superabundance he gave what he could. But Miss Swithin did not figure in his occasional letters to Mrs. Cuthbert Broome, who was too practically occupied with committee meetings and demonstrations of the organized woman's movement, to find time for 'loafing at Antibes.' She would not have understood. Even after twenty years of marriage there were whole tracts in her husband's expansive nature that were entirely outside her comprehension. Yet their marriage was not tragic, nor even a complete failure. Possibly it was a mistake. But marriage is a mystery seemingly outside human volition; and it were rash to dogmatize even so far.

To-night, when the folding-doors were closed, and the crowd broken up into accustomed groups, mainly racial, Broome lit his pipe and strolled over to the cane table that Miss Swithin had fairly made her own. The blue bow, having been fixed on hurriedly, seemed almost to beckon him as its wearer's head nodded in sympathy with Madame de Lisle's account of her boy. Broome had introduced them to each other and was glad to see them making friends. Miss Swithin enjoyed airing her French, and Madame de Lisle her broken English; so it was a capital arrangement, and he went over to enjoy it, sure of a welcome from both.

Sinclair gravitated toward the 'pompadour coiffeur,' for whom he was an oasis in a desert of boredom; young men being scarce at Antibes. He found her pleasant enough in spite of her 'pretty woman' tricks of manner; but caught himself wishing it were Audrey and surreptitiously glancing at the door. Besides, she could talk of the Peri; and he was curious to hear more. It did not occur to him that others could talk of her, too, till 'Semiramide' had hurried to its crashing finale, and the Hen Sparrow leaned eagerly across her niece.

'Have *you* seen our Indian curio yet, Mr. Sinclair? The pretty, little purdah lady who won't defile herself by dining downstairs?'

Mr. Sinclair, who had been looking politely bored, was all attention. Yes, he had seen her, afar off. Did she ever come down, and had Mrs. Heath spoken to her?

'Of *course* I have,' Mrs. Heath twittered triumphantly. 'I made a *point* of it on the first opportunity. Odd specimens. They make up half the fun of hotel life. But this Lilamani girl' (she pronounced it Lillamanny) 'is really quite a sweet creature. She isn't strong. Nerves, I believe. Even India is catching the modern epidemic. Still . . . I *do* think it would be better for her to come down on an evening like this, than to stay moping upstairs. Those three people are going to sing soon. The man with the tambourine is killingly funny—quite a character——'

Then Nevil had an inspiration. 'Couldn't you send up word to Miss Hammond and suggest it?' said he.

'Why, of course. How clever of you! I might write a little note.'

'And I might take it. I know Miss Hammond quite well. We met here before.'

'It *is* a pity she's so self-satisfied,' murmured Miss Blakeney, leaning a sequined and bangled arm over the cane table between them and considering it with interest.

'Is she?' asked Nevil indifferently, and carried off his note.

FOUR

'Les rencontres ici-bas sont souvent preparés de loins.'

—Pierre de Coulevain

He sent it in by Kali Das, with a message that Sinclair Sahib awaited an answer; and before many minutes were out Audrey appeared, in a little flutter of pleased surprise, very rare with her.

'My dear Nevil! Was it your plan?' she asked, scanning him with approval. He looked well in evening dress.

'Partly mine, partly hers. Do come, anyway—all of you.' Then, after a pause: 'Miss Blakeney palls, you know.'

'Yes—I *do* know! And I am to act as antidote?'

'Naturally!'

His frank smile was as frankly returned. 'Very well. I'll try to persuade the child. If we do come, we shan't be long. But don't wait—please.'

Of course he waited, not on the landing, but at the foot of the grand staircase where the lift comes down. And while he stood waiting, wondering, there came over him the strange sense—known to most of us—of having stood thus and waited thus, somewhere, somewhen, for the coming—of what?

At this point the ghost of a memory eluded him, and reality intervened. The iron doors of the lift opened with a clang.

Audrey stepped out, and after her—the 'purdah lady'; no longer a simple evening primrose, but an iridescent vision of grey and gold, shot through with mother-o'-pearl tints that shimmered changefully when she moved. Her *sari*, drawn well forward, had a narrow border of pale gold cunningly inwrought with rose. For, as always, she had chosen a dress to match her mood—her sunset mood of peace tenderly flushed with hope.

Upon Audrey's introduction of Nevil she bowed her head without looking up; and he noted, through the semi-transparency of her veil, the dark, smooth ripple of hair; the red caste mark on her brow; the fine chain at her throat from which one blue moon-stone hung like a great drop of dew. There was not a detail he could have wished otherwise. Even while he shook hands with Sir Lakshman Singh, and appraised the clean-cut strength of the man, he was telling himself that in this dress he must paint her, though only the hand of an Alma Tadema could hope to catch its opalescent sheen.

The great door into the lounge was shut, and through it came the voice of him with the tambourine; not a voice of melody, but of sheer rollicking *joie de vivre*. Four or five hotel servants were flattening their faces against the glass; and an agile waiter pounced upon the door-handle. But Lilamani shrank backward, flushing to the temples. Her fingers closed upon her father's arm; and he turned promptly aside.

'She is right,' he said to Audrey; 'we will go round through the dining-room, and have chairs put in at the back.'

The which they did; slipping in, almost unnoticed, while the whole room clapped and shouted, and the shock-headed Italian, in the shabby dinner-jacket, with a mouth like a slit in a turnip and no stage property save his tambourine, swept a burlesque bow to the woman at his side. For it was a duet—an Italian love-song—trilled and 'tra-la'-ed with dramatic abandon by the tambourinist—an artist after his kind—who could wax playful, reproachful, fervent by turns over a 'Bella' whose middle-aged plumpness was compressed into a puce-coloured cashmere gown of the same doubtful age as herself. No trace in her of the man's madcap surrender to the folly of the moment. Being a woman, and practical, music might be in her throat, but the collection-plate was at her heart. With the laboured zeal of one responsible for the number of francs it might contain, she marshalled her best high notes, her marionette gestures of coquetry, scorn, and final surrender to the triumphal clashing of the tambourine.

Then the real woman emerged; and she threaded her way among the guests, plate in hand. No band on earth could make sweeter music than the tinkle of the silver pieces as they fell. It was her supreme moment, even as the applause had been the man's.

Through it all Lilamani had sat spellbound; shyness and self-consciousness forgotten, in this fresh revealing of the unknown world into which she had flung herself with the valour of ignorance and despair. On the steamer she had rarely ventured out of her deck-cabin, except in those times of peace when hungry passengers gravitated to the saloon table, like filings of steel to a magnet. On *tamasha* evenings, she had heard the sounds of revelry afar off, and watched the passing figures from her window.

Now for the first time, she saw in full—and was amazed: the ugly evening dress of the men, that her father must never wear when they were alone; the women laughing and talking as frankly with them as though all were brothers or cousins of the first degree: the lights, the movement, the waiters whisking away coffee-cups and small glasses. True, Audrey had told her of it all; but to see it, to sit in the midst of it, brought home to her with something of a shock the new conditions of her life. A couple of French women and an Italian wore full evening dress. They sat in a group with three men, leaning bare arms on the cane table before them, puffing cigarettes and gesticulating freely. Young as she was, the sight hurt her in a way few women of the West would understand. In truth, the whole scene, even while it fascinated, troubled her racial sense of dignity and reserve.

But with the end of the song came the end of self-forgetfulness. It dawned on her that people were looking and whispering. Mrs. Heath, peering expectantly through a tortoise-shell lorgnette, caught the sheen of her *sari*, and fluttered across to them, friendly and voluble; while Miss Blakeney, who found Audrey 'superior' and the Indian girl 'insipid,' kept her seat and smiled alluringly at Sinclair, without result.

The devotees of the hat question, lately arrived, could scarcely keep curiosity within the bounds of good manners, and the Hebraic Germans stared so flagrantly that Nevil longed to smite them between the eyes and take the consequences: the more so, when he saw that she noticed it, and drew her *sari* forward, almost hiding her face. During the song he had stood near Audrey talking of old times; though he, too, had been watching under his lids, and drawing comparisons between the sequined fluffy-haired Miss Blakeney, with her self-conscious poses, and the exquisite simplicity of this flower of Indian girlhood, her drooping grace and slenderness, as of a willow by moonlight. And now, smitten by her sensitive shrinking, he deserted Audrey, drew up a chair and sat down boldly beside his picture that was to be.

Unhappily, the end of self-forgetfulness had wrought her to an agony of shyness; and that this strange young man should come and talk to her reduced her almost to the verge of flight. But courtesy forbade. She could only incline her head in recognition of his presence, leaving him to begin.

And he found it astonishingly difficult. He who could talk fluently to anything human, from a guttersnipe to an archbishop, was smitten dumb by the beauty and aloofness of this mere child of another race. He cleared his throat and said lamely: 'You find all this very strange, of course?'

'Yes. It is strange. I am not accustomed——'

She broke off to moisten her lips, and could get no further. Her slim fingers locked and unlocked themselves distressfully.

He tried again. 'The music and the singing pleased you?'

She nodded. 'Your music is very different from ours. I like it. But I like a great deal better the music and dancing of the sun upon the sea.'

'So do I,' he agreed more hopefully. 'You'll get plenty of that here. It was wise of Miss Hammond to choose Antibes.'

'Yes—oh, yes.'

Another dead pause. Something across the room had caught her attention, and he felt himself forgotten. He also felt foolish, and vaguely annoyed. Uphill work with a woman was new to him, and not at all to his taste. If she would only help him forward with a smile, a glance. But her words, low and musically spoken, were seemingly addressed to the locked hands in her lap: and he could not know how her heart was throbbing in her throat beneath the big dew-drop on its chain. In his futile search for a fresh topic he was harassed by the twittering of Mrs. Heath, who believed she was making an impression on Sir Lakshman Singh, while her courteous victim smilingly allowed the waters to flow over his turbaned head.

Then the players in the corner dashed into a spirited mazurka; and Sinclair's next remark passed unheeded, unheard. A chill of disappointment quenched his admiration. As a picture she was incomparable, this child of seclusion; but as an entity she seemed unpromising, almost stupid. None the less did she exhale an atmosphere of her own. He felt it even while resenting, it, because it seemed to exclude himself. More than ever he marvelled how Audrey could hope to make a doctor of her: yet Audrey was no fool.

Of a sudden he saw that she had realized his predicament and was coming to the rescue. He rose at her approach, and Lilamani looked up. It was as if a lamp had been lighted within; and Nevil's flickering spark of interest revived. Audrey laid a reassuring hand on the girl's shoulder; but it was to the man she spoke.

'They are going to clear half the dining-room for dancing after this. Rather nice.'

'Capital!' said he with grateful sense of passing from a too rarified atmosphere into the common light of day. 'The first valse is ours, of course; not to say the second, if you will!'

He turned to Lilamani, his awkwardness gone. 'Have you ever seen English people dance, Miss—Lakshman Singh?'

'No, never. And I think—I would rather not.' She leaned nearer to Miss Hammond, speaking almost under her breath. 'Oh! Audrey, please—there are too many people here. I want to go up again—now.'

'Nonsense, child! You *must* stay a little longer now you've come. Your shyness will soon wear off, and the change will do you good.'

She spoke with kindly decision and with the comfortable conviction that zeal for Lilamani's enlightenment prompted her own wish to remain. It is common as it is consoling, this belief that the thing we would do must, in some way, subserve another's gain: and for all her steady pulses and advanced views Audrey Hammond was yet a woman; glad to recapture, even for a moment, the girlish spirit of enjoyment stolen from her by the strenuous years.

There a stir throughout the room; a scraping of chairs on the tessellated floor. The singers bowed themselves out; the folding-doors were flung wide again; and the band struck up a memory-provoking valse. Audrey patted Lilamani's shoulder, and murmuring: 'Don't be foolish, dear,' went off on her partner's arm.

With feelings that veered between interest and vague distaste, Lilamani watched them go; watched the woman she loved and respected only less than her own mother, spin lightly round upon her toes, like any nautch-girl, in the arms of this strange man, who was neither brother nor betrothed. The reading of occasional novels with her father had taught her that the 'Europe betrothed' might take liberties whereof no Indian would dream; but even so it astounded her that they did not think shame of themselves, capering thus for all the world to look upon. The very waiter-folk, peering in from the hall, showed like grinning emblems of derision. Yet, seemingly, all was well. It was *dastur*, a word that covers more sins than charity's self.

A dozen other couples followed Audrey's lead: whirling in the same graceless fashion; women clinging to the arms of men, even those flagrantly unveiled ones, who had chattered like bazaar folk that come to sell wares in the verandah. In some cases women twirled with women, which puzzled her less, though the distressing publicity remained. And in no case did the dancers dream that the shy strange girl, half hidden in her shimmering drapery, was sitting in judgment on them; weighing their conduct and finding it wanting in dignity, delicacy, and womanly reserve. Even Audrey, of the strong brain and will, did not come off scot-free; and the fact that she could criticize her mentor marked a new phase in Lilamani's progress.

Nevertheless, while pain deepened in her, a reluctant fascination deepened also. Assuredly the music had some sort of magic which even she could feel. The entrancing rhythm of it spoke to the feet, impelling them to move. Doubtless it bewitched those others even as strong wine was said to bewitch men, so that they knew not what they did.

At this point, her trance of thought was broken by the voice of Sir Lakshman—mercifully delivered from the kindest lady alive by one who had persuaded her to dance.

Straightway he came to his daughter, and sitting down beside her, spoke low in their native tongue.

'Thou art troubled, my child? Or doth it please thee, this strange *tamasha*?'

Slowly she shook her head, and turned upon him wide, wondering eyes.

'Strange it is, father mine. And yet—I am here to learn many new things. Is it needful I should become—in all ways—as these——?'

'The Great God forbid!' he said fervently. 'But before long thou wilt better understand how in some matters—this for instance—we see through one glass, they through another. In their eyes this form of *nautch* is harmless as child's play. For them, therefore, it is not evil. And in truth,' he added with a reminiscent smile, 'it is pleasant enough! I myself tried it in student days.'

'You—oh, father! With these white women? But not now——!'
Her light fingers on his coat-sleeve gave her entreaty a hint of command.

'No, no,' he said soothingly. 'In those days, being young, I was eager to drink the waters of pleasure, as of knowledge, at all fountains. Now being old, I eat the fruit of discretion, and it is the daughter of my heart who ventures along strange paths!'

'To-night this daughter of thine heart hath seen enough of strange paths. Why wait we for Audrey? Take me back, quickly—to "the Inside," where alone is peace.'

Her tone had a light touch of petulance, very endearing to him; and the familiar Indian word for the women's quarter struck a note of home that went to his heart. He rose and offered his arm.

'Come, then. I am ready. Miss Hammond can follow when she will. She seems to be enjoying herself after her own fashion.'

So they went forth together, the tall, straight-limbed man in faultless evening dress, with the iridescent vision on his arm; and many curious eyes followed their going.

Audrey Hammond saw it also, not without a passing sense of relief from responsibility. Most certainly she was enjoying herself—in her own fashion; which was not the fashion of Lilamani, or of Miss Blakeney; still less that of Miss Swithin, whose blue bow bobbed jauntily, if a little tremulously, above the elbow of Cuthbert Broome. She found it good to be dancing again with Nevil Sinclair. But no stir of the pulses enhanced the discovery. It is a question whether girls of her type—products of extreme reaction from mid-Victorian ideals—are not cultivating brain and ego at the expense of the natural emotions; a doubtful gain for themselves and for the race, in an age already overloaded with intellectuality and all its works.

Certainly for Audrey Hammond much of Nevil's value lay in the fact, that he could seemingly give and take friendship with as little after-thought as the most inveterate 'bachelor-girl' could wish. The understanding between them seemed curiously complete; and to both it appeared quite natural that they should spend the whole evening together if they chose. Nevil remarked airily:

'Well—shall we go on?' And she:

'Yes, of course. Why not?'

So they went on, to the disgust of Miss Blakeney and the amusement of Cuthbert Broome, who saw Nevil's heart apparently rent and riven at a stroke. Clearly both were enjoying themselves to the top of their bent. For the moment, Sinclair had even forgotten his picture:

and not until the dancing was nearly over did he speak of his wish to see more of the Lakshman Singhs.

'A pity they didn't stay longer,' said he. 'And a pity she's so shy. My attempt at making friends was a dead failure. The deadest I've ever known with a girl.'

'*Very* good for you!' Audrey answered in what Lilamani called her 'medicine voice.' 'But very trying for her, poor child. Her education didn't include the art of talking to strange young men.'

'It must now, though, if you mean to make her a doctor and I offer myself as a dummy to be practised on!'

'You really want to try again?'

'Why, of course.' His hidden motive was almost on his lips; but he knew her capable of thwarting him if she saw fit, and added instead: 'She is charming enough to be worth looking at even if she refuses to talk! How shall we arrange things? Will you all have tea with me in the verandah to-morrow?'

'I doubt that—after to-night! The next day would be more probable. But she's a creature of moods and rather spoilt, as I told you. If you really want them to come you had better ask Sir Lakshman.'

'That I will. He seems a capital fellow.'

Audrey nodded. 'If modern India produced more of his type we should hear little or nothing of political unrest.'

'Very clever of you to bring them here, and very clever of me to turn up at the psychological moment! A thundering good plan all round.'

'Thundering good!' she agreed frankly upon which conclusion they parted; at peace with themselves and the world.

Nevil saw her into the lift; then lit a cigar; and its flavour was enhanced by a pleasant conviction that his impromptu descent upon Antibes bid fair to justify very completely his egregious desertion of Jane.

FIVE

'A spindle of hazel-wood had I.
Into the mill stream it fell one day;
The water has brought it back no more.'

—Roumanian Ballad

'But this is good. Santa Maria, it is good! So slight a thing; yet—entirely alive. If you make not a picture of this, Sinclair, talk no more to me of your aspirations. No longer I shall believe in them.'

Thus Andrea Martino, standing in a flood of afternoon light at his third-floor window, and holding Nevil's sketchbook at arm's length before him. His shock head of hair—jerked now this way, now that—suggested an intelligent blackbird considering a worm; a suggestion heightened by the beak-like nose that sprang boldly out betwixt eyes cavernously set under one dense ink-smudge of eyebrow. The single crease of concentration furrowed his forehead, and dull patches of colour on his cheek-bones, accentuating the hollow beneath, told their own tale. It was a fine head, too fine for the lean, undersized body, producing at times a contrast that bordered on the grotesque.

Sinclair, bestriding a bedroom chair, a cigarette balanced between two fingers, was doing his best not to look foolishly elate, and succeeding fairly well, thanks to a racial heritage of self-repression. Martino's studio was a corner bedroom, roughly metamorphosed by the removal of the washing-stand; a Turkish Djimjim flung over the bed; easel, canvasses and a bare deal table sticky with paints. Two oval windows, looking west, framed sun-saturate visions of the twinkling bay, and white villas of Cannes, backed by the barren ranges and clean-cut peaks of the Alpes Maritimes. A third window looked upon open sea and sky, the twin islands and the carven outline of the Esterelles. Beside it, from a tall vase, rose plumes of mimosa, breathing out faint fragrance.

The one arm-chair was amply filled by Cuthbert Broome, chewing a pipe and correcting proof slips in the intervals of considering Sinclair's profile and wondering which emotion struck deeper—the thrill of Martino's unfeigned approval, or the thrill of laying siege to the self-poised girl with the disconcertingly direct grey eyes. It was a problem congenial to his psychological turn of mind. The girl—if her looks belied her not—stood for politics and a fairly assured parliamentary career. The picture, if achieved, stood for artistry and vagabondage, for possible success, and probable family discord and disapproval. For the moment, Broome felt doubtful which way Sinclair—the essential Sinclair—leaned. Last night he could have sworn to the girl. To-day, watching Nevil's face under Martino's volcanic discharges of encouragement, his assurance wavered: nor could he quite decide which way of leaning his own ripe, unbiased judgment would applaud.

Even from the unfinished sketch it was clear that Sinclair's sleeping talent had genuinely caught fire. But one inspiration, however genuine, never yet made an artist. It is continuity of power that tells; as Broome had good reason to know. He knew, too, that the keystone of all imaginative work worth doing is capacity for great emotion—the furnace that fuses thought and inspiration, form and colour, into one living whole. In a life packed with observation, he had seen and noted how often lack of this very capacity stamps as ineffectual the clever, complex, highly civilized young Englishman of to-day; and, so far, it seemed as though Sinclair had not altogether escaped the disability of his race and age. No doubt smooth going along the line of least resistance had retarded development. But once let him reach the cross-roads, the true man must out. . . .

And while the subconscious brain of the novelist played with probabilities, as a child with the pieces of a puzzle, his hand travelled down the printed slips, scribbling hieroglyphics in the margin with mechanical accuracy, while his ear missed little of the talk, or rather the monologue by the window.

'And she is in the hotel, you say? Under the same roof with us—this houri—this *bellissima*?' Martino had just demanded, slapping-to the sketch-book on one of his extravagant prophecies that set Nevil tingling to the roots of his hair. 'And she walks in the garden?'

'Sometimes; not often,' said Nevil, wondering amusedly, What next?

'Then why not have I seen her—I?'

'Because, my dear fellow,' put in Broome with a friendly twirl of his eye, 'when *you* walk in the garden your expansive soul spreads itself over the whole sea and sky. Incidentally you may be aware of rocks and trees in the foreground. But anything so infinitesimal as a human being——!'

'Chut!' Martino waved him aside with a laugh that broke midway into a cough and brought a crumpled silk handkerchief to his lips. 'It is to Sinclair I talk. You love not to speak your true meaning except with your pen! I remember me now—I have seen a dark man in a turban. He is her father—no?' Nevil nodded. 'Then it is him you have to make believe what a picture this will be. If you are too modest, send him to Martino, who will have a tongue of gold at your service. But, my friend, lose no time. In art you must strike while your iron is hot. You wish in earnest to become an artist. But all these years, I tell you, Sinclair, you have been playing fool with a brush that was made for work. A spark from the fire of God burns in you, waiting to spring into flame. But you have choked it with earth that it cannot burn. And now, see—right out of heaven, this star dropt at your feet. Waste no more time, making glow-worms with your eternal cigarette. Santa Maria! How can you with your insolence of youth and health know— as I know'—he beat upon his damaged chest and coughed again— 'that time is gold and diamonds and all the riches of the earth rolled into one mass. Know it or not, only hear this poor devil with one lung and paint your picture while you can. Paint it that it shall please me, and Jacques Lesseppes—and then——' He stayed for breath, and again it was Broome who interposed, instinctively keeping the balance of things by putting all his weight into the opposite scale.

'You forget, Martino, that as the eldest son of an old English family Sinclair owes it to his father to make an honest bid for a parliamentary career——'

'Huh! Parliamentary candlesticks——!'

'Fiddlesticks, you mean, my dear chap!'

'*Ah, bene!* Fiddlesticks—candlesticks—it is all one.'

'Oh, no; not quite!' Broome's twinkling gravity held its own. Structural differences, you know, to say nothing of value! Besides, in this case——'

The Italian flung up his hands in an ecstasy of impatience, and clapped them over his ears. 'I am a deaf. I hear not anything!' he declared, not all in jest; and Nevil, springing up, gripped his friend by the shoulders from behind.

'What shall we do to him, Martino *mio*? Gag him with his own proofs?'

'If—you—please,' the small man answered with grave emphasis; and at their joint shout of laughter his black brows went up. The gods who gifted him at birth had overlooked the saying grace of humour. 'You are always making some kind of foolishness—you two,' he said, looking from one to the other with puzzled intensity. 'But it remains that for candlesticks or fiddlesticks, I care nothing; and for fathers and parliaments not a great deal either. With art it must be as with religion. To those who are called she speaks as the Great Master to his disciples—"Leave father and mother, leave all—and follow me." You—Broome, you have written books to her dictation. You know that is truth.'

The man's ardour and sincerity were irresistible, and Cuthbert Broome answered in all seriousness: 'Yes, my dear Martino, I know it. But like all counsels of perfection it is "more honoured in the breach than in observance"; except among pseudo-artists, who find it a convenient cloke for egregious disregard of others. And in any case, a man must be very sure of his call.'

'*Ebbene*—it is *I* who am sure—for Sinclair. He doubts, because he has modesty. But give him at least one chance to prove I am right.'

He turned briskly upon Nevil. 'You will speak to that man?'

'Rather! But I believe they have odd prejudices—these Indians.'

Martino dismissed them with a snap of the fingers. 'You show him the sketch, my friend. It will suffice. But when?'

'To-day, I hope. I'm to meet them at tea-time.' He took out his watch. 'By Jove, it's late. I ought to go at once.'

'Be off, then; and bring me word to-morrow that all is arranged.'

'I thought of asking Sir Lakshman to dine with us to-night.'

'Good! Better than all. Then Martino can get in his word—and the thing is done. Go now—and the saints prosper you.'

Nevil Sinclair went whistling along the passage and on down the wide staircase to the first floor. In three days his world had grown singularly interesting and stimulating. More than ever did he bless the house-party that had driven him to Antibes.

It was as Audrey had foreseen; his invitation to tea in the verandah the day after the dance had been refused on the score of Lilamani's shyness. Also, on that afternoon Sir Lakshman had promised her two hours out in a boat with himself: but he hoped Mr. Sinclair would come to them for tea on the following day. Mr. Sinclair had accepted with alacrity; and—Audrey being 'off duty'—had suggested a walk with her along the sharply indented coast to the picturesque old town of Antibes, returning, as of old, via the Lighthouse hill, highest viewpoint of the headland. No word of the picture had been spoken; Martino being too ill, for the moment, to be troubled with such matters; and Nevil preferring to await his verdict before taking any definite steps in the matter. Both had thoroughly enjoyed the easy sense of comradeship, the picking up of dropped threads, and not least the pleasant flavour of reminiscence running through it all.

Only when Audrey had left him to stroll awhile on the gravel path with his cigar, did the wandering thought slip into Sinclair's brain that there went a woman who would make a man 'sit up and do things,' if she cared for him; a wife such as Jane would surely approve, had he any leaning toward marriage in the abstract, which he had not. Hitherto, at all events, the modern man's dread of responsibility and the artist's need of individual freedom had proved stronger than any vagrant impulse of the heart.

Yet the impression made on him by this girl was no light one. In many ways he found her eminently to be desired; and now, looking backward, he wondered vaguely why he had not fallen in love with her years ago. Nor did he guess that other men, who also found her eminently to be desired, had wondered the same thing without stumbling on the discovery that, like many admirable girls of her type, Audrey Hammond lacked altogether that indefinable essence called charm, atmosphere. Even as a landscape at noon fails to thrill the imagination as at sunset or dawn, so does the clear-cut, self-complete woman of transition fail to stir the tumultuous deeps of passion. In one respect, at least, evolving man remains eternally the same—'it is mystery that he chases finally, not beauty or love or any success.' Like to like is for friendship. For love—that can lift a man's heart near to worship—the charm that eludes, and by its very elusiveness, holds him fast.

Not that Sinclair, even now, realized all this any more than the rest had done; but at least it was with a glow of satisfaction that—on entering their sitting-room—he found Audrey alone, standing by the tea-table in broad straw hat and cream serge coat.

'You're not long in, then?' he said as they shook hands. 'I thought I was late.'

'You are late! So are we. Lilamani begged for another ride on the sea though the glare was terrific and it gave her a headache.'

'She's coming in, though—I hope?'

'Oh, yes. Are you so keen?' Her amused eyes scrutinized his face; and in another moment the tale of the picture would have been told. But lo, the door opened and the living picture appeared: simplicity's self this time, in the creamy, clinging softness of Indian muslin; only her *sari's* hem threaded with the gold she loved.

At sight of the tall fair man, whom she had scarcely taken in on that bewildering evening, her head drooped delicately, while the blood glowed under the clear olive of her cheek and throat. For an instant it seemed as if she would turn and fly; then Audrey's protective arm enclosed her, and Audrey's kindly voice of decision was at her ear.

'Come, child, and shake hands with Mr. Sinclair. You mustn't be shy with him. He is an old friend. Almost like my brother. I have been telling him how you love riding on the sea in spite of glare and headaches!'

At the magic word her smile flashed on him like a light and she spoke with the eager spontaneity of a child while Audrey poured out tea.

'Oh, yes—yes. I love it! And to-day—it was wonderful, past telling. No waves to ride upon; only a blue, blue bigness and stillness, like gliding through the sky. How could I mind a little ache of my head when my heart inside was "kuroo-koo-ing" like a dove in spring!' Sinclair's smile at the pretty conceit puzzled her, and she added with shy apology: 'You know there is not any sea in Central India where I come from. It is only since these few weeks I have known it for the first time. When you have known it always, perhaps it does not seem so wonderful.'

'Indeed it does,' he assured her. 'More wonderful the better one knows it; at least to those who have enough imagination to wonder at anything. Audrey must let me introduce you to my artist friend, who has been painting it for fifteen years; and declares he would not come to the end of it if he could paint for a hundred. Then look at sailors, who live on it, year in, year out——'

'Ah, that would be better than all!' she broke in softly. 'I feel always I want to get out far, far, where it is all blue, over and under; not even a trimming of land round the edge.'

Shyness had fallen from her like a cloak. Her serious eyes dwelt confidently upon his face. The subject, the reassuring word 'brother'— most flexible in the Indian language—had wrought like a charm; and Sir Lakshman Singh, entering while she spoke, had a shock of surprise and pleasure, vaguely tinged with apprehension.

'Glad to see you have made friends with my daughter,' he said genially as Sinclair rose to greet him. 'And I hope you will justify to her my high opinion of your country. For her, at present, you are representing the whole English race; which I have taught her to admire as I do myself.'

'A poor look-out for England if she's to be judged by me!' Sinclair retorted, laughing. 'The sooner I introduce your daughter to my friend, Mr. Cuthbert Broome, the better. I shall hardly dare open my lips to her now.'

'Oh, please—please,' Lilamani murmured so distressfully that everyone laughed, and that sent the blood tingling into her cheeks. 'He was praising the sea, father,' she added, bravely ignoring her discomfiture. 'He could not begin better, could he?' The words were for her father; but her shy glance was for Sinclair, who answered it forthwith.

'It's easy talking. But what will you think when I say that my father wished me to serve my country on the sea, and—I refused.'

She shook her head incredulously at the slab of cake she was crumbling with nervous fingers.

'It is hard to believe. But—how can I tell? There might be difficulties——'

'Oh, there were—there were! One of the biggest was that I would rather paint the sea than live on it, any day——'

'Ah,' she looked up again, all eagerness. 'You also paint pictures— like your friend?'

'Yes. I paint pictures; but not like my friend. I wish I could,' he answered ruefully, scanning as he spoke the radiantly receptive face, and wondering how he—the 'double-distilled amateur'—dared aspire to render its quicksilver quality in the lifeless medium of paint and canvas.

Yet the resolve to aspire remained; and mention of his art having slipped in, by a happy chance, he dwelt upon it guilefully in view of that which was to come. To Sir Lakshman the subject was a congenial one. The two men were soon deep in animated talk; while Lilamani sat entranced, drinking it all in as an opening flower drinks in sun and dew; and even taking her own small share in it without a trace of the overwhelming shyness that had baffled and disappointed Nevil at the start. Her intelligence amazed him. Audrey was right. She was more than a picture, after all; more than a child, too, it seemed, though even now he scarce regarded her as woman.

A memorable tea-drinking it was for all; though at the time none guessed its significance save Nevil himself, increasingly aware as he was of hidden depths stirred by the wind of the spirit, that bloweth where it listeth, making music through the children of men as the wind of earth through an Æolian harp.

The invitation to dinner, lightly given and lightly accepted, the suggestion—Lilamani's—that when next they rode upon the great deep he should come also, filled him with a boyish exultation out of all proportion to the bare facts; and the dinner itself confirmed his hopeful mood. Sir Lakshman, having spoken once or twice to Broome, and read much of his work, welcomed a chance of closer intimacy; and Martino, mindful of the hidden houri, plied his tongue of gold to good purpose throughout the meal.

But the subject of the evening was not broached till privacy and the congenial atmosphere of the 'studio' paved the way for confidential talk. Broome had not yet come up, and Martino was rummaging in the adjacent bedroom for a couple of Italian studies, when Nevil took his courage in both hands—and spoke.

'Sir Lakshman Singh, I have a confession to make—and a favour to ask,' he said simply.

'A confession—to me? On so slight acquaintance?' the Indian asked with his kindly smile.

'Yes. It sounds odd. But, you see—it's like this——' A moment of tingling hesitation, then it all came out in straightforward, boyish speech—the vision, the temptation, the resulting sketch, and—with a fresh access of boldness—the final aspiration fostered by Martino's praise.

Sir Lakshman listened with contracted brows, and Martino, returning while the tale was in progress, could scarce restrain his good word till their guest had spoken his mind: no easy matter for a man torn between clear vision of the Western standpoint, and innate recoil from its application to his Jewel of Delight.

'I fear you will not understand me in this matter, so well as I understand you,' he said at last, courteously, yet not without constraint; for the high-caste Hindu does not speak of his women folk to other men. 'If I were English, doubtless I should feel flattered by your request. As it is—well—I have allowed my daughter, for good reasons, to break through the customs of my caste and country. But to remove a screen is not miraculously to remove all—that the screen implies. For the women of India the significance of Purdah is deeper and more complex than we can ever hope to make Westerns believe. It is ingrained in the soul of the race. It is——' He paused, looking from one to the other, increasingly reluctant, and all that was best in Sinclair sprang spontaneously to his aid.

'If the notion distresses you, Sir Lakshman,' said he, 'please think no more of it. In fact—if you really wish it—I will tear up my sketch——'

'By God, Sinclair, you shall do no such madness!' Martino broke in hoarsely; then turning upon the Hindu, twin flames in his eyes: 'Sir, you do not understand what it means for him to say that. He has in him the divine spark. I know it—I. And beauty like that of your daughter——'

'Shut up, Martino, for God's sake!' Sinclair cried out, goaded to irritability by the uncertainty that racked him, as the artist was swift to understand.

'Then talk no more madness,' said he, with less heat. 'And at least show your work to Sir Lakshman Singh, that he may judge if I have not right in what I say.'

'Yes—yes, let me see what you have done.' Repressed eagerness lurked in the father's tone; and Nevil, too perturbed for speech, took up his book, doubled it backwards, and handed it to the arbiter of his Fate. For the moment, he felt as though all things worth anything hung upon Sir Lakshman's 'Yes' or 'No': and in truth more hung upon it than either guessed.

'Thank you,' he said quietly; and rising, went over to the electric light near the bed. Here he stood, with his back half turned, considering the handiwork of this bold young man, who could dare to reproduce his Lilamani—daughter of his heart.

Followed a tense silence, that would have been broken by Martino but for an imperious gesture from his friend. Then Sir Lakshman faced them again, his features schooled to a composure that was far from him. 'It is herself,' he said, as quietly as he had said 'Thank you.' 'Signor Martino is right about your gift. You must use it—use it. But—there are other beautiful subjects; and that you should make a living picture of—of her, for all the world to look on . . .'

'No—no, not *that*,' Nevil interposed, and the sympathetic understanding in his voice brought him nearer his heart's desire than all that had gone before. 'I am not a professional. If you allow me to paint a figure study of your daughter, I would only ask leave to show it to Signor Martino and his friend, a noted painter in Paris; also perhaps, to my father; because their opinions might just prove the turning-point in my life. For the rest, the picture remains my private property; or—if it proves worth accepting—yours, to do with as you please.'

'Mine!' Sir Lakshman echoed in amaze. 'But, my dear sir, I, a stranger, have no right to accept your work—that may be of value——'

'Only in so far as it may justify my choice of a career. If it does that, I can do no less than offer it to you as a token of gratitude for your permission, and as a reminder of your daughter, while she is away from you at college.'

It was a few seconds before the Indian could command his voice; then—'You know too well how to tempt a father, Mr. Sinclair,' he said feelingly. 'And I can do no less than accept, gratefully, your offer and your gift; unless my daughter should shrink altogether from the idea. I would not for the world subject her to such an ordeal against her will. But I will speak to her.'

'When?' The eager question leapt from Sinclair's lips and eyes, and the older man smiled.

'You are young—therefore impatient.' He drew out his watch. 'If I go now, I can talk with her to-night; then you shall have your answer the first thing in the morning.'

'And if all's well—I could start in the afternoon?'

'Yes; in the afternoon.'

'I shan't sleep for thinking of it!' Nevil declared as they shook hands.

But, being young, he did sleep—soundly; though impatience waked him long before his usual hour; and, once awake, the turmoil within gave him no rest. He breakfasted alone with the waiters and one English girl—pretty, and fresh-looking, clearly a lover of the morning. Then, while the tables were filling, he paced the empty pathway to the sea, making glowworms with his cigarette—to no purpose. For the first time in his life the fire of genuine enthusiasm burned in him; and he knew that until now he had not truly lived; that now, if the chance were given him, he could not fail of success. Like most men of the age he had early lost the habit of prayer: but intensity of hope and desire brought him nearer to it than he had been for years.

On turning for the second time in his caged-lion walk, he sighted Audrey's grey figure at the foot of the steps, and hurried forward. Not so she; and her smile, as she drew near, had a touch of constraint as yet unknown to him.

But he could not stay to consider that.

'You have brought Sir Lakshman's consent?' he cried in one breath.

'Yes,' she answered coolly. He had never dreamed her eyes could look so hard.

'And you don't approve?'

Her straight brows went up ever so little.

'I? Do I count at all?'

'Of course you do. But still——'

'But still—not enough to matter; which amounts to not at all. Yet it is I who brought her here, Nevil. It is I who am devoting my hardly-earned leave to her. Surely you might have consulted *me* before making a proposal that is bound to distract her from studies, on which I have trouble enough to hold her attention as it is——'

'I thought so!' Nevil cried, triumphant and quite unrepentant. 'She's not the type. And if they are uncongenial, why press them on her?'

'For very good reasons—that are no concern of yours,' she answered, looking him straight in the eyes. But he wore his elation like a shirt of chain mail, and merely asked with interest:

'Does she mind much—about sitting to me?'

'Yes. She rather dreads it; I can see that. But her father could not conceal his pleasure at the idea, and for his sake she made light of her natural recoil from it. We talked of it afterwards, she and I; but she begged me not to let him know. I confess I did my best to make her retract her consent; you may think what you please of me. But I didn't see why my carefully thought out plans should be put out for the mere whim of an idler——'

He winced. 'I say, Audrey, don't hit so hard. It's more than a whim. You know that. And I do think you're a bit selfish——'

'Selfish? Of course I am!' she flashed out with her formidable directness. 'We're all selfish, whether we admit it or not. It's the main motive power of human achievement. You've as much right to yours, after all—as I have to mine. But still—it does seem hard that the child's studies, which are important for her and may mean a great deal to me, should be interrupted—perhaps upset——'

Genuine emotion checked her, and roused at once the natural kindliness of the man. 'Aren't you making more of it than you need, Audrey?' he asked gently, and she drew in her lips, hiding their tendency to soften at his tone. 'A sitting every other day will do for me, and in between you can cram as much into her as you please. The whole thing won't take much more than a fortnight. I'm no portrait painter; it can only be a study. Then you can wipe me out of your sacred programme altogether, if you choose!'

'That remains to be seen!' she answered, forcing a smile as she turned away. He made as if to go along with her, but she waved him back. 'You're very nice about it, Nevil, or you wouldn't be you. But just at present I shouldn't be good company. We'll be ready for you this afternoon.'

'And will you ask Miss Lakshman Singh to wear that mother-o'-pearl *sari*?'

'Oh, yes.'

'Much ado about nothing,' he mused, looking after her. 'Queer creatures women—even the soundest.'

Then he sauntered back again toward the grey rocks and the myrtle bushes and the many-twinkling smile of ocean, seeing visions and dreaming dreams.

'Drive nature out with a fork;—she comes running back.'

—Horace

Lilamani stood alone upon her balcony—her 'House of Gods,' she had named it—feeling a little lost without her private shrine dear to Hindu womanhood. And here was a shrine indeed: roofed with turquoise of heaven, paved with sapphire of the sea. The trees set about its portals were rough-cut emerald and jade; and the grey-white rocks that broke up the sapphire into foam of diamonds— what were they? Here she was at a loss. The rocks, it seemed, stoutly refused to be anything but rocks; and it pleased her whimsical fancy to set this down to the natural obstinacy of their hearts. Surely no Hindu woman—not even the queens of immemorial times when *purdah* was not—could have possessed a House of Gods so richly jewelled; so vast, yet so intimate in its appeal alike to sense and spirit.

Here she came when the demands of her new life, or intrusive thoughts of troubles ahead, perturbed beyond measure that inner calm which broods at the core of Hindu faith. And here she came now to steady herself for the impending ordeal; accepted with joy, despite hidden tremors, because of the gift that would gladden the father she was so soon to lose—for a time; only for a time. Thought of that parting she had not yet schooled herself to face; and to-day the need of the moment eclipsed all else.

She stood very still, as always in these mystical moods of hers; that were, in truth, but a spontaneous surrender of her whole being to the strong serene influences wherewith light and colour baptize the receptive soul. To-day, from shore-line to sky-line, the sea's vast breadth rose and fell like the breasts of the blue goddess Durga in her sleep. The very wavelets lapping against the rocks were too lazy to laugh in foam. To her it seemed that the Gods of her pantheon blessed her decision, and reassured her tremulous spirit; stilling its nameless fears. She—a brave man's daughter—who had so boldly taken the first step toward freedom, ought by no means to shrink from the lesser penalties involved. And she would not shrink; not even in thought. Her father's willingness to grant so unorthodox a favour should suffice for his child.

The fact that this god-like young man, with threads of sunlight in his hair and the sea's changeful laughter in his eyes, was of an alien race, seemed to make possible that which could else be scarce endured. For, if publicity be thrust upon a *Purdahnashin*, race-distance strangely lessens the sense of impropriety. Besides, this Mr. Sinclair—she named him shyly—was Audrey's friend: almost her brother. No; most certainly she would not shrink. She would look at and speak with him straightly, even as Audrey did. She would be calm, without and within. Not so much as one foolish pulse should flutter——

Then, the door-handle turned; a man's step sounded in the room behind her; and she stood transfixed, while the hammering of her pulses—that were not even to flutter—filled all space. How should she face him, she—the courageous one—who had even now commanded the waves of the sea and believed they would obey her? What had become of Audrey, of her father, that they had left her to face—this, without them?

Then—with a glad start, she recognized her father's footsteps also. Yet could she not bring herself to turn till he came close behind her, and spoke softly in their own tongue.

'Art worshipping, child?'

'Seeking a sign, rather. And the omens be favourable!' Her smile was a triumph of luminous serenity; and the man's last doubts were stilled. 'It is well,' said he; adding in English: 'Come, then. Mr. Sinclair is here, and ready to begin.'

Sinclair, who had busied himself, tactfully, with colour and tubes, came forward.

'I'm afraid you dislike the whole thing,' he said, hoping by frank friendliness to put her at ease. 'And it makes me feel rather like a dentist preparing to operate!'

'I have never seen a dentist,' she answered sweetly, 'And I can't tell if I will dislike it—till I've tried! But I am quite pleased to try. It is so wonderful—' her eyes dwelt thoughtfully upon the clean expanse of canvas. 'Nothing there now! Yet in one week, or two, I will see my own reflection, as in a mirror——'

'I wish I could believe that!' Sinclair was squeezing paints on to his palette. 'You shall see the nearest that my unpractised brush can create.'

'You have the modesty of true talent,' Sir Lakshman interposed. 'Show my daughter the creation of your pencil.'

Nevil, who had not come without his treasure, put the open book into her hands; and while she stood absorbed—fascinated as a child might be at first sight of its own image—he made a few preliminary strokes upon that blank canvas which stood for him as the possible turning-point in his life.

It was at this moment that Audrey entered, and paused in the doorway, watching her pupil with an odd contraction of the heart. Never had book or dissertation of hers brought that wrapt look to Lilamani's face. Was she then, for all her brains and courage, no true pioneer student; but mere woman, such as India breeds by the thousand? At least this annoying interruption might have the merit of putting her to the proof. Here Lilamani, disturbed by the double scrutiny, looked up; and, meeting Sinclair's narrowed gaze, pulled her *sari* forward with the petulant imperiousness of a spoilt child. Dignity and thought of her father alone saved her from ignominious flight.

'Oh, no—that's hard lines—' she heard Sinclair say and the ring of disappointment in his tone smote her sensitiveness more sharply than rebuke.

'I am sorry. I promise not to be foolish any more,' she murmured penitently, and was reassured by the support of Sir Lakshman's arm.

'Sit down, my child,' he said tenderly, drawing her to a chair beside the table. 'Just lean on one elbow, as in the sketch; and if you are not caring to talk, then read. Only Mr. Sinclair must be permitted to see your face!'

'Yes. That is the trouble!' she answered, flushing and smiling tremulously, as she arranged her veil. 'If I may read, I will have my little "Wisdom and Destiny," please.'

But a haunting sense of the man's concentration on her affected her like a lantern flashed in her eyes: and Nevil, keenly aware of her quivering sensibilities, contented himself with as brief a sitting as might be.

Sir Lakshman, having promised to drive with Broome, went out, leaving an abnormally studious daughter behind him; and Nevil devoted himself not unreadily to the delicate task of toning down Audrey's disapproval. It troubled his kindly nature to feel out of gear with any unit of his world; and by way of practical conciliation he suggested driving her into Cannes next day in the motor chartered by himself and Broome.

'You could leave Miss Lakshman Singh with something to prepare for you, and it will give her a nice quiet time for the deep studies I am so wantonly interrupting!' he added, with an irrepressible twinkle, and had the satisfaction of producing the double effect he hoped for. Audrey was manifestly pleased; and Miss Lakshman Singh looked up, an answering gleam in her eyes.

'Audrey knows too well that it would be Browning or Maeterlinck or Miss Sorabji the minute her back was turned!'

Nevil laughed.

'A hopeful pupil! I don't know, Miss Sorabji. But there's a deal to be learnt from the other two—even if it's not physics. Three o'clock suit you, Audrey?'

'I've not accepted yet!'

'Not? Why, your eyes said "yes" the minute I spoke.'

'Pure conceit on your part! They merely said it would be nice; but, in the face of Lilamani's confession, surely—inconsistent?'

'Therefore human! Consistency is the bugbear of small minds and I've always believed yours to be—quite the reverse!'

At that, Audrey, the self-possessed, blushed for the first time in many years; and being awkwardly aware of the fact blushed deeper still. 'Really, Nevil, you are too foolish for words,' was all she said.

But Nevil knew he had gained his point, and made his peace with her, for the moment at least. 'Three o'clock sharp, then,' he said as he covered the easel. 'And for you,' turning to Lilamani, 'Friday at the same time?'

'Yes—yes.'

Her hesitancy distressed him.

'Not unless you feel inclined, of course,' he added at once. 'You've only to send me word. I shall understand.'

'Because you are so kind,' she murmured shyly. 'But I have promised not to be foolish any more; and the Wise Man, Truth-named, says that to break one's word is "damage to Sainthood."'

'Well said—the Wise Man! And who may he be?'

'He's my chosen Guru—since I left India. I found him in Miss Sorabji's book. Some day, if the gods are kind, I may find him in the flesh and tell him how he helped for making me be brave.'

'I ought to thank him too for that. And, look here, since you're so strict about promises, will you promise me something else?'

'Ah—what?'

'Nothing very terrible! Only that you and your father will have tea in the verandah with Audrey and me when we get back, if I engage a table right at the far end. Do!'

'Oh—but——' her startled eyes begged help from Audrey—in vain.

'Try it, Lilamani,' said she, 'and see how it feels.'

'Very well—if I must—I promise.'

And so he took his leave; well pleased, and hopeful, though little enough had been achieved—on canvas.

The next afternoon's programme—motoring with Audrey, the Casino band and a turn at the tables, proved no less enjoyable to this man of catholic tastes; though an undercurrent of longing to be back at the picture that meant so much to him, made him a trifle *distrait* during the drive, and disposed him to talk a good deal about 'that charming child.' For such was still his main view of her; and Audrey found herself singularly ready to encourage it; though, for a woman of her type, the encouragement of a fallacy was as little consistent as motoring into Cannes with a young man, when she ought to have been reading physiology with the brand snatched from the burning.

They went alone, Nevil being an accomplished driver and Broome, with ready tact, refusing the invitation that he was clearly not meant to accept. Not that he had by any means solved his problem yet; but that he preferred to glean such crumbs of observation as Fate flung in his path. The tea-party at the end of the verandah, obviously a Fate-flung morsel, proved irresistible. Nor was he disappointed, when, after greetings and introduction he sat down opposite the 'houri';

and—while talking to her father—absorbed, as through a sixth sense, the essence of her quality, and charm. For to-day, she waxed 'braver' than Nevil had seen her yet; and he made good the chance of watching her expressive face in motion while it was his.

So it befell that Audrey soon found herself the odd man out in the little group: a position uncongenial to all save the speculative observer, and at the moment doubly uncongenial to her. She had come back feeling very much at peace with herself and the world, for no particular reason that she knew of; except that she believed motoring to be good for the nerves. But before tea was over, the restless discomfort that had puzzled her yesterday afternoon was upon her again. Not feverishness; for her blood was cool and her pulses steady. Nor did she feel ill: merely ill at ease; though discomfort amounted to irritation when Mrs. Heath fluttered up with Miss Blakeney, and the burden of making small talk for their benefit fell mainly upon her. Even when Miss Blakeney succeeded in detaching Nevil from 'the Hindu child,' Lilamani—instead of helping—relapsed into shyness and monosyllables; for the which she was rated severely when the two found themselves alone again upstairs.

'It's nonsense being so shy with two women, after talking to Nevil so that I couldn't get in a word.'

Her tone was sterner than need be; and Lilamani listened in wide-eyed dismay.

'Audrey—don't call it nonsense,' she pleaded. 'Mr. Sinclair is seeming to talk another kind of language—I can't explain. Don't you understand?'

Yes; in a measure, Audrey understood. But for the moment she was cross, even with Lilamani, whom she loved, in the repressed undemonstrative fashion that was hers. So she merely said: 'Of course they're less interesting. But if you're going to be so fanciful and fastidious, we shall never get on at all.'

To which Lilamani made answer quite gently: 'I don't like you when you're cross, Audrey; and it's nicer having tea upstairs.'

They had it upstairs next day, and all went well. Sir Lakshman left them afterwards, for a stroll with Broome and Nevil looked to a longer sitting and fuller achievement than before. Only one item was amiss. In place of the mother-o'-pearl *sari*, she wore the primrose and gold in which he had seen her first. But not till he had begun painting and charmed away her self-consciousness did he venture any comment on the fact.

Then he said, as if by the way: 'I wonder whether you realize that I wanted you to wear that grey and gold every time?'

'Yes, I did think so,' she answered, smiling. 'But—it seemed not to fit my mind to-day. You see, for me, colours are nearly same as people. Sometimes you are needing one, sometimes another. And if I am always wearing the one you want, by order, it is same as if you told me what words I must speak whenever you come!'

'Heaven forbid!' cried Nevil laughter in his eyes; and she, with pretty imperiousness, tremors forgotten:

'If you were so much—*zubberdust* as that, I would soon say "no more picture"—even for father's sake!'

'Then I won't be "*zubberdust*"—whatever that may be. I must have my picture now, at any price. But if I'm to achieve that *sari*, I've got to see it sometimes. Perhaps being painted will induce the mother-o'-pearl mood! What do you think?'

'I think you understand my silliness better than anyone—only father,' she answered simply as a child. 'And I think when I am in golden mood, or almond-blossom mood, we might have that *sari* thrown over the sofa, to help you. Is that good?'

'Very, good.'

'Shall I fetch it now?'

'Oh, no—don't trouble.'

'But it's not trouble.'

She ran lightly out; and Audrey, who had opened a book, glanced up, frowning.

'Don't talk too much nonsense to her, Nevil. You'll turn the child's head.'

Her tone had an edge to it that surprised herself as much as him; and provoked him to the retort discourteous.

'It's *you* that are talking nonsense, Audrey. For heaven's sake don't say anything repressive when she comes back, and spoil the pains I've taken to put her at ease.'

Audrey shrugged her shoulders and went on reading; for she—who took pride in her full command of the emotions—dared not trust her own voice. A physical feeling of weight on her chest unsteadied her breathing, while the blood tingled in her veins. It was absurd—almost degrading—that a woman of her good sense and convictions should allow the tone or manner of any man so to disturb her regal equanimity. Clearly, something must be wrong. If only Sir Lakshman would come back, she could go out and walk it off. Till then—what on earth was Lilamani doing? To-day everything and everyone seemed in league to set her nerves on edge.

A few seconds later the girl reappeared; and the reason of her delay was obvious.

'Oh, but I never meant you to put it all on for me!' Nevil exclaimed in such evident delight that she laughed softly and clapped her small hands without sound.

'I did not mean either. It—it simply happened!'

'Great luck—for me! The mood came?'

'Yes—in touching it, I wished suddenly to wear it and also—I knew it would give pleasure—to you.'

Her shy hesitancy added grace to the last words and Audrey did not miss the softening of Nevil's eyes as he answered: 'I can't tell you how much pleasure it gives me. But you must obey your colour-moods. I believe in them. And I'll make the most of my chances when they come.'

The little incident seemed magically to affect her spirits and Nevil drew from her by degrees a hidden store of shy, poetic intuitions as to the eloquence and significance of colour; a topic on which he found her far richer in ideas than himself.

For a while Audrey joined their talk. But the subject was too fanciful for her taste; and soon—quite without intention on their part—she found herself, as it were, edged out. Again that tingling, as of red-hot needle-points under her skin; that longing to move, to shake herself free of this nameless something that oppressed her, body and mind. If only Sir Lakshman would come back!

In the meantime she did not choose to force herself into their *tête-à-tête*; nor would she sit merely on guard, while they laughed and talked. Quietly taking up her book, she went out through the French window on to Lilamani's balcony, and stood with her back to the room, while the wind caressed her burning cheeks. Why this unwonted irritation because Nevil, her friend, had so rapidly succeeded in

lifting a corner of the veil that Lilamani would always wear, figuratively, with strangers, though in fact she had cast it aside? It was so
little-minded, so unlike her normal self——

At this point their voices interrupted her thoughts; and she sat
down, keeping Lilamani's face in view. Nevil was urging her to cap
yesterday afternoon's courage by dining downstairs; and Lilamani's
gentle, decisive refusal soothed Audrey strangely. But Nevil was not
the man to accept it without demur.

'You say you are interested in the people you watch from your
balcony,' he persisted genially. 'Yet you don't want to see more of them
close at hand. Why?'

The girl drew her delicate brows together. 'It does seem all wrong
when you say it. But it's true—both ways. I wonder—can I make you
understand?'

She leaned an elbow on the table; and while she spoke Nevil's hand
moved swiftly, capturing the gracious curves of head and shoulder
and arm.

'I think it is really that I love only to watch them all—far away
down there, and plan my own tales about them. But when they come
close, they make so much noise with talk about foolish little things
that my thoughts all get broken up, like water-reflections when you
put your hand into the tank. From the balcony I see them coming and
going. I see them talking and smiling; but their words are never reaching me. When I like some faces very much I watch for them to come
again, and then . . . sometimes . . . you mustn't laugh!—I make mind-
pictures of their souls.'

'Laugh? Of course not!' The best and gentlest that was in his own
soul looked out of the man's eyes. 'Do we all carry them in our faces
plainly to be seen?'

'Oh no. Many do not seem to be at all. Others are small and hidden,
like pools, grown upon with weeds. But there are some—oh some—
they shine clear and still like lakes making mirrors for sun and skies.
My father's is of that kind. Have you not seen?'

'Yes—I have seen. It is good to know men like your father, even a
little. You would find a picture something like that in the eyes of my
friend Broome.'

Her face lit up. 'That man I saw yesterday with gold in his beard?
Oh yes! But his soul is all sparkling like the sea over here.'

'Good indeed! Yet you hardly spoke to him at all.'

'My pictures come more clearly without speaking. I told you—it interrupts!'

'You're a white witch!' he said, laughing. 'And are all your soul-pictures of water?'

'No. Some are sky and clouds. Some birds. Some walled court-yards——'

'And mine? Have you made a picture of mine? Do tell me.'

Audrey—out on the balcony, frowned at the intrusion of the personal note, and contemplated a return to her post, the more so when she saw that Lilamani veiled her eyes. But curiosity gained the day.

'It is difficult,' the girl said softly; and Nevil wished his picture more advanced that he might catch the veiled blush permeating the olive tint of her skin.

'Why? Because you see it like a mud-puddle with a star or two dropped into it?'

'But no—no!' The imputation unloosed her tongue. 'I see it like one of those glad, quickly-moving rivers in the hills that I am reading about in books. How shall I truly paint it for you? There are rocks, and bending trees, and birds—you know——'

'Yes—I know quite well. And an aimless, chattering stream, dodging to and fro, and achieving nothing——'

Oh no—you are unkind! I did not mean it so——'

The tremor in her voice smote the strongest chord of his manhood.

'Of course you didn't. Forgive my nonsense,' he said hastily. 'I quite understand; and you couldn't have painted a truer picture. Ask Audrey.'

The girl outside started; and to her relief Lilamani sprang up with a cry of joy: 'Here comes my father! And—oh—there is someone else——'

As Sir Lakshman entered with Cuthbert Broome, Audrey stepped in from the balcony, determined on flight. Not that she admitted the ignominious word into her mind. Her ostensible excuse was shopping in Antibes; and before starting, she—who inveighed against stimulant, except in illness—took a dose of Lilamani's sal volatile to still the flutter at her heart. It was bad enough owning to nerves at all. But this haunting discomfort could by no means be ignored; and instinctively she sought a physical basis for most forms of mental disturbance.

The tram, with its chattering 'fares' and the prosaic business of shopping shut out, for a space, the memory of those two voices that had so annoyingly perturbed her: and reduced, at last, to her normal calm, she decided to complete the cure by a brisk walk back along the coast. But she had not gone far before she discovered her mistake. Unquestionably she should have been faithful to the tram. For along this path by the sea she had walked scores of times with Nevil, in the old days; and again only four days earlier in simple, unthinking content. And now——

What folly was this that had gotten hold of her? At each turn of the road some memory waylaid her of Nevil's face, and Nevil's friendly presence; the sympathetic inflections of his voice; the smile lurking always beneath his gravest mood. Breaking wavelets whispered his name at her feet. Sun and sky shouted it overhead. Look where she would, his face smiled back at her, in imperturbable disregard of her bewilderment and distress. With a dry sob in her throat, she sank upon a rock and covered her eyes, as if the vision she would escape came from without, not from within.

But the act was instinctive, merely. She knew now—and raged against the knowledge, like a trapped beast—that she, even she, had fallen in love. Nature, careless of individual conviction, had wrenched the heart out of her body, and given it to a man, who no more needed it than she needed the pebbles at her feet: a man by no means her match in forcefulness of purpose or of will.

The thought burned in her till all her body seemed one flame. What right had he to take possession of her thus, against her will? The thing challenged her pride; her perverted spirit of antagonism against all that man stood for in the average woman's life. From earliest girlhood she had taken her stand with the advanced guard of her kind; had even presumed to despise the average woman and all her works. And now—behold her punishment! Scorn is a slippery weapon; apt to turn in the hand. It was the twisted blade of her own scorn that cut most deeply into Audrey Hammond's heart. With the inherent stoicism that was hers, she repudiated her discovery; denied it; trampled on it—to no purpose. Finally she rose on the decision that at least she could conquer it—unless——

Again that tingling of hot needle-points in her veins. Not even in thought would she complete her broken sentence.

SEVEN

'There stood one with a heart in her hands: there sat another
with hers in a cage:—and the tale goes on.'

—Hewlett

If those two first sittings had proved trying to Audrey, they
were as nothing to the later ones that followed upon her disastrous
walk by the sea.

Whenever Sir Lakshman Singh's presence set her free, she would
find some valid excuse for slipping away to the garden; or the piano;
or better still, to spend an hour with Madame de Lisle and her boy,
whose trouble was of a kind that her practical nature could help and
understand. This is what comes of putting one's life into the hands of
a man, she would reflect, by way of consolation, whenever Monsieur
de Lisle's folly and selfishness reacted more sharply than usual upon
his wife and child. But the consolation did not strike deep, and do
what she might, the thought of the two, left in the sitting-room,
knocked incessantly at her heart. The primitive woman in her—long
repressed and denied—rose up with might and taught her, at first
hand, some plain truths that she had little will to learn. She, who took
her stand upon self-knowledge, found suddenly that she had a stranger to reckon with—and that stranger, Audrey Hammond. For love,
like all great natural disturbances, stirs up best and worst alike from
the deep waters of the human heart. Had it come to this, that she was
actually jealous of Lilamani, because Nevil's eyes and mind were
concentrated upon her with increasing delight as the picture grew under his hand. So much at least was patent; even as the change in her—
smother it how she might—was patent to Nevil. He set it down to her
original disapproval; and was disappointed to find her so obstinate
over a question settled past dispute.

But, for him, every minor consideration was dwarfed by the one
thing that mattered: his picture, that already whispered of success,

and the quickening sense of power that grew by what it fed on. There was a delicate pleasure, also, in the pursuit of an intimacy by no means to be hurried or unduly pressed. For all her young simplicity and flashes of confidence, this alluring child of an ancient race was still, in his eyes, almost as much a thing apart from the common round of life as she had seemed at first sight. Still, for him, she was the Arabian Nights Princess brought hither by a kindly Fate to save him from the ambitions of others and kindle his spark of talent to a flame. Something of this Audrey guessed, and rated herself roundly for the relief it brought her. It was not Lilamani, it was the picture that enthralled him. With its completion, he would retreat to his allegiance; and then—then——

But at this point the old unawakened Audrey would slam the door sternly, upon vain imaginings unworthy an enlightened woman.

And Lilamani?

For her this week—charged with a hidden drama—was a time of mental and spiritual changes the more vital because they were evolving unawares. Nor had they any direct relation to the studies so zealously pressed upon her by Audrey. These traversed only the surface of her mind, leaving few and hazy impressions in their wake. From books more inspiring than any in Audrey's trunk she had learnt astonishingly much for her years; and now her hidden self whispered that it were well to learn something of her fellow-beings direct from life; or, in other words, from the blue eyes and golden speech of the first white man Fate had flung in her path of life.

All unguessed by her the folded flower of her heart was opening, like a lotus to the moon, under an influence silent and irresistible as that which draws petal from petal till the shining secret stands revealed. She only knew that the dreaded sittings had become the pivot round which all lesser lights revolved; that the days between seemed empty and unsatisfying; the more so, because those days were disfigured by Audrey's battalions of the 'ugly words' that hurt her mind. 'Hygiene,' 'oxygen,' 'structural physiology': she grew to hate the sound of them; to wonder how she would ever face those dreadful 'exams,' whose mission was simply to give her a free pass back to India, as a woman qualified to live her own life, and to help those who could not or would not desert the beaten track.

But what if she herself found the unbeaten one too steep, too stony? No—no. That were mere weakness. By some means she must attain her goal; though at present its far-off gleam was dimmed by emotions more immediate in their appeal to her budding womanhood than any she had yet known.

So it befell that she let Sinclair persuade her to join a tea-party in the studio, where she was presented to Martino and ravished his inflammable heart. Nay more, she spent two evenings downstairs, losing, each time, a little of that paralysing shyness induced by strange human beings in the mass. It cost her a greater effort than Audrey or Sir Lakshman knew; and both times she had her reward. Nevil devoted himself to her as gallantly as though he divined that the effort had been made for his pleasure; and Broome began to ask himself, was it, after all, not the picture, but the *houri*?

As for Audrey, it was useless to repeat that the craze would pass, that there could be no possibility of serious complications between such mighty opposites. She was in the grip of an emotion that is deaf to reason, nor regards the great god Common Sense, under whose banner she had lived and moved. On the second occasion she could scarce speak naturally to Lilamani when they reached their rooms; and the girl, who had come up a-flutter with the thrill of her new gladness, had gone to bed chilled, puzzled, almost unhappy.

So day by day the love and confidence that had been between them were dimmed by friction and constraint; and more trying than all— for each in her degree—were the morning hours of study. New faces, new imaginings, and the thrill enhancing both, estranged Lilamani more than ever from Audrey's bone-dry discourses on conditions of health and disease. The call of youth in her blood was ten times more commanding than any appeal to her intellect or ambition. Again and again, in defiance of brave resolves, her fancy would wander off at will, while Audrey's voice, reading or explaining, formed a sonorous accompaniment to the airy visions of her dream.

Audrey, meanwhile, had her own private devils to fight; and the fact that at times they mastered her, bred a smothered irritability that too often flashed out in sarcasm, or sharp speech. Her pupil's increasing absentmindedness annoyed her as never before. Nevil's doing, she could have sworn it. Whether he were merely turning the girl's head or disturbing her heart, some sort of veiled warning seemed advisable. Yet she shrank from engendering by premature speech, ideas that might never occur to this unsophisticated child of seclusion.

In any case the effect upon her studies was obvious. Each morning Audrey was maddened afresh by a sense of ploughing the sands. Each morning, when books, notes, and pencils were put away, the mutual sigh of relief became harder to restrain. Whenever Audrey's vexation flashed out, Lilamani's penitence would have disarmed a stone. But no penitence, however genuine, saved her from relapse next day: and at last, after a week of mingled happiness and strain, the inevitable crisis came.

It was a day of sudden, still heat. Even the persistent light wind of the Riviera seemed too lazy to blow. And it is on just such balmy days that imagination, like the swallow, soars highest into the blue; as Lilamani found to her cost.

To-day her mood was less rebellious than usual. She was making an honest effort to 'be good' and 'attend.' But Audrey's chosen subject was not a happy one; nor had she the art of infusing life into dead facts. Her remarks on sick-room hygiene, illustrated by Indian experiences, were eminently sane, eminently practical; while Lilamani sat still as a mouse under a cat's claw, a pencil in her fingers, her eyes on the brilliant strip of sky and treetops framed by the open French windows. Vainly she clutched at each sentence, trying not to let it slip out of her mind as it passed; till she began to feel like a clumsy child playing at ball, and the foolish fancy whisked her miles away.

For a space Audrey talked on, unaware. But when, in the midst of a technical dissertation on invalid food-values, a dreamy half-smile flitted across her pupil's face, the smothered irritation of days leaped out in flame.

'Lilamani, will you attend!' she cried, slapping the open book so sharply that the girl jumped in her seat. 'Have you heard one word of what I've just said?'

Lilamani puckered her forehead distressfully. 'Oh yes—I heard.'

'Well then—tell me what it was.'

'It was—I——' She passed a hand across her brow as if to brush away cobwebs. 'It was—oh, I forget.'

'Speak the truth, please. You never heard it at all.'

'I did *hear*—only——'

'You weren't listening?'

'I—I suppose not . . . I was thinking——'

'Of carbons and proteids?'

'No . . . no . . . of some small verses I have been trying to make. One had just come so beautifully; and you've startled it away.'

'Verses? Good heavens, you're incorrigible! What about?'

The grey eyes probed the brown ones as a lancet probes a wound— and they drew blood. Lilamani looked down, saw she had scribbled a line or two, and crumpling up the paper thrust it into her bodice.

'I cannot tell you what about, Audrey,' she said, with the gentle dignity that so well became her. 'They are only for my own private heart——'

'Don't distress yourself. I've no wish to see them.' Her tone was cold now, her face a mask. 'But I have at least the right to insist that you shall not write verses when I am talking of far more important subjects and trying to make them clear to you. I wonder if you've taken in anything at all this week? Look at your notebook! Nothing but a few incoherent scribbles. It's a disgrace! And here—verses again——'

Lilamani's hand covered them promptly, and she tore out the page. 'I can't help that. It's my nature,' she said with a touch of heat. 'I am not meaning to write them when you talk. They come.'

'My dear girl, don't ask me to believe such fairy-tales. But if they do come—you must stop them coming—or I must stop teaching you. Frankly, Lilamani, I expected great things of you; and I am disappointed. Girls of your race are generally such eager students—so quick with their brains——'

'My brain is made in another pattern—that's why.'

'It didn't seem so at first. It's all this stupid business of the picture and seeing so many people that has turned your head——'

At that Lilamani pushed aside the hated books and sprang to her feet. Tears stood in her eyes. The crimson of anger stained her cheeks. 'Oh, I am sick of these studies—you are unkind to speak such things. I shall not hear you. My head is not "turned," and the picture is not at all stupid. It is going to be a beautiful gift for my dear father. As for too many people—it was you that made me——'

Her voice broke, and she hid her face from the eyes that seemed to look through her as if she were a pane of glass. A word, even a look of sympathy, might have worked wonders just then. But though Audrey was not so made, she could not see the girl thus, unmoved.

'My dear child,' she said, touching her shoulder and speaking more gently, though scarce tenderly. 'When I "made you," as you say, I couldn't foresee that—that things would move so fast. You're not quite strong yet, and a little overwrought through doing too much. That's all the trouble really. Lie down for an hour, and I'll give you some bromide——'

That last was fatal. Lilamani stepped swiftly backward, and uncovered her face.

'Oh, you *don't* understand! You never do. You think everything is from the body. This trouble is in my soul—and you cannot cure it with any of your stupid medicines——'

Audrey's face hardened again.

'No. I don't understand your behaviour,' she said in chill, even tones. 'But I wish *you* to understand that if you think medicines "stupid" and are already sick of your studies, they will not be forced on you by me. Give up college and medicine, by all means—if you are prepared to go back home and obey your mother's wishes——'

'No—no. I will not—I will kill myself rather!' the girl cried out with sudden passion and fled precipitately, leaving Audrey alone by the table, angry and bewildered as she had rarely been in all the well-regulated years of her life.

Her bewilderment was for Lilamani; her anger was for Nevil, first and last. The emotion of a week, however genuine, was no match for the sex antagonism of ten years. 'When man comes in at the window, Peace goes out at the door,' was her favourite perversion of the old proverb anent Poverty and Love. And behold her wisdom justified: but at what cost! Small consolation to reflect that she had foreseen this result of Sir Lakshman Singh's permission. But there would be some satisfaction in telling Nevil plainly what damage he had done to the girl whom he obviously admired, if nothing more.

Why not seek him out and tell him now—while she could trust her embittered heart to hurt either him or herself with an equal stoicism . . .

Lilamani, leaning against her closed door, a-quiver from head to foot, heard her friend's departing footsteps, and drew a breath of relief.

Never till now had she admitted that there lurked in Audrey some unnameable quality that seemed to rub the bloom off everything, and crush out all the beauty and colour of life. Whether that quality belonged to this Englishwoman or to all, Lilamani could not tell. But there were moments when the prospect of a college full of Audreys, with a Miss Blakeney or two thrown in, seemed hardly less terrifying than the marriage from which she had fled.

While she leaned against the door, with closed eyes and heaving breast, tears stole unheeded over her cheeks that were no more on fire of anger, because anger was drowned in shame at her own loss of self-command. Had not that dear father—whose precepts were sacred to her as the laws of Manu—impressed on her from the earliest childhood that only the low-born or the god-forsaken allow the red mist of anger to darken the light within? Happy for her that he had not seen her five minutes ago. But now, the way being clear, she could slip softly back to her House of Gods, and recapture the virtue she had lost.

There sun and sea gave her greeting, and a little lazy wind whispered of evening coolness not far off. Lying back in her chair, she closed her eyes again, that the last of the sunbeams might caress their lids, while the twin healers—warmth and silence—spoke peace to her soul. Of a sudden, in the heart of silence a sound was born: a footstep. Well, what matter? Let it pass. But she had an almost uncanny ear for footsteps; and this one——

She leaned forward eagerly: eyes wide, lips apart. Yes. It was he, in the greenish-grey flannel suit that she always hoped for when he came. Remembering the afternoon when she had seen him first, she could scarce believe it was but two weeks ago. It seemed as if it must have been another Lilamani in another life. Yet it was indeed she, even to the selfsame yellow *sari*: but how little she had dreamed——Here came a shy thought not to be framed in words; and she slipped past it hurriedly wondering if he would look up; if a vision of her ever visited his mind when she was not present?

It was as if she had spoken aloud. He looked up at once. For a long moment his eyes held hers, while the blood burned in her cheeks.

Then, taking courage, she waved a hand. To her amazement, he replied by a gesture bidding her come down; and all the natural woman in her yearned to obey. But for a Hindu girl of good breeding, yea, though she had dared to rebel against her *dastur*, such boldness were out of the question, even had not her quick ears heard the approach of footsteps more familiar than his own. Shaking her head, she leaned back out of sight just as Audrey came along the path.

She heard their voices at meeting; but no words. Then, cautiously, she peeped between the balustrades, watching unseen. He was smiling, the kind, infectious smile that lighted all his face. But Audrey's eyes showed no answering gleam. They wore the hard masked expression that had grown too familiar to Lilamani in the past week. She asked him something. He assented with raised brows; and, turning about, they walked together down the wide pathway to the sea.

Then she leaned over and looked after them; looked and looked till the tears gathered again in her eyes. What were they talking of, those two favoured ones, free to go where they would and with whom they pleased, while she could only look and long and wonder—like a human bird in a cage? Nay, her true cage had been happier, since she could not see too plainly between the bars. For the first time she, who so loved the land of her birth, regretted her nationality. Of what use to give her freedom, when the dusky skin, and all the hidden differences it implied, could no more be wiped out than the colour of the sea!

Sobs came thick and fast now, and fearing her father's return from Nice, she fled blindly back to her room; flung herself on the bed, and there let grief have its way with her. For the passionate heart of the East slept beneath her girlish gentleness; and already it had turned in its sleep. If there could only have been talk of such a bridegroom—was the stifled cry of her soul: and the next instant she reproached herself for a bold, shameless one, to think thoughts so unworthy of maidenhood. For this cherished daughter of Sir Lakshman Singh was no precocious little woman, like most Indian girls of her age; but something as near the English type of 'sweet seventeen' as the conflicting elements of her life and education could be made to produce. And through all her vague, chaotic misery, her thoughts clave to those two down by the sea. What were they talking of—what?

Only at the sound of her father's footstep afar off did she rise up bravely and bathe her swollen eyes.

EIGHT

'Love, the great volcano, flings
Fires of lower earth to sky;
Love, the sole-permitted, sings
Sovereignly of Me and I.'

—Meredith

And of what were they talking, those two, down by the sea?
Of what else but the girl who agonized alone upon her bed? And
Audrey, in her degree, was agonizing also; though Sinclair was not
suffered to suspect the fact.

Her greeting had been blunt, and to the point. She was in no humour for softening sharp outlines. 'Good evening, Nevil. If you can
spare me half an hour before dinner, I would like a talk with you.'

It was then that he had assented smiling.

'Delighted. My spare half-hours are of no remarkable value. Is it
anything particular?'

'Yes. It's about Lilamani—and your picture.'

'Ah! What of them?'

It was then that they walked off together down the wide path,
ending in a balustrade, beyond which rough slabs of rock fell sheer
to the sea. For a moment Audrey compressed her lips; and Sinclair,
scrutinizing her profile, was puzzled and half annoyed.

'What's wrong with you, Audrey? You've not been a bit the same
girl this week. One could only suppose you were still fussing over the
picture and the studies and all the rest of it. Rather superfluous, surely,
now the thing's half done. Rather hard lines, too, if I mayn't take such
a unique chance without your making a tea-cup tragedy out of an
interlude that's pleasant enough for us all, so far as I can see.'

Audrey regarded him very straightly, without flinching.

'Pleasant for you, no doubt; and—in a sense—for her too. But if you will give me a chance to speak, instead of rating me unheard, I can prove to you that the "tea-cup tragedy"—which may be sufficiently serious for her, poor child, is of your own making, not mine.'

'What d'you mean?' he asked sharply, genuine pain in his voice. 'I wouldn't upset her for the world.'

'It's not a question of what you would do, but of what you have done.'

'Do be more explicit. You're keeping me on hot ploughshares. She seemed quite happy when I saw her just now.'

'Saw her? Where?'

'Looking over the balcony, a minute before you came.'

Audrey made a small sound of vexation. 'I left her lying down. But really I don't know *what* to do about her. When she began to grow home-sick, I thought seeing a little more of people might do her good. But I didn't reckon on this affair of the picture; and now she seems, quite overwrought and unstrung.'

'And it pleases you to throw the blame on me?'

'It doesn't please me, Nevil.' Her voice softened instinctively on his name. 'The facts speak for themselves; and it's as well you should know them.'

'Fire away, then—for God's sake.'

His impatience in no wise hurried her wonted precision of speech, while she sketched for him in outline the week's day-to-day difficulties, ending with an expurgated edition of the final scene that had left her baffled for the moment, and deeply disquieted as regards possible results. To Nevil's half-knowledge the way out appeared sufficiently plain. They had reached the balustrade, and he brought his hand down on it with decision.

'I told you before, Audrey, she's *not* the type. That girl has the temperament of genius. I suspect her verses might be worth seeing. But as for trying to cram her brain with hygienics and physiology, you'd both be better occupied in trying to reach the moon.'

Audrey bit her lip. 'I am beginning to be afraid that's true. But—if you remember, Nevil, I told *you* also that these studies were of special importance to her; and now it seems high time to convince you of the fact by telling you plainly what she came to England to escape.'

'Escape? What was that?'

He spoke rapidly, almost under his breath. All the laughter had gone out of his eyes, that looked steadily seaward, and continued so to look, while Audrey—in phrases deliberately blunt and bald—told him the story that she hoped might disgust him a little; that must, at least, force him to recognize that gateless barrier of race, caste, and creed that divided him from this alluring yet antipodal child of the East.

The story was no easy one to tell. Only a conviction that her duty to both demanded plain speech, and a secret hope that his leaning toward sentiment might be checked in time, gave her strength to carry it through.

She drew an unvarnished picture of the conservative, priest-ridden Hindu mother, who, ever since Lilamani's fourteenth year, had urged betrothal, if not marriage, without avail. She told him of the bridegroom—wealthy, elderly, dissolute—finally brought forward by the Guru, to whom doubtless great gifts had been promised by the husband-elect if the transaction were carried through with success. She spoke of Lilamani's rebellion; of the nerve-shattering struggle which had ended in collapse. And at that the man could control himself no longer.

'Good God!' he muttered between his teeth, but without looking round; for the which she was grateful.

'Yes, it seems incredible to us,' she answered quietly. 'Yet you know next to nothing of what such a marriage would mean for a girl so indulged by her father, so sensitive and fanciful as Lilamani; and even I know little enough. Happily for her Sir Lakshman is as brave as he is broad-minded. But for his championship she could never have stood out against the combined authority of family and religion. He himself, when he called me in, was fairly desperate; or he might not have agreed so readily to my bold suggestion. But he did agree; and after a fresh struggle we three gained the day.'

'Well done, Audrey!' he cried, looking full at her for the first time.

In spite of stern repression her heart throbbed at his praise, and she smiled. 'I'm glad you think that, Nevil. It may help you to realize something of my feelings this week in seeing what I believe to be her one chance of freedom slipping from under her. The ordinary hotel-folk would probably have disturbed her very little. But talk with men

like you, Mr. Broome, and Signor Martino over-stimulates her imagination, her emotions, which *must* be subordinated to her brain and
commonsense if she is to stand on her own feet when her father and
I go back to India. Surely any studies, however uncongenial, are better
than her only alternative—an ignominious return to the arms of a
dissolute, bigoted bridegroom. Not that I think she would go. This
afternoon, when I was driven to speak of it, she said: "I would kill
myself rather." Indian women are like that; and I firmly believe she
spoke the truth.'

'Good God!' the man broke out again. 'It's downright brutal that
a sensitive white-souled girl should be so tormented——' His voice
near failed him; but he steadied it, and went on: 'What are you going
to do about it, Audrey? Speak to her father——?'

'I don't know. I haven't had time to think. Most likely I shall urge
her to speak to him herself. The understanding between them is
singularly perfect; and he may feel less baffled than I do by her deplor-
able change of front. But it's useless for you and me to discuss
possibilities. I merely felt you ought to know; and now——' She consulted her wrist-watch. 'I must hurry back. I shall be late for dinner.
Are you coming in?'

'Not yet. You've given me too much to think about. But I'll see you
to the hotel.'

'Please not. I'd rather be alone. I have a good deal to think about,
too. But it's close upon dinner-time, you know.'

'Is it? Good night. You're a brick, Audrey; and I'm a worthless
good-for-nothing. Forgive me if I've made things harder for you—or
her.'

To that she had no answer save: 'Good night': and he, wringing her
hand, turned down the lesser pathway that winds among shrubs of
myrtle, cytisus, and olive toward that rocky promontory from which
the hotel takes its name.

Flat and tapering, free of sun and wind, with its carpet of sea-laven-
der and scarlet-leaved mesembryanthemum; its cushions of myrtle
and lentisk; its grey-green clumps of aloe and fringe of rugged white
rocks—the Cap d'Antibes reaches farther out into the Mediterranean
than any other headland of Southern France. To sit near its peak at
dusk—with all the coast behind one, looking away to the Esterelles

and hidden Corsica, is almost to believe oneself on a steadygoing vessel in mid-ocean.

As Nevil Sinclair strode rapidly toward this haven of solitude, the fires of sunset were ebbing from a sky tenderly rippled with light cloud, that threw into sharp relief the few outstanding features of the Cap. Here a lone umbrella-pine made a bold smudge of sepia on the delicate pallor beyond; there the crescent-topped outline of a spurious Moorish archway—remnant of some forgotten folly—was bitten out sharp and clear. Farther on, from a black mass of building and bushes the little lighthouse reared its head; and farthest of all, the skeleton of a dead aloe-flower, upspringing boldly from its nest of jagged leaves, was etched as with a fine-pointed pen upon the darkening sea.

Mechanically, the artist's eye noted every detail of the picture, even while brain and heart seethed with such an exalted mingling of rage and rapture as he had never known; a white heat of chivalry that burnt up in its pure flame mere accidents of race and creed; that bade him, at all hazards, snatch this heavenly-sweet flower of girlhood out of the *impasse* for which he was in a measure responsible.

Blessed Fate that had brought her to him! Not that he might paint her merely; but that he might save her from a degradation worse than death. Audrey, plucky Audrey, need not trouble her head about ways and means. He—Nevil Sinclair—would be the god out of the machine. This pearl of womanhood—who had awakened his talent no less than his heart—should not die, but live—and give herself to him. For he could win her; some inner voice assured him of that, even while he marvelled at his own arrogance. The divine intoxication that had put a new song in his month, blinded him to the hundred and one prosaic obstacles that hovered outside the charmed circle of his dream, biding their time. He could have shouted aloud in triumph, there alone with the darkening sky and sea. This was something altogether different from earlier sentimental adventures. So lightly, in his unawakened ignorance, had he taken the name of Love in vain.

One only problem puzzled him. Why had he not discovered the truth until to-day? From the first she had so enthralled his imagination; so satisfied his taste for all that was rare and beautiful. Yet her tender years, her impalpable aura of grace and purity had made her seem a being set apart from the rough and tumble of common life; and always absorption in his picture had stood between him and personal thoughts of her.

But to-day in that direct contact of spirit with spirit, the divine ray had passed between them. They had touched the electric force that vivifies the world and hurls it spinning through the spheres. Then, in that moment, he had first seen her as woman—the one woman, pre-ordained to be his own; brought to him by Fate, in the teeth of opposing circumstances across six thousand miles of sea. Striking sharply upon this revelation, Audrey's story—that was to have disenchanted him—or at least checked sentimental impulses—had wrought the very opposite effect. The rage it engendered sprang, not from chivalry alone, but from the consuming jealousy, that is twin-brother to passion. He had scarce known how to control himself, to hide his secret, as it must be hid till he could win speech of his beloved alone.

And here the first prosaic obstacle reared its head. The thing seemed impossible of achievement. But their destiny was assured; and somehow, somewhen, it must come to pass. If matters looked too hopeless, he could always write, or speak first to her father. But neither alternative was to his taste. It was she to whom he should first tell the secret, that he might watch the rose of her heart blossom in her cheeks, that lamp of her pure spirit lighten in her eyes. . . .

At this point he found himself far out among the last of the broken rocks, whitely fringed with foam. Here he sat him down, lit a cigar and gave himself up to his fairy-tale, while the sky changed imperceptibly from grey to indigo, the stars from silver to gold; and the half-moon, high in the east, took on her borrowed robe of light.

Appetite rather than hunger whispered of dinner that by now must be half over. But in his present mood he was loath to face the heat and noise of the crowded dining-room and the penetrating eyes of Cuthbert Broome. He would go in when it was over, and get a plate of something from his friend the head-waiter; and avoiding the studio, make straight for his own room. In the meantime, his cigar—while it dulled the edge of the body's need, enhanced his mood of dreams, his visions of a purely Bohemian life with this Jewel of Delight here in the glowing South or among the Italian hills. Only let Martino praise the picture he was to see to-morrow, and he, Nevil, would devote himself in earnest to the art that, but for her, might have withered and died in him unrecognized, unfulfilled. Henceforth her temperament of genius would be as oil to the flame of his new-lighted lamp. He would not take her home, or subject her to the ordeal of family disapproval; with a throb of exultation he perceived how completely such a marriage would exonerate him from the rôle of politician and landed proprietor that had hung over him like the sword of Damocles for seven unfruitful years.

And Jane?

He smiled to himself in the darkness at thought of her impotent wrath. But his father's wrath—tinged with bitter disappointment—was another affair altogether. For Nevil—primarily the child of his mother—seemed to have inherited also her indelible tenderness toward the stolid, obstinate, good-hearted man, who had so little true affinity with either wife or son. This same tenderness that had kept him loitering at the cross-roads, surged up in him now and threw the first shadow across his enchanted garden of dreams. . . .

It was close on ten when he ran up the hotel steps on to the balcony-verandah. The hall was nearly empty, and waiters were putting out the lights. He went straight to the restaurant, unearthed a plate of cold tongue and a bottle of Burgundy; asked if there were any letters, and was presented with an envelope addressed in the square, uncompromising hand of Lady Roscoe.

'Damn,' said he softly; and pocketing the missive, went upstairs.

Once in his room, he sat down by the small table that held his books, manuscript, and painting gear. 'Now for Jane's hydrostatics!' he mused, slipping a penknife under the flap. It was her answer to his own first letter, giving chapter and verse for his impulsive flight abroad; and through the curt, vigorous phrases he could hear his sister's familiar tone.

'My dear Boy,—You bolted. That's the plain truth, stripped of lame excuses. But my party isn't coming off after all. So you can safely take the next express home! In fact you must come and do your duty at the election like a man. You should have heard Lord Shandon's inquiries after you the other night. Polite, of course—he wouldn't be otherwise to *me*—but scathing. That I should live to hear a brother of *mine* called "shirker"—even by implication! But what do *you* care for our good name? So long as the sun shines and there's a yard of blank canvas in the market, the dear old Place might go down before the auctioneer's hammer and I might take in washing without your turning a hair. Why I was allowed to be the eldest, and yet not a *man*, passes my comprehension. All I can do is to try and hammer you into the outward semblance of a Sinclair. Little enough use! But it's my duty, and the word carries weight with *some* of us.

'If you've an ounce of right feeling or affection for the dear old Dad, you *ought* to be at home this spring. I don't quite know what's wrong with him, and he refuses to consult Dr. Ransome. He seems just irritable and restless and out of spirits. Not like himself, in fact. Business worries, I fancy, from something Thornbrook said the other day about the estate. But I'm sure it would give him a fillip to have you at the Place for a few weeks, and to feel he had a personal stake in the election. So just pocket your artistic selfishness, and wire "Coming" to my town address. Don't give yourself time to haver and change your mind. Remember I *expect* you. So it's *au revoir*.

'Your affectionate sister,

'JANE ROSCOE.'

'Damn!' her affectionate brother remarked again—not softly this time—flinging the sheet from him as if it burnt his fingers.

Then, rising, he paced the room in a turmoil of conflicting wrath, indecision and dismay. Here was no shadow, but a bomb flung ruthlessly into his enchanted garden. Jane and her exhortations went for nothing. But the poor old man, worried and out of spirits—that was quite another matter. The inherent impulse of tenderness tugged at him; and, but for the tone of Jane's letter, might have overruled 'artistic selfishness,' for all the chains that bound him, and his recoil from the prospect of three or four weeks at Bramleigh Beeches alone with Sir George in his present mood.

The first warmth of greeting over, he would probably be sworn at, and certainly bored to extinction by the old futile effort at playing good comrade to the father with whom he had nothing in common save the mysterious tie of blood and their unspoken allegiance to her who was gone. For, even when Nevil exasperated him most, the stubborn heart of Sir George clave to the son who spoke the language of his dead wife, and smiled upon him with her eyes. A sore point, this last, for Jane who, in secret, sympathized acutely with the immaculate elder brother in the parable. For her, the loyal, the ever-present, neither fatted calf nor feasting. But for Nevil, the defaulter——. Eyebrows and shoulders, mutely eloquent, implied the rest.

Could she have witnessed his present perturbation, she might have admitted a rudiment of conscience in his spiritual anatomy. Certain it is that, in the face of such a call, his picture alone would not have held him back. But—there remained Lilamani; her possible love for him; and the cruel alternations between which she stood.

So half the night long he agonized and deliberated over the age-old problem—that loses no whit of its tragedy through repetition—how far a man is constrained to cripple the fulfilment of his own life and love, out of respect for his father's wishes. Can filial duty condemn a son to live unhappy that his father may die happy? All the undiluted Nevil in his blood cried out, No, a thousand times. How, then, if he went home immediately for a week or two and thrashed out the whole matter with his father once for all? A few days earlier such a step had been conceivable, if uncongenial; but now—on the eve of his divine discovery—! No, again.

Should Lilamani prove indifferent, or marriage with an Englishman beyond the pale of possibility, time enough then to think of fathers and of flight. For the present two events only filled all his horizon: Martino's verdict, and Lilamani's answer. On the morrow a wire should speed homeward: 'Immediate return impossible. Writing': nor would he put pen to paper till his fate was sealed.

NINE

'O little more, and how much it is!
    And the little less, and what worlds away!
How a sound can quicken content to bliss,
    Or a word suspend the blood's best play—
And life be a proof of this.'

—Browning

For all her decision of character, Audrey Hammond fell asleep that night in a painfully unsettled frame of mind. Obviously Lilamani's story had shocked and perturbed Nevil Sinclair in no small degree. But to what end, or with what probable result?

Heavy-laden with pain and perplexity, she had stood watching him as he strode away from her toward the Cap, secure in the bitter certainty that he would not dream of looking back; and upstairs, in their sitting-room, fresh perplexity had been her portion. In place of the passionate girl she had left, behold a smiling, faintly-repressed Lilamani, who, after dinner, read to Sir Lakshman from her favourite 'Wisdom and Destiny'; discussing with him—in her quaintly poetic turns of phrase—the roots of happiness and the hidden springs of peace, as though the storm of two hours earlier had never been. In the circumstances, Audrey had thought well to bid her good night without their occasional after-talk over the day's events. Whatever conclusions the girl had arrived at were best slept upon before being submitted to the test of speech.

Not till she began setting out her books next morning did Audrey broach the subject.

'Does this mean you have thought better of yesterday, child?' she asked smilingly; and Lilamani bowed her head.

'I was too much mistaken,' said she, still looking down and twirling a pencil between fingers and thumb. 'My father's heart cannot be hurt just for the wandering of my brain. So please not say any more,

Audrey. I will try to keep my thoughts in chains. But if I am still stupid—perhaps—some small punishment——'

'My dear girl! I may have been impatient with you, but I draw the line at battering medicine into your head! We can try again, and see how things go.'

They did not go brilliantly that morning. Though Lilamani zealously held her 'thoughts in chains,' and Audrey was patience incarnate, each was aware of an invisible 'Something' between them that made for division. Lunch ended, Audrey excused herself on the plea of a promised outing with Madame de Lisle: and Nevil, arriving well ahead of his time, was relieved to find father and daughter alone.

They also were to have their first sight of his picture today; an event made ten times more significant by his newly-awakened passion. For the moment, artist and artistry were eclipsed by the natural man's eagerness to gauge her share in the divine discovery.

At the first meeting of hands and eyes he knew himself predestined victor: knew that the shy, virgin heart of her was astir, if not yet awake; and gloried in the privilege, that would be his, of revealing to her, by tender and delicious degrees, the golden secret that gleams at the core of life.

In the meantime he must curb imagination, and sun himself in the twofold triumph of the moment. For it was no less than a triumph to lift the embroidered curtain from his canvas, to watch the dawn of wonder and delight in the faces of those two, who had, in so short a space, become the nucleus of his world.

To Lilamani it seemed that she beheld her very self leaning there upon the balcony's edge, looking away out of the picture with uplifted eyes, wherein—oh, miracle of miracles!—she caught reflected glimpses of her own most hidden thoughts and dreams. Tint of skin, sheen of *sari*, all her tender curves of budding womanhood, were rendered with an astonishing delicacy and truth. For if Sinclair's pencil had wrought excellently, his brush had verily been inspired; so that he himself stood amazed; marvelling helplessly—as every true artist marvels more than once in his life—how the thing had come about, and whether he could ever hope to touch so high a point of excellence again.

Before Sir Lakshman could find voice, Nevil had found Lilamani's eyes, that gazed on him with a young, unveiled adoration; and even as her whole face lit up in response to his smile, Sir Lakshman spoke.

'My dear Mr. Sinclair—it is many times more wonderful than I was imagining. Almost, to me—she lives and breathes.' Then, drawing Lilamani nearer, he looked steadfastly from counterfeit to reality, till the colour flooded her face.

Nevil took a deep breath to steady himself, and heard his everyday voice make answer: 'Honestly, I believe it's good; and I'm delighted that it pleases you. If only Martino, the hypercritical, thinks half so well of it——'

'That he will, beyond doubting: and then——?'

'Oh then, there shall be no more havering. All along I have looked on this picture as the touchstone of my talent. So you see'—his glance dwelt a moment on the girl, rejoicing in the swift warmth of her cheek—'it has been *yours* to decide the question of my career!'

'If that means I am deciding you to paint more pictures, and always more,' she answered, plucking at the border of her *sari*, 'then I am—glad.'

'It does mean that; if Martino approves,' said he: and Sir Laksh-man, glancing from one to the other, felt a sudden twinge of appre-hension that impelled him to draw his child away from this magnetic young Englishman, and set her down in her usual seat.

Then he turned to Sinclair. 'You are wishing, perhaps, to do some work before they come?'

'I think not, to-day.' He covered his canvas with a smiling glance at the original. 'I feel too restless. Besides—it would be a pity to risk superfluous tinkering, till I've heard what Broome and Martino have to say. They'll be here early, I know. And that reminds me—a very old friend of mine, a Mrs. Despard, who arrived yesterday, begged to come too. She's always been keen for me to take up painting in earn-est. So you can imagine my news pleased her. Hope it wasn't very cool of me to invite her?'

'My dear sir, any friend of yours must be welcome to us. Despard—you say? I must have known some relation of hers in India.'

'Probably her husband. A civilian somewhere down your way. Had to retire not long ago on account of heart-trouble, poor chap. But Mrs. Despard was out there a good many years, and is naturally interested to meet you and your daughter.'

Sir Lakshman's smile had a hint of scepticism. 'That does not al-ways follow. Anglo-Indians are of many kinds, and many minds. Not all are so wide-hearted as to break through the official shell that checks intimacy with the native of the country; less than ever, strange to say, if he shall show any taste for ideals or education of the West. But, as I said, there are many exceptions——'

'And Mrs. Despard is one,' Sinclair broke in warmly. 'They live quite close to us at home. She and I have had endless talks about India and its peoples; her favourite subject. There's no question about how she will feel towards you and your daughter; or I assure you I would not have asked her up.'

'That I should have known. I think it is they who are coming now.'

It was so: and three minutes later Lilamani looked upon the one daughter of England destined to love and understand her, from the moment of meeting; while her own soul—young, ardent, steeped in poetic fancy—was bowed down in worshipful admiration before this lissome slip of an Englishwoman, whose delicate-featured face, with its softly shining eyes, was crowned with a mass of dull gold hair, through which ran threads of fire. A clinging gown of tussore silk, finely embroidered, such as Audrey never wore; and old lace at her throat—where an aquamarine pendant hung from a silver chain— completed a picture distinctive enough to impress brains and hearts less susceptible than those of a Hindu girl of seventeen.

And she, scarce waiting for Sinclair's introduction, swept toward the shyly smiling creature in the mother-o'-pearl *sari* and took the slender hand in both her own.

'Welcome to Europe,' said she in a voice of singular sweetness. 'How brave and wise of you to cross "the black water!" And how lucky for my friend, Mr. Sinclair, that he happened to be here at the time!'

'Greatly I hope it is,' Lilamani murmured with a fervour that even shyness could not quite subdue.

'And I am sure it is!' the other declared, as she turned to greet Sir Lakshman, who was shaking hands with Broome.

Then, while the four fell into friendly talk, Martino plucked Sinclair by the sleeve, and, with an impatient jerk of his head, signified his wish to have done with superfluities and come at the real thing.

Lilamani, watching them covertly through the curtain of her lashes, saw them move towards the easel; saw Nevil Sinclair fling back the covering as before. Then—her heart leaped at the light that flashed in Martino's eyes. With an inarticulate grunt he stepped back a space, and stood so, looking, looking, and still looking, while the other two hurried forward, eager to see that which had smitten the volcanic Martino dumb.

Greater triumph Nevil Sinclair could not have desired: yet was there pleasure almost as keen in Broome's curt tribute: 'Good Heavens—what a likeness!'

The words seemed to rouse Martino. His eyes flashed again.

'Likeness?—*Sapristi!* It is interpretation.' Then he swung round on Nevil. 'Your handshake, *amico mio*. No further doubts now—is it? I—Martino—salute the inspired artist!' the which he did with a grip of steel. 'Pity it cannot be shown. But after this—you are pledged. There must be others.'

'I hope to Heaven there may be,' Nevil answered, overwhelmed. 'But the thing's not done yet. There must be faults; room for improvement. It's criticism I want, man. You know that.'

Martino's vigorous nod signified fullness of understanding. 'The last infirmity of the true artist—no? *Ebbene*, you shall have it—without sparing. For by all the saints in the calendar your work is worth it.'

So they two, regardless of the rest, plunged into their private jargon of tones and values and the critical nature of those last touches that may spoil the whole: while the rest, being human, gravitated to the tea-tray, that wooed them with gleam of polished plate and delicate tints of *petits fours*, ordered daily by an indulgent father for his daughter's special delectation.

Mrs. Despard, increasingly drawn towards this child of the *purdah*—who seemed, yet, so fully a woman—laid a friendly hand on her as they sat down.

'When I talked of Mr. Sinclair's luck just now, I had no idea that you had actually done for him what he has failed to do for himself in the last seven years. I am one of the few who have always urged him to follow his natural bent in earnest; undutiful though it might seem! Between money and position, one feared he would never achieve anything. But now—through you—he has found himself. And I can't tell you how delighted I am!'

Neither could the girl—with eyes demurely intent on three carnations at her breast—tell this angel of the golden halo how delight unspeakable sang within her like a hidden bird. She could only answer in the same low tone: 'You are mistaking. It is not I. It is Mr. Sinclair who has done all.'

Then, because the room was large, and the two behind the easel and the two on the hearthrug much engrossed in their own talk, she drew from her new friend, by a shy question or two, more of Nevil Sinclair's home and history than she had yet heard; till he himself joined them and the rest followed suit.

Seldom had there been so festal and frivolous a tea-drinking in the quiet sitting-room, mainly dedicated to study and art. Martino's triumph brimmed over in a fireworks display of his quaintly characteristic English, whenever he could command the field; and Mrs. Despard, glowed openly when the East was her theme.

Sir Lakshman, stirred alike by her beauty and enthusiasm, cast aside, for once, his mask of polite reserve. He spoke frankly, warmly, on the subject that lies nearest the heart of all thoughtful Indians in this our day of agitation and transition. His zealous championship of British rule, and fervent belief in ultimate concord between 'mother and eldest daughter,' woke an answering echo in the hearts of two, whose fate hung upon his readiness to give personal proof of the faith that was in him.

But it was Mrs. Despard alone who voiced her approval. 'If only there were more men of your mind on both sides,' said she, and her smile was in itself a reward, 'how much disastrous friction we might have been spared all round. But though you are in a minority, it is you, and men like you, who may end in saving the situation, unless we ourselves—or those who misgovern us—bring the whole Empire crashing about our ears!'

'May the Great God forbid such calamity!' Sir Lakshman spoke with unusual warmth. 'Yet, my dear lady, because I have shown you all the good feeling that is in my heart for that England who made India what she is, you must please not to misjudge me in respect of my own country. You must believe that I am as zealous for her welfare as any Bengal agitators or inflammatory news-writers, who, in blind perversity, are trying to break up the only influence which can make possible that national unity they cry for, among the Indian peoples. It is only that I see one manner of welfare: they another. In my belief— and I am sharing it with scores of men better than myself—no worse harm could befall to India than that Great Britain should cease to be paramount power. But only this—in order for being paramount she must be, in best sense, a *power*; not mere figure-head or rash experimentalist, shifting now to this foot, now to that. Even in your own Book is it not written, if the trumpet give an uncertain sound, who shall prepare themselves for battle?'

'Who, indeed?' the daughter of England assented ruefully. 'And of late years the sound has been less imperious, less inspiring than it should be if we are to hold our own.'

'Unhappily—yes. I cannot help but agree. It is not that I am disloyal, as you know. It is that we are troubled—we Indians, who believe in England's power—to see how such a great land is seeming to lose grasp on those noble ideals of straightforward strength and courage that we learnt in early days to couple with the name of the British Raj. Trouble it is also to see how blessings of enlightenment and patriotic feeling, are now made weapons against her supremacy, that she won by those ideals, and cannot keep except through the same. Let us hope it is only by appearance that she is losing hold on them; that the true England, yes, and the true India, may wake up and grasp hands together before it is too late.'

'Hear, hear!' was echoed by all: then Martino thrust in his oar again, and the talk became general.

Only Nevil, the ready of tongue, had singularly little to say. For if Lilamani found her private ecstasy hard to conceal, her lover was in much the same case. The hearts of both were too full for speech of any kind. But though the door of the lips be locked, there are windows through which the hidden self looks forth. The girl—a little startled by her own emotions—kept her windows veiled. Not so the man. Transported beyond pedestrian counsels of prudence, he could not withhold his eyes from her face and form. Neither could he compel hers to meet his own. Primitive instinct whispered that that way danger lay. But Nevil was in no mood to be baulked; and now that general conversation was in full swing again, he boldly drew a chair up close to her, and spoke under his breath.

'I know you are almost as glad as I am. But I want above everything to hear you say so.'

The flagrant lover's folly of it, and the dawning sense of her woman's power to give and to withhold brought her heart thrilling into her throat.

'If you know it, that is enough. The rest is only nonsense!'

'It's not. It's truth, serious truth. I——' he checked himself, realizing that this was no moment to unveil the shining secret. 'Well, today I've a right to be foolish!' he added more lightly. 'And you might do what I ask. Just to please me.'

'Of course, if you make it like that, I could not be so discourteous. And . . . I *am* glad that your success has come . . . through my picture: much more than I could say. So it is no use trying.'

Her shifting colour, and refusal to meet his gaze, pricked him to further boldness. He knew, and gloried in the knowledge, that—by every means of mute confession given to woman—this girl was showing the very truth she strove to hide. Never before had he been quite so close to her; and the fresh, faint scent of sandalwood that pervaded her went to his head like wine. Once get the whole party down into the garden, and he could trust himself to contrive some flying chance of speech.

He set his hand on the tea-tray's rim within an inch of her own, and noted how her glance travelled from one to the other while he spoke.

'It is just because this has come . . . through you, that it means so much to me. I never dreamed how it would be when I had the audacity to begin. But I want one thing more to complete my great day. Can you guess?'

'No.' The full lower lip was indrawn demurely, and an uplift of her lashes revealed laughter in her eyes.

'Perhaps you don't want to hear!' he challenged her with increasing boldness.

'That is quite possible! All the same . . . you will tell it!'

'Of course I shall. And you will grant it.'

'That is not at all so sure.'

'Oh, but it is. I want to end with a walk down by the sea . . . all of us. I've not bothered you much about coming down these few days. But I want this immensely. Will you come?'

She drew in a quick, startled breath as if he had touched her. 'No—no, please. Not to-day.'

'And why not to-day?'

His voice took a deeper note that filled her with nameless fear both of herself and him.

'I cannot tell,' she whispered, glancing instinctively towards her father, who was too absorbed in his subject to be aware of the magnetic young Englishman's latest move. 'Only . . . it has been very wonderful . . . for me also; and I am wanting to be alone with it all, in my House of Gods, for sunset time. Please understand.'

'I'm doing my best,' he said ruefully. 'But still—it's unkind to disappoint me, and spoil everything.'

'Oh, *don't* say that! It hurts——'

Her hand went to the carnations at her breast, as if indicating the point of pain; and that small gesture took the sting out of refusal and disappointment alike.

'Not enough to make you say "Yes"?'

She shook her head.

'Well, then . . . to-morrow? You shall ride on the sea in my boat. Your father shall come, and Mrs. Despard, and Broome. There now! In common decency you can't say "No" again.'

'Then I can only say "Yes"! If father will come.'

'Promise!'

'How unbelieving you are! I promise.'

Before he could answer, Sir Lakshman had become aware of them; and the hand he laid on his daughter's arm had a movement, as though he would draw her away.

'Mrs. Despard is suggesting a walk now it is cooler; and I have agreed. Do you feel inclined?'

'Mr. Sinclair was just asking that same!' the girl answered with admirable composure. 'But I said . . . not to-day.'

'She has promised to come out in my boat to-morrow, instead,' Nevil hastened to add—unaware, as yet, of hidden antagonism.

'Only if you would like it, father,' from Lilamani, on a note of irresistible eagerness.

'Decidedly, I should like it; and there is good chance of my being free, unless a heavy mail comes in. But then, no doubt, Miss Hammond could go. I would not like you to lose a ride on the sea.'

Broome and Mrs. Despard accepted readily: but Martino, who worshipped the sea as a Titanic force, rather than a means of locomotion, refused point-blank.

In the leave-taking that followed, Nevil—with a lover's ingenuity—contrived to secure the last touch, the last word; and that small cool hand, once captured, was singularly hard to relinquish.

'To-morrow . . . whatever happens,' was all he dared to say. For answer he had the rose-flush on her half-averted face; and he went forth as one who goes to victory; secure in his belief that the morrow could not pass till her lips had confirmed the avowal of her cheeks and eyes. Almost, in that moment, he felt capable of bidding the sun stand still and expecting it to obey him.

And she?

So soon as the door had closed behind them all, she went swiftly to the threshold of her shrine, and stood there, cooling her face against the glass of the open door, one hand upon her heart that throbbed and sang as though it would burst the bounds of flesh.

What it all meant, whither it would lead them, she dared not ask herself in set terms. As yet it sufficed that she shared his triumph; and he, in turn, shared with her the nameless thrill of touch, and speech, and glance. Nor was that all. Something within whispered that he craved more than this sublimated essence of emotion, so satisfying to her. Was it conceivable that he craved all—might even dare to ask all?—he, the inspired English artist, of her, the Indian girl-student, divided from him by immovable barriers of country and creed?

Then the door was flung open briskly; and she turned to meet Audrey's inquiring eyes.

'It's all over, then?' was her greeting, and her very voice brought Lilamani to earth with a thud. 'Was it a success? What's come to you, child? You look transfigured!'

'Do I?' Lilamani tried to smile, but tears sprang unbidden from the deeps. 'It has all been so wonderful! Signor Martino spoke such praises. And—I am so happy——'

Her voice broke.

'What is there to cry about, then?' asked practical Audrey: and the girl swept a hand across her lashes.

'Oh, how can I tell? You would never understand.'

She made as if to go, but Audrey's hand closed upon her arm.

'Don't run away, dear, the minute I come back,' she said a little wistfully. 'I'm not so stupid as that amounts to; and I want to hear about this afternoon. Signor Martino is pleased? And your father?'

'Yes. He says—it lives and breathes.'

Audrey's hand was on the silken covering. 'I suppose I may look since everyone else has seen it?' said she; and proceeded to look, long and silently, defying the ache within; while Lilamani, in broken, half-coherent phrases, told her of Martino's enthusiasm, of Mrs. Despard's conviction that through this—her picture—Mr. Sinclair had 'found himself' at last.

Audrey listened without interruption. Then she nodded, compressing her lips.

'Yes. It's a very remarkable bit of work. But still——'

'But still—*what?*' Lilamani spoke almost sharply. The cool tone maddened her so. Yet now she must endure the worse ordeal of the cool glance that discerned something, at least, of the agitation within.

'What I mean is this——' Audrey handled her words steadily, as the surgeon his knife. 'It is a cruel kindness for them all to inflame Nevil with their enthusiasm on the strength of one exceptional success. They only make it harder for him to remember his *real* duty——'

'What is that?' The low voice was toneless now, the sweet submissive face a mask.

'The duty he owes to his father and his family at home as you, a daughter of Hindu tradition, very well understand. Nevil is the eldest son of a distinguished house——'

'Mrs. Despard told me that; and all his father's wishes. Only—she thinks——'

'In my opinion she thinks too much of Nevil, and of his art; which makes it a pity she turned up just now. No right-minded person can doubt that it is high time for him to drop philandering with paint and canvas, and knocking aimlessly about the Continent, achieving nothing. He ought to go home, and stand for Parliament, and then marry the right sort of girl—in his own position. The marriage of an eldest son is an important matter in England. He is less free to choose haphazard than other men.'

Then, kindly but inexorably, she enlarged upon the subject; doing her own duty by friend and pupil without stint; and while Lilamani listened meekly, expressing a mild interest from time to time, all her vague rose-coloured possibilities shrivelled and died.

No sunset peace was to be hers. Better had she accepted the walk by the sea. The afternoon had quickened all her deepest sensibilities into passionate life; and Audrey's dutiful dissertation was like a chill hand upon her quivering heart.

TEN

'O sun of heaven, above the worldly sea,
O very love, what light is this of thee!
My sea of soul is deep as thou art high,
But all thy light is shed through all of me,
As love's thro' love while day shall live and die.'

—Swinburne

But the heart of seventeen is nothing if not resilient; and the thin coating of ice, dutifully laid on by Audrey, could not choose but melt again in the light of Nevil Sinclair's eyes. Then the laughter of sun and sea; the boat, pulling lightly at its mooring-rope, like a playful child; all glad things seemed wooing her to forgetfulness of a pillow wet with tears, and carefully turned over lest Audrey discover the fact.

One thing disappointed her. There were but four of them. Mrs. Despard's husband was too ill to be left; and a heavy mail, that Sir Lakshman wished to grapple with at leisure, had made him beg Audrey to take his place. She could not well refuse; and now the four stood ready to embark from the toy bay scooped out of the headland where Nevil had sat with his 'divine discovery' two nights ago.

Vivid against the broken white rocks, the sea that Lilamani loved so, shone blue and green, like her favourite peacock's breast, and her golden butterflies flickered, in their millions, along the wide path of light travelling westward with the sun. But the silken calm of yesterday was gone. Out in the open, heaving billows rose and fell, hinting lazily at huge forces in reserve. A brisk little breeze from the southwest tipped them here and there with feathers of foam; and away towards Italy a harmless-looking flock of grey-white clouds dappled the blue. A day that justified in full Lilamani's phrase of riding on the sea; and she could scarce restrain her impatience to be afloat. But, the boatman, with eloquent hands and eyebrows, appeared to be dissuading the Englishmen from going out. He detected promise of storm in that brisk little breeze, with its affectation of playful frivolity; and Audrey made haste to put in her word.

'If he thinks it best not to go, Nevil, don't be unwise enough to insist.'

But Nevil was mysteriously aware of the cloud that shadowed Lilamani's face.

'My dear girl, I know what I'm about. It's merely a case of not going too far. But, of course, if you feel nervous——'

She silenced him with a glance; and he, turning to Lilamani, added, with manifest change of tone, 'You rather enjoy a little tossing, don't you? And we can turn the minute our friend here gives the word—eh, Broome?'

'Right. I see no symptoms myself of serious derangement of the elements. Our friend may be more lazy than weather-wise, after all.'

That happy suggestion clinched matters, and they set out: the women in the stern; Nevil rowing stroke; the pessimist reclining in the bows, to keep a sharp look-out on the heavens and lend a hand if need be. By this arrangement Sinclair's eyes were free of the beloved face; and he had promised himself, by interplay of stolen glances, to prepare the way for speech.

But he reckoned without the effect of Audrey's presence on the girl, and the yet more repressive effect of her words. To Lilamani, however rebellious at heart, one thing was certain: if there were the remotest fear of injuring his family or his fame, then yesterday's wonder of revelation must be, for her, as though it had never been. And without speech she must contrive to make him understand. So she refused, stoically, to meet the eyes that sought hers, at first in glad certainty of response; then in a growing bewilderment that verged on despair. This was not the Lilamani of last night. It was the Lilamani of earlier sittings: and he did not hold the key to the change. Instinctively, he blamed Audrey; though what she had said or done he was too distracted to guess.

It may be imagined that conversation fell flat: while Nevil—shuffling and discarding wild conjectures—handled his oar more casually every moment.

Broome, amusedly trying to keep time with him, gave it up at last, and balancing his own blade, smote his friend upon the shoulder.

'Come out of that, Nevil!' cried he. 'I'm tired of playing second fiddle to a stroke who indulges in a *scherzo*, with variations, under the delusion that he is propelling a boat. I've not sworn at you once—audibly. And I claim my reward. Come out of it, and let me give the ladies a taste of my quality! Good Lord, man, steady on! You'll have us all in the water.'

For Sinclair had risen impetuously, with a swift darkening of his whole face, duly noted by Audrey. One last look at Lilamani—unreturned, like the rest—and pulling himself together, he exchanged seats, with all due precaution, and a twisted smile in response to Broome's friendly pressure of his arm. Then did the boat bound forward to some purpose; and flagging conversation revived: though not for long.

Of a sudden that brisk little breeze from the south dropped its pretence at frivolity, and raced full speed across the open sea, lashing the long lazy billows to crested waves. They caught the green and white pleasure-boat broadside on with a force that set it shuddering from end to end; and the pessimist in the bows had his moment of triumph.

'*Voyez donc, Messieurs, tournez—tournez vîte!*' he cried in unfeigned alarm. '*Ca vient comme un ouragon.*'

Before the words were out, both Englishmen had gripped their oars and bowed themselves to the task with a will. But the leaping, rocking boat seemed animated by a will of its own. Every moment the onrush of wind and waves grew fiercer; while the harmless flock of clouds sped across the sky, their dark edges blurred with rain. Audrey, gripping the gunwale, paled a little; not on her own account, but on account of the girl at her side, who—for her part—was lost in sheer delight at the beauty and movement and tense excitement of it all.

The two men battled and failed; battled and failed again, swearing inaudibly, between their teeth. Then—even as a curling monster broke over the boat, wetting Audrey to the skin—will and muscle triumphed. With a perilous lurch they swung round, and headed for the shore, as speedily as a broadside gale and wave on toppling wave would allow.

Not till then did Nevil dare snatch a glimpse of Lilamani, round the intervening bulk of his friend. Alert and upright she sat, this fragile being in her silken draperies; head uplifted, lips apart. One small hand had followed Audrey's lead; the other held her *sari*, that flapped and billowed about her fantastically with each fresh gust of the gale. And now the eyes that had been denied him, met his own fearlessly, all shadow of self-consciousness swept from them by the keen joy in things elemental that drives out the spirit of fear: and her lips flashed him a smile of such clear confidence as redoubled his own. With zest renewed he fought his way through the surging waters. All would yet be well; though this confounded hurricane had upset his cherished plans, and might conceivably upset the whole boat-load into the bargain.

Once—yea, twice, when a green wall of water bore down upon them, implacable as Fate, the end seemed a matter of minutes; and the natural, human dread of Death clutched at their hearts. But light craft, like certain light natures, will weather a sea that would sink a sturdier vessel; and, at each crisis, their cockle-shell rose gaily on the wave that should have whelmed it; shuddered down the far side with no worse punishment than a blinding shower of spray; and still headed gallantly for the Cap. But here, in the toy bay, where breakers laughed and thundered among the rocks, fresh danger confronted them. Almost it seemed as if landing were impossible; and to attempt rounding the point were certain destruction. But Cuthbert Broome was more than a mere weaver of fiction; and as they neared the danger-zone, his voice rang out, clear and commanding, above the sonorous laughter of the sea.

'*Attendez bien!*' he shouted over his shoulder to the weather-wise one in the bows, bidding him take fast hold of the rope and leap or plunge ashore on the first ghost of an opportunity. He and the other *monsieur* would manage the rest. A command tipped with gold; two louis, no less: and the son of old Antibes laughed in his sleeve. Certainly a wetting would be a nuisance. But gold was gold. And, though the breakers ran high, they were child's play to others he had weathered in fifteen years of intimacy with their kind. So long as '*les messieurs Anglais*' did not expect him to help with the women-folk—who would certainly shriek and struggle at the last—all was well; and he promised two whole candles to his patron saint, who had plainly made these fools of foreigners deaf to his warning out of pure consideration for his own empty pocket and recent ill-luck.

Before three minutes were out, he had seen his chance and taken it, with the agility of a chamois. Then, as the boat's keel screeched and jarred upon hidden rocks, Broome shipped his oar, and leaned forward, speaking with quiet decision.

'You must let me carry you across, Miss Hammond. It's imperative. Nevil can take Miss Lakshman Singh.'

Revolt against the indignity of the first, and determination to prevent the second, made Audrey thrust out both hands, as if to ward him off by force. But, in such a case, might is right.

'For God's sake don't make a fuss,' the man said sternly and a moment later she was in his arms, held high like a child, while he slipped and staggered among the last of the breakers; till a hand thrust out by him of Antibes pulled them safe ashore.

Then—as Broome released her, and the boatman pocketed his gold—down came the rain: not mere drops, but steely shafts of water that flogged the earth and the tossing, shuddering trees. Sinclair, still in the boat, found time to hurl Audrey's parasol at his friend. The wind swept it yards ahead of them: and Broome, with a backward glance of pure amusement, secured his thankless captive by the arm.

'Come on, Miss Hammond. It's a case of running for all we're worth. That toy of yours won't be much use.'

But Audrey stirred not an inch. 'I'm wet through already,' she answered coolly. 'And I don't mind rain. I must wait for Miss Lakshman Singh.'

'Nonsense, nonsense——' The masterful hand on her arm propelled her rapidly forward would she or no. 'Seawater's one thing; rain's another. At my advanced age it spells rheumatism and Nevil, of all men, may be trusted to take good care of your friend.'

'What do you mean? You don't understand,' she panted. They were fairly running now; and as they passed under the archway of Moorish design—set where headland merges into mainland—Audrey snatched a last look over her shoulder at the two, who were so annoyingly far behind.

Nevil stood safely on the pathway now, with the treasure he coveted in his arms. Jealousy stung her, like a scorpion, jealousy that gave place to anger, and the old antagonism, as she was ruthlessly hurried along. Why did he not put the girl down at once? What shadow of right had he to hold her an instant longer than need be? What right, indeed, beyond the primeval one of a heart that is set on fire of love, and feels the only other heart on earth throbbing close against it, to the same immemorial tune.

Chivalrous gentleman though he was, the primal man triumphed in Nevil Sinclair just then. Instead of relinquishing his heaven-sent burden, he set off at a round trot—without leave asked or spoken word—for the archway a hundred yards off, whose width promised shelter and a chance of speech. Odd that, although he had flung his own coat about her shoulders, he should have forgot her parasol; but the boatman chased him with it and thrust it open into the girl's hand.

As for her—shyness, amazement, and a thrill of fear, that was rapture, had smitten her dumb. But now, as he began to run, she dutifully strove for freedom; pushing herself from him with one ineffectual hand pressed against his drenched silk shirt.

'Let me walk. Put me down. Oh, please, please!'

'When we get to the arch,' he assured her, smiling, as he hurried on. And all the while his arms that held her, lightly, yet so closely, were telling her things not to be uttered save through that mystery of contact which is love's daily bread.

Then the arch loomed darkly above them. There was respite from the lash of the rain, that fell now in a steady downpour; for the wind had dropped. And the man was constrained to set her down, to loose his hold upon her yielding slenderness—for a time. Before they went on he would have her promise; not in words alone.

The blood drummed in his temples, and the whisper of her quickened breathing was music in his ears. But speech was difficult; more so than he could have believed. His flannel coat slipped unheeded from her shoulders as she stood before him, wind-tossed and palpitating, a flower shaken by the storm.

Then he drew a step nearer, and dared all.

'Lilamani——'

The word swept through her like triumphal music; and he saw the whole rose of the woman blossom in her cheeks. Then—remembrance stabbed her: remembrance that as far as the East is from the West, so far had Destiny set them asunder.

'Oh . . . but you must not——' she pleaded, veiling her eyes lest they contradict her tongue. 'And . . . we ought to go on, please. At once.'

'Why? You're very little wet; and the storm will soon pass over.'

'But Audrey will be angry——'

He dismissed Audrey with a gesture of impatience.

'I'll settle with her, if only you will give me leave to tell her——' He came closer and she stepped back a space. 'Lilamani!' he cried again, his voice breaking with passion held in check. 'You know—you must know that those sweet, small hands of yours have plucked the heart out of my body. Will you throw it down and break it? Will you—will you?'

Still she denied him her eyes. 'Oh, do not ask me such things. How shall I say? It is to my father you should speak.'

'But it is from his daughter I must have my answer first.'

Experience of her kind tempted him to enforce his plea by persuasion more compelling. But never had he realized more poignantly her delicate aura of apartness than in this, their first moment alone, when it seemed that he had but to go forward, with tender mastery, and take her to himself. Opportunity beckoned; temptation was keen; and he readier, by nature, to yield than to resist. Yet he merely put out a hand and passed caressing finger-tips along the edge of her *sari*.

He had his reward. For a small shiver of ecstasy ran through her; and he knew—exultingly he knew——!

'Beloved—let me see your eyes.' He spoke low and eagerly. 'Let them promise me that you will be . . . my wife, in spite of everything. Put out of your mind all foolish scruples about difference of race—and colour. They are unworthy of you—of me—of the great countries to which we belong. Oh, my beautiful love! Don't keep me in suspense——'

At that she let fall her hands, and he cherished their chill moisture, while those dark unfathomable eyes of hers dwelt upon his face in a passion of adoration, such as the modern man rarely looks for in marriage, and still more rarely receives. Nevil Sinclair had seen enough of counterfeit coin to realize that—worthy or unworthy—he had struck pure gold at last.

He let out his breath in a sigh of supreme content.

'Now nothing in Heaven or earth can come between us,' he said; and, still holding her, leaned nearer for the crowning assurance.

But she, with a broken sound, stepped backward against the brickwork; and, freeing one hand, warded him off with a gesture that for him was a command.

'Oh, I must not—I may not! There is not yet any betrothal. And—and—there never *can* be——'

'In God's name, why not?' he cried out desperately. 'If you wish it . . . and I wish it——'

Again that appealing gesture. 'Oh, please—please not to speak, and—try to understand. You are asking if—if I—love you; and—how shall I deny? But—for marriage——' The sob that struggled in her throat was bravely driven back. 'In my country it is not just to the pleasure of two people. It is to union of families, of same religion, same caste. But . . . how can we . . . for sake of my father, and—and—for yours——'

'Mine? What d'you know of him——?'

'Not a great deal; but—enough. Audrey told me——'

'Audrey——? Good Lord——!' Fire that was not passion blazed in his eyes and her lips quivered at this new revealing.

'Have I said wrong? Please not be angry——'

'With you? Never!' Betrothal or no, his arm went round her shoulders, and, in defiance of gentle resistance, held her so. 'But I'll not put up with Audrey's interference. My home affairs are no concern of hers, and I shall tell her so in straighter language than she'll care about. What has she said already? Tell me honestly. I have every right to know.'

The measure of an Eastern woman's submission is the measure of her love; and, in faltering, tailless phrases, she told him honestly of the half-hour's talk that had jolted her from heaven to earth, adding, on her own account, a tremulous plea for duty and family honour, and—hardest of all—for the girl in his own rank of life. . . .

But this he would not endure, even from her.

'Lilamani—how dare you, after—just now! As for my father, no doubt he would rather I chose a girl in my own set; you see, I am frank with you. But in my country, a man marries to please himself, not to please his father.'

She sighed; then, smiling bravely up at him: 'In my country it is not so: at least—not with women——'

'I know that. Audrey told me also—of you——'

'Of me?'

A wave of hot colour flooded her face: and his hold upon her tightened.

'Darling, we won't speak of that, or think of it even,' he whispered; and through the thin veil she felt his lips upon her hair. 'You are mine now—for always. Your father will never be blind to your true happiness! He is so courageous, so wide-minded——'

'Yes—yes. But—in this, it is not him; it is our law, our custom. If I, a Hindu, marry to a foreigner, I am cut off for always from family, from caste, from religion—from ever going back to my home. This he cannot change with all his wishing and his courage; and for this—he would surely break his heart. But he shall not—he shall not——' her voice vibrated on a low note of passion—'that is why I can only—break—my own.'

'And mine, by the way. Does that go for nothing?'

At the thrill of pain in his tone, the sob so bravely beaten back rose up again, striking away her pitiful defences of pride and maidenly aloofness. Then—how it came about she never quite knew, though he perchance could have enlightened her—she found herself crying her heart out on the shoulder of the man who could never be her betrothed; burning face hidden against his damp silk shirt; distraught spirit soothed by the magic of his touch. And, for a while, beyond murmured endearments, he made no attempt to check her tears. He blessed them, rather, in that they brought relief to her, and to him the privilege of such caresses as a smiling Lilamani would never have allowed. Only when the sobs had died down to shuddering sighs, he brought his head close again and pleaded his cause with hope renewed.

'Beloved—if . . . supposing . . . your father is not dead against me as a son-in-law, you would be willing to sacrifice . . . all you said——?'

Her passionate whisper, 'Yes—oh yes——' lifted him to such heights of humility as it is good for a man to reach once in a life. 'But he will never—never——' she sighed out her tragic conviction. 'And without his consenting, I will never—make promise . . . even for you——' A tremor shook her stoical resolve. But she checked his threatened interruption, and went on, with a lift of her small, proud head: 'For me there can be no marriage. Punishment of gods doubtless for going against my mother. I must only be thankful for freedom to do Audrey's plan. I will conquer these ugly studies. Then—I go back to my father and—my country; and I will bring health and light to my less free sisters, who are sick of body or of mind——'

'You will do nothing of the sort, you blessed little saint,' he assured her; and his conviction, though a smiling one, equalled her own. 'You will stay where Fate has sent you, to give health and light to one unworthy Englishman, who can't live without you. Lilamani——!' He drew near again and stood before her, very straight and virile in the clinging silk shirt and *kummerbund*. 'Have you quite grasped the fact, even now, that I want you more than I have ever wanted anything on earth? Why should we meet tragedy half-way? Seeing how you are placed, your father might be readier than you think. . . . Only give me a chance to ask him, to-morrow—to-night even——'

'Not you. It is for me now,' she said softly. 'It is I that can give him less pain in telling. Also—it is only I that might—perhaps—bring him to see this thing with our eyes——'

'Yes—yes. You are right. You will speak soon?'

'I could not sleep to-night without telling him all that is in my heart.'

Her eyes had a far-away look, wrapt and tender. He felt himself forgotten, and knew the prick of jealousy.

'Dearest,' he said with sudden intensity, 'will you ever love *me* half as well as that?'

'Foolish one!' she rebuked him tenderly, and the play of blood in her cheeks was an uplifting thing to see. 'How shall I know—yet? But this I know—we are staying here too long. Audrey will be so wondering and so angry.'

'What a calamity! And your news won't mend matters, I'm afraid.'

'No. That is the pity. But still—we must go quickly. Look—the wind is almost dead.'

'Is it?' he asked, looking instead at the delicate pencillings of distress between her brows.

'And the rain also,' she went on, stepping out for a fuller view of sea and sky. 'Look how the sun is sparkling it like jewels! And there— over there—more beautiful than all! So great a rainbow! Two rainbows. Such as I have never seen!'

It was true. Arched across the eastern sky, where rent clouds unveiled a vision of frail, storm-washed blue, a double rainbow spanned the heavens in two unbroken arcs. Not blurred and misty, but astonishingly clear, gleamed each ring of those primal colours that rightly fused create the miracle men call light; even as love and courage, faith and truth, in perfect fusion, create that other miracle men call a human soul.

And while they stood watching, awed to silence, these two who had touched the secret springs of life, sea and sky grew calmer, till all the blue was stippled with footprints of the vanished wind—umber and grey and white, smitten by the passing sun to luminous tints of pearl.

'"Bride of the Rain," that is how Arabs call it,' Lilamani whispered at last; and the man's hand closed upon hers that hung at her side.

'Very beautiful,' he said in the same tone, as if they stood on the threshold of a temple. 'For *you* are my Bride of the Rain! And it's a good omen. You know our Bible legend?'

'Yes. I have read.'

'The bow of promise—you remember? Well, there it is—twice over. Yours and mine.'

Smiling, she shook her head; and the eyes she turned upon him had their own rainbow-light of love gleaming through tears.

'You have the more courage. But you cannot see, so clear as I see, all the frowning mountains——'

'Love and faith can move mountains, Lilamani.'

For a fleeting instant, her glance caressed him. 'It is possible. And you must believe that I will do all I can except go against my father. Come now——' the hand that nestled in his own was gently withdrawn. 'And please—if Audrey is waiting me downstairs, will you come up with us—that she shall not ask me questions? I cannot speak with her—of you, till I have spoken with my father. Will you come?'

He beamed at the request. 'At least, then, you allow my right to protect you?'

'I am allowing—every right,' she answered very low. 'Only—I have so little hope——'

'Well, I have enough for us both and to spare!'

'Ah—that is a thought to shame my weakness. Come, quickly.'

So they went together up the broad path from the sea, keeping farther apart than need be, lest any recognize them as lovers stepping downwards from the hill of dreams into the valley of stones. And Miss Blakeney, smiling distantly upon them, as they mounted the steps, was moved to righteous disapproval at the increasing forwardness of the 'Indian curio,' who by rights should be safely shut away from the sight of man, 'Instead of flagrantly fishing for an English husband—whom she would certainly never catch!' A spiteful touch evoked by the transfigured aspect of Nevil Sinclair's face.

ELEVEN

'C'est un ordre des dieux qui jamais ne se rompe
De nous vendre bien cher les grands biens qu'ils nous font.'

—Victor Hugo

No sign of Audrey below stairs, to their exceeding relief. Lilamani hoped secretly that practical considerations had driven her to her room. So might the culprit escape unchallenged to her own. But when jealousy and curiosity join hands with an unwavering sense of duty, the culprit's chances of escape are small: and Audrey Hammond had every intention of speaking out her mind to both.

Reaching the hotel, saturate and rebellious, she had looked round for a sight of them, in vain. Dignity and the state of her own heart alone withheld her from going straight back through the rain; and she may be forgiven if irritation triumphed.

'What on earth can Nevil be doing,' she broke out hotly. 'It is abominable of him to detain Lilamani like this, when she's wet through——'

'Not half so wet as you are,' Broome said soothingly. 'You got the full brunt of it, being on the weather side and no doubt Nevil thought it better to take shelter till the worst was over.'

'He had no business to think——!'

'Make allowances, Miss Hammond. It's a talent worth cultivating. I was nine-and-twenty once myself, and one remembers a thing or two. Seeing that shelter included ten minutes alone with a charming girl, I don't blame Nevil for taking it. No young fellow worth his salt would have done otherwise.'

'Of course not. That's the exalted way you men look at things!' The concentrated superiority of modern girlhood tinged her tone. 'But with Lilamani it is different, as he knows well enough. She is an Indian girl——'

'And Nevil is an English gentleman,' Broome reproved her quietly. 'Miss Lakshman Singh is perfectly safe with him; and I see no reason why we should risk catching severe colds on their account. If a layman of advanced age may presume to prescribe to a doctor—I should advise immediate change of clothes, and ammoniated quinine. May I see you to your room?' Again he had her metaphorically by the arm. Refusal would have been folly—undignified folly; and of that Audrey was incapable. At her door he had left her; and she, hurriedly exchanging a wet coat and skirt for a dry one, was out again on the landing before five minutes were up.

The lift halted; an elderly lady emerged, closing the door behind her.

Cool as she was by temperament, anger burned in Audrey Hammond like a white flame; anger against the man who had stolen her own heart unawares, and now—in the teeth of her straight-speaking—seemed set upon wrecking her dearest project, to say nothing of Lilamani's happiness. That he would be mad enough to offer his distinguished name to a Hindu girl-student—however well-bred—she could not bring herself to believe. He was simply indulging his masculine privilege of stealing with one hand the priceless thing he must needs throw away with the other. Oh, these men—these self-styled 'lords of creation!'—with their unconscionable assumption that women, whose meed is worship, were created solely for their personal delectation! And the heresy dies hard; despite the pains taken by a subversive minority to refine away from man, the over-grown schoolboy, all the true masculinity, the essential barbaric, that spells national power.

Not that Audrey would have admitted this last. She merely rejected on principle the 'lord of creation' theory of life: raged against it, rather, in her present mood. But so long as the bulk of 'unenlightened' women persist in setting the needs of others above their own, what hope for the champions of self-assertion and so-called equality? What hope indeed, seeing that Nature—who abhors equality as heartily and justly as she abhors a vacuum—framed the other-regarding woman for her own great ends: a fact more frankly recognized in the East than in the West, as Audrey had good reason to know.

And Lilamani, angelic little fool, was, in this respect, Eastern to the core: misguided past hope of redemption! If Nevil had won her love, she would quite conceivably take a pride in prostrating herself at his feet, while he stepped over her quivering heart into more eligible arms.

Thus Audrey, pacing the empty passage; listening for the unconscionable two, who came not; and longing for the relief of speech, however inadequate.

Ah!—the lift again. She swung round, steeled to fresh disappointment; and lo, they were coming towards her. But there was that in both faces which proclaimed the futility of reproof. Baulked at all points, she could only listen, with impassive interest, to the transparent lameness of Nevil's explanation, that explained nothing save the one fact obviously suppressed.

'We were afraid you might be wondering what had come to us,' he concluded airily. 'But it was a punishing downpour; and Miss Lilamani is wet enough as it is.'

'Yes, I will go at once and change. Good-bye for now; and thank you.' She gave him her hand, but not her eyes; adding, for Audrey's benefit, with a desperate attempt at lightness: 'I will make sure and remember the quinine!'

Two minutes later, she stood alone, behind the blessed shelter of her bedroom door; and Audrey heard the key turned softly. A knife turned in an open wound could hardly have hurt her more.

But Nevil was speaking again; apologizing for his disregard of advice, and for the anxiety it must have caused her, to say nothing of the wetting.

'But I sincerely hope you'll neither of you be the worse for that,' he added with a fervour that hardened her heart afresh.

'Make your mind easy. Lilamani won't die of it,' she answered him gravely. 'But rain or no rain, you ought to have brought her straight in. You had no right whatever to do anything else.'

A light she had not yet seen sprang to his eyes. But he controlled himself and said coolly: 'That remains to be proved.'

'Nevil! What on earth do you mean?'

He answered her with a direct look that drew the blood to her cheeks. 'I can't give you a full explanation yet, Audrey. What's more, I'm not responsible to you for my actions.'

'To me? No. But what of Sir Lakshman Singh?'

'We can settle that—when I see him to-morrow. Good night.'

He was gone; and she stood alone, deliberately shut out from the confidence of the two human beings who, at the moment, made up more than half her world. Incredible that he could be in earnest. And Sir Lakshman Singh? If she knew anything of the man he would not hear of it. But still—it might be well to see Nevil before the morrow, in spite of his rebuff; and make him understand that, for Lilamani's sake, he must not persevere in so crazy a proposal. She would go down after dinner; leaving the father and daughter alone. Her heart cried out that she could not sleep till she had the truth from Nevil himself.

Fortified by this decision, she looked into the sitting-room, told Sir Lakshman (who was growing anxious) they had escaped with nothing worse than a wetting, and that Lilamani was lying down; then went on to change for dinner.

The meal that followed was not enlivening: Sir Lakshman preoccupied with the business that had kept him at home; Lilamani patently ill at ease; and Audrey, between snatches of machine-made talk, counting the minutes till she could decently make her escape.

On the arrival of coffee she rose with a hurried murmur about promising a book to Madame de Lisle, picked one up at random, and sped down the broad, shallow staircase, rating herself for the flutter of trepidation within.

Disappointment again. The Spinners of Destiny seemed in league against her all round. Nevil was nowhere to be seen.

He had dined early, in the restaurant, to evade the X-ray glances of his friends; and at the moment of Audrey's descent he was pacing the long path by the sea, 'making glowworms' with an unimpeachable cigar and living the afternoon's triumph over again.

On this night of nights, the claims of father, family, social position, and trifles of a like significance to both, suffered total eclipse. The man saw nothing but Lilamani; his indubitably, by virtue of that dumb adoration in her eyes. To-morrow he would claim her openly, regardless of conventional arched eyebrows and uplifted hands—if only she could win the consent of Sir Lakshman. In this direction alone he admitted possibility of failure. Not all Love's sovereign egoism could blind him to the truth that upon those hidden rocks of duty and devotion to her father the storm-waves of passion would beat without avail. But surely if the man idolized her, as Audrey had said, all must be well.

Impatience racked him. How could he wait till morning, when by now his fate might be sealed!

And even while he paced and smoked, and built aircastles under the wistful stars, Lilamani knelt beside her father's chair, lids lowered demurely, hands resting lightly on his arm.

'Father mine—there is a thing I must tell before sleeping: a thing my heart is aching to tell. And yet—it is afraid——'

'Of me? Since when has it learnt such foolishness, joy of my life?' His free hand covered hers.

'Since a few days only; and now still more—because, in returning from the boat—Mr. Sinclair——'

'Ah—what of him?'

The sharpness of his tone startled her. She looked up in dismay.

'Kindest, please not be too quick to blame, or how shall I find courage for the truth? To-day, after landing, when Mr. Broome and Audrey hurried on, he . . . he waited me, under the arch, because of rain; and then he told me . . . asked me. . . . How *can* I say all? Only that he wishes, very much . . . oh, very much . . . that I give him promise—of betrothal——'

Sir Lakshman felt the small hands quiver beneath his own, that closed upon them firmly in token of assurance, while, for her sake, he mastered his amazed indignation and spoke.

'My child, I have been fearing, these last days, that some such madness was in his mind. But this I did not look for, that he should presume, without my leave, to speak so freely——'

'He says . . . English custom,' she pleaded softly, not daring, now, to hint at freedom other than speech.

'With their own women, it is true. But in such a case, quite outside experience, he did wrong to make use of closer intimacy, permitted only for a time, by reason of his urgent wish. Yet, after all . . . *I* should have foreknown. Lacking true detachment, by reason of love's frailty, I had not courage to resist the offer of this picture, when your image in my heart should have sufficed. Seeing how your beauty had smitten him from the first, I should have been steadfast in refusal: and now—because the gods strike through our best-beloved—behold my punishment laid on you, who have already suffered enough. Is it not so, Lilamani? Is it he alone who wishes, very much—this impossible thing? Or do you also——?'

'I also.'

The words were a mere whisper. She had bowed her forehead upon his hand; and it was wet with her tears.

'You told him this?'

'I told him.'

A stifled sound escaped Sir Lakshman Singh: and she, choking back her grief, knelt upright, the tear-drowned eyes challenging his with a courage of his own bestowing.

'Kindest—if I did wrong, you will forgive. How should one heart lie to another, when both stand unveiled? Yet I gave no promise, except I would plead your consent to this, which you call impossible. Oh, Father . . . to us it does not seem so.'

'Kama, godling of the arrows, has thrown dust in your eyes,' the man answered, smiling sadly. 'And this Mr. Sinclair has not the smallest knowledge of what such marriage would mean—for *you*——'

'But I told him; saying also I was ready . . . to forgo all; in certainty nothing could quite cut me off—from you. Could it—could it?'

'No, sweetest one. With us, no division can come between soul and soul. Yet spirits are constrained to dwell in the house of the body. And the ocean is wide as you know, now——'

Her tears overflowed. 'I know . . . bitterly I know. Only . . . you would come more often, for my sake——'

'Assuredly: whenever possible. But what of your mother, your brothers, your religion? True, I have shown you sacred books of many creeds, that you might perceive how the light of the One great Unseen dwelling behind the veil of the seen shines alike through all forms of doctrine and worship. Yet for each man the form received from his own ancestors, his own country, is best. Believing this, as I do, daughter of my heart—you would surely not wish to change even though you must lose all except essence of our faith?'

She drew in a tremulous lip.

'Oh, it is easy with lips alone to make sacrifice! But marriage and religion are one; and unless—by accepting the last, how shall I gain the first?'

'There is yet a way: only it is as if to cure one ill with another. In Europe they have an evil practice of making marriage by law, without ceremonies of consecration——'

'No—oh no! We could not have it thus. Sooner, I would make any sacrifice. From him I will learn of his creed, that his God may be as my God. In this first great matter husband and wife must be of same mind.'

'Truly spoken, wise one. You have seen enough in your own home of the trouble that comes when they are not so, even though of same creed. But faith is not as a garment, to be taken up or cast aside—even at command of love. Believe me, child, yours would not change, though you deck it in new words and give it a new name. You would not ever have one mind with this man of traditions and ideals far away from your own. Knowing these things, I do well to say such union is not possible for this daughter of mine.'

'Oh, Father—Father!' All the newly-awakened passion of her woman's heart, dutifully repressed till now voiced itself in that despairing cry. 'I will never go against you. But you said . . . I have suffered enough. Now . . . will you kill me right out?'

He winced: then gathered her close.

'Hush, dearest one; that is wild talk. If I am seeming cruel for a moment, it is only that I may save you from worse suffering—when too late. No, not to interrupt. Listen a little longer; remembering that I have lived in England and speak of what I understand. Even if you are ready to renounce all, endure all—and I am believing you capable of both—there are, for Mr. Sinclair, difficulties not to be brushed aside like cobwebs. Audrey tells me he is eldest son of a Baronet and by duty to his family——'

'That she told me, too——' For some reason Audrey's name pricked her to impatience, 'and to-day, I tried to speak of it; but *he* said——'

'Yes, yes. I know well what young men of all nations say when their blood is on fire for passion of a beautiful woman. And you are a woman now, little one, beautiful as a half-blown lotus-bud in the moon. More than that, remember you are light of my eyes, the most priceless jewel of my heart; and you are asking that I shall bestow this upon a stranger, a foreigner, of other creed and race——'

'But Father—are you not forgetting he is of the race you admire more than all?' she pleaded eagerly, inspired by despair to one last eloquent appeal. 'Is it not from your own so big mind I have been learning, all these years, to join your admiration of this great England and those her ideals you told of only yesterday? Is it not you that have shown me, by stories and poems of her highest writers, how it is beautiful, this love-made marriage between freely-consenting hearts of woman and man? Is it not you who saved me from that other marriage, worse than death, and gave leave for the picture that has brought to me this—crown of life? Have I not heard you speak often against those lines about East and West, that the two may not meet; because you must believe there might one day come closer understanding, through sympathy—through love? Is it only from your *lips* this believing, Father mine? And if from the heart—how better to prove such belief than by giving even your most priceless jewel to a man of this fine race——' Her voice broke on the words; her flash of eloquence died out. 'Oh, Father, I beg you not take away all hope!' she cried piteously, and hid her face upon his breast.

For many minutes she lay thus, a quivering sheaf of sensibilities, soothed by the strong pressure of his hand upon her head; praying passionately to Mai Lakshmi, goddess of Fortune, who, being a woman, must surely hear and make him understand. Then, in a tense expectancy, she waited—waited for the words that seemed as though they would never come: not realizing, in her anxiety, that his silence proved the strength of her appeal.

In language the more arresting for its simplicity, she had set before him the truth that unwittingly he himself had led her, step by step, toward this undreamed of consummation. He saw her—his priceless jewel—set between the devil and the deep sea; between the hideous marriage from which he had snatched her, and a life of barren womanhood, devoted to uncongenial work. To this pass he had brought her through insistence on a Western education, and delight in her sweet companionship; or, in the language of his own creed, through lack of detachment, whereby all evils come.

Dare he deny her so miraculous, if questionable, a chance of escape? No student, it was plain—this lovely and lovable child of his begetting; but just true woman, who, having found her lode-star, must follow it, 'to her triumph or her undoing.' And he who so heartily wished to see concord replace conflict between East and West, could it be thus that the gods bade him give proof of the desire, the belief that was in him—as she had said?

'Lilamani.' He spoke at last, lifting her head from its shelter and framing her face with his hands. 'Habit is master even of the strongest. I have never denied you in small things. How should I deny you in this—greatest of all? Your words have the force belonging to truth.

That which my own acts have brought about, I have no right, no power to undo. Marry this man, child, if you cannot find happiness except in taking such tremendous risk. I was hoping in time you would get more pleasure from your studies. Selfish hope, because in the end they would bring my uncaged bird back to the nest.'

'I also was hoping, and for that same reason—dearest,' she made answer steadily, though tears gleamed on her lashes. 'But ask your private heart only—is woman created for wisdom in book-lore, or in heart-lore? Is she, before all things, Life-healer, or Life-bringer? Audrey might think—the first. But I . . . never! And will it be great harm for England if I give to her a few children with best blood of India in their veins?'

For such a mingling of young simplicity and womanly wisdom he could find no answer but a lingering kiss on her brow.

'That is the seal of your consenting?' she whispered. And he: 'It is the seal of your freedom, rather, to make your own decision. Only this I counsel, that you give no promise of betrothal till you have considered, with cooler brain and heart, all that you must lose for this one gain. Best wisdom, believe me, child, is that you should go without any sight of him for one whole week. Abstinence will bring surer knowledge of your own heart; also, in detachment of spirit, you will see more clearly to judge true judgment.'

'And—he?'

'I will myself see him to-morrow. I must know something more of him and of his own people, before I can fully give consent. After seeing him, I will ask him to go right away for one week. Not too long, little one?'

She shook her head with compressed lips and puckered brows.

'I shall put very clearly to him all you must forgo, and see that he too is ready to face his share of difficulties like a man. Because . . . if he should make you unhappy——?'

Murder gleamed in the dark of Sir Lakshman's eyes; and she leaned to him, lightly smoothing his brow.

'On that account, Father, have no fear.'

'Yet even so—there is too much that might bring you trouble; and I not by to help. Think, my child, if the Gods in anger should take him from you, leaving you a widow—young, beautiful, cut off from home and country——'

'Oh, please, please hush!' she cried out, covering her ears. Then, with a sudden dawn of inspiration in her face, she added low and fervently: 'Shall the flesh survive when the soul is gone? If the Gods smite me through him—I go also. I am *suttee*. There are other ways than the funeral pyre.'

She set her small hands palm to palm; and he pressed them between his own, knowing well that she spoke truth. Yet, for all his enlightenment, was he too innately a Hindu to voice his conviction that surely she was of those whom the Gods themselves could not wittingly harm.

TWELVE

'He which observes the wind shall hardly sow;
He which regards the clouds shall hardly reap,
Risk all, who all would gain: and blindly. Be it so.'

—Francis Thompson

There were at least four people in the Hotel du Cap who slept very ill that Friday night, and welcomed the smile of morning with the peculiar gratitude of those who have been at odds with their pillow through the small hours.

Perhaps, of the four, Audrey Hammond had the worst of it. A sense of being shut out from the confidence of those, who in a peculiar sense belonged to her, added poignancy to suspense; and, by the time Annette's knock gladdened her ears, all she asked was certain knowledge— good or bad.

The maid handed her a note. She paused a moment to steady herself before opening it; then she read the few lines writ in pencil—and knew the worst.

'DEAR AUDREY,—I slept too little in the night, and this morning I will stay in my room *alone*. You will hear from father all that came to me yesterday, still too wonderful to believe. It will make you sad. Perhaps angry. But I am hoping you will understand that heart must come before head when it is a woman. And please forgive, if you can, your stupid and disappointing, but so grateful,

LILAMANI.'

She read the note twice over, tears clutching at her throat. But she would not suffer them to fall, though such kindly rain would have been her best medicine of healing just then. Strange how all jealousy, all thought of the man seemed suddenly eclipsed by the pain of losing this 'stupid and disappointing' Lilamani, whose heart must come before her head. Instinctively her latent motherhood had gone out to this unmothered child, whom Nevil—with characteristic disregard of complex issues—must have asked to be his wife. But what of Sir Lakshman? Could even Lilamani persuade him to countenance such madness?

With Audrey dressing was always a rapid operation: but this morning she broke her record.

Sir Lakshman stood awaiting her, composed and courteous as usual, but with creases of worry on his brow. Her own mask of cheerful practical interest did credit to her powers of self-control.

'Lilamani sent me a line,' she remarked, pouring coffee and milk into Sir Lakshman's cup. 'The child slept badly and won't hurry up. She says you have news for me. Is it—Nevil?'

'Yes. He wishes to marry her.'

'And—can you bring yourself to consent?'

At that direct attack, composure deserted him.

'Miss Hammond, situated as she is—can I bring myself to refuse?'

Audrey considered the question while helping herself to honey.

'That complicates matters,' she admitted grudgingly. 'It is disappointing that the study of medicine is so little to her taste. Yet—I suppose you would hardly let her marry into a family that might refuse to receive her as one of themselves?'

'Is it likely?' the man asked sharply.

'Well—possible, from what I know of Sir George Sinclair and Lady Roscoe. Arrogance, and narrow prejudice, you will say. But you have to remember that many intelligent and cultivated people, who have had no connection with India, would not see much difference between an Englishman's marriage with an Indian girl of good breeding, like Lilamani, or—say—with a superior ayah.'

The fighting gleam in Sir Lakshman's eye told her the shot had gone home.

'It is precisely about this that I must speak to Mr. Sinclair,' said he, and the fighting note was in his voice.

'Oh, you can trust Nevil to make light of family disapproval! But it will be no light matter for Lilamani. And, for them—well, Nevil is the eldest son. It is only natural they should think . . . of his children.'

'Believe me—I think of them also. In India marriage is for that purpose. Yet consider, for her sake, if I refuse—what then? Stumbling-blocks at every turn,' he muttered, frowning. 'I have been breaking my shins against them all night long. I have sent word I will see Mr. Sinclair. And, at all events, I send him away for a week. Then—we shall see.'

'A week? Poor Nevil!'

'Yes. I can enter in his feelings. But she is worth waiting for.'

With which conclusion he fell back upon silence. Plainly his pride of caste and of fatherhood were up in arms—which was well, from Audrey's point of view.

The instant breakfast was over she made haste to be gone. If she knew anything of Nevil that message would bring him upstairs three steps at a time; and she prayed to be spared from meeting him as she ran down.

To-day her *kismet* was kinder. She was safe in the little olive wood near the tennis-courts when Nevil Sinclair sped along the passage to the corner sitting-room, marshalling arguments that might convince the man who had power to crush or crown him with a word. Rather odd, having a Hindu for a father-in-law, he reflected; and hardly knew whether he relished the idea. Still—Sir Lakshman was the father of Lilamani, and in many respects far above the average semi-Anglicized Asiatic. His enlightenment was not a mere matter of Bond Street suits, slang phrases and a motor-car. He was of the very few who assimilate the spirit of culture with its forms; and without question he had passed on the lighted torch to his child.

Certainly he appeared a father-in-law of whom no man need feel ashamed as he rose to greet the bold young Englishman, who was displaying one of the essential qualities of his race in his readiness to take a risk and face the consequences: a quality that breeds great mistakes, and, by the same token, great achievements also.

'Good morning, Sir Lakshman. Glad to get your message,' Sinclair said, with a valiant show of assurance. Then, irresistibly, his glance travelled towards the balcony.

'No, she is not there,' Sir Lakshman said, smiling, yet with a touch of constraint. He had not been prepared for sudden recrudescence of the keen primeval antagonism that for the moment made further speech difficult. His passing awkwardness gave Sinclair courage, and unloosed his tongue.

'I believe I did wrong in speaking first to your daughter, Sir Lakshman,' said he, plunging valiantly into the heart of the matter. 'And I apologize. Frankly, though, I don't regret it. If I had come to you first, you would probably have sent me about my business.'

'That is possible.' Sir Lakshman smiled more kindly. In the face of such manly straight-speaking how should antagonism hold its own?

'But now that I have spoken, for God's sake don't say you can't trust her to me!' Nevil cried out; his assurance changed to sudden fear.

'Sit down, Mr. Sinclair,' said the Indian, laying a hand on the young man's shoulder and gently pushing him into the arm-chair. 'It is of this that we must speak. You come to me asking the greatest gift one man can make to another. Well—I have strong prejudice in favour of your country; and to yourself I took great liking on that first evening, when you drove in your thin end of wedge. Yet I hesitated very much even then. Better, perhaps, for all—had I refused.'

'Can you honestly think that, sir, seeing how she is placed!'

'Honestly—perhaps not. But now, if I hesitate still more, do me justice to believe it is not from doubt of trusting her to you, but because such trusting would involve many difficulties over which you can have no control.'

'Yes—yes. That's the pith of the problem,' Nevil admitted with a frankness that raised him many degrees in the Hindu's esteem. 'I hardly slept last night for thinking of it all. It seems she must pay a big price for the privilege of accepting a worthless chap like me. But she's willing to pay it. That I know—since yesterday. And I suppose you know it too?'

'Without a doubt. She is pure Hindu woman in her capacity for sacrifice of self. But her eyes are dazzled. They cannot see all it will mean. And her great loss makes greater responsibility for you.'

Nevil nodded feelingly. He stood at the cross-roads now with a vengeance. But the last vestige of hesitation had been burnt up by the flame within.

'That's true enough,' said he. 'And responsibility's new to me. Audrey would tell you I don't know the meaning of the word. But I do know that in these few weeks, your daughter has awakened more than my heart. Isn't my picture proof of that? And can I do more than give you my word of honour to make her happiness my first consideration? I admit there are difficulties I can't control. But there are still a good few that I have power to soften. In the first place, we could live mainly abroad. The climate and the general atmosphere would suit her better than England—don't you think?'

'Yes: much better. But what about your people? Your career?'

'My career—if I achieve such a thing—was decided on Thursday, by Martino's verdict on my picture. No more amateur work for me after that. So, in any case, remaining abroad gives me a double advantage. Better scope for study, and escape from family friction at close quarters.'

Sir Lakshman suppressed a sigh. 'You are claiming heavy price for your gift, Mr. Sinclair. For you the substance. For me the shadow. And I am to understand there would be even more "family friction" as you say, if I permit this marriage?'

Nevil hesitated, tugging at his moustache; and for a second or so they confronted each other in silence, these two, who so deeply and diversely loved the girl to whom the murmur of their voices through the wall came as the sound of an unresting sea, that had power to float or to capsize her rosy-sailed bark of life.

'I have the right to expect frankness from you,' the Indian began, and Nevil broke in eagerly—fearful of what might follow:

'You shall have it, sir; only . . . such things are not easily said. I'm afraid my people would be as much against the marriage as against the artistry. But—I'm my own master; and their annoyance would blow over. I promise you I would not take her home until I made sure they would give her the right sort of greeting.'

'That is well. I should demand it. Yet there is always possibility it might not "blow over"; and anyway, from my point of view it is most distasteful to think of letting daughter of mine marry in a family that will look on her as what you call—*mésalliance*. It is true what Miss Hammond said this morning. They would probably have no knowledge of caste distinction. They would think you have demeaned yourself——'

'They may think what they thundering well please!' Nevil flashed out, goaded by suspense.

'Of yourself, certainly; if you are indifferent;' Sir Lakshman conceded with his imperturbable dignity. 'But of her—by no means. You have to remember that although I give much respect to your country, and am inclining to consent, for Lilamani's sake, yet, if your father has his pride, I too have mine. To me it seems no more honour for her to marry with you than with any fine young fellow of her own country. She is of old Rajput family, therefore of good birth and lineage, like yourself. In fact, if you had not been her equal in that, I would never give consent. But there are other obstacles serious enough. In the first place her religion. For the Indian woman religion is all; and marriage is a chief part of that religion. It is consecration for this life and all other lives. That is the inmost reason of *suttee*. The wife, being spiritually higher than her husband, has all power over the welfare of his soul in future incarnations; he, without her, having none. These are not matters spoken of in my country between one man and another. But only I do so because you most honestly love my child, and because Westerns so ignorantly misjudge our motives in the matter of our women; thinking we hold them in contempt, because we are giving them so little material power, which is what you peoples chiefly prize, in spite of Christian faith. But now consider—how shall there be marriage of consecration without unity of creed? See then, what loss for her, that she can have no power for the welfare of your soul.'

Nevil frowned; his fingers once more at his moustache. Dimly he began to perceive the full complexity of a matter he had hoped, if not expected, to settle out of hand.

'Seems a sorry affair for her all round,' he said ruefully. 'I quite thought a civil marriage would meet the difficulty.'

'So I was imagining. But to her, marriage unconsecrated is so distasteful that rather would she change her religion for your own, and would learn from you——'

'My dear sir, I'm afraid my faith, what there is of it, is as unorthodox and formless as the faith of most men nowadays. But hers is the biggest part of her; and if she wants a voice in the welfare of my soul, I'd almost as soon turn Hindu myself——'

Sir Lakshman raised a protesting hand.

'Put that from your mind,' he said with great kindliness. 'I appreciate it as proof of your feelings. But if religion means not a great deal to you, better, most certainly, to keep what you have of your own. It is want of vitality in religion that is causing so much harm in all progressive countries to-day. But you will not mend that by change of name, which also would do no good in the matter I spoke of. By this marriage she would be cut off—as she told you—from all religious rites and privileges. She can keep only the spirit of her belief. Better therefore, civil marriage, and for both to accept that in this case, as in too many others, you cannot be of one mind.'

'God knows I'm willing to accept anything sooner than lose her,' Nevil made answer fervently. 'And if she's willing too, why shouldn't we have the courage of our convictions and make the experiment?'

Sir Lakshman had a smile of sympathetic understanding for the eager confidence of youth that is at once so enviable and so pathetic to the middle-aged.

'A big matter for experiment. You have to consider also that marriage is for more than for personal companionship. With us in India that counts perhaps for too little. But at least we do very well in recognizing that chief purpose of marriage is for continuing the race; though unhappily there are too many signs it is not so regarded among better classes of modern Europe and America. You will please not take my frankness amiss. For this is a very serious difficulty about which your father would have right to feel strongly, you being his eldest son.'

Fresh confusion of face here for Nevil, who, in the ardour of personal desire, had overlooked the most obvious stumbling-block of all.

'Jove, I didn't get as far as that!' he confessed, so ruefully that the elder man's smile deepened to pure amusement. 'But all the same,' he added, valiantly ignoring the momentary jar, 'whatever my father's prejudices may be, I'd stake my life on it that—her children and your grandchildren couldn't have very much wrong with them, inside or out.'

'You are more wide-minded than most men of your race,' Sir Lakshman answered, plainly gratified by such wholesale loyalty to his Jewel of Delight. 'Yet there is one thing not to be escaped. In spite of good blood on both sides those children must suffer the stigma of half-breed, which Nature herself is said to abhor.'

Nevil winced: but his courage held good. 'Why any more of a stigma than if I married a well-born Spaniard or Italian?'

'That has always been a puzzle for me, seeing that Indians are no less of Aryan stock than southern races of Europe. But fact remains that in one case there is stigma; in the other, not. Still, in my great wish to promote closer sympathy between two so fine countries as England and India I have often wondered would this be helped or hindered by occasional marriage, between best on both sides. It is very hard to tell.

And, in my thinking, chief difficulty is not so much race as religion, that is the soul of a race. From idealist standpoint it seems as if such combination ought to produce fine result: if only because soul of the West is masculine and soul of the East, feminine. Yet look how unsatisfactory the mixed race created in India by such crossing——'

'In most cases, surely, the wrong kind of crossing. A marriage like ours would be quite another affair. *You* know that. I declare you're on our side in heart, sir: and it's you that should have the courage of your belief and give your daughter a chance to work it out.'

Sir Lakshman shook his head. 'Strange that she said much the same last night; and between both of you, it seems as if I shall be driven to it, after all. The Moslems have a proverb, true enough: 'When a man and a woman are agreed, what can the Kazi do?''

'Give 'em their way, and wish them luck!' cried Nevil, in open triumph.

'So it appears! Yet the theory-maker is not often so eager to put his theory in practice, fearing his pretty bubble might break; and no father worthy of that name is eager to make experiment with his own daughter. Also in my theory-weaving I have been checked too often by a thought that even if some of us were willing to bestow our daughters, as I mine, how should it fare with a high-caste Hindu who should ask an English father what you ask from me. Now, you—who are wide-minded—what answer to that?'

Nevil hesitated, plainly at a loss.

'There—you see!' Sir Lakshman turned out his hands in expressive Eastern fashion. 'Little use of readiness on one side. It must be also on the other. And it is not.'

'But—surely—there is a difference. Indians admit it, tacitly, when they speak of Western views and customs as enlightened. One, say your daughter's case, seems an advance: the other—if you'll forgive me—would be, in measure, retrogression.'

'You think that? Well—I forgive. But I do not entirely admit. I think only that for people of each country their own customs are suited best. If we seem to Westerns too much jealous for the honour of the Inside, it is partly because marriage, as I said, is for the woman a consecration to motherhood, almost like Roman taking of veil; and no Hindu would allow mother of his sons to run into such risk and temptation as English husbands permit. For them it may be well; their men having cooler blood and more restraint. Yet how often come tragedies! How often family life—chief of all sanctities—is ruined by consequence. Believe me, something can be said for both sides: and always there is risk of suffering, if not harm, from change that is not first prepared by development. In my daughter's case there has been preparation— a small measure; chiefly in hope I might one day bring her to England and lead her to wider life. Of such means as this I did not dream. Yet it might seem as if without knowledge I had most carefully prepared the path. Such mystery is in the ways of Fate.'

'I believe it was ordained from the beginning—on both sides,' Nevil declared, with indomitable conviction forged upon the anvil of desire. 'And now may I see her, sir—and claim her promise?'

'No, not to-day,' spoke the voice of inexorable calm, so maddening when the blood is on fire. 'In fact—not until to-day week.'

'To-day week——! Why the devil——?'

'My dear Sinclair, contain yourself.'

'Was it *her* wish?'

'The suggestion was my own; and she—in spite of her few years— has enough of wisdom to know how it is needful to consider such important question without too much disturbance of emotion, which nearness must bring. I cannot let her make so great sacrifice with dazzled eyes, even if to gain the desire of her heart. You also have to consider, with cooler mind, your own share of sacrifice. Because if it should happen that you are regretting when too late; and she came to know it—as she surely would—then by all the Gods of my fathers——!' Sir Lakshman checked himself sharply; but the set of his jaw and the sheet-lightning in his eyes spoke his thought more forcefully than words. For all his lover's egoism Nevil Sinclair recognized, beneath the schooled detachment of Eastern fatherhood, a devotion no less ardent than his own.

'I'm not a mere boy, sir. I'm close on thirty,' he said quietly. 'I've seen something of the world, and of women. Any chance of regret, on my side, is out of the question. Consideration for her—is another matter. It'll be a black week for me. But I'll pull through it somehow, for her sake.'

'Bravely said,' Sir Lakshman applauded, rising to his feet. 'Better for both if you could go right away. Make some little motor expedition with your friend Broome. No?'

Nevil's relief was obvious.

'A happy thought. I'll ask him. I mayn't write a line?'

'Better not.'

'And you won't over-persuade her?'

'You can trust me for that, Sinclair. I may call you so now?'

'Wish you'd make it Nevil, sir. It would sound a bit more promising.'

'That I shall do with pleasure—when Lilamani gives me the right.' The kindness of Sir Lakshman's smile seemed a promise in itself. 'Now good-bye, and good luck for you, till this day week. You shall hear from me if you let me have address.'

'Thank you, sir. You've been uncommonly good to me,' Nevil answered, frankly returning the other's grasp.

Then, in a mood of sadly-chastened exaltation, he went forth in search of Cuthbert Broome.

THIRTEEN

'Take each man's censure, but reserve thy judgement.'

—Shakespeare

No sign of Broome in the lounge-hall; and Sinclair, passing out on to the wide balcony-verandah, scanned the seats where smokers and newspaper readers basked in the strong unclouded sun of early March. Two of the benches on the path below had been transformed into open-air stalls; and toward these Sinclair was lured by the lover's imperious need of giving, that is, in its essence, divine. But choice was difficult, for a beloved so far removed from the usual type. The trinkets were too trumpery; hairpins, combs and brushes a trifle too intimate—as yet; paper-knives, and their like, too impersonal, too prosaic.

Then—while the rival pedlars volubly assailed him with impossibilities, his eyes lighted on a pair of oval buckles in mother-o'-pearl. By divine right of fitness, they were made for her small golden shoes; and pushing aside the human flies that buzzed at his ears, he picked up his treasures.

While he stood so, querying the man's preposterous demands, behold Audrey, emerging from the olive wood, where she had been remodelling her 'sacred programme,' and metaphorically fighting the beasts, like any early Christian, without the stage properties of arena, audience, and the martyr's crown.

At sight of Nevil, appraising those shimmering trifles on his open palm, she set her lips and stood still. Escape were impossible; nor was she in the mood for it now. There are moments when self-chastisement dulls the edge of self-pity. Besides—she wanted to know.

He looked up and recognized her.

'Hullo, Audrey,' he said, flushing awkwardly and closing his left hand.

'Too late. I saw them!' she rallied him, with a forced lightness that had its undernote of pathos and pluck. 'Has the modern dandy progressed from striped silk socks to buckles on his pumps?'

'Not yet! No doubt he will—in time! But—if you saw them——' his boyish awkwardness was vexatiously engaging—'you must know— they weren't the right size——!'

'Yes. It puzzled me. Does it mean—congratulations?' she moistened her lips. 'I understood you were to be banished for a week.'

'So I am—bad luck to it.'

'And yet——?'

'Oh, hang it all, it comes natural to a man. And I thought—I'd give a hostage to fortune. You might wish me luck, Audrey,' he went on, paying for his hostages, and moving away with her, 'though I *have* so egregiously upset your apple-cart. It's awfully tactless of me; and I apologize humbly. But one couldn't foresee—this.'

'No, indeed!'

'Well then——? Are you quite too angry to wish me well? Or do you disapprove, as usual—root and branch?'

She lifted her shoulders. 'Yes. I disapprove. But I'm not angry. I've no right to be. Only disappointed, for the moment. Though I don't see that my disappointment or disapproval need matter much—to either of you.'

She had turned down toward the sea in speaking; preferring the pain of his nearness to the pain of his absence; and she stepped beside him in resolute fashion, with long leisurely strides. But the calm of her tone did not carry conviction; and Nevil scrutinized her well-cut profile with troubled gaze.

'I wonder why you say that, Audrey?' he asked in the voice of sympathy against which she steeled herself in vain. 'Seeing that we owe pretty nearly everything to your pluck, in persuading Sir Lakshman to bring her home. And yet—I'm hanged if I know what's gone wrong with you!' he broke out in honest bewilderment. 'A fortnight ago we were such good friends, I'd have sworn nothing could come between us. But ever since I started the picture——'

'My dear Nevil, it's not like you to make mountains out of mole-hills!' Only a show of anger and open speech could save her from betrayal. 'Naturally I was anxious about Lilamani when I saw what was happening to her. I never believed for a moment you would dream of asking her to become—the future Lady Sinclair; and I dreaded another emotional crisis, that would upset her studies and her health——'

'Well, then—now, you ought to be satisfied. And you're not.'

'No. You've only turned my anxieties into a fresh channel. To me such a marriage seems little short of madness—for you both.'

'You think I'll not understand her—that I'll make her unhappy?'

'God knows! If Lilamani were more like the average Indian girl— a precocious little woman, graceful and gentle on the surface, sensuous and subtle underneath, my chief concern would be—for you. But she has a personality, a rare spiritual power that may just possibly enable her to transcend the limitations of race. I'm not over-fanciful or impressionable; and at first I looked upon her simply as an attractive child, with brains that I was keen to develop for the service of her country-women. But of late I have been compelled to recognise—quite against my will!—that this mere child, ten years my junior, could teach me deeper things than I could ever teach her. Nevil— when that girl gives herself, she will give all, without reservation or stint, as few English girls can, or will, in these days. It's this that makes me tremble for her: and I confess I half resent such a complete burnt-offering of personality being made for the sake of—any man.'

'Even if he feels his own unworthiness in every fibre?'

Sinclair cried out with sudden fervour: and for a second or two— her own pain forgotten—she regarded this new Nevil of Lilamani's making.

'If you honestly feel that,' she said slowly, 'if I could only believe you might *continue* to feel it—after the gift has been given, my own loss would be easier to bear. It will be a big loss in many ways; how big I hardly knew—till I read that.'

Obedient, for once, to an impulse she did not stay to analyse, Audrey Hammond handed Lilamani's note of the morning to Lilamani's lover, and watched him while he scanned it; the ache of jealousy clashing with the ache of mother-love.

Nevil Sinclair read the note twice through, lingeringly, before handing it back.

'Hindu or no—she's an angel of God,' he said under his breath. 'Thank you for letting me see it. But it makes me feel madder than ever at being banished for a whole week!'

'The best thing that could happen, all the same,' said she. 'I admire Sir Lakshman's wisdom. When d'you go?'

'This afternoon, I think; if I can fix it up with Broome. I came out to look for him. But I'm glad I stumbled on you first. It's been a relief, and a pleasure, to have a friendly talk with you again. Have you seen anything of Broome?'

'Yes. He went past, while I was in the wood, with Mrs. Despard and Signor Martino, who had his easel. I believe he's painting on the Cap.'

'Good. Let's join them.'

'You can. I'll turn back.'

'Why? Don't you like Mrs. Despard?'

'Yes. She's charming. But we don't see life from the same angle. She'll prophesy much smoother things to you, and wipe out all the effect of my foreboding! Goodbye!'

'No—not that: *au revoir!* And you won't wish me luck—even now?'

'I can only wish—what is best, for you and her; and honestly I don't yet know what that is.'

'But you won't frighten her off with your forebodings, will you, Audrey? You'll play the game?'

'I've too much of the boy in me to do anything else,' she answered, half proudly, half in bitterness. 'If she is really—yours, nothing will keep her from you.'

The last words gave an added warmth to his hand-clasp.

'If you believe that, Audrey, it should soften your disappointment. She wasn't yours from the start. I'm convinced you brought her all the way from India, simply that we might meet. And some day what is really yours will come to you for a reward.'

'Will it? I wonder.'

Her eyes and tone had a strange softness.

'Take my word for it,' he assured her, smiling: and again, as on that first night of revelation, she stood watching him while he left her—alone.

Yet was Sinclair thinking more of her, in that moment, than of his banished love. This was not the Audrey who had greeted him, and rated him, less than a month ago. There were new inflections in her voice; and, just now, he could have sworn to the gleam of tears in her eyes. Then—a sudden suspicion darted into light. Did it mean——? Could it be . . . that she . . .? Nonsense! He thrust away the thought as an impertinent ebullition of masculine vanity; and hurried on to the gleaming headland where Martino's easel and small figure were silhouetted against the blue, while Broome and Mrs. Despard lounged near at hand on a fragrant cushion of lentisk.

They waved letters and newspapers at his approach, and Helen Despard patted the empty space at her side.

'Good morning, Mr. Sinclair. Come and laze with us on the most luxurious spring couch in Europe! How that Colossus of industry, Signor Martino, can stand and paint, hour after hour, in this lotus-eating atmosphere is beyond me altogether. But *you* have earned the right to loaf; and I want you to talk to me about that charming girl.'

'I'm ready!' Nevil answered, sinking easefully down beside her, and sniffing the aromatic sweetness of crushed leaves.

Broome, leaning round on one elbow, eyed him keenly.

'Thought I noticed a glorified air about you this morning,' said he.

'The best it could be. I've asked Miss Lakshman Singh to be my wife.'

'Good Lord, Nevil! You don't mean that! I thought——'

'You thought I was amusing myself—legitimately?'

All a lover's indignation burned in his tone. 'I've just been trying to persuade Sir Lakshman to let me marry her at once.'

'Well?'

'He's turned me off the premises for a week to think things out with a cool mind, and give her a chance of doing the same.'

Broome nodded three times decisively. '"A Daniel come to judgment!" You mean to leave the Cap?'

'Yes. A week's spin in the motor would meet the case, if it suits you.'

'Right. I'm your man. The last of my proofs went off yesterday, which leaves me a free agent—till next time!'

Helen Despard, prone upon her cushion, looked from one to the other with sympathetic interest, awaiting her cue. But Martino, hearing vague snatches of their talk, suddenly caught the drift of it and pounced round upon them as a dog upon a bone.

'*What* is that you are talking, Sinclair? Not enough that you have painted such a wonderful picture, but you are marrying the *houri* herself?'

'The minute her father gives me leave,' Nevil answered, proudly content.

'*Sapristi!* But that is true romance; too seldom seen in this age of dry bones! And I applaud your choice. I—Martino—would have done same myself, only that I have—lost my one lung.'

It was as if he had said 'I have lost my umbrella'; and his stoical coolness smote so sharply upon Nevil's sensitized heart that it cost him an effort to answer, laughing: 'No fear, Martino *mio!* Not while I was alive and could wield a pistol!'

The Italian shrugged his lean shoulders. '*Ebbene!* The better for my art; even like my lame inside, that forbids me from unfaithfulness, such as you will fall into, my friend, when that *houri* makes you the necklace of her arms, and you cannot see the stars of heaven for the shining in her eyes.'

But for Sinclair the vision eclipsed the warning.

'It's my belief I shall see them ten times more clearly,' said he.

'Ah, the incomparable lover! For that I shall petition the Holy Virgin and all the Saints. Only through some great emotion, some lightning-flash into Heaven or Hell—small matter which—is great achievement born. So! If you can make full surrender, you gain the more. For myself, I paint for your bride a sea-piece—the finest that Martino's brush can achieve. It would please her—no?'

'Beyond everything!' Nevil glowed visibly, Englishman though he was. 'Let it be all sea and sky, Martino. That's how she likes it best.'

It was then that Helen Despard leaned forward, laying a hand on his arm.

'This makes the fairy-tale sound astonishingly real,' she said, with softly smiling eyes. 'I was charmed at first sight. I always found Indian women curiously appealing: but I have met few of *her* quality. I had my suspicions on Thursday—about you both; and I wondered very much how far the Bohemian element in you would dominate the average Englishman's instinct for the beaten track. It's a daring venture. But, like Signor Martino, I applaud your choice.'

'Thank you. I felt sure you would,' Nevil said simply. But though his words were for Mrs. Despard, his eyes were questioning Cuthbert Broome.

'You don't feel quite so sure of me—eh, old chap?' quoth the novelist, pensively tapping his pipe against a rock. 'Well, it's always been the trouble—hasn't it?—the Bohemian element under your Park Lane surface! I admit the girl's attractive enough to knock any man off his centre. But still—what of Sir George?'

Sinclair winced. 'My affair, surely,' said he, with a touch of constraint. Then, because Broome was Broome, and licensed to say what others might not, he added in a changed tone: 'It's rough luck on the old man, of course. But I'm free to choose for myself. He'll admit that, if I know him, when the first vexation's over; and I shan't take her home till it is. Once get 'em together, I can trust her for the rest.'

'H'm. It's conceivable—after a time. What's more, if you leap into fame with a picture or two, as Martino prophesies, and turn up in town with a beautiful Eastern wife, it's quite on the cards that, in this day of volatile fads and crazes, she might become the rage. I can just picture certain hyper-cultivated, esoteric hostesses of my acquaintance thrilled to the tips of their French suede gloves over "a new find," and discovering, with enthusiasm, that *saris* and Hindu philosophy are the only wear——'

'Confound you, Broome!' Nevil broke in hotly—a new Nevil indeed. 'D'you think I'd let her be exploited by a parcel of society women?'

'No, no, my dear boy, he doesn't think anything of the kind!' Thus Helen Despard extinguishing the egregious author with wave of her hand. 'He's only talking ribald nonsense because it is his nature to! Let him alone, and listen to *me*. I didn't spend fifteen years in India with my eyes glued to one side of the picture, as some of us do. I made many friends among high-caste native ladies and girls, who are entering on a phase of transition as full of disadvantages and difficulties as our own; and even more fertile in distressing incongruities. Anklets jingling above heavy Oxford shoes. *Saris* draped over unspeakable "English jackets." A smattering of music, and a veneer of education from Zenana schools. But this girl—like most Indian women of real distinction—seems to have been educated mainly by her father, a very remarkable specimen of the Anglicized native. Still—if you *do* marry her, don't Westernize her more than you can help. Keep her away from superficial English influences——'

'Yes, yes, that's my notion,' Nevil assented eagerly, with a triumphant glance at Broome, the extinguished, who was consoling himself with a second pipe. 'I wouldn't change one iota of her unique, delicately-poised personality. Her pretty poetic fancies and her quaint turns of phrase are as much a part of her as the scent and colour are of a flower.'

'Happy for her that you are poet enough to discern the essence of her charm—once lost, never to be recaptured. Again and again I have been puzzled and distressed to see how all that is vivid, beautiful, and alluring in the Indian woman's personality becomes crude, inartistic, and inadequate through too close contact with Western things: the wrong things, no doubt. But it's hard to discriminate. Keep your *houri* Eastern, in thought and feeling—*and dress*, Mr. Sinclair, and it's possible you may learn much from her that will make you a better man and a finer artist. There's rank heresy for you!'

'Then you may write me down the rankest heretic that ever stepped.' And while Broome chuckled in his beard, Mrs. Despard patted the artist's sleeve.

'In that case, it won't shock you if I add that we have more to learn from the East—especially perhaps from its women-folk—than our native arrogance will let us admit. There! my sermon's over; and I shall see all I can of Miss Lakshman Singh while you're away. When d'you go? At once?'

'This afternoon; eh, Broome?'

'M—yes. By the way. I promised to run over to Monte Carlo for the night, on the trail of that mis-begotten lunatic, de Lisle, who went off three days ago with some infallible new system in his pocket, and every penny of his wife's spare cash. Not a line from him since; and she seems afraid he might make away with himself if he lost it all. Best thing that could happen for her, in my private opinion.'

'Poor soul! But how is she managing without the spare cash?'

It was Helen Despard who spoke; and Broome, studying the horizon with interest, made answer gruffly: 'Oh, that's been squared—for the present. And, for her sake, I've agreed to hunt for a needle in a haystack. It's worth trying on the chance. You don't mind, Nevil?'

'Rather not. We can put in the week-end there; and then take a run into the low hills—Cagnes, La Tourelle, Gorge du Loup. Good to see all the old places again, with new eyes.'

'That's fixed up, then. Two o'clock sharp.'

And on the stroke of the hour a snorting motor whirled them forth upon their pilgrimage, through the iron gates of the Cap Hotel; while a girl in a primrose *sari* looked after them from the corner balcony, and knew, for the first time, that strange and terrible feeling, as of the heart being dragged out of the body and flung quivering into space.

FOURTEEN

'We are children of splendour and flame,
Of shuddering also and tears.'

—William Watson

In the week of shifting scenes that followed, Nevil Sinclair saw many things with new eyes. For love—the true, other-regarding love that lasts—is an adjusting glass, the most delicate and infallible given to man.

The two hours' drive, through Nice and on along the Dantesque magnificence of the Grand Corniche road, with the peacock-breasted sea flashing a thousand feet below, set him yearning for the presence of his beloved, for her young, untarnished delight in it all. Not so Monte Carlo, where the world, the flesh, and the devil stalk naked and unashamed; where clean sea-breezes and life-giving sunshine seem tainted with the greed of gold, the feverish pursuit of pleasures, artificial and meretricious, that satiate, without satisfying, creatures designed for better things. Even to think of Lilamani in such an atmosphere seemed desecration; and Sinclair privately cursed de Lisle for dragging him straight out of Paradise into this glorified human dustbin, where men and women of all nations and temperaments scrabbled shamelessly for notes and gold. A man in love is apt to resent the intrusion of ugly realities; and, in his present mood, Sinclair marvelled how he could ever have found the place amusing, even as a panorama of varied, if distasteful, life.

They spent Saturday evening in the heart of the dust-bin—the great Casino; passing from room to room, hot and heavy-laden with mingled odours of orris-root and patchouli; from table to table, where silent intent men and women massed three and four deep, automatically set down and received doles of silver, paper or gold; their movements regulated by the reiterate cry of the croupiers: '*Faites vos jeux, messieurs. Faites vos jeux!*'

Anxiously they scanned the close-packed rows of faces, frivolous or haggard, tense or stoical, according to the player's race, temperament, or immediate run of luck; themselves staking here a five-franc, there a ten-franc piece, and winning, most often, because they cared little for the game. It needed some grit on Nevil's part not to desert his purposeful, great-hearted friend for the more cheerful distraction of the theatre, or the divine serenity of stars and sea faintly silvered by a moon nearing the full. But he had promised to help; and for over an hour they pursued the needle through the mazes of that unsavoury hay-stack.

No sign of de Lisle.

'Come out of this soul-destroying temple of lust, my son,' Broome said at last, taking Sinclair by the arm. Then—as the heavy swing doors fell to behind them, and a whiff of cool night air gave them delicate greeting: 'Phew-ew! But it's a pestilential atmosphere, offensive to the nostils of sense and spirit. Tempts a man to endorse the fool who said in his heart "There is no God." And we must go again to-morrow evening—if it *is* the Lord's Day.'

Sinclair sighed. 'Yes, worst luck. I suppose I'm a fool not to find it amusing. But I don't.'

'Sorry, Nevil. But if you'd seen that poor woman at Antibes, agonizing over her boy, you'd not grudge a couple of days spent in her service. And a man's not half a man if he can't look in the face of sin and pain without his muscles turning to jelly and his blood to gall. You young fellows of a hyper-civilized age need reminding, at times, that there is such a thing as wholesome brutality—and an unwholesome delicacy. Now come on, to the Hotel de Paris, and I'll stand you a champagne supper to take the taste out.'

Sunday was a nightmare of fruitless, unremitting search. Casino, gendarmerie, likely hotels were ransacked for a husband—lost, stolen, or strayed: without avail.

'Give it up, man. You've done enough,' Sinclair urged, as they commanded *chocolat* and *patisserie*, preparatory to a fresh start.

'Have I?' quoth Broome, carefully choosing a sugared cake.

The man had the persistence of natures born to succeed. More or less Southern in temperament, he was emphatically British in his refusal to accept defeat: and an hour later they ran their quarry to earth, in a fourth-floor bedroom of a second-rate Pension. But his wife—who knew de Lisle too tragically well—had been justified of her forebodings.

It was the shell of that which had once been a man that lay stiff, dishevelled, and unshorn upon the neat white coverlet: the glazed eyes half-open, the lean hands clenched, as in impotent defiance of the Power that made and broke so poor a creature on the wheel of things. The untidy dressing-table was littered with brushes, razor, a half-empty coffee-cup, the unpaid hotel bill, and scraps of paper, covered with hieroglyphic proofs of the infallible system that had driven him to his death.

Broome closed the unseeing eyes, and slipped a hand under the gaping shirt.

'Not long gone,' he mused aloud. 'Poison, most likely. Not a word to his wife, I'll swear!' he added between his teeth; while Nevil, with a sick sensation, compact of pity and disgust, went over to the window that looked down into a narrow street, and away across a forest of chimney-stacks to a gleaming line of sea.

The horrible sense of uncertainty, of unreality, that assails the young and imaginative in face of the one awful actuality, clutched at his throat. And while he wrestled with it, ashamed of his own weakness, Broome had collected the dead man's belongings, and rung for a waiter, who testified that *Monsieur* had been present at *déjeuner*. Then they went down, and out again, into the common, reassuring world of life, after Broome had interviewed the manager, written out a wire for Madame de Lisle, and made all needful arrangements for the morrow.

'Now then, Nevil, old man,' said he, as they stepped forth into the street. 'Back you come to the Casino; fork out your last night's winnings, and stake 'em for all you're worth.' He held up a five-franc piece. 'That's all I found in the poor chap's pockets: and, between us, we've got to swell it into a sum worth passing on to Madame and her boy. She's proud. But if we've honestly won the money, we knock that pedestal from under her brave feet. Monte Carlo's a devilish awkward place to die in; and if we mean to see Madame through, we must put up with delays. Come on, my son. Early dinner at the café. Then we'll back our streak of luck till it turns.'

Two hours later they were backing it still; regardless of the pestilential, over-scented atmosphere that stirs the senses and lulls the brain; regardless of the thronging faces, that had so painfully absorbed their attention the night before; eye and brain concentrated upon the devil's own pastime—hallowed, momentarily, by the hidden motive that glorifies or debases every act of man.

Save for an inevitable failure or two they won steadily from first to last. Broome, in particular, played like a man inspired; and fell asleep, near midnight, on the justifiable conviction that the Lord's Day had not been ill spent after all.

Monday brought Madame de Lisle, pale, red-eyed, yet stoically composed. In her speechless amazement and gratitude, over their joint achievement, both men reaped full and sufficient reward for a day that neither would readily forget. On Tuesday Sinclair took possession of the motor and scoured the stark, stately heights above Mentone, while Broome did all that mortal man may do to smooth the ground under a proud and suffering woman's feet. But if Monte Carlo is an awkward place to die in, it is a still more awkward place to be buried in. The endless inquiries and formalities could neither be evaded, nor hurried. So it came about that Nevil's interminable week was more than half over before the blunt-nosed motor turned its back upon the sea, and sped, purring, up and up into the green heart of the hills.

Crowned and fulfilled with an all-pervading peace were the sun-kissed valleys and majestically unfolding heights of the Alpes Maritimes, after the fret and stir of Monte Carlo, where pain struck sharp on pleasure makes jangling music to sensitive ears. Here were no jarring contrasts; but on every hand, upon every tree-top, and in every cranny of rock, the secret music and laughter of life renewing itself with unwearied zest. Everywhere unseen forces yearned up towards the light: and Nevil, controlling with skilful hands the car, that throbbed under him like a live thing, felt his own pulses chiming in tune with the season that, in tree and bird and flower, is a festival of love made manifest.

Skirting the low spur where the brown, flat-topped houses of Cagnes huddled, in picturesque disorder, among gardens and vineyards more than half awake, they swept up and round to the far side of that noble valley, past the waterfall and rocky hamlet of La Tourelle, where they stayed to unpack their lunch-basket, to smoke and lounge among the rocks, while Nevil achieved a lightning sketch for his beloved.

Then down and down again into a sterner region of volcanic rock-walls, ochre, and red, and grey, towering higher with each mile of their descent, till they reached their Ultima Thule, the Gorge du Loup; a gorge as wild in nature as in name, where the Loup leaped in thunder, over rocks and stones, between glowing cliffs, at whose feet nestled terraced orange groves and fields of mild flowers, in all their new bravery of purple and yellow and white: the narrow dip spanned by great railway arches two hundred feet up.

Here, in the one little hotel overhanging the boisterous torrent, they spent the night; completing their pilgrimage by a 'spin' through Grasse and Cannes, and on along the red, fantastic coast-line of the Esterelles.

Here, too, before leaving, Nevil achieved a long explanatory letter to Sir George; denouncing himself, in his father's own phrase, for 'a damned unsatisfactory son'; and justifying the denunciation by news of a picture, appraised of Martino; a picture that plainly indicated the one career in which he was like to attain distinction. He had decided, therefore, to stay abroad for the present, and devote himself to something better than spoiling of canvas. As for the election; surely none of them had really believed he would stand. They knew him for a duffer at politics. But he had hopes of proving that he could handle a brush to some purpose. And withal, he remained Sir George's most affectionate, if undutiful, son . . .

A brief note of regret to Jane referred her to his father for details; and thereafter he vented his repressed impatience in a fervent plea to Sir Lakshman for a few lines of assurance, that should reach him at Valescure, and enable him, on the return journey, to ransack Cannes for a ring approximately worthy his Jewel of Delight.

FIFTEEN

'O king, thy kingdom who from thee can wrest?
What fate shall dare uncrown thee from this breast;
O god-born lover,—whom my love doth gird
And armour with impregnable delight
Of Hope's triumphant, keen, flame-carven sword?'

—Sarojini Naidu

And of her, who looked shyly for his return, what record through those days of waiting; of quickened breath and fluttering pulse?

While Sinclair, with the restless energy that is the hallmark of the male throughout creation, sought distraction in movement from the fever of longing, Lilamani went softly down the days of her appointed week, accepting it with all the fundamental woman's capacity for still endurance and folded wings. While Sinclair looked without, she looked within; marvelling, now at her own daring, now at her unworthiness—unrepentant rebel as she was. The wonder of it all, the miracle of unlooked-for escape from those grey studies dazzled heart and brain, as Sir Lakshman had said. It was as if enclosing walls had crumbled at a touch, setting her in a blaze of sunlight, that warmed and cheered and—above all—gave promise of womanhood made perfect through renewal of life. Yet it demanded no small venture of faith to go forward, irrevocably, along this unknown, if alluring, way of the heart. Like all ways leading to the next-door House of Life it must needs have ups and downs; stones also, it might be—and shadows.

The first of these—a mere cloudlet—blurred already her clear sky of dawning. It had hurt her inexpressibly to realize that her lover had taken for granted the unconsecrate marriage by law; that their difference of religion affected him little, if at all. Tactfully and delicately as her father had broken the truth to her, there had been need of much silent wrestling and praying to induce the conviction that she could endure all things sooner than face the blank of life without him. To such fullness of knowledge she had attained in those first bewildering days of his absence: and, recognizing this, gloried, woman-like, in the wisdom of that dear father, who was her 'Wise Man, Truth-named': father and Guru in one.

As for that other, chosen lord of her life—not yet to be named, even in thought—her Eastern woman's instinct of worship, and skill in glossing over flaws, convinced her finally that his ready acceptance of mere legal marriage had arisen from reluctance to suggest the supreme renunciation on her part that a religious ceremony would involve. And through her secret pain and shrinking ran the one gold thread of consolation that, loyalty at least would be permitted to the faith of her country and her ancestors; excommunicate though she would be from the rites, feastings, and sacrifices that absorb more than half the Hindu woman's life. These she had learnt to regard as garments of religion; and Sir Lakshman assured her that the gods, not being man-made like priests, would surely not reject sacrifice and incense of the soul. So he believed; while yet he prayed—with human inconsistency—that if fatherly love had led him into 'benevolent falsehood,' his lapse from accuracy might not be visited on her.

And she—having wrestled and overcome—quietly set about preparing herself for the great consecration, in much the same spirit as a novice might prepare for the veil. True, in her case no stricter retirement would follow upon betrothal: yet could not a few months of freedom dispel that instinct for purdah, so deeply ingrained in the soul of her race, that the word has become a synonym for family honour, modesty, prestige. Of the customary prelude—the colourful pageant of sacrifice, feastings, and gift-bringings—she could have none. Greater need therefore, to her mind, for personal purifying by prayer, fasting, and meditation, that body might become subordinate to spirit; even as she, Life-bringer, would become subordinate to him, Life-giver, when the days were accomplished that she should be his. Symbolism, always symbolism. It is the Hindu woman's breath of being. For where complexities of outer life are denied, the soul must live by thought and feeling, or die outright.

But East and West agree at least in this, that a good deed is twice itself when the right hand knows not what the left hand doeth. So did Lilamani, quite simply and instinctively, devote the night to her spiritual preparation; reducing sleep to a minimum, and reserving only the first hour of the morning and the last hour of light for reading, or meditation, alone in her House of Gods.

In addition to translations of her own sacred books, she renewed her acquaintance with the Holy Book of her lover's country, choosing her favourite Gospel of John and St. Paul's dissertations on wifely submission and womanly modesty; finding in both, as always, fresh confirmation of her father's teaching, that the light of the one great Unseen dwelling behind the veil of the seen shines alike through all forms of doctrine and worship.

Then with the quaint incongruity that belongs to transition, her study of St. Paul would culminate in a form of prayer to Sarasvati, Goddess of Wisdom: 'She who, robed in white, sets far all ignorance. She who abides with the Creator, may she abide with me——'; or Mai Lakshmi, Goddess of Fortune, would be entreated to make her a wife not less perfect in devotion and mighty in renunciation than Sita, the ideal woman of Hindu legend, and heroine of India's great Epic the Ramayana. Even from dim days of childhood, Rama's unsullied queen had reigned supreme in Lilamani's heart—had been, as it were, her chosen patron saint, upon whose character she must strive to model her own. It is in this fashion that India's two great Epics have become so closely inwoven with her national life and religion. To be called by her father his little Sita Dévi, had been, and still was, Lilamani's crowning reward for an act of self-suppression, or a day well spent; so now it was Sita who dwelt constantly in her thoughts during her hours of secret vigil.

But the fasting, not to be foregone, could by no means be achieved in secret. Her father she could trust to see without seeing, and say no word. Not so Audrey, who was bound in honour to protest on the score of her own private godling—Health; and the girl shrank from speech on the subject, with one who could not be expected to understand. She supposed that even the unveiled bride of the West could not approach so great an event without some form of sanctification. But to her, the subject seemed too intimate for discussion.

With the smiling *insouciance* of one who does quite the ordinary thing, she drank tea at breakfast, milk at lunch, and ate no food till after sundown. Even then her meal was of the lightest and to Audrey's anxious remonstrance she answered with sweet reasonableness; 'Why must I eat—if not hungry?'

Had not Audrey been herself in love with the prospective bridegroom, it is possible she would have jarred the Eastern girl, by attributing this to his absence. For, while we of the West profess to hold love sacred, there remains the paradox that we hold it also fair game for the most inept form of humour, aptly called 'chaff.' Happily, Audrey's lips were sealed: but a repetition of no breakfast and no lunch brought the direct question Lilamani dreaded. She gave the direct answer, briefly as might be, with eyes downcast and cheeks that burned; while Audrey, unversed in certain phases of Indian life, realized, as never yet, that this poetic, passionate child, deeply imbued with the primitive woman-soul of the East, could never have been hers to mould and make into a student of medicine, a pioneer of the brain. In that realization she could, and did, forgive Nevil much; though her own disappointment was none the less keen.

'You are thinking me a too much foolish Lilamani?' the soft voice ended on a note of pleading. 'But with us—it is custom. Father understands.'

And Audrey recognized by now the finality of that last. She could only counteract it by a tentative appeal to vanity, quite against her principles. But of late these had been tumbling about her like a house of cards.

'No, dear, I've never thought you foolish,' she said with unwonted gentleness. 'Only remember you are marrying—an Englishman, who won't understand such things. He will come back expecting to find the same beautiful bright-eyed Lilamani. But if you starve you won't sleep; and where will your bright eyes be then? Do what you think right. But I advise you to eat and sleep normally the last two days; or the very joy of it all may upset you, and make you ill. Not pleasant for him; and as I've done my best to get you strong, it would be sad to go away and leave you more or less of a wreck——'

'Leave me? But Audrey—why that?'

Her dark eyes echoed the question, in pained surprise and Audrey looked deep into them before answering. She had her own confession to make.

'Dear child, what else?' she asked, forcing a smile. 'No more studies after next Saturday; so no more need of me. I met a friend in Cannes yesterday, who is stopping at Mentone. She wants me to go over and see her; and I thought of leaving on Friday——'

'So soon? Leaving your Lilamani, for always?'

Audrey Hammond's arm went round the girl's slender shoulders. 'Do you really mind as much as all that?' she asked.

Tears welled up into the great brown eyes. Caresses from Audrey were rare enough to make both feel a little shy of them; and Lilamani looked down again, choking back her 'foolishness.'

'How could I not mind?' said she. 'It is all through you—this wonderful thing. But it will not be yet! Father said so. And—I was hoping——'

She hesitated; and Audrey caught her breath. 'What were you hoping, child?'

'If only—you could come too, for a little time—and teach me, that I should not feel so strange for that lonely fashion—of English marriage. Oh, are you angry? I didn't mean . . .'

For Audrey had looked up sharply, white to the lips.

'Lilamani, that's impossible. You don't understand.' Then seeing a quiver of pain on the sensitive face, she added more quietly, 'Is it only that you are afraid of the strangeness, or—that you want me a little too?'

'It is half—I am afraid; and half, I am greedy, wanting you too. But if that is wrong, then I must not make storms in the tea-cup, like you say. Only when I am trying to think it all, my mind comes quite in a fog. No mother-in-law to teach new-made wife. No brothers and sisters—of him. No women—peoples for companion or for home duties——' She smiled a little wistfully, shaking her head.

Even here in the hotel, with studies for home-duties and one 'woman-person' to replace the small colony of relations—by blood and marriage—she had missed, at times, the cloistered seclusion and intricate etiquette and deference to the claims of others that are the key-notes of Hindu home-life; and Audrey, recognizing this, felt the more anxious as to the outcome of Nevil's daring leap in the dark. But for Lilamani's sake at least she would do her best to make the crooked straight and the rough places plain.

'You will have women-peoples in time, dear,' said she. 'If you manage to make friends. But, though the Englishman denounces purdah, he has his own variation of it. If an Indian wife may not go abroad, your joint-family system gives you a little world of life under your own roof. The English wife has her world of people outside; but in the home her husband, if he loves her, wants her for himself, especially in the first few years. You see, with us marriage is a much personal affair. An English husband wants more than a mother for his sons. He wants a woman companion, specially devoted to him.'

Lilamani nodded pensively, though still with puzzled brows.

'Yes. That I have come to know a little, from your novel stories. It is beautiful; and—I must learn. But sometimes, I am thinking—with us it is even more beautiful; to become, by sacredness of bond, even from childhood, so truthfully one that both are almost seeming to forget each other, in welfare of family. Only in their secret hearts they carry the light.'

Moved beyond her wont, Audrey Hammond drew the girl closer and kissed her forehead.

'Well, child, whatever happens, I believe you will always carry your light,' said she; and Lilamani, shyly, in the midst of her blushes:

'Perhaps one day—you also——'

'No, no. I'm not the type.'

A hint of bitterness in her tone saddened the girl, who was herself so essentially 'the type,' primal yet eternal, that inspires, through the ages, the worshipful love of men.

'Is it that you really like better the way of the brain?' she hazarded gently, surprised and pleased at such intimate talk with Audrey, the inaccessible. 'Or—have you no father to make arrangement—to give dowry?'

A smile, half-amused, half-wistful lightened Audrey's gravity. 'No, I have no father. And if I had, he would not "make arrangement"! We English think we believe in marriage. But we believe still more in personal freedom; and our women are left to shift for themselves. As for the compulsory dowry—in that matter we might very well take a lesson from India. If English fathers were bound to provide for their daughters, the Woman Question might be less acute than it is.'

'Woman Question? What is that?'

'Happy little ignoramus! It's a disease of modern civilization. A riddle without an answer; and I'm a part of it. But don't trouble your pretty head about me, dear. After all, the life I've chosen gives me a kind of satisfaction it could never give you. When my leave is up, I shall go back to Hyderabad; and perhaps find another brave girl among your women-folk to help me with my work.'

'Yes, yes—there are so many in these nowadays, eager for way of the brain. You will surely find a much more commonsense Lilamani, not so troubled by ugly words.'

'But, never, I think, one with such a talent for creeping into other people's hearts!' Audrey answered with so rare a tenderness that—for the first time, in months of close intercourse—the girl's arms went round her in a young spontaneous caress.

'Please not quite leave me,' she whispered. 'Since I was coming from India, you have been for me like—like Mataji; and I can't forget you ever.'

That was Audrey Hammond's good minute; though Lilamani guessed it not; a reward quite other than she looked for, as is the way, of rewards; the gain through loss, in which it is so difficult to believe till the heart responds to its touch. Persistence along the stormy paths of study would have ended in alienation; but one touch of nature, shared unconsciously, though decreeing separation, drew them closer than either could have believed three weeks ago.

Thus, illumined by the white joy of a closer understanding, the days slipped peacefully by. Audrey made no further protest; though her medical conscience pricked her at sight of paling cheeks and darkly-shadowed eyes. But when Friday brought the parting, she pleaded once more for normal meals, these last two days, if only on account of someone, never directly named between them: and Lilamani, feeling not a little unstrung by recent austerities, could not say her nay. Mrs. Despard had gladly undertaken to 'mother' her during Audrey's absence; but so soon as dates were fixed she would write, and Audrey must come back. Audrey would. She promised. And so an end.

Lilamani had meant to sleep that night, having given her word. But habit prevailed; and she lay, acutely awake, with sealed lids, counting the hours, that seemed to elongate, like stretched elastic, as they neared the dawn. Then she slept heavily; and Sir Lakshman, who guessed at the week's programme, allowed her to sleep till noon.

It was tea-time—thronged tables under the white, wide awning proclaimed the fact—when a much-travelled motor drew up at the foot of the hotel steps. Broome grasped the wheel—having refused to trust the life of an invaluable parent to the hands of an accepted lover; and Sir Lakshman met them in the deserted hall.

'I may go up and claim her?' Sinclair demanded eagerly, when Broome had passed on.

'You may. That is her wish.'

'And yours, I hope?'

'Yes—mine also. Since she is trusting you from her heart, I am agreeing to trust you also, with biggest proof father can give.'

'Thank God you see it that way, sir——' They were nearing the lift now. 'My thanks to you I can only prove—through her.'

'That is how I look for you to prove them,' the other answered almost sternly, his hand upon the doors.

'I'll do my utmost. On my honour, I will. And—I may see her alone? It's our way, you know.'

'Yes. But it is her wish that first there should be some small formality of giving. With us betrothal is not mere personal promise; but religious ceremony. It is, in fact, true marriage, sanctifying union—if consummated or no—through all lives to come. This it will mean for her. Therefore she is wishing that first I make my gift, joining your hands, in our own fashion; then, conforming to your custom, I leave her with you.'

On that understanding they went up together, and along the passage to the corner room; Sir Lakshman ahead, Nevil following, his thumb and finger at the waistcoat pocket where two rings were nestling—merely to assure himself they were there.

Then the door opened and he had the desire of his eyes. . . .

Alone upon the hearthrug she stood, her drooping head turned from the door, *sari* drawn forward, as of old, half hiding her face, restless fingers shifting her bangles up and down the bare slenderness of her arms. There were more bangles than usual—in honour of his coming; delicate trifles of jade and glass and gold. Above the soft silk under-robe of palest green, shot through with golden light, was wound and draped a *sari*, quite new to Nevil, of true deep indigo, like the night sky, gold-bordered and flecked with golden stars. No shoes upon the small feet, slender and shapely as her hands; silk stockings only, green like her skirt, and anklets of gold; the first he had seen. For she had learnt the unfitness of wearing them over English shoes.

Very still she stood, and from the whole of her, from curved instep to veiled head, emanated the peculiarly Eastern mingling of demure aloofness with a delicately direct appeal to the senses and the heart.

Possibly some instinct had impelled her, before it was too late, to bid him remember the gulf between; and he, who had drawn so close to her in spirit, since that day of mutual revealing, was arrested by a sudden sense of strangeness, of the veil down-dropt between them, as at first.

All the week long he had been picturing over and over this moment of vision: the first glance, the first words, the first rapture of reunion: nor was he analytical enough to realize how the very intensity of anticipation robs reality of its due. For the space of a heart-beat or two, he saw this marriage as through the eyes of Jane: and for that space—he was afraid.

Then—hearing them enter—she turned with an audible catch in her breath, and fear fled, stricken and shamefaced, once for all.

Framed in the dusk of the *sari* her beauty shone out with a moon-like pallor that intensified the red of her lips, as the faint shadows, left by sleepless nights, intensified the deeps of her eyes, when they flashed a smile at him for greeting. Four rows of pearls made a gleaming collar round her throat; and beneath it on a fine chain one great diamond shone out, five-pointed, like a star. Clearly she no more dreamed of speaking at such a moment than an English bride would dream of bidding her groom good morning at the altar rails. If her wedding must perforce be an affair of registration, she could, and did, impart to this simple ceremony of giving her own deep sense of the moment's sanctity; while Nevil Sinclair, touched to the heart, was thankful to defer speech till he could have her to himself.

And now her head was bowed again; for Sir Lakshman had taken her hand, joining it with her lover's, and enclosing them in both his own.

'Nevil Sinclair,' he said with simple dignity, looking the Englishman in the eyes, 'I, Lakshman Singh, give you this most priceless daughter of mine, confiding that you will cherish and protect her through your whole life; and in fervent belief that she will fulfil to you all duties of wifehood with loyal and loving heart. Give both hands, Lilamani, in token that nothing is kept back.'

Both hands she gave him, and Sinclair, bereft of words, could only press them to his lips; while Sir Lakshman, conferring a mute benediction on his daughter's head, went quietly out, leaving them alone.

For a space they stood so, in a throbbing silence, that enfolded them like a spell of enchantment, difficult to break. Then very softly, Sinclair spoke her name.

'Lilamani.'

For answer came her passionate murmur: 'Live for ever, my Lord and my King.'

The sheer unexpectedness of it unloosed his tongue.

'Beloved! You shame me to earth!' he cried in genuine distress. '*I'm* no fit subject for a woman's worship. Yours less than any.'

Smiling, though without looking up, she shook her small wise head.

'That is no matter at all. In my country—husband of every true woman is even as her God.'

'It's not so in mine, by any means,' he answered drawing her close, yet restraining himself because of the delicate tremor that ran through her.

'No? How pity! The woman is losing so much——' the right to serve and worship and the glory of it, that was her Eastern view. 'But with me you will permit——? You could not prevent——!'

'I'm afraid I wouldn't, if I could,' he said with sudden fervour. Then, taking out the ring, that had delayed his coming a full hour, he slipped it gently on to her marriage finger. 'That is my form of betrothal, Lilamani. The ring of promise.'

It was a heart-shaped aquamarine, limpid as a drop of sea-water, set in brilliants: and at sight of it she caught her breath.

'Oh, but how kind! How beautiful beyond telling! Like Mrs. Despard's pendant that I must be looking at—always.'

'You shall have one—soon,' he told her, exulting in his power to please her every way. 'But now'—she was drawn closer still—'I want something in return for my ring of promise. Something you would not give me under the arch. I've been wanting and waiting for it a whole week. Tell me I may have it now—Jewel of Delight!'

She told him. And he, taking her veiled head between his hands, set the seal of their compact first upon her down-dropped lids, and last upon her lips, claiming to the full their shy, soft passion of surrender. Then, with a low, broken sound, she withdrew them and fell sobbing on his breast.

Lightly lifting her in his arms, as if in fear that she might break on too strong pressure, he carried her to a low chair that looked upon her balcony, and away, over tree-tops to the sea. There he set her down, kneeling beside her, and whispering persuasively at her ear: 'My Bride of the Rain—is it only a sun shower? Or is she broken-hearted at having promised herself to a barbarous English husband?'

'Yes—oh yes—she is too much broken-hearted!'—laughter gleamed suddenly through her tears—'and also—too much foolish. A little, how Audrey calls "run down," by not sleeping a great deal, these few nights——'

'Thinking of me?'

'Yes,' she answered, with truth; then veiling her eyes: 'And . . . how to make myself good wife in such unknown fashion, hard to understand——'

'Not so very hard. Trust me to make it easy for you, darling, once you give me the right. When is that to be, Lilamani—when? I've an ideal home all ready for you.'

'A home?'

'Yes, true. That good chap Broome has offered me his châlet on Lake Como for the summer. A little lone place, under a great rock, close to the water's edge, opposite Cadenabbia, in Italy, where Martino lives. Think of that: a real home, waiting for the bride. When will she come? Next week?'

'Oh no—no! How you are impatient!' She put forth a shy hand and caressed the dull gold of his hair. 'Have you not spoken with father?'

'Only a word or two. I came back to claim his child. What's the delay? What must we wait for now?'

'Oh, so much; and you must please not make trouble for that. Father wishes that first I should get stronger; and I wish, from home, our Indian wedding-ring: bangle of iron, covered in gold; also—other things for this kind of other life so different to my expecting. That must mean five weeks, or six.'

'A lifetime! But at least I shall be here. I shall see you.'

'For two weeks—yes. After that he is thinking better for both if you go to Paris for studying, and put this troublesome Lilamani a little from your head——.'

Sinclair sighed, 'He's a horribly wise man, that father of yours. And does this troublesome Lilamani honestly wish to be put out of my head, even for a little?'

'No. Not for one smallest minute,' she murmured, and was caught close again for reward. And again her exquisite fragility held his ardour in restraint. So yielding, so unsubstantial a creature was she, in her soft natural draperies, that it was as if he enfolded some fragrant ethereal essence of the eternal feminine rather than a woman of flesh and blood.

This he told her, in lover's language, his lips at her ear: and she—drawing herself away from him with pretty dignity: 'At the same time it is truthfully a woman; and inside it . . . there is fire . . . of so great love that not all the waters from my beautiful sea could put out ever—ever——. That is what my *sari* has been telling you, without speech, all this while. But your eyes are still too deaf for language of colour——'

'They're not blind anyway! They saw, and admired. What is it telling me, Lilamani, this beautiful new dress? I want to know.'

'Listen then—lord of my life,' she answered very softly. 'With us, indigo is for constancy of love, because it is dye that nothing will remove. This green of my skirt, like young leaves, is for hope—for new life. Gold and pearls are for purity: and this'—touching the star that flashed like a prisoned sunbeam—'gift of my father, is for happiness with . . . with . . . '

Shyness overwhelmed her.

'Nevil?' he prompted tenderly.

'Yes.'

'Well then, let me hear you say it. I've been waiting all this time.'

'With us, it is not custom even when married to take the name of—beloved,' she told him with averted eyes; and stooping he kissed her with sudden passion.

'Beloved's good enough for me. But still . . . as the promised wife of an Englishman, it's only fair—isn't it?—that you should study our customs a little, too?'

'Yes—yes. With all my heart I am wishing it—Nevil.' And at that, he kissed her again.

BOOK TWO

The Blossoming

ONE

'And now my cheek is warm against thy cheek;
Yet, is Love satisfied? Nay,—evermore
Thy hands are full of promise; . . .
Joy hath joy in store
And heaven another heaven within its skies.'

Every detail in the little room—save the well-grate with its plain oak mantel—breathed of India, even to the warmth and fragrance of an atmosphere charged with spices, sandalwood and attar of rose.

Over one door a Punjab *phulkari* made a blaze of gold. Over another hung a priceless embroidered panel—green and purple cunningly inwrought. On the walls, two pictures only; one of Sir Lakshman Singh, in State dress, and an old Indian painting of the sacred three—Rama, Sita, and the devoted Lakshman—setting out, in 'coats of bark,' for their fourteen years of banishment. Over the mantelpiece, with its gleaming rows of *lotahs*, a square of vellum, gold bordered and lettered in gold, 'There is no likeness of Him whose name is great glory. Deathless they become who, in heart and mind, know him as heart-dwelling.'

For the rest, an octagonal table, bearing a sandalwood casket and the Bhagavad Gita; velvet-soft prayer-rugs on the matted floor; a native bedstead of red lacquer, and a low square stool of the same, whereon sat the guardian of the place, in pearl-white robe, and *sari* golden-edged: Lilamani Sinclair, bride of six weeks' standing. The magic circlet of gold gleamed beneath the drop of sea-water shaped like her heart; and upon her slender wrist, the wedding-bracelet of her own land. At her throat hung the promised pendant, shimmering drops of water and light; and her father's star of happiness transformed into a brooch fastened the drapery on her left shoulder; a modern innovation, worn for the first time.

Little of the West about this girl-bride beyond her ring and her English name. But even had she chosen to exchange her *sari* for a Paris 'coiffure,' and her simple robe for a Paquin 'creation,' her doings would have bewrayed her. Crouched upon the stool before a primitive brick oven, set up under her own supervision, she was absorbed in cooking her lord's dinner; a service so sacred to the Hindu wife that a special garment of silk fibre is reserved for that function and for prayer.

Europe nominally endorses the Divine command: 'He that is greatest among you let him be your servant.' Asia acts upon it. In a Hindu household domestic service—as the West understands it—is not. All home duties, save the most menial, are carried out by sisters, daughters, daughters-in-law, under supervision of their ruler-in-chief—the mother; though here, as elsewhere, change is creeping in. Drudgery? She of Asia would resent the implication. Her law of life rests upon one basic principle: The highest may serve the lowest, but may accept service only from the highest.

And woman stands, spiritually, higher than man, because 'she alone is capable of conquest—for others.' Logically, then—and Asia is nothing if not logical—'to accept service and devotion of any is the highest honour you can pay her.' That is the core of the Indian woman's *credo*; the lamp hidden in her heart; and by the light of it many perplexities are made plain.

But when a woman, for whom service and worship are birthright and crown of glory, mates with a man in whom the Western idea of chivalry has not been quite crushed out by the haste and pressure of an unchivalrous age, complications are born.

That the wife of Nevil Sinclair of Bramleigh Beeches should cook her husband's dinner—only his dinner, she urged, deeming the request a modest one—did not square with his British sense of fitness, Bohemian though he was. What is more, he distrusted amateur cookery; little dreaming of the talent he bade her hide under a bushel; and of which she had been too shy to speak. 'What would his valet think?' he had asked, 'and Broome's Italian chef and the little waiting-maid?' Dread questions, for which she could find no answer. Only, beneath her wifely submission, had dwelt a faint hope that possibly when he should see the contents of those boxes from India——!

Two weeks after their first shy home-coming these had arrived; and from out of them had come the store of simple home belongings, that had brought a sense of familiar sweetness into her new nest. Then had she laid before him the shining row of brass plates and *lotahs*, the boxes of spices, of shredded coconut and herbs.

'All the way from India they came for you. Must they not be used ever? Even if only sometimes for game of play?' Then, with a captivating honesty and confusion of face, she denied that last. 'No, for me it is not play. With us, I have told you, worship of husband is worship of Life-force. And if food is fuel for keeping that flame alight, shall it not be sacred duty and privilege for wife to prepare it?'

And he, without waste of words, had set the seal of permission upon her lips.

'Not every day,' had been his sole stipulation; 'once or twice a week; or on great occasions'; thus instinctively annulling domestic comment. Intermittent ebullitions of cookery might be accepted as an Indian lady's whim.

And Lilamani, lifted far beyond thought of comment, had enjoyed her small triumph to the full. Her first curry and *pillau*, her irresistible sweets and lightly-tossed *chupattis* had been a revelation to Nevil, shaming his distrust; and upon the third great occasion, when she had won leave to cook all three courses of their simple meal, he had laughingly warned her that it might end in his refusing to eat a dinner prepared by any hands but her own.

'That is how it should be for true honour of the house,' she had answered, smiling, demurely.

And this golden 14th of June, that completed her eighteenth year and her sixth week of marriage, was a day of privilege, past question.

Six beatific weeks, sun-filled and love-enchanted, they had spent in Broome's châlet, set in a shelving cove, under the lee of a rugged hill, its balconies and verandah overlooking Como's blue stillness, now blurred with pearl-white films, now pierced by a million quivering points of light. Too still almost, it seemed to Lilamani, after the changeful majesty of her sea. Yet that very stillness, as of some harmonized Yogi purged from passion, spoke to her heart of the palm-girt lakes in her own Hyderabad; and through them, of dear, far and familiar things never again to be seen, or heard, or felt while breath remained in her body. What this completeness of severance meant to her she dared not admit even in her most secret thoughts. There were inevitable moments when the prick of remembrance intruded upon her joy. Yet each day that passed deepened her conviction that she had chosen aright; and this 'lonely fashion of English marriage' proved itself not so hard to understand, after all.

But even the devotion of a new-made husband had not availed to soften the wrench of parting from that father, who had been parent, comrade and spiritual guide in one. Each smallest happening of that last unwedded week was graven upon the tablets of her heart: a week of tangled emotions, overlaid with a smiling stillness that had almost deceived Sir Lakshman himself. Once only had her self-control gone to pieces. The mail that brought her wedding-bangle and other necessaries, had brought no word to her from Mataji. How should it? Yet, with the divine inconsistency of human nature, she had hoped against hope. She could not know that all Mataji's bitterness had been vented in a vehement, incoherent letter to Sir Lakshman that had cut her husband to the heart, while it revivified all the devils of misgiving he had trampled under foot in the days following upon Nevil's declaration. Not for a kingdom would he have spoken of it to his child, who was sufficiently upset by her sole word of greeting from home.

Even Ram Singh, favourite elder brother and playmate, could not write otherwise than in sorrow of an event that, at one stroke, cut every thread binding his sister to home and country. Some day, perhaps, Destiny would bring him to England. There they might meet, if her English husband would permit. Till then he would write without fail: and, in a tear-blotted postscript, Vimala—blowing her a kiss across the 'black water'—promised to write also, though pens were not her favourite toys, and it was not letters she wanted, but her 'dear own Lilamani' who would never come home again.

Impossible to hide from Sir Lakshman the turmoil wrought by such letters and by Mataji's tacit repudiation of her child. But at least he should not see her tears. It was on Audrey's shoulder that she had cried till the black demons of fear and disloyalty had been washed clean out of her anguished heart.

For Audrey, true to her word, had come back just before Nevil started for Paris, and had left again—upon a flawless pretext—on the eve of his return. Her going broke yet another link with India, and the pain of it was acute. But with the coming of Nevil, love's warmth and light had enveloped the girl, till the day of days, arising out the East, called on her to quit her dream Paradise and grasp the shining, implacable facts of life; to make good her irrevocable gift, and break the last link, the last link——

Something of this final pang Sir Lakshman had foreseen, and his had been the happy idea of shipping home the modest contents of her room in India, supplemented by rugs and embroideries of his own bestowing.

On that day of days Mrs. Despard had been all a mother to the tremulous girl-bride, deprived alike of mother's blessing and bridal rights. Together they had hidden away all trace of what Lilamani called her 'Hindu-ness' under the hood and long cloak devised by Audrey for her first flight. A fine lace veil tied beneath her hood shielded the girl from curious eyes; and in the after-hours she had blessed that kindly veil from her heart.

Vividly it all came back to her, while she sat alone, in her shrine: the early start; the motor-drive to Nice; the brief, unromantic formalities, of that had joined them irrevocably as any immemorial rites, or sevenfold circling of the sacred fire; and afterwards, the lifting of her veil, while he—her husband—set the ring upon her finger, the bracelet on her wrist, the sacramental kiss upon her lips. Then—the wrench of parting from Mrs. Despard, who must return to Antibes, while they three fared on to Milan in luxurious privacy; the two men, tenderly considerate, leaving her to absorb, as in a dream, the colourful beauties of Italy's coast-line, till a sudden, overpowering weariness blotted out all things; and she knew no more.

Not until the following morning had she awakened fully from that blessed spell of stupor—Nature's reaction from another week of secret austerities. Dimly she had been aware of the journey's ending, of noise and flashing lights; of a glass held to her lips; then the vague thrill of her husband's arms, the cool softness of the bed that received her; the touch of hands that freed her deftly from cloak and hood, unwound her *sari* and covered her with a quilt. By that time she was too far gone again in sleep to feel his kiss on her eyelids and on the dear, unveiled head, seen so for the first time.

Next morning she awoke in full sunlight to find herself alone on the great white bed. And while she lay wondering mistily over it all, he— Nevil—had come to her from an adjoining room; an unknown Nevil, wearing a long *choga*; his hair, damp from bathing, crisped into fugitive curls, and in his eyes a gladness beyond speech. Then only had there flashed upon her the full significance of yesterday's doings, that had stripped her of all things familiar and set her alone in an untried world with this deeply adored stranger, lord of her life in very deed.

Sir Lakshman had seen them into the train for Como, promising on his return from London to be their first visitor. But while he spoke, the inexorable engine drowned his voice; her desperate clutch upon his hand relaxed, some chord within her seemed to snap, and she lay back dazed, tearless; the rattle and clank of machinery seeming to beat upon her bared nerves.

Six weeks she had lived without him; six weeks of happiness unspeakable. Yet in one secret corner, the ache remained. Even in memory she drew a veil over that moment's anguish, softened though it was by the peculiar tenderness that Nevil Sinclair had gotten from his mother. She preferred to dwell on the journey up the Lake in the pellucid end of a May evening that conjured the grey-green water into gold. And oh! before starting—the sight and smell of the white bullocks, in Como town! Dignity and reserve alone had withheld her from open worship—there, on the cobblestone of Italy, that knew nothing of Shiva or his sacred bull.

In early spring the winding reaches of Lake Como have the grey-green tone of Italy—of olive and rock, stone cottage and pebbled paths. Here, white incidents of hotels or villas, there, black incidents of cypress, flashed like exclamation marks on some jutting headland, or grouped like sentinels about a shrine. But by now the grey was jewelled everywhere with green, enamelled brightly and delicately with every tint of every flower that blows. Only the Northward view showed a gleam of the high Alps; gods of the upper heaven untroubled by the season's ebb and flow.

At last, slipping round a fir-capped island, they had sighted their villa set upon the water's edge like a brooding bird. And lo, at Tremezzo landing-stage, a slim white boat awaiting them, its gay little flag aflutter at the stern. In the deepening stillness, they had been rowed across to their own private oasis, where nightingales were already at evensong among the bushes, and fire-flies dipped and darted in irregular flashes like stars gone mad. Without spoken word Nevil had slipped a hand through his bride's arm, leading her in and up to

the room that would be his studio. He had shut the door behind them.
And they were alone.

Then, as he turned, with that in his eyes that made her heart stand
still, it had come upon her afresh—the fear and the ecstasy. In one
appealing look she had besought him to understand. And he had
understood: most tenderly and amazingly he had understood. For in
the best men, and in all true artists, there lurks some hidden touch of
the woman, some impress of the mother that bore them; and it had
needed just this touch in Lilamani's husband to ensure that the ecstasy
should outweigh the fear; nay, drive it out for good.

He had succeeded; and that so completely as to leave her wondering, now, if she really had been afraid—ever. As for the ecstasy, it stood
revealed in her eyes as she paused in the deft scraping of a carrot, arrested by the low, clear whistling that came from behind the *phulkari*
hanging over his studio door.

The key was turned in the lock—on her side; a daring act of coer-
cion achieved, with delicious tremors, after his fourth incursion, just
to see how things were going. It was the only way to ensure his getting
any dinner at all, she had explained sweetly—from the other side. For
the *chef* had been given a holiday, leaving her, Lilamani, mistress of
the situation. It had been her chosen birthday treat; and the simplicity
of it smote her husband's heart.

For two hours he had worked contentedly, on his side of the barrier,
at the new picture—'Dreaming': a bevy of Eastern girls asleep, suggested by a descriptive passage in the 'Light of Asia.' His month in
Paris had justified to the full Sir Lakshman's decree. Immersed in his
natural element, his talent had blossomed and expanded with a readiness that surprised none more than himself, and delighted none more
than his girl-bride, self-dedicated high-priestess of the sacred flame.

In those first days of divine idleness, when they had lived mainly
in the little white boat, it had been decided that he should make his
name as a painter of Eastern subjects, having become enamoured of
half a hemisphere in the person of one small woman. It was then that
she had reillumined for him the familiar 'Light of Asia,' and pleaded
for a painting of the great Prince's 'pleasure-home,' with its walls of
pearl-shell and lace-worked stone, through which moonbeams fil-
tered, making tender light and shade upon a group of sleeping dancers, fairest and most favoured *houris* of the royal household.

She herself, in her loveliest *saris* would be model for all, if he could change the faces a little 'from his own imagining': and for him remained the joy of painting six sleeping Lilamanis, each in some new pose of girlish grace and beauty. Then, as the work progressed, she had written to Sir Lakshman for a full and an abridged translation of the Ramayana—Saga of princely heroism and wifely devotion, that lies nearest to India's heart. The full translation, sumptuously bound, had been her birthday gift: and thence they would cull fresh subjects for his brush when he had completed his dream of one fair woman multiplied by six.

It was nearing completion now: and while he worked lovingly at shadows of marble tracery and silver lamps that swung like censers from the dim roof, she, on her side, chopped vegetables, washed rice, and measured out spices with the ardour of a devotee and the absorption of a happy-hearted child at play. But she knew what that whistling meant. He was tired of his 'Dream.' He wanted reality. She wanted it too; yet she made no sign.

Then the tune broke off short, and through the curtain his voice came to her, appealing as a caress.

'Little wife! I'm tired of seeing you asleep. Come out of your shrine.'

'Wait only a small time—impatient one! Or curry will spoil.'

'Hang curry! I want *you*.'

'Then no dinner. Only soup and cream pudding. Think how squash!'

'Cheese and pâté,' said the curtain, clinching the argument in a fashion beneath contempt. 'Come along.'

She smiled enchantingly at the mixture she was tossing in the pan and hurried on with her work.

Silence for half a minute: then the curtain spoke again.

'I say, Lilamani. Giulietta's brought the tea. Your cake, with coffee icing, and a box of fondants from Martino with a thousand compliments. There now!'

Supreme conviction in that last. He could see the delicate disdain upon her face before speech confirmed it.

'You think if I will not come—for you, I come for cakes and fondants?'

But her fingers were unfastening the brooch at her shoulder, and the *sari* sacred to cooking was whisked off with surprising alacrity. For answer he began crooning with guileful intent her favourite song:

> "'My heart, my heart is like a singing-bird,
> Whose nest is in a watered shoot;
> My heart, my heart is like an apple-tree
> Whose boughs are hung with thick-set fruit;
> My heart, my heart is like a rainbow shell
> That paddles on a halcyon sea.
> My heart, my heart is gladder than all these
> Because my Love, my Love has come to me——'"

Ah!—so you *have* come, after all!'

The key had turned softly in the lock, and now she stood before him: a slender, iridescent vision with lids dutifully downcast, awaiting his pleasure.

At the first he had been puzzled, then increasingly charmed, this English husband, by the worshipful aloofness with which the Hindu bride approaches her lord, at least until the crown of motherhood is hers. To the Indian husband this attitude is merely a part of the im-memorial nature of things: but for Nevil Sinclair, used to the casual camaraderie of the West, there were moments when it went to his head. He had to temper elation with the reminder that it was ins-tinctive, impersonal; homage to husband-hood rather than to himself. But, enchanting though it was, he would not always have it so. She must learn his ways also. And she was learning—shyly, proudly; her woman's adaptability quickened by the impulse of love. For a heart-beat or two he watched her where she stood. Then, smiling, he indi-cated the tea-table.

'I angled well! You couldn't resist them—eh?'

'That is as my lord pleases!' she answered demurely, imps of laughter in her eyes; and he held out both hands.

'A shame to insult her on her birthday! Come then—English wife.'

It was their private password; and straightway she obeyed its hidden command; laying light hands upon him and lifting her face for his kiss.

'The necklace of your arms,' he whispered, caressing their silken softness. 'D'you know Martino, said one day, at the Cap, that when the *houri* made this necklace for me I should be faithless to art; and I contradicted him flat. Was I Truth-named, Jewel of Delight?'

She nestled closer.

'Even at the first you were so clever to know your Lilamani. Now he must believe, when he sees, in one little month—how beautiful picture——!'

'To say nothing of the masterpieces we mean to paint from your Ramayana before the summer's out.'

That 'we' sent a shiver of joy through her. It united her, not only with his manhood, but with the art that was his crown of manhood; the art dear to her, as to himself. Had it not brought her this—her crown of womanhood?

'About those other pictures, I have a new thought to tell. It came in my mind—God-bestowed—when making your curry——'

'My curry! You inimitable high-priestess of a brick oven! While you were chopping onions, I suppose?'

'Yes. Just exactly by that time.' She assumed an adorable gravity. 'It is bad to make joke of my sacred service—worthless one! I shall not tell.'

'Oh, but you will.'

His lips brushed hers in a fugitive caress; and the 'God-bestowed' thought found utterance. She had seen, in fancy, a group of pictures, each with Sita for central figure; the whole, when complete, setting forth India's ideal of womanhood in the ascent of that gracious spirit from steep to steep of renunciation, unsullied, unafraid, even until the end.

Lilamani's whole face glowed as she warmed to her subject.

'Sita, when begging of Rama to share banishment,' she went on eagerly. 'Sita, alone in forest hut when That Terrible is approaching in guise of Brahman. Sita out from fire of ordeal, in great God's arms. Think how splendid!'

'Jove, yes—*if* it's possible.' His ardour caught fire from hers. 'Arrogant high-flying, of course. But we'll lay the scheme before Martino to-morrow and see what he thinks. You shall give us an outline idea of the story and the special scenes you want.'

'Yes. Only . . . Sita is like patron saint to me; like a piece of my own heart. And how difficult! When all is so big——'

'Not a bit of it. You'll manage beautifully. Think it all out when you get back to your sacred curry! And you would be my Sita? Is that it?'

'Yes, I would—oh, I would—in all things. If there came a need.' She brooded on the thought with luminous eyes.

'But, Lilamani, suppose I paint you, yourself, how about letting all the world see? Wouldn't you hate that?'

Her scarlet flush gave answer, and she hid her moment; then looking up again, spoke bravely. 'Not—if I shall be Sita. Think how small thing for honour of your name, comparing with ordeal of fire.'

'And you wouldn't stick at that either,' he said, 'if such barbarism still existed.'

'No,' she answered simply. 'I am *Suttee*.'

'Lilamani—what d'you mean?'

'Only—in old days, when *Suttee* was not outside law, girl-brides would fear sometimes were they strong enough, were they worthy? Then they would make test; holding smallest finger in fire till flesh burnt from bone; or stirring with bare hand rice when boiling. And I—I have done—that last; though never I told to anyone—till now.'

'You? My little one!' In a passion of protection he held her close.

'Such a small thing!' she murmured, not ill-pleased at his concern. 'But now—I am glad; and perhaps a little more worthy for being Sita in your so beautiful pictures, that I long to see.'

'*Our* pictures,' he corrected her in a sudden humility. 'It's you that are the true artist, Lilamani—the inspired brain. Without you I should never have painted a thing worth looking at. But with you there's no limit to the insolence of my aspiration—.'

TWO

'My heart in me was held at restless rest,
Presageful of some prize beyond its quest,
Prophetic still with promise, fain to find the best.'

—Swinburne

Martino's approval of the *houri*, and something more, dated from his first sight of Nevil's sketch. Constrained by that something, he had wrought, in the sea-piece that was his wedding-gift, a symbolic portrayal of his own soul, untamed and untameable as the waters that cover the earth. All wind-driven wave and cloud it was; save for one down-sweeping sword of radiance that struck a path of gold through the turmoil: the whole smitten into life by the illusion of light and movement that was fast gaining him recognition as one of the master-painters of his time. This much, at least, of himself should be hers: the quintessence of his nature purged from the dross. For outside his art, and his touch of heroic fortitude, Martino's code of morals did not bear critical inspection.

It was Sinclair's mention of her 'soul-pictures' that had inspired his attempt at symbolical portraiture, in the hope that she might see and understand. She had seen and understood. On the day of its bestowal he had watched discovery creep into her eyes; had heard from her lips the tribute he coveted: 'But, Signor Martino, it is *you*—yourself!'

'For which reason, Signorina—it is yours,' he had answered with his awkward little bow of gallantry. And today, as he sipped his *chocolat* in Broome's familiar study, he felt a thrill of pleasure in seeing 'himself' hung in the right light, at the right angle; the only picture added, by Nevil, to the chosen few that adorned Broome's grey-green walls.

The French windows were flung wide; and the two men sat just within them. Out on the balcony, in full sunshine, gleamed the silver tea-tray, and beside it, on her lacquer stool, sat the *houri*; Signorina no longer, but bride of another; shyly conscious of her new dignity, shyly aloof, for all her flutter of pleasure at sight of one who recalled Antibes.

Lovelier and more desirable than ever she seemed to Martino, in her subdued glow of happiness and health renewed; the olive and rose-madder tints of her skin set off by a *sari*, delicately pink as the lining of a shell; its narrow border of almond-buds, breaking at each corner into a full-blown spray. Whatever pangs of envy may have pricked the man, the artist, at least, could find pure pleasure in watching her, while Sinclair unfolded her God-bestowed conviction that, between them, they could achieve a set of paintings from the great Hindu Epic, choosing scenes that should not involve an overcrowded canvas, or technical knowledge of detail, hard to acquire out of India.

'It's flagrantly ambitious, I admit,' Nevil concluded, lighting a cigarette and holding his vesta to Martino's cigar. 'But Sir Lakshman is a keen student of ancient literature; and—she is astonishingly well up in it all. She tells me he has a remarkable collection of old books, native pictures, and curios; and thinks he would gladly send out for some of them to act as 'stage properties' and give me a better grasp of the subject. What d'you think, Martino *mio*? Is it a credible venture? Or has too much good-fortune turned my head?'

Martino considered the question a moment, his ragged moustache thrust out.

'Difficult to answer,' he said at last. 'It is I who am lost, confounded, by your so rapid advance. Your new picture!—how remarkable! . . . All in one month. After that, it is not for Martino to say possible or impossible. In Paris you shall have worked like anything else than the Sinclair known to me these three years.'

'Jove, I did! But then, I had a very special inducement—waiting for me at Antibes.'

Nevil's eyes dwelt an instant on his wife's half-averted face; and Martino coughed till the tears came.

'That one can understand,' he muttered gruffly. 'But you painted no picture there—was it?'

'No. Only studies and sketches—scores of them. But without Leseppes I'd have been nowhere. He called himself my godfather. Even let his own work slide a bit on my account.'

Martino nodded. 'H'm. That is Leseppes—when the finger touches his heart. Which is not too often, I can tell you, Sinclair. It is—how you call?—feather in your cap. He knew it would be worth. And he knew right. One can trace Jacques Leseppes in that.' He jerked his cigar towards the dreamers. 'But I—Martino—knew it first. That is my *panache*. The surprise to me is how you were content, those many years, to play fool with a gift so precious——'

'My dear fellow, I wasn't content. That was the deuce of it all. Often and often I felt the ache and stirring of a power, that seemed as if it must work itself out—somehow, some day. But in between times conviction went to pieces; and I cursed myself for an imaginative, conceited fool——'

'Surest proof you could *not* be!' Martino broke in with a short laugh.

'Horribly disconcerting all the same. Without proof of unusual talent I could hardly ask my father to spend money on a gift he didn't believe in. So there I was! A failure in my father's eyes. Worse than that in my own. Only when I got into touch with you and your kind, I used to feel like a man who has a treasure locked up in a secret room of which he has lost the key——'

'And, by God, you have got it now, *amico mio!* Not often is it that an artist shall have the unique good fortune to find himself—in his wife.'

He jerked out the last with an effort; and the half-averted face was turned gently away. It was the custom of her new world, this open fashion of speech: but not soon would her sensitiveness become inured to personal allusions impermissible among Hindus of good breeding.

Her husband, keenly alive to the significance of that slight movement, answered, without direct mention of her: 'I'm quite as much confounded as you are, Martino *mio*; and perhaps a little intoxicated with the wine of the gods, or I could hardly take this new notion seriously. But I do. Honestly, I do——'

'*Sapristi!* That picture gives you right. And to take seriously, is to achieve. Will you or . . . the Signora tell me more of this Epic, Saga—what you call it?'

'Yes. I want my wife to give you an outline of the story. Will you—Lilamani?'

She turned, aflush to the temples; her ringed hands moving nervously in her lap.

'If Signor Martino is wishing—I will try. But—it is so great and beautiful; and my telling so clumsy. I am not clever to such things.'

'Your telling's good enough for us. Eh, Martino?' Nevil said, smiling.

The small man nodded vigorously.

'No fear for Martino to be critical, Signora,' he said with unusual gentleness. 'Outside of form and colour there lives no great knowledge in my black bullet head. Tell me, please, this Epic of your country. History, is it? Or legend?'

'Hard to say how much from each,' she answered, clasping her hands to steady herself. 'It is mixture of all things; war and philosophy and family love. But almost for us it is religion. Because Rama, prince and hero, was incarnation of Vishnu, called Preserver, second great god of Hindu Trinity; and this poem tells of his many adventures in ancient forest of Dandak. There he was living fourteen years in banishment, because of long-ago promise made by that old king, his father, to second queen, who was favourite, and was wishing to see her own son in Rama's place.

'Then, because royal word cannot be broken, Rama must fulfil that promise; even if father, mother, and all the peoples break their hearts for losing such a Prince. In rough guise of pilgrim he chose to go; leaving all possessions, even Sita, beautiful and beloved wife. She must stay safely with his mother because forest life was too much rough and dangerous for high-bred woman. But now there came difficulty——'

Lilamani paused and drew in a low soft breath. The sacredness of Sita, of all communion between wife and husband, made the telling of so impassioned a love-story more difficult than she had foreseen. Nevil, divining her thought, frowned imperatively at Martino, checking comment on his lips.

And she, leaning forward, chin cradled in one hand, found courage to speak on; her eyes intent upon a fairy fleet of clouds, her voice hushed to a musical monotone, as if thinking aloud.

'Sita, dutiful beyond all women, refused in this one matter to obey her lord, caring nothing for danger or rough life if only she may behold his face. Rama, too much anxious, would not hear such thing. Only at last, by saying she will take poison, even fainting with grief, she won consent. Lakshman, own brother to Rama, said he will go also; and they three, in coats of bark, went forth to their strange adventures. There might come one picture. Another might come, months after, when Sita was sitting alone in forest hut, built by Lakshman, while

Rama has gone in search of wonderful deer, seen by her, and greatly wished. But this deer was only form taken by a Wicked One to draw Rama far from his beloved. Because of his strength, no evil giants of that wood were able to conquer him; and they were desiring vengeance, because he spurned offered love of hideous giantess, sister of Ravan, that ogre-king of Ceylon. By his devising was such cruel trick played on Rama, all-conquering one; only to be caught by deceit because his spirit was too clear for such muddy thoughts.

'So he was leaving his Queen in care of Lakshman, and following that deer. But at first prick of arrow, the Wicked One cried out, in voice of Rama: "Ah Sita, ah Lakshmana —help! help!" This they heard with fearful hearts; and Sita was insisting that Lakshman shall leave charge of her and follow that call. But even for her command, he would not disobey Rama and desert his Queen; till Sita became angry, saying she must believe he wishes that brother's death, so he may marry with herself. Heartbroken from such suspicion, Lakshman must go.

'Then while Sita was sitting alone, beautiful as full moon, in robes of amber silk, with lotus-wreath upon her hair, came That Terrible, stealthily up from river, in guise of Brahman. First he was begging food, as holy man, that none may refuse. Then, throwing off disguise, he was speaking shameful things to that most loyal wife. In scornful anger she spurned him, as her lord had spurned his sister. More than this, weak woman could not do. So That Terrible—catching her by waist and by hair—carried her off in his flying car, over tree-tops to Lanka, now called Ceylon. Only one great vulture, friend to Rama, saw them go and made battle with Ravan. But no use. He fell, with many wounds and arrows, killed almost to death——'

Another pause. Half-unconsciously Lilamani was identifying Sita with herself, Rama with her lord; and now it was as if the actual sword of division pierced her heart.

'See a fresh picture—sorrowful beyond telling,' she murmured, the thrill of oncoming tragedy in her voice. 'Sita, broken of heart and hope—true wife still, pure as snow newly fallen—grieving alone in that garden of Ravan, where all was beautiful, except only the she-fiends—with head of wild beast and bodies of women—who must guard her and torment her with insult and cruelty; because not all flatterings or gifts or threatenings could make her disloyal by even look or word. Only one thing kept That Terrible from taking her in his palace by force. He feared she was daughter of high gods who would punish him for such sacrilege. Therefore he tried every way for winning her consent. But no use. So he grew angry, and gave her in charge of she-fiends that she might not escape.

'But on this day, unknown to her, there sat one among the branches with message from her lord: Hanuman, general of the monkey-peoples, by which is meant wild forest tribes. Lightly leaping down, he knelt before that sorrowful lady, telling her how one great prince Rama had been searching many months all over South India for stolen wife dearly-loved; how he, general of monkey-peoples, had leapt across the sea to make search in country of Ravan. Hearing of beautiful prisoner in Asoka garden, he came, by his littleness and cunning, through the treetops to see. And now, if she is that lost Queen, he is begging token for her husband that she is still alive and true wife. Then he will bring great army and win her back. By this news, joy came once more to Sita's heart; and most precious jewel, gift of her father, she sent for greeting and proof of faithful love.

'Then, through many months the story is filled with noise of battle and chariot-wheels, and death and victory. No pictures here. Till, at last, came day of meeting between Sita and her lord. By his orders she was carried in litter to greet him on field of victory. And he, not approaching, called her to come forth, with face uncovered, before those many folk. From this so strange command she had fear of trouble; yet, shrinking greatly, she came forth. With eyes veiled, though face must be seen, she went proudly to her lord; heart and thought unstained as when her father made the gift.

'Then fell that unspeakable thing. There, in cruel speech, that all his army shall hear, he told her not for great love had he fought and conquered, but only to avenge insult and theft. There, before all, he named her faithless wife, Queen of Ravan, that could never any more be Queen for him. Oh, cruel! *Too cruel*——!'

Lilamani's voice vibrated with pain and scorn. The hand that lay on her lap clenched itself in passionate protest. Martino, pictures, Nevil himself forgotten, she was seeing all, hearing all; translated in spirit back to the morning of the world.

'Surely Rama, true husband, must be lost in Rama, proud Prince, to speak so. And Sita was answering, in such noble meekness, that he may doubt others, if he will; but not that truth which all her life has shown. "Why," she was asking, "had he not sent such word through Hanuman, that she might die and be spared from deepest insult and shame?" Then she was pleading remembrance for early days of happiness and love: "O King, is all forgotten—all?"

'From Rama no word; and she, peerless one, turned to Lakshman, begging him, in broken voice, make ready funeral pyre. For loving woman, hurt beyond healing, what else was left?

'So there, before all, it was made ready, none daring to disobey: and Sita, not shrinking now, drew near those leaping flames, praying with uplifted hands to the God within.

> "Universal witness, Fire,
> Protect my body on the pyre
> As Raghu's son has lightly laid
> This charge on Sita—hear, and aid!"'

'When those cruel flames closed upon her loveliness, most piercing cry went up from all; and tears came in Rama's eyes. Then down from heaven came the great Gods, in cars golden like sunbeams, revealing to Rama he is no mortal man—but Vishnu himself in human shape; reproaching him for such treatment of his Queen, like man of common clay.

'But see—see! Those flames are rolling backward, and out of their burning heart came the Lord of Fire himself, carrying that stainless one, no fire could harm. Fresh, like she came from the litter; not one flower of wreath scorched nor hair of eyelash singed, that Universal Witness gave her again to her lord of life. Then Rama was proclaiming, before those many peoples, that never had he been doubting her word and her love; only for princely honour there was need that searching fire shall give proof to all. Now he will cleave to her as hero cleaves to glory; and never leave her again. Oh, if he kept that word . . . if he kept it——!'

The low cry ended in a broken sound; and Lilamani sat motionless, her face hidden.

Martino glanced at Sinclair. His cigarette had gone out. He leaned back in his chair lost to everything but this fresh revealing of his girl-wife; and the Italian, more poignantly moved by her distress than by Sita's sufferings, leaned impulsively towards her.

'It was not kept? That demi-god, was he so despicable? Tell me, Signora—is that the end?'

Nevil frowned sharply. Lilamani started and looked up. Tears hung on her lashes.

'That is the ending—for my pictures,' she said quietly. 'True ending of story also, in my belief. But in such faraway times, who can tell? Long after death of that great poet was added *Uttra Kanda*, after-part, telling of triumphal return to their own kingdom, where they two lived in happiness, too perfect, one year only. Then came to Rama's ears that people were murmuring doubts of his Queen in spite of all. Not one doubt had Rama. But for honour of his kinghood, he was believing Sita must go. So he sent her, even before birth of his child, to that far hermitage; and she, in great grief of her heart, said only: "Husband is God of the wife; what seems right to him she must do even at cost of life."

'So for twenty long years she was living, without anger or complaint, in that hermitage of early days; till twin sons of Rama had become men. Then they, without knowing, went to sing glorious deeds of their father at his Court. There came recognition: and Rama was crying out that he will bear separation no longer; that Sita must come back to grant forgiveness, and once more reign as his Queen.

'She came; proud, but sad from too much pain and waiting. There, before chiefs and kings and all subjects, she stood in crimson robe, still beautiful as dawn. But—oh terrible!—even while Rama was greeting her, came the people's murmur: "Let her be tried by fire." Even for such a great heart that was too much. Like one pierced with a sword, she covered her face, crying in broken voice: "If unstained in thought and action—Mother Earth, receive thy child!"

'Then that great Earth-Mother, quick to answer, cleft the ground and came up, there, at her daughter's feet. Beautiful beyond telling her throne: wide her arms of welcome. Vain, all vain, outcry of Rama and his people. The earth was closing on mother and child. She is gone that stainless one——!'

With a shuddering sob Lilamani sprang to her feet, flung both arms heavenward in a gesture half triumph, half despair: then, stabbed awake by sudden acute self-consciousness, turned and fled.

In the silence she left behind her, the hush of sun-sinking seemed still to palpitate with ghosts of dead emotions interwoven with live ones. The breathing of both men sounded curiously distinct. Nevil lit a fresh cigarette, mechanically, as if his mind were elsewhere. Martino sat gazing at the empty chair; then, with awkward haste, brushed a hand across his eyes.

It was Nevil who stepped first out of the cloud.

'Well, Martino—it's a big thing, isn't it? What do you think?'

Martino grunted. Then he coughed.

'My friend, at this moment, I think not at all. But this I know. Through her clearness of vision you shall paint those pictures in such a fashion that they shall make your name. I, Martino, have said. Let your strong imagining take colour from her. She is like flame to your mind—to your life. No?'

'She is.'

'*Bene*. That I thought. Of lesser matters we shall speak another time.'

THREE

'Oh laisse frapper à la porte
La main, qui frappe avec ses doigts futiles.
Notre heure est si unique; et le reste, qu'importe
Le reste, avec ses doigts futiles?

. . .

L'instant est si rare, de lumière première,
Dans notre coeur, an fond de nous.'

—Emile Verhaeren

It was after sunset when the little white boat 'Marietta' slipped out of the rocky cove, as it had done almost every evening for the
past six weeks. Nevil rowed. Martino sat beside his *houri* in the stern;
since rowing was apt to catch his breath and make him cough.

The hush and glow of early evening, in sky and lake, cast its spell
upon all three. The Western hills wore a halo of light, shell-pink melting to amethyst. In the east an orange-golden moon hung poised
above the rugged heights as if loath to lose touch with earth. The
watchword of the evening was Peace.

The three in the boat talked fitfully of passing things. But of the
great scheme no one spoke, till the keel grated on the pebbles. Then
said Martino abruptly, gripping his friend's hand:

'When my spirit shall have digested that wonderful recital, I shall
better be able to speak of details—possibilities. You understand?'

'Very much so. You've only to send word across when the process
is complete!'

'That will be soon, I hope,' softly, from Lilamani.

'The sooner the better for me, Signora. *Buon riposo.*' From the top
of the stone steps he watched their departing boat cleave the shining,
sensitive silver below, while the black worm of envy gnawed at his

heart. Fame, recognition—the one great good he had wrested from life in defiance of his 'lost lung,'— seemed of a sudden chilly, unsatisfying, like a glass of water on a cold day. *Santa Maria!* To be young and strong, with such a wife to feed the sacred flame! As if in jeering comment a violent fit of coughing shook him, as a dog shakes a rat. Then, with a curse, he turned homeward to supper and probable recriminations from a devoted if sharp-tongued sister: sole genie of his lamp.

Out on the lake, in the vanishing boat, silence had fallen again. But at the heart of it was understanding. To stir a man's imagination, is to seal his lips: and to-day Nevil Sinclair's imagination had been profoundly stirred. The rapture of the artist was his; his vision of things, beautiful beyond expression, entreating to be expressed; of things vital clamouring to be born.

And it was her doing—hers. He worshipped her with his eyes while she lay back against her cushion, watching the birth of star upon quivering star.

Who that saw her, without prejudice, could doubt that his unique experiment seemed like to prove a unique success? Martino did not doubt. But Martino was of the elect. It was thought of the Philistines that chilled him; one Philistine in particular, brimful of prejudice. He thrust her impatiently aside. His decision for art had made him permanently a black sheep in her eyes. What matter one smudge the more? And his father? A twinge of pain here, tempered with annoyance. Why in the name of commonsense couldn't folk who swore by it let a man be happy in his own way? He was, and would be, none the less. Nay more, he would make the name of Sinclair famous. Perhaps they would be satisfied then. For himself the glowing golden present was satisfaction enough. It is at once the strength and weakness of the artist nature, this full surrender to the spell of the moment.

Beyond this enchanted summer he refused to look definitely. Vague visions of a winter in Rome, or Egypt, sufficed. What matter where? The secret charm lay in seeing the whole world afresh, through her eyes; in realizing, through her, as never yet, the sanctity and sanity of the common, primal bond between man and woman that is at once keystone and pinnacle of the house of life.

Mighty opposites were they—irreconcilables? By no means. Six weeks of closest intimacy, of spelling out letter by letter the unknown quantity he had taken to wife, inclined him to believe rather that East and West are not antagonistic, but complementary: heart and head, thought and action, woman and man. Between all these 'pairs of opposites' fusion is rare, difficult, yet eminently possible. Why not, then, between East and West?

In the strength of that analogy he could go forward, unafraid; still more so because the poetic temperament common to both implied a certain imaginative insight and flexibility, favourable to the bridging of gulfs; and the fact that, in Broome's phrase, he had 'too little of the average Englishman under his Park Lane surface,' was no longer a stone of stumbling, but his most valuable asset. In less than six months of marriage with the average Briton—say his own brother George—Lilamani's fairy boat of happiness would almost certainly have run aground upon the rocks. Even with himself, to whom a great love had given understanding, its fragility was a thing to tremble at; and he dreaded the risk of impact with sharp-cornered headlands that loomed vaguely through the golden mist.

Yet, for all his understanding, he did not dream that already two intrusive actualities threatened the fragile thing; did not dream of her troubled wonder in divining that the vital, motive power of her own life seemed to count for little in his.

Six weeks; and, to her knowledge, no form of devotion or prayer. A Bible lived among his books; an old Bible, solidly bound and clasped, with Christina Nevil writ in faded ink on the fly-leaf. But though Lilamani had read it—with an awed thrill in touching a book handled by his mother in her girlhood—she had only seen Nevil open it once. It was strange. Were all Englishmen thus? Or was it a part of his tender consideration for her that had been the crowning revelation of their union? Shyness and innate shrinking from the least hint of criticism made her fear to ask him—yet.

The second intrusive reality was more personal, more poignantly disturbing; one that might compel her to speak.

Six weeks; and no word of recognition from that father and sister, henceforth to be dear as her own; dearer, if that were possible. For in theory, if not always in fact, her husband's people become paramount to the Hindu wife; only a degree less honoured, less sacred than her lord himself. But then . . . the home-coming of an Indian bride sets her in the heart of his family: an additional daughter, modestly self-suppressed; handmaiden in chief to the Queen-mother of that human hive. And Lilamani Sinclair—child of transition—found herself, instead, alone with this one man upon an unknown road, with never a signpost for guidance, and never a word from that England to which she must now belong.

For the first three weeks, secure in her certainty, she had not given the matter a thought. Then she had begun to watch her husband a little fearfully, whenever a post came in. Days passed. Eagerness faded into a wistful anxiety. Surely, even in England, some form of greeting, of 'friendly wishings,' was due to bride of eldest son? Could it be that he had never written of his marriage? And if not, why—why?

Day after day that question had tormented her waking, and bred grotesque nightmares when she slept. More than once it had been upon her lips. But her own conviction that he ought to have written made her dread his answer. Better they should be in the wrong than he. Yet—she must know; she must! And to-night, while she sat silent in the dusk, watching the birth of the stars, she was wondering, wondering—dared she ask him now?

The moment seemed propitious for touching upon intimate things. Courage waxed, as the glow of evening waned, and earth-stars came out along the water's edge. She stirred softly, and sat upright, clasping her hands; a trick she had when nervous. But it was Nevil who spoke.

'Such a silent little wife! Dreaming? Thinking of Sita?'

'No. Of Lilamani.'

'So was I! Anything wrong with Lilamani? Isn't she quite happy?'

Her eyes dwelt a moment on his moon-lit face. Her own was half in shadow.

'Dearest,' she said softly, 'why ask so strange thing?'

'Only because I wish it so tremendously; and because—well, when a man stands at the summit of desire he's always half afraid of the next turning. *You* understand that—don't you?'

'Yes, too much. But . . . we have . . . not to be afraid.' She drew a deep breath. 'Nevil . . . King of me . . . have I leave to say all that is in my heart?'

'Beloved, why not? What is it?'

'Something I must ask. Only—if it vex you——'

'Ask any mortal thing you please.'

A pause. Nevil, intent upon her shadowed face, let the boat drift at will.

'It is only—these many days I have been waiting, hoping . . . some small word of greeting for new wife . . . from England——'

'Lilamani! Forgive me—!'

The pain and self-reproach in his cry told her all. She leaned forward, steadying her breath.

'Oh, Nevil! Is it——? You have not written?'

'No. I have not written.'

'Why?'

He merely saw the word; and his free hand covered both hers.

'Darling, how *shall* I make you understand? With you, in India, it is so different. You see, my decision about the painting upset them a good deal at home. I was honestly sorry. But it had to be. Then came my marriage, which I knew they would not see—quite as I see it; and I wanted no outside worries disturbing our first spell of happiness. But it was wrong of me to forget how my not writing might affect *you*. I fancied you would be too happy in these honeymoon weeks to bother your head about strangers you had never seen.'

'Oh, I am happy, beyond all dreaming. But Nevil——. Father of you, sister of you—my own being like lost—how could I not wish——?'

His grasp on her hands tightened. 'I never thought of that, selfish duffer that I am. But truly, if they'd been a different sort I would have written sooner.'

'Different sort? What is that?'

'Nowadays English, little wife!' He smiled, longing to win her from her anxious mood. 'My meaning is that I'm a kind of freak in my family. They're not much like me, any of 'em, except my youngest sister, Christina, who might come out to us later on. She has more of my mother in her than the rest.'

'How many—the rest?'

'Two brothers; a sailor and a soldier, besides Jane.'

'And you also—very like your mother?'

'Very like. And proud of it. But I've always been out of gear with my father and Jane. They worship a godling called the Right Thing, whose first commandment is "Thou shalt respect the whole beaten track, and nothing but the beaten track." And we're not exactly respecting it—are we, Jewel of Delight?'

'No—I am afraid. But . . . you were meaning to write . . . sometime?'

'Naturally. I've been wondering this last week how much longer I would be justified in keeping our sanctuary sacred from the touch of outside things. That's how I look at it. Life is none too prodigal of happiness like ours. Are you in such a mortal hurry to admit the world, the flesh, and the devil?'

'Oh, no—no!' she cried out with sudden passion. 'It was because I thought . . . it must be right, and——' The small even teeth closed on her lower lip.

'And what?' he asked almost sharply.

'Not anything more.'

'There was something. I heard it in your voice. You asked leave to speak out all your thought. As you love me, Lilamani, keep nothing back.'

'But it is such a small thing; a little private ache, because I had feared, through your not writing, you began to be . . . ashamed——'

The hands he held were crushed against his lips. 'I'll write tomorrow,' was all he said.

Then, releasing her, he gripped his sculls and the boat sped forward, away from the thickly clustered constellations of Cadenabbia and Tremezzo, toward the lone twin lights that beckoned to them from the farther shore, as yet untouched by the moon.

After a short silence Lilamani spoke.

'You did not sing to-night. Will you—now?'

He balanced the sculls at her bidding; lifted his head and sang softly, with tender inflections, the old Scots' ballad, so simple in phrasing, so extravagant in protest:

'My love is like a red, red rose that's newly sprung in June.
My love is like a melody that's sweetly played in tune——'

So singing and so floating, star-encompassed above and below, the watchword of the evening descended again upon them like a beatitude. The voices of the outer world seemed far away and unreal: themselves, and this their transient Eden, the sole realities.

The song ceased, and Nevil's oars plashed again, scattering stars. A few swift strokes carried them out of the moonlight into the shadow of their hill. Both were imaginative; both susceptible to the mood of the hour; and, in that moment of passing, a little breeze of dread blew chill upon their hearts.

As the keel grounded, Lilamani leaned forward, putting out a hand. 'Nevil,' she began, then checked herself.

'What is it?' he asked, his ear quick to catch the trouble in her tone.

'Not anything,' she answered as before.

'Lilamani, is that true?'

'Nearly true. Only some woman's foolishness, of . . . perhaps . . . Pity to break so heavenly evening with "perhaps"——'

'Wise one!' he commended, turning to moor the boat. Sincerely he hoped that her trouble was no more than 'woman's foolishness.' But, being man, he was grateful for the reserve or consideration that had checked her impulse of speech.

Springing out, he drew the boat well in-shore; secured it and returning, leaned to her again.

'Is it still there—the foolishness?'

'No.'

'Did you drive it away?'

'Yes. Like it deserved.'

'Don't let it come back. This is our perfect hour. Let us keep it so.'

Above them, from massed bushes of rhododendron and azalea, the love-music of nightingales echoed his plea and she sighed.

'Yes. That I am feeling too. Almost it is like enchantment. One little touch might break——'

'That's why I put off writing. Must I now?'

'It is not for wife to command her lord,' she breathed. 'But think only . . . dearest, your father——'

Without a word he lifted her in his arms and carried her up through the fragrant dark, jewelled with aerial gold of fire-flies.

To both came the thought of that first time he had carried her thus, in the rush and swirl of the storm, that had led them into this deep heart of peace: and Lilamani, remembering all that his arms had told her then, found tonight, in their enfolding pressure, an answer to the question she could not bring herself to ask.

FOUR

'Oh, I would be to thee
As gentle as the grass above the dead,
And have I been but darkness and a sword?'

—Stephen Phillips

It was the last of June; the last lingering hour of a radiant evening. Not often does the queen of months fulfil herself so royally as she had done for these two, with whom the very gods seemed to have fallen in love. In the heavens a lazy light-filled cloud or two, by way of reminder that tears must fall again some day. On earth increasing fervour of heat and fragrance of a million roses. And over all brooded that spirit of peace, of a sanctuary enclosed, peculiar to hill-girt lakes in the zenith of summer.

Even the passing flutter of holiday life on steamers and on hotel terraces had ceased—for a time. Lilamani basked and blossomed in the heat like some exotic plant of her own land. Nevil, less inured, had suggested a move up to the Dolomites. But she clung to her nest, fearing to 'break the enchantment' and waken the forgetful Gods. They were growing a little superstitious about 'the enchantment'; so pathetically certain is human nature that the perfect moment is of all things most fragile, most impossible to regain when lost.

In high hope, tempered with awe at their own daring, the Ramayana pictures had been begun. Nevil had chosen for his first venture, Sita in the forest hut; the scene being one of the simplest, yet imbued with the thrill of approaching drama. By now the groundwork had been roughly blocked in; the forest hut, with massed trees darkly looming; their black trunks and branches barring the red glow of sunset fire. Sita, in amber draperies and lotus-crown, was as yet merely indicated; as also was the stealthily nearing form of That Terrible, with staff and begging-bowl and matted locks. Rapello, Broome's stalwart young boatman, pressed into service as model, had accepted with alacrity and repented at leisure; consoling himself, for hours snatched from a promising courtship of Giulietta, with reflections on the *Inglese's* proverbial liberality, and the honour of having his portrait painted by a genuine artist. At moments when he looked particularly handsome and complacent, Nevil had been tempted to let him see his 'portrait'; and only the risk of losing a good model had held the impulse in check.

Colour-books on India had been sent for, and Sir Lakshman, greatly interested, had promised to do his share. He was back in Paris now, appreciably nearer. Yet another week and he would be with them. Father and husband under one roof! Lilamani hugged the blessed thought. Could the most exigent bride ask for more?

And while the last evening of June burned its heart out, the most exigent bride was curled up in Broome's big chair frowning at a slip of paper, and chewing the point of her pencil in quest of inspiration. She was alone in the little châlet for the first time in her brief married life. Two hours ago an urgent message had come from Cadenabbia. Martino, prostrated by one of his worst attacks, had begged his sister to send for Nevil Sinclair; and Sinclair had gone, promising to return as soon as might be to the lone bird in her nest.

The first hour she had spent in her shrine, praying Vishnu the Preserver to save Martino's life. Then for a space she had worshipped the image of the Baby-God Krishna, that lived in her sandalwood casket; dreaming shyly, yet with passionate hope, of the day when the Shining Ones should vouchsafe her a Baby-god of flesh and blood, to worship in its stead. Then, because time lagged sadly without her Light of Life, she had gone back into the studio, where all things spoke feelingly of him: picture and easel; brushes and palette, flung hastily aside; slippers and the holland coat in which he worked.

Here the happy idea had come to her of completing a June lovesong, written in secret. Then, if Signor Martino lived, she would surprise Nevil with it on his return. Grateful for the distraction, she settled to her task in the hope of charming away a little restless ache that tugged at the back of her mind like a spoilt child at its mother's skirts.

Ten days since Nevil had written to Jane; leaving her to judge whether Sir George's state of health made it advisable to tell him—yet. Ten days; and no answer, to Lilamani's knowledge. But, yesterday, she had seen a shadow in her lord's eyes, not there before; and had longed to ask—yet dared not. Now, in her hour of loneliness, they tugged at her afresh—the longing and the fear. With the delicate passion of her own love-music she strove to banish them; reading her small achievement through for the twentieth time, in hopes of capturing two spontaneous last lines:

SONG: IN LOVE-TIME

'As the new-blown rose at noon-day
　　To the passion of the Sun,
Yields the fragrance of her spirit
　　To that All-compelling One—
So, in ecstasy of giving,—mine to thee, O my King.

'As the nightingale new-nested,
　　In a rapture of delight,
Coins heart-love into music,
　　Through the star-enchanted night:—
So the music of thy silence is to me, O my King.

As the full-blown moon at midnight,—
　　(Lotus plucked from Sita's crown,)—'

How to make an ending? How to put in best words that image of moon in the lake was like image of him in her heart? It was at this pause that she had sought inspiration from her pencil-tip—and found the missing couplet. Yes. That would please him. With a half-smile she set it down:

As the full-blown moon at midnight,
　　(Lotus plucked from Sita's crown,)
Sees, in darkly dreaming waters,
　　His radiant image thrown:
So thine image deeply dwells in heart of me, O my King.'

Not so beautiful as she wished. But if she put away the verse at the back of her head for a while, new lines would come singing to her, from the Beyond, and that at the most incongruous moments, even as they had come while Audrey discoursed of carbons, and *pro tems*, and other invisible bogies whose names she had joyfully dismissed from her mind. Poor kind Audrey—so full of knowledge, so empty of true heart's riches—had written more than once from England and seemed content with her barren 'way of the brain.' Well—to each the good they craved; and to herself that good had been given in fullest measure.

Then, springing from her chair, she went over to the writing-table, with intent to slip her love-song inside his blotter—'for a surprise.'

Opening it, her eyes fell upon a letter just begun. Half a dozen lines only; and her quick brain seized them at a glance:

'DEAR JANE,

'I am quite at a loss how to answer your confoundedly sisterly letter of congratulation! You brandish your zeal for the honour of our house like a two-edged sword. As for the unspeakable brother you have hacked into little pieces, I can only say——'

What—what could he only say, this priceless husband who, on her account, had been 'hacked into little pieces'? Would hard words from his people make him angry or sorry? Would they ever. . . make him regret . . .?

There sprang the question she had refrained from asking on that evening whose watchword was Peace. Now the blow had fallen: and he had said no word. Yet she had seen the shadow of it in his eyes. Rigid, almost without breathing, she stood scanning those few lines, in the dear familiar hand, while the blood stole slowly from cheeks and lips, back to her stunned heart and froze there . . .

But the moment's merciful numbness could not last. A new and poignant question stabbed her back to an agony of sensation. What had she said, this 'Jane,' who must be called 'sister'? What manner of blows had she dealt with her two-edged sword?

It was plain that Nevil did not mean her to know. And yet—she must know. The rebel strain in her—overlaid by happiness and wifely devotion—uprose again with power; the fighting spirit of her race that bids even its women-folk set honour and self-respect above the duty of self-subjection and makes the *purdahnashin* of Rajputana more of an entity than her of Bengal. For his sake, to keep stainless the honour of his name, she could and would defy all things—even himself.

But the letter——! It came yesterday. His eyes told her that. If it were not utterly destroyed, she intended to find and read it; not staying to consider was it right or wrong. Once or twice she had chidden him gently for his casual, untidy ways. Now they alone gave her hope of success.

With fingers that trembled and pale lips compressed, she felt in the pockets of his holland coat, caressing it with her cheek the while, as if to ask pardon for intruding upon its privacies. Not there. She drew a breath of relief. And yet—it must be found.

Drawers, the blotter, other pockets were shrinkingly invaded. Then her glance fell upon the waste-paper basket—and she knew. Its plethoric state proved that it had not been lately emptied. The letter was there. Yet she hesitated. Something seemed to turn over inside her. Must she . . . dared she . . . push her quest so far?

The next instant she was on her knees among fragments of transient words that yet have power to wreck the happiness of a life. She had not seen Lady Roscoe's writing. Broken sentences must be her guide. Straightening a severely crumpled morsel of paper, the words 'Bramleigh Beeches' caught her attention. Ah—this was it——!

Then—with a sharp cry, she dropped the paper as if it had stung her, and kneeling upright pressed both hands tightly over her eyes.

But the words she had seen danced in letters of flame upon the blackness. 'A native mistress at Bramleigh Beeches! Half-caste sons to carry on the name of which we are so rightly proud——'

Tremulous no longer, but with a tragically steadfast deliberation, she straightened out four other fragments of the same paper, the same writing; badly crumpled all. He had been angry, then. A gleam of comfort in that. The four fragments pieced themselves into a half-sheet. Evidently not the whole letter. But she could find no more; and this would suffice.

It did more than suffice. For it was a large half-sheet and, in spite of crumpling, easy to be read.

DEAR NEVIL (it ran),

'You have *surpassed* your own record! I could not bring myself to write sooner, and now—what on earth *can* one say? Your last bombshell was bad enough, though I always had a lurking belief things would end so. *But this!* Had you *no* thought for the future? A native mistress at Bramleigh Beeches! Half-caste sons to carry on the name of which we are so rightly proud! In my opinion father would be justified in cutting off your inheritance; even in cutting you off with a shilling!'

Lilamani puckered her brows over the cryptic utterance. Was that what Nevil meant by hacking him into little bits? None was by to enlighten her; and, still with her tragical steadfastness, she read on:

'When estates *are* free, it seems only common-sense that they should go to the fittest. In our case, George, without question. Compare his sound satisfactory engagement and your own crazy marriage! Even if the girl had been English, the whole affair is fatally precipitate for an inflammable man like you.' Inflammable? Precipitate? More dread-sounding words without sense. Yet those that followed were cruelly clear; and in reading she bit her lip till it bled. 'But a *native!* Who in their senses could dream of your picking one up on the Riviera, where you might so easily have picked up a presentable American heiress, who would have been of some use to the estate. Certainly I shall say nothing to father yet. In his present state of health I believe the shock might kill him. When he is stronger you can tell him yourself. As for you, *your* real punishment will come later, when you wake up from your infatuation—it *can* be nothing else—to find yourself tied hand and foot for life——'

Here the sheet ended; and the girl-wife was thankful that the rest could not be found. In that last broken sentence she saw her own death-warrant: no less.

Pushing the pieces from her, she rose and paced the room; the dear room, almost alive with the presence of him who must be freed from the impending dilemma, when he should wake up from infatuation. . . . Another strange word. What . . . exactly . . . did it mean?

Mechanically she sought her dictionary and turned the pages with hurried nervous fingers. Ah, there it was. No mist of tears blurred the small print. 'A foolish passion, beyond the control of reason and judgment.' She formed the words with her lips, frowning a little, as if to bring back her mind from a long way off. Her hands were steady when she laid down the book.

Fresh confirmation—that was all—of the resolve that had brought the tragical steadfastness into her eyes. Child though she was, and passionately in love with life, there could be no struggle; no hesitation. To her clear, uncomplicated mind, it was all so heartrendingly simple. Sooner than shadow of stain upon his family, his name, obliteration of herself beyond recall. The detached stoicism of centuries dominated her; blinding her to side issues; impelling her toward the inevitable end.

She stepped out on to the balcony that the peace of evening might lay its balm upon her anguished heart. But tonight there was no peace even here. To her overstrung fancy, Nature's self seemed imbued with the spirit of Jane Roscoe. Black against the sky's clear amber, the great kindly hills loomed stern and forbidding. The placid lake cared not one iota whether it should bear on its bosom a radiant Lilamani or hurry a desperate one into the next-door House of Life.

Twilight was fading into dusk. Earth stars glowed here and there. Shadowy boats moved upon the darkening water. One of them might be his. Why, oh why was he so long in coming? For the first time in her short, sheltered life a great horror of loneliness overwhelmed her; and she fled back into the study like a hunted thing.

Her few words of farewell came with a strange spontaneity, simple as speech: 'Beloved—By chance I saw your letter in blotter. By purpose I found that of your sister, and read—because I *must* know truth. Now I go, that the way may be clear for honour of your house. At first you will grieve. But that will pass. There are many women of your own land better for wife than your Lilamani. Good-bye.'

Without tear or tremor she folded that pitiful scrap of paper; and set it on his blotter, together with her love-song and Jane's mangled half-sheet. Then—with wide eyes and slim hands clenched, she stood as if smitten to stone.

He was coming! One of those boats had been his. Reprieve? Alas, no. Merely the added anguish of enduring his touch, his glance, before . . .

The door was flung open, and he hurried towards her. Still she did not move. His hands were on her shoulders. His voice seemed to come from far away.

'Dear little wife. A shame to leave her alone so long! But poor Martino was in a bad way when I got there. He's better now; and I believe he'll pull through this time. I knew you wouldn't grudge him an hour or two of my valuable company!'

'Oh, no . . . I am glad——'

Her tone betrayed her, and he brought his face nearer, searching hers in the dim light.

'Lilamani—you don't sound glad. And why were you standing there like a little statue in the dusk? Tell me.'

'It is hard to tell.'

'Why? Has anything gone wrong?'

'Yes. I have seen ... I have read ... that letter of your sister——'

'Good God!' he cried in a fury of dismay. Then he remembered. 'But, my dear, you must be dreaming. I tore it up on the spot.'

'Yes. Only—it is still there. I found it—one half-sheet. Oh, how shall I ever call name of sister, woman who wrote such cruel thing!'

'You poor darling!' he drew her closer. But what possessed you to go ferreting it out like that? How on earth did you know it was there?'

She hesitated. The anger in his tone was more against the circumstance than against her. But she was in no mood to make distinctions.

'I—I saw first your own few lines in the blotter. Then—then I was looking everywhere, because—I had to know full truth——'

'Not if *I* didn't wish you to. If I'd meant you to see that letter I should have shown it to you myself. But I'd have died sooner! And can't you see that it was wrong and dishonourable to go hunting among my private papers when my back was turned——'

'Oh no—not say that!' She shrank from his touch that was robbing her of courage. 'Only when I had seen yours——'

'What devil's luck led you to see mine? Of course, I ought to have been more careful. But you don't meddle with my writing-table as a rule. What on earth took you there to-day?'

She covered her face, and for the first time her voice lost its steadiness.

'If you will speak more gently, and leave off from hurting me—with your eyes——'

'My darling! I wouldn't hurt you for the world. It's you who have hurt yourself so cruelly in spite of the pains I was at to spare you. That's what makes me angry; that and Jane's egregious effusion——. But tell me—what took you to that wretched blotter?'

'Only I wanted to put inside, for a surprise—some verses I had made——'

'Verses? Let me see them.' He moved swiftly to the table, thankful for the welcome change of subject. 'Where are they, little wife?'

But she sprang past him, and snatching at the papery crumpled it in her hand. 'No. Not now.'

'Why not now?'

'Oh—it is all different——'

'It is *not* all different. You made those verses for me?'

'Yes.'

'Then they are mine. I want them. Give them to me at once!'

The half-playful note of command hurt more than all.

'But not to read—yet,' she pleaded, so earnestly, that he must needs humour her, puzzled and distressed though he was.

'Very well, if you really wish it, we'll read them together later to take the taste of all this out of our minds.'

'Together!' The word was like a javelin flung at her. But he, all unwitting, proceeded to smooth his crumpled treasure on the table, and so caught sight of her note.

'Hullo! What's this?' he said.

And she, with a quick-drawn breath: 'That—you may see now.'

Then, with the soft rush of a winged thing, she sped past him—out, and down into the night.

For a moment, knowing her shy ways, he fancied she had merely slipped into her shrine, and drew nearer the window to decipher his note. One hurried glance enlightened him. With an oath he crushed the paper into his pocket; and, turning, beheld her, flitting like a pale moth, through the dark of the garden.

'Lilamani, stop! I command you!' he shouted. 'I'm coming down.'

Then he sped after her, clearing the short flight of stairs almost at a bound. He believed her capable, at such a crisis, of carrying out her fell purpose in defiance of his command; and those few moments of poignant fear lit up his whole consciousness as a searchlight illumines a night of stars. Deeply and honestly as he loved her, he had not known how terribly dear she was to him—till now. So much, at least, Jane's letter had achieved——

'Lilamani! Stop, for God's sake!' he shouted again, once he was clear of the house. But she fled on. . . .

When he came up with her, she was clambering on to a rock, whence she could jump straight into deep water.

Swiftly his arms closed round her from behind, drawing her down to his level. Desperately, and in silence, she fought for freedom; submission of wifehood swept aside by the fierce resolve not to spoil his life. Her delicate body seemed animated with superhuman strength: and he, hoping to soften her tearless passion of resistance, tried to win possession of her lips. But she turned her head away sharply; speaking at last, between quick-coming breaths.

'Go, go—leave me! Hard now—but afterwards——'

A swift shudder convulsed her; and, lest he notice it, she began struggling afresh.

'Beloved—have you *quite* lost your senses?' he cried, a sharp ring of fear in his voice.

'It is possible. So much better—that I go. But not say—beloved.'

By sheer force he held her to him.

'I shall say it. Because it's true. And you *shall not go*.'

No fear in his tone now; but the deep strong note of command, that called to the primitive deeps in her: nor called in vain. He felt her tense limbs relax—ever so little and pressed his advantage home.

'Lilamani, conquer your madness, and listen to me. Is it lip-service when you call me lord of your life?'

'Nevil! It is truth—from my heart.'

'Then you have no right, no power to fling away that most precious gift against my wish; and to sacrifice my life as well——'

'But no. With men it is otherwise. Afterwards—because of others—you would be grateful for courage of that Lilamani——'

He closed her lips with his own, and felt the whole of her melt into yielding softness at their touch.

'I will not hear such things,' he said, and drew her to a rough seat, still holding her cautiously, as one holds a prisoned bird, lest her madness return. 'Besides,' he urged in tender reproof, 'don't you know that it is very wrong to take your own life—for any reason?'

'No, not so—with us; by right motive,' she answered with rare steadiness, for all the turmoil in her breast. 'Also, to us, death is not such great matter. Only passing on—to next-door House.'

'But think—in that next-door House you would find no Nevil.' He felt her tremble and was glad. 'You would leave him here, alone, not able to finish his great pictures without Sita. Did you think of that?'

'N—no——' The word was disjointed by a sob.

'And would you make a sister of mine,' he went on, drawing her closer still, 'though she did write harsh, abominable things in her bitterness and vexation—would you make her virtually a murderer in my eyes—and in the eyes of God?'

That last thawed the frozen fountains of a grief too deep-seated for tears. With a broken cry she clung to him as one drowning to a spar.

'O King of me! Forgive . . . forgive . . .!'

FIVE

'Her strength with weakness is overlaid,
Meek compliances veil her might,
Him she stays by whom she is stayed.'

—'True Woman.' C. Rossetti

They spent a long evening in their balcony, watched over by the wistful stars. There was much to talk of now that she knew all: and their happiness, snatched from the verge of extinction, had a new depth and consciousness, that is the guerdon of pain shared and conquered.

So far as might be, Nevil expounded Jane, and the remoteness of her view-point from his own; an assurance that was balm to the hurt soul of his wife. He bade her, for his sake, forget those unjust, ugly words that the writer would surely regret when she knew his Lilamani. But she answered truthfully that were impossible. She could only promise not to let them poison her thoughts or embitter her spirit. And he knew of old the value of her given word.

Her love-song, with its musical cadences, at once delighted him and wrung his heart. That Jane's unvarnished candour should have struck sharp on that impassioned out-pouring, infuriated him afresh. But she should not have the satisfaction of provoking him to a retort. Silence would at once annoy her and convince her that, for him, the subject was outside the pale of discussion. In the meantime, with the dear dark head against his shoulder, the cool clinging hand at rest within his own, he would fain forget the existence of Jane and all her works. The high encompassing heavens, the passionate jubilance of nightingales, thrilling up through the dark, weaned him from thought of trivial things; stirred within the body of his manhood, the pulse of the Divine. . . .

When it came to 'good night,' they whispered that the enchantment was not broken, after all: whispered it, lest the Gods hear and snatch away the precious thing.

But it seemed that the Gods were sleeping, or on a journey. For three unclouded days they rowed and read and painted at will. Sita and Ravan emerged from their background of hut and forest. Sita, more especially, grew in beauty and power with each fresh sitting; nor did Nevil Sinclair guess how much he owed to his wife's trick of identifying herself so innately with Rama's queen that a sense of approaching tragedy weighed upon her heart; while, in her misty imagining, That Terrible stood for Jane Roscoe and her two-edged sword.

Three unclouded days: and upon the fourth day, fell a bolt from the blue.

Breakfast was not long over. Lilamani sat on Sita's stool, ready for the morning's work, and her husband stood at his easel, when there came a telegram from England that took all the healthy colour out of Nevil Sinclair's face.

'My God!' he groaned under his breath; then, sinking into a chair beside the writing-table, pressed a hand over his eyes.

The flimsy, yellowish paper slipped unheeded to the floor and lay there, harmless—looking as a dead leaf, till Lilamani, treading softly, picked it up and read the curt summons twice over, in a stunned bewilderment, before the sense penetrated—and the pain.

'Father has had a stroke. Serious. Come immediately.'

What a 'stroke' might mean, she did not know. But two facts were plain: grave illness, and Nevil's instant departure—with or without her? Which would it be? For answer, she had only the leaping hammer-strokes of her heart.

A second or two she stood, while all things seemed smitten into a sudden unnatural silence. Then, softlier still, she drew near her husband.

Feeling her nearness, he looked up; and she saw the brave blue of his eyes veiled in tears. The pang that smote her was not all grief: it was the birth-pang of that mother-tenderness which is the diviner half of woman's love for man. To the Eastern wife it is impermissible till actual motherhood add a cubit to her stature; and, with a thrill at her own presumption, Lilamani Sinclair slipped a hand round her husband's head, drawing it close into the softness of her breast and cradling it there, as though he were indeed her son.

'The dear old man. Always such a tower of strength,' Nevil said at last, without looking up. 'When Jane wrote that he was not quite himself, one never thought—of *this*. God knows I've been a disappointing son to him. But I felt sure—if only he could see you—Well, there's hope still——' He drew himself up, brushing the mist from his lashes. 'Time's everything. I'll wire to Jane and we must start to-night.'

'We?' The word was little more than a breath; and her eyes, quick with love's clairvoyance, dwelt on his. 'Were you really meaning——? Is it not better—in such time of trouble—not to make more . . .?'

'But Lilamani!' He gathered her close. 'How on earth can I leave you here—alone?'

'"Can" is always making a way, when there is "must"!' she answered, smiling bravely. She had seen a ghost of indecision in his eyes, had heard it in his tone.

'But there's no "must,"' he persisted, love and chivalry conquering his suspicion that she spoke truth. 'You're my wife; and I'm proud of the fact. Even Jane couldn't be otherwise than decent to you—at a time like this. As for the dear old man—he needn't know till he's fit to see you himself. And if—— There's no "if." And there's no "must" either—is there—now I've made things clear?'

He was talking valiantly against his own conviction. She saw it too clearly: saw that, for all his dread of parting, her presence now at Bramleigh Beeches would but serve to pile anxiety upon anxiety, pain on pain for the husband who was her all.

'Perhaps not "must,"' she admitted wistfully. 'Yet still—because of your father . . . better to go alone. Also for me—it is too soon—meeting Lady Roscoe—after that letter——'

'You're right. It *is* too soon!' He spoke with sudden heat. 'Too soon for me, if it comes to that. But this is no time for squabbling; and of course—if you're not there. . . . I believe you're right, little wife. Better have the wrench now than risk spoiling everything by taking you home at the wrong moment. But you shan't be left alone. I'll wire to your father. Lucky he's in Paris. Shall I ask him if he can come at once, or take you along to join him?'

'No—not that!' She shrank from so complete a break. 'Tell him "Come soon." He will. Somehow, he will. For his Lilamani.'

'But at soonest he can't be here before to-morrow night. Twenty-four hours. You—who have never been alone in your life! I should be haunted by the thought of you. . . .'

'No—oh no. You must believe I am brave Lilamani for your sake. Signor Martino and his sister will be kind; and in the evening time I will write you longest letter you ever had!'

Smiling, he pressed her hands between his own. Then they must needs forget themselves and each other in telegrams, time-tables, and flying orders; hateful, merciful trivialities that thrust themselves in between the anguished heart and the too nimble imagination, the terrible second self that stands outside the picture—watching, pitying, recording, and so intensifying emotion.

The telegrams written, Barnes must be told. Barnes was Sinclair's valet; faithful, but of late, mildly remonstrant. He received the news from home with a decorous air of sympathy due to any trouble that shadowed the prospective owner of Bramleigh Beeches, even if he had 'married beneath him, in a manner of speaking.' Mrs. Sinclair's taste for cookery was suspicious—to say the least; and—he wondered, discreetly, how much they knew 'at home.' Well he would soon find out now: and, on the whole, though that there Miss Juliet *was* a 'taking piece, and pretty well up to the balcony-trick,' he could do with a few weeks' return to British Bass and an honest cut off the Sunday joint.

In the meantime, he advertised his sympathy by an elaborate lightness of tread and a voice pitched half a tone lower than usual. Discovering that the journey was to be a single affair, he patted himself on the back for 'a knowing bird.' It was a hole-and-corner business. He had suspicioned as much from the first. Peculiar, when you came to think of it; but there hadn't bin no letters with the Bramleigh postmark addressed to Mrs. Nevil Sinclair so far as *he* knew. The young master wasn't quite such a fool as *that* amounted to. Trust him. A courtesy marriage: he, Horatio Barnes, would have took his Bible oath; only that the lady's father was obviously 'in it'—whatever 'it' might be. But then—Lord love you!—when it come to heathens, however well-turned out, there was always dark possibilities in lurk; as he had gleaned from certain of the young master's books. For Barnes was a bit of a scholard in his own esteem. He had read of

Japanese and Burmese marriages, in which parents were quite agree-
able to a temporary arrangement. The notion occurred to him now:
and he chuckled inwardly at his own astuteness. You never knew
when an odd bit of reading might nip in handy. At all events—mum
was the word. A bat in daylight could see as much. And mum it should
be for him till the lay of the land seemed to justify speech: which he
didn't go for to suppose it would.

Thus Horatio Barnes, moving like Agag, between the portmanteau
and the chest of drawers: while Nevil Sinclair, stunned and miserable,
gave not a moment's thought to the inferences a valet might draw
from his latest move. He only saw that Lilamani was right; astonishingly, beautifully right, as she was apt to be in matters seemingly outside her ken. By some instinct of the spirit, that took the place of
worldly wisdom, she had seen more instantly than he the impossibility
of arriving at such a crisis with an unacknowledged wife, in the face
of Jane's unacknowledged letter. For himself, eyes and judgment had
been blinded by grief, by chivalrous consideration, and the natural
desire that he had of her.

And how long would he be gone? Neither dared approach that
question till Sir Lakshman's answering telegram forced them back
upon a topic too painful for gratuitous talk. When it came, Nevil—
still pale and shaken—was mechanically swallowing a biscuit and a
glass of sherry, while they talked in the jerky, unnatural manner of
those about to part; carefully avoiding each other's eyes. Only yesterday, at tea-time, they had been behaving like two children; she, perched lightly on his knee; and he, insisting that she should 'bless' each
cake he ate by daintily biting off a corner herself. Only yesterday! It
seemed a week away. Now he swallowed unblessed morsels without
tasting them, and handed Sir Lakshman's answer to his wife.

'He'll be with you this time to-morrow. Thank God for that much,'
he said without looking at her, while he fumbled at the clasp of his
cigarette case. 'I suppose—I hope to goodness he can stay—till I come
back.'

'How soon is that?' she whispered, folding the paper into diminish-
ing parallelograms with minute care. 'One week—or two?'

'Impossible to tell, little wife.' He had lighted his cigarette now and
coming nearer laid a sustaining hand on her shoulder. 'Everything
depends—on him. But you may trust me to come straight back to you
the first moment I honestly can.'

'Yes—yes. But so long as they are needing you—please stay . . .'

At this point they were interrupted by Agag with another telegram from the stationmaster at Lucerne; and once more the hateful, merciful actualities cleft them apart. Sinclair blessed his wife's tearless composure even while he marvelled at it in one so young, and withal so passionate, as he had discovered her to be. But the Eastern temperament is a thing of extremes. Either it will beat the breast and wail unrestrainedly upon the least provocation, or it will endure to the utmost with a stoicism almost sublime. Much hangs on caste. In Lilamani Sinclair, inherited instinct forbade the indignity of uncontrolled outcry or lament; and his pain, his need of small services, eclipsed all thought of—afterwards.

But there came the dread inevitable moment when the last label was writ, the last key turned in its lock, and they two stood alone in her shrine, dumbly, acutely aware that here was an end—not of their love, but of that sublimated phase of it that comes once only, and by no means to all.

To Nevil came also a sudden unreasoning fear of the lake. It was too soon to leave her—too soon. True, her madness was past; yet, in their after-talk, he had discerned at the heart of it, a deep, underlying idea that at once lifted it above a mere desperate impulse and made it the more liable to recur. The oppressive sense of Death's immanence, of life's instability, that was upon him, quickened his dread.

'Lilamani,' he said hoarsely, gripping her two hands with a force that was pain, 'I *can't* leave you alone here, even for one night, unless you promise me, by whatever you hold most sacred, not to let—that madness of yours come back. Think of me—of the Sita pictures, of—of Jane, if the Devil tempts you to imagine that I could ever—oh, it's impossible! But give me your sacred word, and drive the ugly fear out of my heart——'

'Lord of my life,' she answered, a thrill of passion in her low tone, 'I promise . . . by most sacred thing of all . . . that gift I shall one day give you——'

A faint tremor here: and he—with an inarticulate sound—gathered her into his arms; held her so, for one measureless moment; then, whispering 'God keep you, little wife,' drew her down and out into their sun-filled garden.

The waiting boat received him. He waved as it pushed off. She waved back, achieving a smile. Then—he was gone; gone into the vague, unknown world of actualities: and for many minutes she stood where he had left her, straining to keep his boat in view through the mist that gathered in her eyes.

SIX

'Life struck sharp on death makes awful lightning.'

—E.B. Browning

Cherton is the station for Bramleigh; a small station with a small shelter on the 'down' side. When Nevil Sinclair alighted—heartsick and travel-sick, after interminable hours of ceaseless, and almost sleepless, rushing through space—it was raining, uneffusively, yet persistently, as it can rain in July. The clouds hung low and positive, here thinned to a whitish-grey, there heavy with unshed tears. No bustling wind threatened to interrupt their superfluous zeal for earth and trees and new-mown hay already saturate to repletion. They wore a settled, sullen look, as if they meant to stay there on and off for days.

Sinclair, followed by Barnes, hurried under the shelter and commanded a fly. It arrived out of space, with the leisurely dignity of its kind; and, for Nevil, that four-mile drive in a superannuated brougham, smelling at once stuffy and damp, almost broke the back of his endurance. Yet it was his own doing that he had not been 'met' by the landau and the greys. In wiring from Paris his probable hour of arrival, haunting thoughts of his father had impelled him to add 'if wet don't send.' For at that time the evolving motor had not quite changed the face of the landscape, and the stench and snort of one was as smoke to the eyes and vinegar to the teeth of the dear old man. By way of protest, he emphasized the sanctity of his greys and their driver: a faithful tyrant of twenty years' service. Hence Nevil's impulse of consideration. And it was just such endearing acts of graciousness— foreign to Jane and George—that had gone far to keep his first-born supreme in the father's heart, for all his tiresome perversity in matters of greater moment.

And now, while Nevil leaned back uneasily in the brougham-that-was, watching dejected hedges and tearful trees trail past him through the rain-blurred landscape, he found himself praying, instinctively, incoherently, to the dim God of his boyhood that he might, at worst, be granted living sight and sound of the father he had disappointed and deceived, before the Great Silence fell between them for ever. No wire awaiting him in Paris seemed to augur possible improvement. But he had been travelling for eight hours since then; and eight minutes would suffice . . .

While his ark of safety, lurching through the pillared gateway, rumbled on between drenched battalions of cypress and fir, Nevil Sinclair held thought suspended. One last lurch, and the house loomed into view; flat-fronted, creeper-covered, with short wings at either end: the east wing culminating in a tower. Familiar, every line and corner of it: yet now—tragically unfamiliar. For as Nevil leaned out into the rain a dozen sightless windows attested the futility of that broken prayer.

Sir George Sinclair was dead: and the spirit of the place, the spirits of unnumbered Sinclairs, who had lived and died there, called mutely on Sir Nevil to rise up and reign in his stead. But in that first shock of realization, he was simply a son bereft of a father—hard to please or understand, yet honestly beloved, in the queer, shamefaced fashion of his race.

Barnes, with eyes discreetly lowered, opened the brougham door; and at sight of him a jarring thought intruded on Nevil's misery. The man must be warned not to speak of the Como establishment. It was a detestable necessity; implying, as it did, a slur on Lilamani's fair name from which his every instinct shrank. Yet, hateful or no, speak he must.

'Look here, Barnes,' he said under his breath, 'no chattering about my private affairs in the servants' hall—you understand?'

Distaste lent an unusual curtness to his tone; and Barnes infused into his own a hint of mild reproach.

'That might ha' gone without sayin', Sir Nevil,' he answered, still considering the wet gravel; and the new-made baronet winced. He could have struck the man for his glib change of address. But instead, he hurried forward into the dim hall, smitten by a sudden acute fear that, by some unforeseen chance, his marriage had become known; that, he, Nevil, might even be responsible——He could not complete the hideous thought. Nor could he dismiss it, till he knew——.

But in this stronghold of the conventions all must be done decently and in order. Through the dimness came Madgwick, butler and major-domo, a small, shrewd-faced man, with kindly eyes and a suspicion of red about his eyelids. Nevil, frank and friendly always to those who served him, shook hands in silence with the pillar of the house.

'Wish you could ha' got here sooner, sir,' Madgwick muttered huskily. No glib change of address for him. 'Her la'ship's waiting tea for you in the dining-room.'

He led the way and Nevil followed into a lofty, oval space—lit by skylights and ringed by a gallery—known as the large hall. Though not the smoking-room proper, it had been the dead man's favourite 'den'; and his spirit clung about it in the faint, familiar smell of leather, tobacco, and dogs. Two setters rose from the hearthrug to greet Nevil; their tails, at a melancholy angle, wagged mere recognition. They missed the cheerful voice and heavy tread of their master, and the sensitiveness of humanized animals told them something was wrong.

As Nevil stooped to caress them, the dining-room door opened; Madgwick obliterated himself, and Jane looked out.

'That you, Nevil?'

' Yes.'

She came forward to meet him; a feminine counterpart of Sir George; square-cut and decisive; with strong, blunt nose, cleft chin and a lower lip that would obviously 'stand no nonsense' from woman or man. Though only five years older than her brother, she looked more, was more, in fact, from having lost, too early, if she had ever possessed, the elasticity of youth. Plain, at her best, she looked plainer than usual in an old black dress, hastily donned; her brown hair brushed well off an uncompromising brow; her eyes, like Madgwick's, betraying the weakness of secret tears. In spite of mutual grief, that unanswered letter hung between them like a bared sword.

There was a perceptible moment of embarrassment as they clasped hands; an embarrassment that would have proved more awkward, but that Jane distrusted emotion, and had not kissed her brothers since she came of age. Determination not to let grief master her, increased her natural air of assertion as she scrutinized Nevil's tired face and the dumb anxiety in his eyes.

'Poor boy! You looked fagged out,' she said.

'Yes. I got no sleep.'

'You came straight through, of course?'

'Yes. I couldn't possibly have got here sooner.'

'We were afraid not. Yet—one hoped. He—he seemed to want you.'

'*Did he?*' She had not the key to his suppressed eagerness. 'I wish to God I could have been here. When—when was it over?'

'About an hour ago.'

'Only an hour?' He bit his lower lip to steady it, and she turned back to the dining-room.

'Better have some tea before we talk any more,' she said, forcing the common-sense note.

'A brandy and soda. No food, thanks,' he answered, following her.

'Nonsense! There are sandwiches—and scones. I kept them hot——' She lifted the dish from the grate, where a wood-fire crackled and sputtered in defiance of July. 'Makes the room a shade less dismal,' she explained, setting the chicken before him and returning to warm her hands; for they were cold. 'It's been raining steadily for three days.'

There was a pause. Lady Roscoe, still warming her hands, tried to ignore a recurrent ache in her throat; while her brother obediently swallowed sandwiches that tasted like shavings, and threatened to choke him.

Then, leaning suddenly forward, he said huskily: 'Jane—what was it—that upset him? A shock?'

'Yes. Speculation. A big failure.'

'Thank God!' He spoke under his breath; but with such fervour of relief that she rounded on him sharply.

'Nevil! Are you quite mad?'

'No. I was afraid—by some chance, he might have heard—that it might have been——'

'No. It's not as bad as that. You're responsible for enough as it is.'

She turned back to the fire. She heard Nevil push aside his plate and empty his tumbler. Then, without looking round, she spoke again.

'If you really thought it might have that effect on him, how could you bring yourself——'

Nevil's hand came down upon the table. 'We don't want to quarrel at a time like this, Jane. The thing's done and I shall never regret it.'

'Never's a long word. You are sure it's binding—legally?'

'If it were not, I should at once take steps to make it so. That's enough.'

The quiet note of command surprised Jane, Being of the downright, athletic type, that observes little and reflects less, except on matters of practical moment, it did not occur to her that love and husbandhood had naturally made her irresponsible brother more of a man. But man or no, Jane Roscoe was in the habit of going her own way.

'Well, I'm glad you had the good sense and good taste to come by yourself,' she remarked, ignoring his last two words.

'The good sense was not mine. It was hers,' he answered with repressed heat. 'Nothing but her own express wish would have induced me to leave her alone. Luckily her father could come.' He lit a cigar. 'But Jane—about the speculation—the failure? D'you know any details?'

'No. One knew he speculated, of course. But not on such a big scale. He was writing to you when—when the stroke came.' She drew an envelope from her bag. 'I didn't read the letter. Perhaps it explains.'

He held out his hand for it, a strained hunger in his eyes. But Jane saw only the outstretched hand. For her, eyes were not windows of that heavenly stranger, the soul. They were features in the human face. She knew when they flashed anger, or held tears. The finer shades of expression escaped her. And, while she stood pondering on matters practical, which Death emphasises rather than sweeps aside, Nevil was reading his father's last words to him, shielding his face from view.

'My dear Boy,' wrote Sir George, ten minutes before his hand was stricken powerless. 'It's bad news I have to tell you, and I'm not much use on paper. Never was. Often as I've rated at your unpractical disregard of money, I'm thankful for it now. It may help to soften the blow. My own regard for the "dirty shekels" has pushed me deeper into the hell of speculation than any of you have guessed. I took to it, like dram-drinking, when your mother died, and I've kept on at it ever since. Bigger ventures each year. The luck lured me on. That and my ambition to put you into Parliament with a small fortune at your back. Money's everything these days, and when I'm gone I should turn in my grave if you couldn't keep the old Place going in the old style.'

'Well—you knocked Parliament on the head, and now a parcel of muddle-headed fools in South Africa have robbed you of the fortune I was scheming to leave you. Don't be too down on your old father, boy. I've had a black time of it, these five years, since the luck deserted me. This last plunge was a desperation stroke. But I took the soundest advice available and worried myself half crazy over it. You must believe that, old boy. It was kill or cure——'

The word that followed was a meaningless scrawl. Nevil set his teeth and breathed deeply, while all the letters on the page ran together into one blur. But he mastered himself and looked up.

'Jane—it's awful. What he must have suffered—these last months!'

Lady Roscoe nodded. 'I told you something was wrong. If you had come home—he might have spoken.'

Nevil winced at that.

'Too late for "if's",' he said a trifle hurriedly. 'Besides—how could one imagine—— It looks like a bad business. But this doesn't explain much.' He held it out to her. 'Let me have it back. George here?'

'Yes. Hal couldn't get away. But he hopes to come—later. Gee's gone into Bramleigh—on business. He's good at doing things. But you must take your right place now, Nevil.'

'Of course.'

He frowned. He was tired, jarred, unstrung. She would have liked to put a hand on his shoulder, to take the edge, if might be, off her cruel letter.

But it is the penalty of those who are afraid of emotion, that at rare moments of true feeling they are tongue-tied, prisoned in the fortress themselves have built.

So Jane Roscoe mechanically re-read the address on her father's letter, and Nevil Sinclair pushed back his chair with a sigh. 'Where's Christina?' he asked.

'Kit? She's back from Germany. Arrived this morning: just in time. Nevil'—she hesitated between pain and embarrassment—'won't you come up—to his room?'

'Yes—yes——' there were light steps in the large hall. 'That must be the Kitten,' he said in a changed tone. 'I'll see her first.'

And as Christina entered, Jane passed out.

They were as little alike as sisters could well be. Slim and fair as her brother, Christina had the Nevil eyes and brow where imagination sat enthroned; though tempered by a modified edition of the Sinclair mouth and chin. She was three-and-twenty, fresh from studying music in Germany; well up in modern theories and philosophies, but a tyro, as yet, in the greater philosophies of the heart and of life. Christina she had been baptized. Kit she was called; the longer name, however beautiful, having small chance of survival in a century dominated by the snippet, the postcard, and the monosyllable. Harold became Hal, and even George had been reduced to 'Gee.' Nevil, who was artist enough to object, had always been thankful that his own name triumphantly withstood the 'potting' process. At sight of him Christina gave a little cry.

'Oh, Nevil, my dear, I never knew you had come!'

As he rose, she flew to him, and cried a little on his shoulder, while he patted her head.

'Such a comfort to have you,' she murmured between two sniffs. 'Jane's so hard. I know she's miserable. But she wears chain-mail under her clothes, and makes one feel a hysterical fool if one breaks down.' She lifted her head and saw tears in his eyes. 'Oh, Nevil—it was awful! He—he never knew me; and—I almost wished—I had come too late. Am I a despicable coward?'

'No, no,' he said, recalling his own sensations at Monte Carlo. 'It is a natural shrinking. I quite understand.'

'You always do.' She dabbed her eyes with an ineffectual wisp of lawn, already saturate, and regarded him lovingly. 'I can hardly believe it's a whole year since I said good-bye to you at Dover. Yet you look older, graver; and I'm glad you've taken up art in earnest. It's a sort of "rainbow bridge," joining the prose and poetry in us, isn't it?'

Nevil nodded.

'But you've been a fiend about writing,' she went on, pressing his arm. 'Not a letter worth speaking of in the last three months.'

'Sorry, Christina. But we were both busy studying, weren't we?' he answered, looking thoughtfully at an impish blue flame that spurted from the crevice of a log. Then, because Christina was his sister every way, truth must out. 'Besides, two months ago—I got married.'

'Nevil! You—married?' Eager curiosity gleamed through her tears. 'But what on earth made you keep it so dark?'

'Well—there were difficulties——' he said uneasily, still studying the flame. Then thought of Lilamani shamed him, and he looked his sister in the face. 'The truth is—I've married a beautiful Indian girl of eighteen. A Hindu. I wouldn't let her change.'

'Good heavens! And you never told *any*one?'

'Only Jane. She's furious, of course.'

'Not—not father?' Voice and eyes were lowered.

'No. I knew it would upset him. I was waiting——' He bit his lip. 'Look here, Christina—I had to tell you. But we won't talk of it—yet. When—when all's over, I must announce it. Then you shall hear more——Are you horrified?' he added hastily.

'N—no. I'm sort of stupefied with amazement. But it's so romantic. So interesting. I want to hear lots more.'

'You shall. Later on. I'm going up now——' She shut her eyes and shivered. 'Sit you down there, old girl,' he said tenderly, 'and try to read.'

'Oh, I can't read. Nevil, you *are* a dear! Come back soon.'

'All right.'

Through the large hall he went, into the lesser one, and on up the broad staircase with reluctant feet.

He had felt the fact so far: not realized it. He dreaded the realization, that grew with every step through the unnatural silence of the house. The dear old man! It seemed incredible, even in the face of overwhelming proof. Instinctively the human soul rejects the fact of death, that seals the door of the charnel-house yet opens a window towards infinity. Mind and senses assert glibly: 'Dust thou art——' The soul, unconvinced, whispers: 'If in this life only we have hope——' And between both the heart of man swings like a pendulum, now this way, now that, inclining always toward the larger view; realizing, in moments of lucid vision, that the impersonal force men call death is not merely the King of Terrors, but the King of Life, which, without that inexorable shadow at the crossroads, would be shorn of half its meaning and more than half its glory.

Nevil Sinclair—man of misty beliefs and clear intuitions—had recognized this aforetime. To-day, mounting the staircase of Bramleigh Beeches, he recognized only that he had lost his father: a loss no faith in immortality could lessen or make good.

As he neared the door, Jane's black, square figure retreated down the passage. For a second or two he stood looking after her. Then he softly turned the handle and went in——.

SEVEN

'A man's foes shall be they of his own household.'

—St. Matthew

It was over. Everything was over: formalities, letters of condolence, wreaths and crosses, the thud of falling earth on Sir George's last sleeping-place, the dismal trail of carriages, the no less dismal crowds of villagers about the old church and graveyard. All the dreary panoply of woe, that is gall and wormwood to the real sufferers, boasts one justification only. It is a clumsy fashion of showing respect to the dead. Let the living endure it as best they may.

Sir Nevil Sinclair, the worst man on earth for public functions, had endured it with a fortitude and tact approved even of Jane: but this afternoon—pacing the vast lawn, where twin-cedars made a fragrant drawing-room—he was undeniably thankful to be 'through with it all.' Summer, having got over her fit of ill-temper, was once more a thing of sweetness and light. Rainbow sparkles flashed from every leaf and petal; and all the birds were out after their harvest of worms.

Ten days, now, since he had left Como and his girl-bride. More like a month, it seemed; so absolute, so abrupt had been his change of atmosphere and surroundings. The 'longest letter he ever had' reposed in his breast-pocket and a second had arrived that morning, brimful of sympathy for his loss. Brave letters, both; though beneath the surface cheerfulness, he discerned the ache of love and longing, to which his own heart throbbed passionate response. For the sake of his father it had been possible to leave her. But now that father was gone, he grudged every hour of his truancy.

And yet——!

A new sense—dormant hitherto—had been sending up green shoots through the dark and pain of this past week; the sense of possession, inherent in his race. For the mere title he cared little; for the house—with its insistence on minor tyrannies, domestic and social—less than he ought. It was the good earth herself, the good great trees of her begetting, the wide spaces of heather, beyond the pine plantation, that climbed up and up behind stables and kitchen-garden: it was these he rejoiced to have and to hold, to shield from the desecration of promiscuous building that is fast converting the Queen of Home Counties into a suburban paradise.

More than all Nevil loved the beeches that had given the place its name. Beyond a rose-garden that flanked the east wing, sprang and outspread the gracious symmetry of their trunks and limbs, grey and dull silver, dappled with mosaic of pale lichens, robed and crowned with satin-bright cascades of a million leaves. In May their emerald carpet was alight with sheets of bluebells; in early autumn brown with beech-mast, flecked with scarlet of moss-cups and fungi; and at all times patterned with every conceivable shade of green. Temple and storehouse of squirrels, song-birds, pigeons, and pheasants—religiously preserved by Sir George—the noble wood stretched on and up a bold sweep of rising ground; ending, as the pine plantation ended, in wind-swept spaces of heather, gorse, and broom.

And it was his own: all his own. Magic words that no democratic zest for parcelling out the earth in snippets will ever rob of their deep significance. But for Nevil Sinclair the legitimate joy of ownership was marred by revelations brought to light during a long morning with Reynolds, the family lawyer. He had taken his client through Sir George's papers the day after the funeral and had made the whole situation painfully clear to the new baronet, whose heritage was but a fraction of the well-ordered estate left by his grandfather, Sir Robert; an early Victorian politician of simple tastes and rigid sense of duty.

Hard not to censure the dead while those revelations were in progress. Not that Sir George had been wilfully extravagant or careless of the old Place, that was nearer and dearer to him than his God. But the Sinclairs had never been men of wealth; and from early days of possession 'things' had gone against him; a phrase conveniently comprehensive and vague. Blind to moral and spiritual values—with the complacent blindness of a certain sturdy British type, that sees life in clear-cut unlinked fragments—he had determined that his sons should not be 'hampered' by the pinch that makes character. Their allowances had been more liberal than the estate could afford. Nevil, in particular, with his artist hobbies and zest for travel, had been a costly item. But from year to year, pride and generosity combined had withheld Sir George from telling the truth. Then, in the loneliness following upon his wife's death, had come the temptation—inspiration he had deemed it then—to mend matters by gambling discreetly on the big scale. It was the one weak point in a shrewd, level-headed, if limited, nature. Secretly indulged in, it had exacted penalty to the uttermost, and poisoned the whole.

Pitiful beyond speech, it seemed to Nevil—and to Jane, the crowning irony—that the poor old man should have lost his life in straining after a fortune for which the son cared little; while the heritage, for which he did care, was flung on his hands shorn of its immemorial dignity: one-third heavily mortgaged; the rest a costly burden hard to maintain on the dwindled income left to him out of the wreck. There remained, also, his pictures, and Martino's prophecy of leaping into fame. How wise, beyond expecting, had been his undutiful decision! Jane herself must admit that; if not now, at least by the summer's end, when the Ramayana series would be near completion. A special exhibition of them, should the subject happen to 'catch on,' would at least help towards paying off the mortgage that withheld him from full mastery of his own.

But here a fresh dilemma tripped him up. Clearly it seemed his duty to remain at home for the present, to inaugurate in person the new *régime*. And behind the sense of duty lurked a natural longing to share this new possession with Lilamani, to instal her here as Queen. Yet he had given his word to her, and to her father, that this more critical phase of her transplanting should not be hastily carried out; and well he knew that the time was not yet ripe for her, or for Jane, the unappeased; possibly the unappeasable.

For although the public ordeal was over, the private ordeal had yet to come. Not until this morning had she reverted to the subject of his marriage. Throughout the week he had discerned a touch of sisterly fellow-feeling beneath her chain-mail. But the revelation in her father's last letter rankled sore; and this morning, when she requested a word or two with Nevil after breakfast, there could be no mistaking the repressed hostility in her tone. She supposed that since he had married to please himself, and was thoroughly satisfied with the arrangement, he would now see fit to announce the fact. Distressing though it was, to conceal it any longer might give a bad impression; and it had occurred to her that this afternoon, when they would all be together for tea in the large hall, would be a suitable time.

'A detailed confession of what you are pleased to consider my delinquency, in full family conclave? Is that the programme?' he asked, frowning, and looking out across the lawn where a solitary blackbird pranced and piped, serenely indifferent to everything but worms.

'Put it that way, if you like,' she answered with composure. 'I merely meant it would be as well that you should tell your news in person, before the boys and Uncle Bob go away. I haven't even mentioned it yet to Ned.'

'Very considerate of you!' said Nevil in an even tone. 'Ned' was Lord Roscoe, a milder, less formidable person than his wife; and Nevil, seeing her determination to make things hard for him, denied her the satisfaction of knowing how well she was succeeding.

'I'm quite ready, when they are,' he had concluded casually, as he left her.

And now—he knew that they were ready; very much ready—and that he was not.

They had been marshalled into the large hall, nine of them; for the Sinclairs were a clannish family, and those who did not live in or near London had stayed on a few days at Jane's request. While he flagrantly kept them waiting, Nevil pictured them all discussing him in subdued tones; mildly curious; and thankful, in secret, for some thing, fresh to think of; though none but Christina would honestly have confessed the fact.

From all save her he anticipated disapproval, if not hostility. She and he had sat up till midnight in the study one evening and had talked it all out. He had shown her the big carbon photo of his portrait and converted her into a hot partisan. But of the rest there was little hope: his two brothers, well-groomed, conventional types of the professions they adorned; George's fiancée, Phillippa Weston—commonly called Phil; Miss Julia Sinclair, cultured, within due limits, and devoted to good works; Sir Robert Sinclair, a leading light of the Foreign Office, lately retired, and his wife, Lady Margaret, daughter of a Scottish peer, mannered, suave, unimpeachably correct. Beyond these remained only Jane herself, Lord Roscoe—a sound Conservative, though too purely a student and a philosopher to approve his wife's vehement party-spirit; and Jeffrey Moss, Vicar of Bramleigh, a second cousin once removed. For the Bramleigh living was in the Sinclairs' gift, and it behoved them to 'keep it in the family.' Nevil suspected that Sunday's casual invitation for Tuesday had been given with this event in view; a suspicion that did not allay his repressed irritation or facilitate the task in hand.

Not all his loyalty to Lilamani could make so public a confession other than distasteful to a man of Nevil's temperament. His very insight put him at a disadvantage. He understood these Sinclairs far better than they understood him. He could see the thing through their eyes; could gauge to a nicety their half-nervous, half-resentful attitude towards the abnormal, more especially when that particular devil entered into a pillar of the house.

He drew out his watch and whistled softly. In common decency he could keep away no longer; and passing through the great domed conservatory, he entered the large hall.

Sir Robert—thick-set and slightly convex, with clipped beard and *pince-nez* perched at an inquiring angle—dominated the hearth-rug, by instinct, though no fire justified his attitude. The rest made dismal black patches about the room; and Jane stood at the heavy gate-leg table, dispensing tea. Her eyes challenged Nevil's as he entered. He returned her look without flinching; greeted the Vicar and joined Sir Robert on the hearthrug.

'Well, my lad, we've been wondering what had come to you,' said the leading light of the Foreign Office; and a heavy hand on Nevil's shoulder, acutely reminiscent of Sir George, sent a pang through his son's heart, 'Where've you been—eh?'

'Strolling round the place. Taking things in,' Nevil answered in a level tone, so unusual with him that Christina looked up and Sir Robert remarked, as one who makes a discovery:

'A goodly heritage, boy.'

His nephew nodded absently, one hand stroking and twisting his moustache, a gesture Christina, knew of old.

'Tea, Nevil?' from Jane.

'Please.'

He roused himself; fetched it, and made room for his cup among a crowd of small bronzes on the mantelpiece: pheasants, dogs, foxes, and others. They had been a weakness of his father's; and most of them were his own boyish gifts.

While he displaced them thoughtfully, an under-current of talk revived between Lord Roscoe and the Vicar, George and Miss Weston.

Then fell the question he dreaded. It was Sir Robert again: Chairman of the Committee, thought his disrespectful nephew, in half-amused irritation.

'Well, Nevil, what's the great secret you've got up your sleeve? Jane's been making us curious. Good news, I hope. We need it.'

'The best possible news, so far as I'm concerned,' Nevil answered, not without a hint of defiance. Dread confession as he might; to apologize, even remotely, for Lilamani, was an insult nothing should induce him to offer her. 'The fact is—while I was abroad I got married.'

'The devil you did!' Sir Robert's amazement rippled round the room in a broken murmur. 'That's news indeed! Nothing like marriage to check your craze for continental life. Money—I hope? The Place calls for it. But what have you done with the lady? She ought to be here.'

'She ought; I admit; if the circumstances were normal. But—they're not.'

'Eh—what's that? Not normal?' Sir Robert peered distressfully over his nippers at the two girls. 'What the deuce have you been up to now, Nevil? Don't tell *me* you've married a variety actress, or a foreigner?'

'I suppose you want the truth,' Nevil said, sipping his tea. 'My wife happens to be an Indian girl; a Hindu of very good family, cultivated, beautiful——'

'But—but—good Lord! A native! Good Lord!' Sir Robert broke in testily, his dismay echoed by minor explosions from Harold and George; while Miss Sinclair dropped her knitting with a gasp. She rather prided herself on being broad-minded; had lately called on two Romanists in her neighbourhood, and found them 'really quite estimable people—up to their lights——' But a Hindu! And poor George's son——!

'Perhaps—a converted Hindu, dear Nevil?' she ventured, dreading an outburst from her hot-tempered brother at a moment when even raised voices jarred her sense of fitness and decorum.

'No. She's not converted. Nor likely to be,' Nevil answered bluntly.

'But, dear boy, surely it would be possible to——? Our good Jeffrey is so convincing; and Hindus, I have always heard, are remarkably intelligent and open to reason——'

'Yes, Aunt Julia. My wife is quite remarkably intelligent.' A spark of the Sinclair temper flashed in Nevil's eyes, and lent an edge to his quiet tone. 'She knows the Bible better than some of us do; and religion means a great deal more to her than to the average Christian——'

'Come, come, Nevil! No blasphemy——' Sir Robert interposed with repressed heat.

'Blasphemy, Uncle? I am stating a fact; and I want to make it clear that there will not be any call for Jeffrey's good offices, when I do see fit to bring my wife home.'

'You mean to bring her *here*, then? A heathen Lady Sinclair, under your father's roof?'

'Certainly. In time. What else?'

'The devil knows what else! Thank God George has been spared *this*,' he added, lowering his voice. Then he swung round sharply. 'What do you think of your brother's madness, Jane?'

'I have told Nevil quite frankly what I think,' said she. 'Outside his own infatuation, there can be no two opinions on the subject.'

But such arrogant assumption of certainty was too much for Christina, who, for Nevil's sake, had repressed herself valiantly so far. Now she leaned forward, defiance in her eyes.

'There *can* be two opinions, outside infatuation. Because there's mine. I don't want to seem impertinent, but I never thought you would all be so narrow-minded, so insular——'

'Be quiet, Kit,' sharply, from Jane. 'You *are* impertinent; and your opinion goes for nothing.'

'Doesn't it, indeed? I'm not so sure,' quoth the nineteenth-century rebel, less easily quenched than her of the eighties.

In vain she tried to catch Nevil's eye. He had half turned his back, and was rearranging the small bronzes, seemingly indifferent to the tea-cup tempest. But Christina knew better. She longed to hit out furiously at them all; or to get up and throw her arms round his neck. But again she knew better.

'More tea, George?' came the voice of Jane, the inexorable.

Captain Sinclair handed his cup, and Lord Roscoe went quietly out. As a peace-loving man, family dissensions offended his taste, and a certain look in Jane's eyes was always a signal for retreat. A glance over his shoulder drew the Vicar after him. Lady Margaret, bored and a little disgusted, followed in their wake. Phillippa glanced tentatively at her lover, who was scowling into his tea-cup; and she, being young and curious, kept her seat.

Then Sir Robert—seeing that nothing remained but to accept the lamentable fact—said with less heat: 'Well, Nevil, your minor eccentricities have been a joke to this one. But since you've tied yourself for life to an Asiatic, there's no more to be said. A civil marriage, I suppose?'

'Yes.'

'And may we be allowed to know your immediate plans?'

'I must return to Italy as soon as things are more or less in order. Probably the end of this week.'

'And shut up the Beeches?'

'Why not? But as George is on leave, he might as well put in his time here and see to things a bit. Jane, I know, considers him a good deal fitter for that sort of thing than myself.'

'Thanks, old chap. Awfully good of you.' George's tone suggested sarcasm. 'Leave you free to devote yourself to the enchantress—eh?'

'I'm hard at work on a series of pictures,' Nevil answered, addressing his uncle and ignoring the thrust. 'I hope to exhibit them this winter. I've done one since my marriage of which Signor Martino thinks very highly.'

'The picture you wrote of?' asked Jane.

'No. That was her portrait. I gave it to her father.'

'H'm.'

This was more than Christina could stand. 'He's got a ripping big photo of it upstairs,' she broke out eagerly. 'You *ought* to see it. Nevil, really they ought. Mayn't I fetch it?'

'Yes, if you like,' he answered indifferently, chilled to disgust by their reception of his news.

Miss Sinclair glanced up, mildly expectant.

'Dear Nevil, I am *so* glad there is a picture—' Devotion to the entire family tree, even unto the remotest tips of its many branches, was a part of her creed. Hindu or no, by some means she must manage to assimilate this new niece.

Christina reappeared in no time, lifting her trophy high, for all to see, and a murmur of reluctant admiration went round the room.

Miss Sinclair held out a hand. 'Let me look at it closer, dear. My sight is not what it was.'

She looked closer and her brown eyes grew wide. 'Why, Nevil, she is really beautiful! And this is *your* work?'

'Yes.'

'No wonder your Italian friend thinks well of it. Remarkable. Look, Robert.'

'H'm. Very good-looking. Quite life-like. You've come on extra-ordinarily, Nevil, I must say.'

'Yes. Thanks to my wife. Leseppes, the great French painter and critic, expects me to make a name. Lucky—as things stand—that I did take up art seriously. Bramleigh Beeches needs the shekels, eh, Jane?'

'Very much so. If they ever come in,' she answered, her gaze fixed searchingly on the new Lady Sinclair's face. 'This is promising. Very. It's your staying power I doubt.'

Without further comment, she passed the picture on to George; who glanced at it half in disdain; then whistled softly.

'My word, but she's a beauty! Trust Nevil! What age, old chap?'

'Eighteen,' said Nevil, jarred by a savour of the stable in his brother's tone. But George, serenely unobservant, added, with the experienced sagacity of four years' service in India: 'M', yes. From seventeen to twenty native girls are about as alluring as they make 'em, even the commoner sort. The deuce of it is they're middle-aged by thirty. Run to flesh, and——'

'Damn you, shut up!' Nevil flashed out, losing control of himself at last.

'Nevil—*dear*!' she protested in dismay; and Christina, snatching away the photo, muttered wrathfully: 'Upon my word, George! You *are* a beast!'

'Sorry, Nevil,' the delinquent remarked grudgingly. 'I was only telling you the truth.'

'It's not the truth—altogether. The—the premature ageing is chiefly the country; their feeding; their way of life. It doesn't follow that Lilamani——'

'Lila—which?' from Harold, who had been more amused than otherwise by what he privately dubbed 'a family scrap.'

'Lilamani,' Nevil repeated with quiet emphasis, and was thankful that just then Sir Robert emerged abruptly from his reflections.

'Look here, my dear boy. I'm still in a fog. You haven't told us yet how this incredible affair came to pass.'

'Another time, Uncle Bob,' replied Nevil, unfeigned weariness in his tone. 'I've had about all I can put up with at a sitting.'

At that Jane rose, decision in every square inch of her. 'If you don't mind, I'll ask you all to go now. Nevil and I must finish talking this out alone.'

'Quite so, my dear; quite so,' fussily, from Sir Robert. 'Whatever you think best.'

And they went.

Then Jane turned to her brother.

'Now, Nevil.'

'Well? What?'

Both spoke quietly; yet it was as if a pair of duellists had unsheathed swords.

'How *can* you talk calmly of returning to Italy this week, when you know quite well that your rightful place is here?'

'Of course it is. If there were not very good reasons for my being elsewhere—just now. My rightful place, if it comes to that, is—with my wife.'

'And she refuses——?'

Nevil smiled, in spite of himself.

'If you knew her, even slightly, you wouldn't ask such an absurd question. It is *I* who refuse to bring her here—yet. In the first place, if Martino isn't quite misguided, the set of pictures I am working at should be worth more to Bramleigh Beeches than my presence here this summer; and I want to get them done, or nearly done, in the right atmosphere. Then——' he hesitated. 'You may as well have it straight. I refuse point-blank to bring my wife to her future home till

I have clear proof that she will be decently received by you and all the rest of them.'

It was Jane's turn to hesitate.

'What—precisely do you mean by that?' she asked without looking at him.

'I mean kindly, affectionately. Just as you would receive Miss Weston if George were in my place.'

'My dear Nevil, there's a difference! You ask a good deal——'

'I don't ask. I am stating conditions.'

'And suppose the conditions—fail to satisfy you?'

'I am supposing,' he answered coldly, 'that my relatives, even if narrow and prejudiced, are at least human beings; that they will— later, if not now—give the woman, who is to fill my mother's place, a fair chance of proving that she too is human, lovable, admirable—— Good Lord, Jane,' he broke out, maddened past endurance by her chill antagonism. 'If I'd married a Hottentot or an American negro, I could excuse you. But I presume even you will acknowledge that there's some racial connection between Indians and Europeans, which makes all the difference in the world.'

Jane drew herself up.

'Of course I see that, Nevil. I may be prejudiced. I'm not ignorant. It's quite bad enough, in any case. But after all—we gain nothing by recriminations. And as this child of eighteen will be virtually the head of the family, we can but make the best of her.'

'Make her *feel welcome*,' Nevil corrected, with emphasis. 'Write to her before she comes.'

'Yes. If you wish it. One can say the usual polite things. Kit, at least, can say them honestly. Does she read English with ease?'

'She's as well-read as Christina.' He drew out his lettercase and handed her—not without reluctance—Lilamani's June Love-Song. 'She wrote that.'

Jane read it, with raised brows: evidently impressed though so unrestrained an outpouring of 'sentiment' was, in her view, almost indecent.

'Talented. And very devoted,' she said in a changed tone, handing it back. 'I'll write to her, Nevil—later on, as nicely as I can.'

But her brother, though mollified, was still sore from the afternoon's ordeal, which was her doing.

'It's just as well you should write her a decent letter or two, Jane,' said he with a direct look, not to be misread. 'Considering all things, you owe that much, at least, to her—*and* to me.'

For once in her life Jane Roscoe was quite put out of countenance; and before she could recover herself—Nevil was gone.

Four days later he left for Italy: for Lilamani, and the Ramayana pictures—and peace.

EIGHT

'In two little rooms my heart divides,
Joy, wide awake, in one resides,
While slumbering Sorrow in the other hides.
Oh, joy, sing gently in thy glee,
Lest Sorrow wake through hearing thee.'

—Heine

The Lake of Como in July is only for the native born; or for banished Lilamanis, who rejoice alike in the heat and the absence of vagrant humanity. But for all Sir Lakshman's fatherly indulgence, that fortnight had seemed to the bird with one wing the longest two weeks in her life.

While irate and bewildered Sinclairs were passing their parochial, though not unnatural judgment upon her, she lay alone in the night, wondering sore whether 'That Terrible' were trying to wean her lord from his 'foolish passion beyond control of reason.' His letters were full of tender devotion: but when night came, the spirit of Jane prevailed. That haunting sentence pricked her like a thorn left under the skin, and would continue so to do till time should prove things definitely one way or another. But by day she smiled bravely, because her father must not guess; and, as often happens, in sowing courage, she reaped happiness—of a kind.

Sir Lakshman, intent on distracting her thoughts, had lured her into excursions up and down the Lake, and even across to Lugano. Then, in the quiet of their chalet, they had enjoyed an informal reversion to the 'studies' of early days, peculiarly welcome to the man, who by rights, should have been back in India weeks ago. But the lure of the West, that grew in him with the years, was intensified now by the wish to remain within reach of his child. Stifling the voice of conscience, therefore, he had secured leave for a longer stay, and had written smooth things to Mataji, who tyrannized triumphantly in his absence, yet hated, with a vitriolic hate, the unseen power that took him oftener and oftener from her side. And, in a sense, she was justified of her hate: she—mother of his sons, controller of his household, guardian of his immortal soul, whose after-fate he imperilled year upon year by these futile journeys across the 'black water,' with its mysterious power to defile. Loyal though he was to his own Motherland, the Big Mother drew him, as she draws all who drink of the well of knowledge; drew him into the vortex of that unresting flux, which, while satisfying desire—of mind and body, if not of soul—recreates it at every turn. Multiplicity of desire—that is the Alpha and Omega of our mercurial civilization, that runs ceaselessly to and fro, in quest of fresh stimulant, fresh satisfaction of a hunger that grows by what it feeds on. Hence the insidious danger of Western education for the keen brain and sensuous nature of the East.

After the dazzling complexity and movement of Paris and London, the fundamental simplicity of Indian life beneath all its barbaric splendour, is apt to lack flavour; and though, in a sense, discontent may be divine, it does not touch all spirits to fine issues. Unhappily for awakening India the average result hitherto is sterile dissatisfaction; time and money spent out of the country; home duties left undone. That the exceptions are most often brilliant exceptions—doubly endowed, with the wisdom of the East by heritage, and the knowledge of the West by acquisition—does not disprove the critical nature of the ordeal. Sir Lakshman—himself a brilliant exception—was yet, in some ways, a less satisfactory working force in the great native state he served, than men of half his ability whose hearts and minds were not torn between opposing interests and beliefs. As a husband, also, he wearied increasingly of the dissonance inherent in a house divided against itself: a dissonance that makes the home-life of the 'England-returned' one of the saddest features of a progress-at-any-price age. But, when all is said of drawbacks and dissonance, there remains the existence of a real Indian renaissance, working, like all true growth, from within outward, to what ultimate end who shall prophesy—as yet?

In Sir Lakshman's home, the daughter after his own heart had been the main redeeming feature; and, bereft of her, he came near to dreading return. The fortnight she found so long had, for him, been all too short.

It was over now. To-night the man who had robbed him of his treasure would return to claim his own. To-morrow he supposed he must be gone. But Lilamani would not hear of that. Nevil would surely have much to ask him of the Ramayana pictures. He need not think to escape so easily!

Would she not like to go over and meet her lord, he asked, the little station of Menaggio—or even at Lugano. But she shook her head; eyes darkly shining; and he understood. This meeting, after long absence, was a thing too charged with sacred emotion to take place anywhere but in their garden of dreams. Let her have patience, only a little, and he would come in the Hour of Union—their veriest hour; even as the sun, husband of earth, descends after day's work to meet her at the time of sleep.

And so it was. In the Hour of Union, he came. Sitting on the balcony they sighted the little white boat afar off. She fluttered a handkerchief, leaning over the rails; and he, standing up recklessly, waved his hat.

Down she sped into the garden, and there awaited him in a shadowed corner near the bench where he had won her back to life and love. She heard the keel kiss the shore; saw the slim, alert figure—dark now, because of his loss—hurrying up the slope with long strides.

Then, as he sighted her—his low call: 'Lilamani'; and her throbbing answer:

'King of me. I am here.'

The rest was sacred to themselves and the unheeding stars, that trembled into life one after one, while they two lingered, heart against heart, humanly loath to let the good minute go.

'Darling, did it seem so long?'

'Endless ages—to me, waiting. For you it was different. So much to think, to do—to suffer.' She stroked the dark sleeve of his coat. 'But now—all is past. Come in the little nest. Father will be waiting us. He is saying he must go to-morrow. But we will not push him away first minute, will we?'

'Of course not. He likes the picture?'

'Yes. He is so pleased over all. Not sorry now for trusting me to English husband! Oh—and Nevil, he will tell you—such a plan! I hope you agree.'

'Something to do with you?'

'Yes, yes. With all three.'

'Come on then. Let's hear it. I couldn't refuse you anything to-night—Lady Sinclair!'

But having brought father and husband together, she left them 'to talk the plan' at leisure. She herself had inevitably some mysterious dish on hand in honour of her lord's return.

Sir Lakshman greeted his son-in-law with genuine, if restrained friendliness, and regret for his loss; regret privately increased by a natural anxiety as to its effect upon his daughter's immediate future. They spoke for a while of Sir George, of the crippled estate, of Nevil's prospects as artist and landowner. Then came the crucial question.

'You ought now to remain in England, and look after this home of your ancestors?'

'Yes—I believe I ought,' Nevil answered, pensively twisting his father's signet-ring.

'Then you came back only to fetch Lilamani, and other belongings?'

Nevil's direct look put the Hindu out of countenance.

'Sir Lakshman, I gave you my word.'

'H'm. The word of an Englishman. I should have known. But remember, Nevil, I have had dealings with all kinds of humans. Even the Englishman is not immaculate! And men of all races, desiring some great gift, are ready for big promises that afterwards they may conveniently forget.'

Nevil smiled.

'True enough. But I think you may trust me, sir. Not that I'm any better than the rest. Only—I love my wife a deal too well to run risks with her happiness.' He flushed awkwardly in making the confession; adding, yet more awkwardly: 'A man doesn't speak of such things. But I *do* want to give you confidence in me.'

'That I have more and more; especially since these days spent alone with her. And—your family——?'

Nevil, not unprepared, looked steadily out of the window.

'My elder sister will write and make her welcome—and be good to her, though they won't have much in common. My younger sister—more like myself—is longing to know her. My brothers are seldom at home. They all admired her picture. Then—there is Mrs. Despard——'

'Yes. That is good. She understands like few of your race. And you mean to return—by what time?'

'Not till the summer's over—they're having a wretched one at home—and my new picture's nearly done. But what's the great plan she spoke of that concerns all three of us?'

'Ah, that——' Sir Lakshman's face lit up. 'Since I do not now sail till September, I was thinking how delightful if you and she shall come only to Egypt. There we shall all spend a week together. Then I go on by next mail; you returning same time—if you will. You have seen Egypt?'

'No. I should like it of all things, only——' renewed awkwardness here—'I must think it over. I believe we might manage.'

But Sir Lakshman, guessing his thought, took him kindly by the arm.

'You do not quite take my meaning, Nevil. It is not for you to manage. The plan is mine altogether. My parting gift—you may call it—to the child. For her it will be greatest pleasure imaginable. For myself—I need not say! And you—with these bold pictures in your brain—though Egypt is much different from India, yet how excellent to feel for yourself the spirit—what you artists call atmosphere—of the East. Now—you will come?'

'Thank you, sir. It'll be splendid. Lilamani will love it, of course——' A minute prick of apprehension checked him. Would she love it more than he quite cared about? How would it affect him to see his Eastern wife among Easterns, even though not her own people?

He thrust the disturbing questions aside; and Sir Lakshman, not enlightened this time, added: 'Of course, in September it will still be hot. But that you would not mind?'

'Not a bit.'

Vaguely disconcerted, he strolled over to his easel, and they talked Ramayana till the door of the shrine opened softly, and a mother-o'-pearl Lilamani, with the buckles of Antibes on her shoes, stood looking from one to the other with questioning eyes.

It was to Nevil she spoke.

'Have you planned the plan? Is it real and true?'

'As real and true and delightful as *you* are, little wife!' he answered, smiling; and in the quaint young fashion that he loved, she clapped her small hands lightly, without sound.

Sir Lakshman stayed three days longer; and the pain of parting was alleviated by visions of 'the plan.' On the Sunday that followed, Nevil asked a question that surprised his wife.

'Lilamani, would you mind much if I deserted you this morning, and went to church?'

'To church?' She could only regard him in open-eyed amazement; and he smiled, a queer, half-sad smile, unusual with him.

'Well, darling? Did you think your Christian husband was a rank unbeliever?'

'Oh, Nevil! Please not say such things. But—I could not help from wondering—did you ever——'

The words would not come; and he, slipping an arm round her, gently kissed her cheek.

'Dear little saint! I did—and I do,' he assured her none too lucidly: yet she understood. 'The trouble with our religion nowadays is that, being a live thing, it is growing and changing its form like all other live things: breaking through husks, throwing out new leaves. But the Church says: No. The one ancient form must be kept sacred from all change, like an embalmed mummy. And in consequence, many thinking Christians have little use for Church, however honestly they believe in the things that matter. You understand?'

'I do,' she answered thoughtfully. 'Same with us. It is always so with priests. Nevil—I would like to hear more.'

'That you shall. Another time. It would need a long talk and rather a deep one, if I'm to make things clear. But you mustn't doubt my belief in the Great Unseen: and now will you spare me to go and worship Him in my own fashion?'

'Yes. I am so pleased——' She spoke without looking up; and there fell a pause.

'Well—what more?' he asked, regarding her with a quizzical tenderness.

'Only . . . I am shy to ask . . . is it quite beyond possible . . . that I come also?'

'You? My dear little wife! Will you?'

'If—if it would not make shock to the Christian peoples?'

'I think the Christian peoples might survive it!' he answered, kissing her again. 'There won't be half a dozen at this time of year.'

'And I can hide all Hindu-ness with my cloak and hood. Oh, Nevil—I hardly believe! I never thought——'

'No more did I!' He pushed her gently toward the door. 'Hurry up, little woman. We've none too much time.'

So Sir Nevil and Lady Sinclair rowed across to the little English Church at Cadenabbia; and if the Christian peoples were pricked to undue curiosity by the veiled and hooded figure in a pew near the door, the subject of their scrutiny was lifted beyond all consciousness of the fact. To-day the presence of others troubled her not at all. For to-day, by her husband's wish, she was privileged to worship, with him, that Great One, that 'Brilliance at the core of Brilliance,' whose diverse names and forms are but the manifold garments of His revealing.

The handful of 'Christian peoples,' hypnotized by ceaseless repetition, found the service, with its scanty music and unimpressive sermon, a rather lifeless affair. But to one privileged 'heathen' it seemed a thing of beauty and awe. The church itself, plain and unpretentious, like most of its kind abroad—had yet its pervasive atmosphere of sanctuary, above all in the region of the altar—shrine, she named it— where the white-robed figure, tall candlesticks and sober embroideries were glorified by sun-rays streaming through stained glass.

As for the simple hymns and chants—it was her first hearing of organ music, and the deep-toned reverberations set all her sensitive nerves a-thrill. The hidden magician—bald and spectacled—chose for voluntary a stately Largo by Beethoven; and Lilamani's hand, slipping into her husband's, kept him seated till the last note shuddered through the empty church.

Then they went forth into the blaze of noon, and rowed homeward, too deeply and diversely stirred for common speech. Only once he intercepted her brooding gaze and asked, smiling:

'Well, does our fashion of worship please you?'

'Yes. It is more simple—more solemn than ours. It speaks to the soul.'

Her husband's smile had a touch of envy. He had not found it so.

'Some day I will take you to a really great service in our Abbey,' he said; and the promise wafted her on a dream-journey that only ended when the keel touched ground.

A small event; yet of no small significance in an experiment more vital and far-reaching than they two, in their charmed seclusion, had quite recognized as yet. That first church-going led to others, at intervals; led also to more intimate talk of the 'big-little things'; a strengthening of links for the long after-strain of marriage.

For the rest, throughout the blazing stillness of July and August, they dwelt in an atmosphere of ordered peace, as needful to artistic achievement as emotion and experience to artistic conception. And it was just this absorption in a subject quite outside themselves that saved them from those lavish overdrafts on the emotions that are the peculiar danger of honeymoon conditions indefinitely prolonged. They talked Ramayana, read Ramayana, and lived Ramayana, without fear that either could weary of the obsession. Sir Lakshman's treasures from India supplied fresh fuel for the divine fire, that burned clearer and stronger as the bold pictures came to life under Nevil's hand. Martino—vindictively jealous of all who trespassed on his sacred sea and sky—could rejoice whole-heartedly in the growing vigour and beauty of his friend's work. His monologues became more volcanic; his prophecies more extravagant. He spent more time in Nevil's studio than in his own; now and again bringing a brother artist to confirm his verdict, lest it seem mere partiality to the man who felt himself in the grip of a power greater than he knew.

Outside the pictures, worked at day by day and dreamed of at night, their only events were constant letters from Sir Lakshman and rarer ones from the house of Sinclair. Christina, zealous to atone for Jane, wrote in genuine sisterly fashion to her 'dearest Lilamani,' regretting that she must be back in Germany by October, not to return again for good till early spring. And Jane wrote also; kindly—yet with a difference, which 'the Hindu child' was not considered capable of detecting. But she did. She discovered, also, that, while she had supposed herself to be obeying Nevil in regard to that first letter, it had in truth so tinctured all her thoughts of Lady Roscoe, that mere sight of the square handwriting awakened a fierce antagonism, personal and racial, that boded ill for the days to come. Between the formal phrases of welcome her quick spirit caught flashes of the two-edged sword. Yet, for Nevil's sake, she must seem convinced; must even devise an answer, not too carefully studied, lest he suspect. What the writing of it cost her, he never knew. Nor did he know how, when it was written, she tore Jane's compulsory welcome across and across; then burned the pieces one by one in her brick oven, holding them in her dwarf tongs; watching them curl and blaze with a gleam of primitive hate in her eyes that her husband must never see. Could he have seen it, he might have thought twice about taking his wife home at all.

As it was, Lilamani's answer pleased him; and the ardour of work—that, for the moment, eclipsed all else—flowed over the incident, as the rising tide over a rock that will rear its head anew in the time of shallows.

NINE

'Naught is done that has not seeds in it.'

—Morley Roberts

For both husband and wife, as for Sir Lakshman, September arrived too soon. Not even the lure of Egypt could make Lilamani other than loath to leave a corner of earth saturate with memories, sacred and imperishable as her love itself: and to Nevil, as the time drew near, there returned that faint prick of apprehension for which he hated himself the more because he could not disregard it altogether. But Lilamani on the sea was a revelation enchanting enough to banish all forebodings for a time; and present content was deepened by the knowledge that—conceit apart—he had achieved a remarkable summer's work.

In the seven weeks following on his return, three more pictures had been added to Sita in the hut: her first pleading with Rama—that, as a portrait of Lilamani, excelled his study at Antibes; the setting forth of the three; and the abduction of Sita by Ravan. The completion of each had bred a larger confidence, a deeper understanding of the great subject chosen and inspired by his wife: while into the fourth he had infused a strange mingling of beauty and terror that at once amazed him and fired his ambition to bolder flights. A fifth picture, even, had been started: Sita, broken with grief, in the garden of Asoka, while she-fiends, on guard among the high enclosing bushes, leered at her through the dusk; their hideous shapes, half human, half bestial, grimly suggested rather than seen. They had given Lilamani nightmares; and her self-identification with Sita had so wrought upon her nerves, that she was not sorry to escape from the haunting nearness of Ravan and his myrmidons, for a time.

With Nevil it was otherwise. To tear himself from easel and canvas and the idea that dominated him was a greater wrench than he would have credited six months ago. But, in this crowning summer of his life, a very rage of work possessed him; a spontaneous flow of inspiration, not to be denied. It was as if all the thwarted and dammed-up energies of those priceless years between twenty and thirty, having at last found their natural outlet, would give him no rest till they had atoned, in some measure, for achievement stultified and opportunities lost.

Happily for Lilamani, she herself was the mainspring of her husband's inspiration; while her absorption in his subject and her Eastern capacity for long spells of stillness made her an invaluable asset to his actual work. And afar, on the horizon of his golden present, the promise of the future glowed like a lamp. In Egypt he looked to imbibe large draughts of the colourful East; not in the self-conscious, note-book-and-pencil fashion of the journalist, but with all his creative fervour in abeyance, that the receptive faculties might have full play. Then, returning by Brindisi, they would spend a last fortnight in their land of enchantment before putting the Great Experiment to its ultimate test.

It had already been arranged that 'Dreaming' should make its appearance in the Goupil Gallery at an autumn exhibition of English painters; and Martino looked that this picture alone should bring Sinclair's name into notice among the elect; thus preparing the way for his bold design of showing the Sita series independently when complete. Pamphlets, giving a brief outline of the Epic, should be supplied to all-comers, with a special description of each chosen scene; and Martino himself would brave the unspeakable English climate that he might have the pride and pleasure of inaugurating the Unique Event! Even Leseppes, prince of egoists, had shown keen interest in the new venture and promised a flying visit to Cadenabbia before Sinclair left.

With such stimulating visions and a radiant Lilamani for company, Nevil paid small heed to the whisper of apprehension during the brief voyage from Brindisi to Cairo; and through the first few days of varied and leisurely sightseeing, he strove loyally to convince himself that all was well. But upon the fourth day conviction went to pieces. Too late he recognized the wisdom of his instinctive recoil from Sir Lakshman's plan.

Hitherto he had seen the East through Lilamani's eyes, veiled and glorified by her idealism. Now he saw it in the fierce unsparing glare of its own sunlight; saw, too, how potently it drew and held the woman who had renounced it for love of him. True, it was not India; and the familiar-looking folk in street and desert spoke an unknown tongue. But the East, Near or Far, has its own indefinable atmosphere; and to Nevil Sinclair it was obvious that Lilamani drank it in as though it were the breath of life. An under-current of suppressed excitement vibrated in her low voice, and glowed fitfully in the brooding softness of her eyes. Acute consciousness of it pricked her husband to a not unreasoning jealousy, and even checked in a measure his own ardour of enjoyment.

On the fourth day in question, he found her standing at the window of Sir Lakshman's private sitting-room, so absorbed in the street scene below that his entrance passed unheeded. He was almost at her elbow when she turned with a startled sound; and though her lips smiled a greeting, he saw the gleam of tears in her eyes.

'What is it, dear?' he asked.

'Not anything,' she replied mendaciously, for she missed the note of sympathy in his voice.

The touch of her fingers on his coat sleeve elicited no response; and, after a second's hesitation, he said: 'I'd sooner have the truth, Lilamani. You're not like yourself since you came. It excites you, upsets you, all this perhaps—makes you regret——?'

'Oh Nevil! Could you think such a thing?' Her fingers closed sharply on his arm. 'Only—how can I help?—if it aches me sometimes, with reminding of my own country, my own peoples. Even though I cannot know their language; still, by their colour and movement—even by smell of shops and streets—all is speaking to me in the language of my heart. Have I made you understand?'

'Yes—yes. It's only natural. So long as it doesn't spoil your pleasure, I am content.'

But although he patted the hand that held him, his tone belied his words, and he spoke looking down into the street, with its flow of noisy, leisurely life, its blinding patches of light and clear-cut, blue-black shadows.

A puzzled distress and the nearness of tears kept her silent; and he, with a muttered plea of letters to write, went out, leaving her a shade more puzzled, more distressed.

What was wrong? What was the nameless shadow that had come between them, dimming the radiance of her perfect week? For the past two days she had been vaguely aware of it; and now—his words, his manner, so unlike himself.

She brushed away the disturbing thought as if it were a fly that buzzed at her ear. But even as the fly returns, after futile circling, so the feeling came back, whenever some spontaneous outburst on her part forced Nevil to a show of response. Months of the real thing made her fatally quick to detect the counterfeit; and it saddened her beyond speech.

On the next night, when Sir Lakshman offered them another week at the hotel after he left, Sinclair would not see the eager pleading in his wife's face, while he thanked his father-in-law, and urged the need of finishing the picture on hand before going home in October. Yet after all, touched by her loyal seconding of his refusal, he stayed on three days—and regretted it. There were moments of unreasoning, yet invincible revulsion, when he could scarcely endure the sight of those other Eastern women who, in a dozen trifling ways, so subtly reminded him of his wife; robbing her, thus, of the unique quality that was for him an essential part of her charm. True, in happier intervals, he had absorbed much and observed much that was invaluable to an artist who aspired to interpret the East: but it was with a sense of undiluted relief that he trod the deck of their homeward-bound steamer and felt the hidden heart of it throb beneath his feet.

Not so Lilamani. Standing alone at the taffrail, while her husband interviewed the head-steward, she drank in every detail of the fast-retreating coast-line, as if by intensity of looking she would stamp it for ever on her brain—that fervent and colourful East which spoke to her so feelingly in the language of her heart. No denying that this brief return to the atmosphere of her girlhood and the subsequent parting with her father had brought home to her the completeness of her own severance as nothing else could have done; had stirred afresh the ache of longing drugged, of late, by happiness almost beyond belief.

Yet did she not forget the price of return; the *impasse* from which her husband's love had so miraculously saved her: and even had it not been thus, regret were unthinkable. To belong body and soul to Nevil was, without question, the best fate that could befall a woman. Only, at this moment of parting, a perplexing conflict of emotions so perturbed her that when, at length, her husband came to her side, she could not turn and greet him because of chill tears that crept down her cheeks.

Nevil saw them, and for the first time they moved him to irritation rather than pity. His tone betrayed him.

'Crying again, Lilamani? Wishing you could have gone on with your father, I suppose, instead of having to come back with me?'

She winced and bit her lip. 'Unkind to speak so,' she murmured without looking round.

'I'm sorry. But you provoke it. You seem so heartbroken——'

'Not that. Only—a little sad. How can I help?'—then controlling herself, she looked up at him, smiling mistily. 'But it is foolishness. And surely—we shall come again?'

He frowned. 'I don't know. There won't be much surplus money for pleasure trips just at present. I've a big place to keep up, you see, and precious little to keep it on.'

'How pity,' she said softly, not quite following the drift of his last remark.

Again the vanishing coast-line absorbed her; and he, still frowning, regarded her delicate profile in a speculative silence. Then he turned abruptly away; and strolling down the deck, soon fell into talk with the first officer.

Left alone again, the tears fell faster; till, in shame at her own weakness, and fearful of discovery, though dusk had fallen, she stumbled blindly down to their cabin—alone. In crossing the hatchway, she caught sight of Nevil and his companion pacing the deck. He saw her go. She knew it. But the minutes passed and he did not come. He was content to walk and talk with a stranger, while she lay crying softly in the half-dark; not only because the East was slipping farther from her with every throb of the ship's pulses, but because the radiance of her wonderful ten days had been dimmed by a shadow whose substance she could not divine.

So deeply and entirely had they lived hitherto in the world of imagination and emotion, wherein their unity was complete, that she scarce recognized, as yet, the possibility of serious divergence. She only knew that for near a week they had been living in a tangle of cross purposes which she was powerless to unravel; that now, for the first time, her tears had moved him to vexation, and he had left her to find her way about this strange ship alone: events of no mean significance in the early stage of marriage. But why? What harm had she done to cause this break in his unfailing tenderness; this first real sense of apartness from him who was more than ever her all, since India had claimed her father? Only one answer suggested itself. Always, at such moments, that unforgettable sentence in Jane's letter would prick softly, like a thorn left under the skin, reminding her—'I am here.'

By the time he came into the cabin, tears had ceased and bending down he kissed her flushed cheek; then, without a word, passed a soothing hand over her hair. She caught the hand and pressed it passionately to her lips. So, once again, comfort was restored—for the moment. Yet still—she did not understand: and therein lay the seeds of tragedy.

Egypt once out of sight things readjusted themselves insensibly, though the effect produced on Nevil could not be lightly shaken off. There was no more jarring irritability. But there were times when his wife was still aware of that intangible barrier; times when he was so absent and distrait that she felt as if the real Nevil had slipped miles away from her and only the shell of him lay beside her in the long deck-chair. Once, when she ventured on comment, he had frowned as if interrupted in a train of thought, and answered that between digesting new impressions and heavy responsibilities ahead, he had a good deal on his mind just then: which was true, though not the whole truth, as she was quick to divine.

Thenceforward she kept silence. But her thoughts were less easily bridled than speech, and during that short return voyage, she found herself too often at their mercy. On most nights Nevil would take her down to the cabin, and there leave her, while he himself returned to pace the deck in troubled meditation; faintly, indefinably alienated by a nameless something too elusive for definition; hating himself heartily; yet temporarily at the mercy of his mood. More than ever was he thankful for the few weeks of seclusion in store for them at Cadenabbia. Both being hypersensitive to the spirit of place, and of association, he relied confidently on these to restore that completeness of harmony, of fusion, without which he scarce dared contemplate the last great test of England and Bramleigh Beeches.

In this reliance they were unconsciously at one. Through the long hours when she was supposed to be asleep, Lilamani lay listening, instead, to the rhythmical swish-swish under her port-hole and the heart-throbs of the ship that bore her, minute by minute, nearer to the familiar peace of their sanctuary. There at least she had reigned supreme; there she had been essential both to his life and work; the woman's incurable need. There, surely, this shadow of division, of disappointment, would pass.

Yes, it was disappointment; that she had decided; having arrived at her own solution of the problem in those wakeful hours; a solution characteristic of her race. Six months a wife and yet no promise of that other—the supreme gift, that should crown her first one, the finding of himself. For the Eastern woman, marriage means motherhood, or an abiding sense of failure: and the least delay in the fulfilment of her divine mission breeds a lurking anxiety lest the worst befall. Already it knocked softly at the door of Lilamani's heart, and that it should visit her husband also seemed to her the most natural thing imaginable. He too had hoped. He too was disappointed. And although his tender consideration forbade speech, he could not hide it altogether from one who loved and understood.

Thus she wove around his perplexing mood her primitive-womanly myth that was leagues removed from the truth; and longed only for courage to broach the subject, that pain might be lessened by sharing. But the mere imagining wrought her to such agony of shyness that she knew speech could not be between them—as yet. She could only wait—and pray. In the meantime she hoped great things from the spirit of peace that dwelt in their balcony, their little white boat, and their garden of dreams. Absorbed once more in their joint enterprise, the evil demons of vexation and disappointment must be driven out— if only for a time.

And it was so. The spirit of place and the very real love Nevil Sinclair had for his wife achieved their perfect work. The mood of aloofness vanished as though it had never been; and again, as after the lesser interruption of Jane's letter, the ardour of work flowed on over the incident, blotting it almost out of memory.

Lesseppes' promised visit proved a foretaste of triumphs to come. He applauded Martino's verdict; insisted upon hearing long extracts from the Ramayana; and covered Lilamani with confusion by advertising his admiration with a frankness of gaze that in her view amounted to insolence. For himself, he enjoyed her embarrassment. It added a provocative quality to her beauty; and to stare a pretty woman into a Crimson silence was a delectable amusement that never palled. But of this by-play his host was unaware. He took good care of that, and Lilamani was too shy to speak.

For Nevil, in truth, the artist eclipsed the man. For him Leseppes the prince of egoists, the reputed libertine, was submerged in Leseppes the inimitable colourist, the godfather of his own lesser gift; and the great man's words at parting exalted him as the praise of no other living painter could have done.

'I tell you this, *mon ami*, and I speak from wide knowledge,' said he, wringing the younger man's hand in the effusive fashion of his race—'those pictures of yours are unique, of their kind. They have the colour and sensuousness, the emotion and idealism of the East. *Mon Dieu!* They shall stir the blood even of those colossal Philistines, your own countrymen! I shall be over with Martino when your exhibition opens.'

It was a very elated husband and wife that drank 'Success to Sita' at dinner that evening.

'And it's all your doing—yours, my own little Sita Devi,' he assured her, silencing her protest, as it deserved. 'We'll block out the Hanuman scene to-morrow. I wish to God we could stay on here till the whole thing was done!'

How passionately Lilamani echoed that wish she dared not confess. Yet a flicker of hope gleamed in her eyes as she asked: 'If you are so much wishing, Nevil—could it not be?'

''Fraid not. Don't tempt me, sweetheart. Jane would have a fit; and there's a deal that needs my personal supervision. No joke playing the double rôle of artist and impoverished landowner. But after all it's high time we started our real life together in our real home. I've picked a capital room in the East Tower for the studio; and we'll have one blessed fortnight all to ourselves before the new Lady Sinclair takes the family by storm!'

Lilamani shook her head, smiling uncertainly. 'Lady Sinclair is afraid——'

'Afraid? Nonsense! She is going to be an unqualified success all round!'

His serene optimism stilled her qualms—for the moment at least. The date of their departure was fixed; and on a golden afternoon of

October the little white boat set out for the last time. Lilamani, crouched in the stern, elbows planted on the cushioned seat, watched their châlet recede and dwindle till all outlines were blurred, and in spite of herself a muffled sob betrayed her 'foolishness.' This time it did not move Nevil to irritation. Balancing his sculls he leaned forward and caressed her shoulder.

'Why break your heart over the good days gone, beloved?' he reproved her gently. 'There are plenty more ahead; and we'll come back here again, I promise you.'

'Yes—yes; we must come back,' she murmured, choking down her tears. But young as she was, already she began to perceive that the scheme of life does not admit of 'coming back.' It is an eternal, inexorable passing on.

BOOK THREE

The Fruit

ONE

'Whom does love concern beyond the beloved and the lover?
Yet its impact deluges a thousand shores.'

—E.M. Forster

'Lilamani! You're a moonbeam incarnate! I don't wonder
Nevil went crazy over you; and if the rest don't follow suit—in their
sober Sinclair fashion—I shall disinherit them forthwith!'

Thus Christina, appraising her sister-in-law with Nevil's own smile
in her eyes. It was evening; and the new Lady Sinclair stood before her
cheval glass at Bramleigh Beeches arrayed for the supreme ordeal of
her marriage: a dinner-party of fourteen, all members of the clan, save
two.

A special dress lately arrived from India had been set aside for the
critical occasion; and the pale golden sheen of it in the light of two tall
candles justified Christina's simile. Unable to mourn for her husband's
father in 'English fashion,' she could only forswear the least touch
of colour, to the secret regret of Nevil the artist; though Nevil the
man loved her the more. He had explained regretfully that gold was
not mourning; and she that Hindu women wear silver only on the feet
with the result that they had compromised in borders and embroideries of palest gold like the new-risen moon. To-night, the shimmery
under-dress was shot with it; and through the filmy *sari* ran a network
of gleaming threads, that, more closely woven, formed the narrow
border. Only the vermilion caste-mark glowed, as always, between
her brows. For jewellery—her father's star, Nevil's pendant, and his
last flagrant extravagance, a bracelet-watch set in diamonds.

No beautiful girl so arrayed, and blessed with a wholesome share
of vanity, could feel other than elate; and gratified by Christina's frank
approval, she answered softly with her veiled blush:

'I shall be getting too much spoilt—if all were like you——'

'Oh, but they're *not* like me, poor dears!' Christina's equally frank commiseration was far removed from conceit. 'And none of them recognize their misfortune! Still—Jane isn't half bad really; straight and strong-minded and as common-sensible as a chest of drawers. She's fond of Nevil too—in her queer way; and probably wants to be fond of you. But the door of her heart is a bit rusty on its hinges. No doubt she'll just shake hands, and ask how you like Bramleigh; while, if she had half an ounce of real mother-feeling in her—which she hasn't in spite of two plain children—she would take you in her arms and kiss you straight away.'

A faint involuntary change came over Lilamani's face.

'That I should not like at all. Though relation by marriage, I am quite stranger—with Lady Roscoe.'

'Lady Roscoe! My dear, you *must* call her Jane. You call me Christina.'

'But how different! Through many letters we became like sisters before meeting; and for me, you could never be stranger. You are too like—like Nevil in a girl.'

Even now, racial instinct made her shy of 'taking her lord's name' before others; custom impermissible for wife or husband among her own people, as Christina had come to know.

'Does that make you love me very much, little Moonbeam?' she asked, slipping an arm round the slender shoulders; and for answer two warm lips pressed her cheek. 'It was awfully good of Nevil to give me this quiet time alone with you two before the influx of the clan,' she went on, well content. 'And I half wish I could put off going back to Germany. But now I must fly and dress. Are you going down? Or will you wait here for your "lord"?'

Lilamani did not miss the gleam of amusement in her eyes.

'Why do you make fun for that?' she asked simply. 'Does my husband-worship seem to all English peoples—foolishness?'

'I don't know about all English peoples! To me it seems rather beautiful. Rather enviable. And I'm quite sure Nevil's in luck to have picked up a wife who believes in that kind of foolishness. At the rate we're going, they'll soon be as extinct as the dodo.'

Lilamani puckered her brows. 'Extinct—gone out, is it? How pity! But who is the dodo?'

Christina laughed.

'I give it up! Ask Nevil, you angelic little anachronism. Now go down and knock the bottom out of my noble sister's condescension; and *don't* forget to call her "Jane!" '

Lilamani's answering smile did not imply acquiescence. But Christina was gone; and soon—far too soon—Nevil would come to take her downstairs. There she would meet face to face the woman whose poisoned shafts of speech still pricked her heart. Knowing all, she must yet appear unknowing. She must endure the touch of hands; the meeting of eyes; but the touch of lips—never! For beneath her surface gentleness throbbed the passionate, unforgiving heart of a soldier race, strong to smite, swift to revenge.

With a last lingering glance at her own reflection, she smiled, sighed, and sank into a chintz-covered arm-chair, heartily wishing the evening well over. And not this one evening alone; but the next few days, which she must learn to call 'week-end.' It was her first dinner-party; and the mere crowd of strangers dismayed her, apart from the fact that all were her husband's relations and friends; curious, interested, or disapproving, even as those who had come in carriages to 'inspect her' and deposit bits of paste-board on the hall table.

Nevil had prepared her to the best of his ability; had sketched them all for her, with touches of not unkindly humour; and had much to tell her of two artist friends, Miss de Winton and Frank Norris, who would come on the Saturday, and were eager to see the pictures destined to establish the impression already made by 'Dreaming,' at the Goupil Gallery. Jane alone, Nevil had left to his wife's imagination; merely remarking that she was a 'good woman under chain-mail,' and that Lilamani must make allowances, for his sake.

And now—the time was at hand. The 'blessed fortnight' all to themselves had melted like snow in a thaw. Even then, they had only been nominally alone; and she had found it hard to hide from Nevil how the great rambling house and its retinue of servants oppressed her. Mrs. Lunn, Queen-Regent of the household—grown portly and domineering in the service of her widowed master—filled Lilamani with awe unspeakable. Her scrupulously respectful bearing was tinctured with too perceptible a pinch of condescension toward this 'heathen chit of a child, from goodness-knows-where,' whom she, Sarah Lunn, was called upon to serve.

'Enough to make pore dear old master turn in 'is grave *that* it is!' she confided to Barnes over their nightly glass of wine in her sanctum. 'If it wasn't but what I firmly believe he'd *feel* it, even where he is, I'd 'a given notice the first day I set eyes on her.'

Barnes nodded in sympathetic comprehension. The discovery that his astuteness was superfluous had put a severe strain on his own loyalty.

'That's your magananimus sense o' duty all over, Mrs. Lunn! An' Sir Nevil he may be thankful. Without you the old place 'ud fall to racking ruin.' He sipped meditatively and shook his head. 'It's bin a quare business all along. At first I thought——' No. His thoughts on the subject would scarce bear retailing to the Queen-Regent of all the proprieties. 'Well—I *had* me qualms. Who wouldn't? But I own I *did* give Sir Nevil credit for more good sense than this 'ere fiasker amounts to.'

'Good sense, Mr. Barnes?' Mrs. Lunn's sniff expressed the quintessence of contempt. 'You, with your experience, didn't ought to be looking for good sense from a master that wastes his time messin' about with dirty paints, instead of tramping or riding round the old Place natural-like, with the dogs at his heels; a master that can't even use 'is droring-room after dinner like a gentleman; 'e's so set on them heathen pictures of his, and that mucked-up room in the Tower.'

It was true. The great drawing-room still languished, empty and desolate, while the misguided pair spent their evenings in the studio, with its friendly litter of books and painting gear; its memory-provoking atmosphere of cigarette smoke and attar of roses. For the artist in Nevil Sinclair, having survived the barren years of discouragement, could challenge even the sacred obligations of heritage. It would not suffer the real man to be entirely overridden by the thing possessed.

As for Lilamani, that sacred hour or two of isolation in the Tower room had come to be the crowning-point of her day; a light toward which she moved, with a deep and conscious yearning that pervaded her every thought, her every act. For she of the East lives in and through the one supreme emotion with a singleness of soul scarce credible to the many-faceted woman of the West and despite Mrs. Lunn's lamentations, 'the old Place' inevitably absorbed more of Nevil's time and attention than seemed good to a young wife little used to rival interests that took him from her side. For Nevil Sinclair, temperament or no, was at core an Englishman true to his breed, as Lilamani to her own. Yet withal, they must contrive to be true to each other. There lay the pith of their problem.

There were mornings spent in the saddle with Thornbrook—land-agent and confidential adviser; tramps through the beech-wood with Mills, the gamekeeper; a visit from Reynolds; a call from a bachelor landowner, who must be asked to lunch, and whose talk of bags, coverts, and meets was pure gibberish to the 'ripping little beauty,' who sat with lids downcast, praying for his departure. Worse than all—just when she had secured Nevil to herself—were the superfluous strangers—who 'came only to look what queer kind of creature Indian bride might be.' This conviction—which at once hurt her sensitiveness and fired her pride of race—was proof against Nevil's most tactful denials. At this time he discovered in her a fund of quiet, unreasoning obstinacy, unsuspected hitherto; and great was her joy when, in pity, he revealed how she could frustrate 'those needless ones' by the magic formula 'Not at Home.' Thereafter she was insatiable—when he would permit; and her childish joy in pronouncing the shibboleth made refusal seem sheer brutality.

Only one thing had failed them entirely: the one thing most like to fail home-comers in an English autumn.

In place of Italy's passionate, unfathomable blue, a shifting greyness hung low over the tree-tops; a reservoir, it seemed, for all the tears of all the earth. Most often Lilamani's great event, the coming of the sun, could only be known by a stealthy, half-hearted change from grey to a whitish pallor, through which, as daylight grew, a moonlike disc peered, ghost-like; his passing, by a gleam in the west, as it were a lifting of tired lids flushed a little with sweeping. Then the slow onset of dark; renewed patter of raindrops; the unresting murmur of wind-swayed trees. Nevil Sinclair—sun-lover though he was—could not know that for Lilamani these changed conditions meant no mere deprivation of light and heat, but temporary eclipse of the reigning gods of her Pantheon. Instinctively her excommunicate soul had slipped back into the primal nature-worship of Vedantic times; satisfying thus her racial instinct for religion, and the deeper human need of worshipping, through the medium of the seen, that 'Great Unfading, who unseen sees, unheard hears, unthought thinks, uncomprehended comprehends.'

And now behold temple and gods alike obliterate! Only for a time, she hoped; yet this fresh deprivation added not a little to the difficulty and strangeness of the new phase of wifehood she was called upon to fulfil. She said little to Nevil; lest she seem to disparage the cradle of his birth. Only upon the fourth day of weeping skies and whirling leaves she had asked half in joke: 'Do sun and moon nearly always keep purdah in your England?'

'Why, of course not!' said he, and the sympathetic note in his voice assured her that he had not taken the question amiss. 'Wait till the autumn gales are over. Then you'll see!'

And the very next day, as if in ratification, behold the sun-god, smiling genially, in a clear sky, flaked with drifting cloud. She must come for a walk, Nevil decreed, through the beech-wood and up on to the moor. It was sodden underfoot; and Lilamani, who had never worn boots in her life, was chary as a cat about wetting her silver-shod feet. But Nevil—not to be gain said—assured her that walking in the wet was an accomplishment all who aspired to live in England must learn forthwith. A pair of Christina's goleshes had been unearthed; and for near two hours they had tramped, like a pair of happy children, through the dominion over which they were king and queen. Through the stately beech-wood, already on fire with burnt sienna and gold, with here and there the bronze gleam of a pheasant among the leaves: then out on to the open moor, where the October sun had awakened a host of midges, that danced like winged motes in his beams; and, from tip to tip of the mummied heath-bells, undiscouraged spiders had woven their gossamer snares, that swayed and lifted, changefully iridescent, in the afternoon light.

Standing silent and entranced, with the sun in her eyes, the mother-longing had stirred in the young wife afresh; conjuring up visions of a day when children's voices—her sons and his—should fill moor and wood with the divinest music on earth. And he? Did he also dream and hope? She stole a shy glance at him. But his thoughts had gone off on a journey of their own; and he did not see.

When at length his eyes sought hers, the transfigured light in them thrilled him strangely. But no word was said.

Returning, he had slipped an arm round her, secure in their vast privacy; and they had walked home like lovers, oblivious of everything in earth and heaven save themselves. Then, all too soon, the house closed over them; the house with its mute reminder of responsibilities, 'needless ones,' the minor tyrannies of possession—changing them into Sir Nevil and Lady Sinclair once more.

On the second clear day he drove with her to return the visit of a 'needless one' who plagued her with the two reiterate, unanswerable questions that seemed a part of this particular ritual: What did she think of England, and how did she like Bramleigh? Then on to tea with Helen Despard, in the rambling black and white oak-panelled bungalow, that Lilamani loved at sight, like its mistress, and secretly preferred to the spacious desolation of her own ancestral home. There was endlessly much to be said, when the men left them alone: but alas, the adopted mother, on whose sympathy and help Lilamani had reckoned, would not be long at hand. The Despards rarely spent a winter in England; and, like Christina, they would not be back till early spring. In this double deprivation, Lilamani saw the malice of her outraged gods. Yet how propitiate them without offering or penance? For her the problem was a serious one, beyond her power to solve.

Thus, between work and play, between driven clouds and fitful sunshine, their fortnight had evaporated. In spite of interruptions, the Token scene had progressed near to completion; and no longer, in Nevil's opinion, could the crucial 'week-end' party be postponed.

On Wednesday had come Christina—true spirit-sister, flower of purely Western culture though she was. This afternoon had brought Sir Robert and his wife, with 'Aunt Julia,' who had kissed her, a little nervously, and called her dear child, but had failed to set her at her ease. Then, before the arrival of the later train—bringing George and 'Phil,' the Roscoes and Broome—she had pleaded headache and fled to the solitude of her shrine, above the studio, arranged exactly as in Italy.

Here, in one of her Yoga moods of receptive quiet, she had striven to still the flutter of anxiety, lest in word or bearing she should not satisfy her lord and those he loved: excepting only 'That Terrible,' whose secret antagonism, she felt convinced, would equal her own. Nevil, divining her need, had not only refrained from seeking her out; but had checked Christina's mistaken impulse of sisterly kindness.

So, for an hour or more, there had been respite; the indefinable refreshment of solitude and silence, and, by a merciful oversight of the gods—a blazing sunset that fired all the west. Slipping a shawl round her shoulders, she had flung the window wide, and sat there in a carven stillness, till eyes and brain and spirit were saturate with the molten brilliance; till all sense of self was lost in that miracle of fusion which only intense gazers know; till living light faded to a dull orange-crimson that glowed beneath the curtain of cloud like the heart of a forge seen through an open door.

Even now, so long after, the ethereal fire seemed to glow in her veins. But imagination makes cowards of the bravest—before action; and detachment was hard to maintain when Nevil's footstep was at her very door.

She rose as he entered and stood before him; breath suspended, eyes veiled. He had not been allowed to see the dress till now; and he stood a moment, appraising her with a long look, felt even through her sheltering lids. Then he came quickly forward, took her in his arms and kissed her with a lover's fervour on lips and eyes and brow.

'You are satisfied with your Lilamani?' she whispered, craving, woman-like, the full need of praise.

'More than satisfied. She is inimitable. Come.'

Laughingly, he offered her his arm, and led her thus down the broad shallow staircase.

Just outside the drawing-room door he felt her hand tremble, and pressed it against his side. 'Be a plucky little wife, for my sake,' he pleaded; and they went in.

Lilamani had an impression of a graceless figure, uncompromisingly black, that turned as they entered, and stood still. She heard Nevil's voice say: 'Well, Jane, here she is—the new Lady Sinclair!' She felt a hand, harder than Audrey's, close upon her own; while Nevil, fearing that his presence would only multiply embarrassment, passed on to where the three elders were discussing the latest evening paper, brought by George.

There was a moment's dead weight of silence between the two he left behind. Opposite as the black and white they wore, they had yet one trait in common. Both were too innately honest for surface insincerities. Lilamani startled by the fierce flame of hate that had leaped in her at the touch of hands—was smitten dumb; leaving Jane, woman of the world, to hit the happy mean between rank hypocrisy and truth.

'I'm so glad you're both really home at last,' said she. 'We were

beginning to think we should never see you in the flesh!' Her attempt
at lightness rang false; and the new Lady Sinclair's small, polite smile
was a little disconcerting. But Jane Roscoe was not the woman to be
lightly put out of countenance.

'I suppose Nevil has shown you all round the dear old Place by this
time?' she asked conversationally.

'Yes; so much as possible in such uncomfortable kind of weather.
With sunshine it is beautiful.'

Lady Roscoe nodded. 'Autumn's a bad time, of course. Nevil
should have brought you home long ago.'

'There was too much work in Italy.'

'Was there? I'm sure he could have done it just as well here. Some
artist's fad about "atmosphere." Simply an excuse. He's incorrigible
over the Continent. But now we've got him into his proper place at
last, we must keep him there. We shall expect *you* to use your influence!'

The soft mouth hardened ever so little.

'Best surely for—husband to do what he thinks right.'

Her instinctive avoidance of Nevil's name gave an air of stiffness,
of sententiousness to her small remark; and Jane flashed out with a
touch of ungovernable asperity: 'A good deal depends upon the husband. *Some* men have a convenient knack of thinking "right" any
mortal thing they feel inclined to do at the moment.'

Lilamani's brows went up a fraction of an inch.

'Have they?' she murmured with a laming indifference that effectively tripped up the subject.

Another dead weight of silence. Her eyes had wandered to the slim
figure on the hearthrug, and Jane's chill antagonism was pricked to
active irritation. What an insipid little fool the girl was! And why on
earth had not Nevil insisted on a more decent show of mourning? She
herself still abjured white, except at throat and wrists. By broaching
the subject, she lightly fingered the gossamer *sari*; and Lilamani needed all her self-control not to shrink visibly from her touch.

'Very beautiful, indeed,' she said, not without a shade of condescension. 'You never wear black in India?'

'No. Not custom. It is too sad, and too ugly with dark skin. So I
could only leave off from colour, though for me almost like breath of
life.'

It was Lady Roscoe's turn to lift her brows. She stigmatized all such phrases as 'artist's jargon,' and supposed the child had caught up, parrot-wise, scraps of her husband's tall talk. She merely said: 'H'm! I suppose you *can* live without it for a time—out of respect for Nevil's loss?'

'But naturally. What else?' Lilamani made answer with such transparent simplicity that again Lady Roscoe had an annoying sense of disconcertion, of being politely set at arm's length by this mere child, who, but for Nevil's madness, had no business to be reigning at Bramleigh Beeches at all.

'I was suggesting thin line of black along this border,' the soft voice went on; 'but—*he* did not wish.'

'H'm!' Jane remarked afresh, and on her lips that ungracious monosyllable had an eloquence of its own. 'I can quite believe it! He always *does*——'

But what he always did his wife never learnt; for at this point the door opened to admit Cuthbert Broome, who came eagerly forward, his sailor eyes agleam.

'Ah—there you are, my runaway bride of Antibes!' said he, enclosing her hand in his great friendly grasp, while Lady Roscoe, to their mutual relief, passed on. 'And here's my girl, Morna, dying to make your acquaintance.'

Morna Broome—tawny-haired and blue-eyed like her father—flushed up to her eyebrows. 'It's all father's doing,' said she. 'He's a great admirer! And his enthusiasms are so infectious.'

'Yes. That I remember well!' Lilamani answered, the morsel of ice at her heart dissolving like magic in the geniality that breathed from both. 'I cannot ever be thankful enough to your father for this most beautiful summer in my first home.'

She bestowed on the big man a look of melting tenderness, through which laughter gleamed; and Broome nodded down at her, well content. Jane, watching covertly from the hearthrug, saw that look through the distorting glass of prejudice; and misread it altogether.

'The harem type all over,' was her thought. 'Shamming shyness with *me*—her husband's sister. But all smiles and sugar for a man—though he's *not* one of us.'

For Jane, like Aunt Julia, spoke the sacred pronoun in capitals. Tonight it was Lilamani's patent duty to ingratiate herself with Nevil's

People; and she would probably spend half the evening talking Antibes with Broome! Nevil should have coached her in advance. Just like his casual ways!

The three near the piano, joined by Christina, were soon engrossed in easy, happy talk, the real Lilamani flashing out spontaneously, at moments, in low laughter, and shy, playful sallies, to the further confounding of Jane. Nevil—after praiseworthy efforts to discuss Egyptian unrest with Lord Roscoe—drifted irresistibly back to the piano, leaving the five elders regnant on the hearthrug: immemorial throne of the British home.

Sir Robert had twice consulted his watch, a trifle ostentatiously, when George and Phillippa sauntered in, serenely unhurried; and there was only time for a brief introduction before Lord Roscoe offered Lady Sinclair his arm.

Phillippa's first thought was an unconscious echo of Jane's: 'The harem type all over.' It is the brand wherewith the essential woman is branded by an emergent minority; to which Phillippa Weston preeminently belonged. A good shot, a straight rider, and mistress of a clear five thousand a year—she was, as Jane had written, a 'sound and satisfactory' family asset. And if Jane's conviction *plus* the thousands were, in a measure, responsible for George's fervour, Phillippa had no inkling of the fact. She had the modern girl's tendency to admire her own sex; and Lady Roscoe stood scarcely second to George in her esteem. On one point alone were they at variance. Jane was a passive advocate of women's right to vote; Phillippa an active one. But it was quite understood that the martyr's crown must be foregone if she desired to become Mrs. George Sinclair: the which she did as heartily as any unit of the unenlightened mass. She was woman enough also to note and resent the fact that George's glance lingered unduly on his new sister-in-law, even while he gave his arm to Morna Broome, who looked a trifle overgrown and rough-cut by contrast.

As for Lilamani, bringing up the solemn procession on Lord Roscoe's arm, she had thoughts for nothing but the lean, grave-eyed man, whose over-punctilious politeness reduced her to monosyllables and murmured platitudes; the more so because Jane, given over to Broome, walked just ahead.

The hour that followed was one of undiluted misery for the zenana-bred hostess of eighteen, condemned to sit through a six-course dinner with a mixed party of strangers, who talked and laughed incessantly while eating, and—worse still—had all of them a covertly curious eye to their kinsman's bride.

Alone with Lord Roscoe, the veil of shyness might have been lifted. But the noise and lights bewildered her, while Jane's proximity froze all spontaneous speech upon her lips. Broome—who had not the clue to her discomfiture—did his utmost to dispel it, with small success. Once or twice Nevil caught her eye and smiled encouragement across leagues of chrysanthemum-decked table-cloth. But he was so far off, and That Terrible, with eyes that probed like gimlets, so perturbingly near! Lord Roscoe, scholarly and unprejudiced, had to own himself disappointed; and Miss Sinclair, who found dear Edward's conversation so stimulating, reaped the benefit accordingly.

It seemed as if dessert would never arrive! But it did. And with it came the alarming recollection that it would be hers to make the move, to catch Lady Margaret's eye. From the moment the wine began to circulate her mind became so concentrated on this achievement that she could hardly hear what Cuthbert Broome was saying.

In the end it was Nevil who saw, and came to her rescue and the thing was done. They were all filing out, the black-robed figures, in the midst of which she gleamed like a ray of light; and Christina, hanging back, slipped a sheltering arm round her as they went out.

George, holding the door open, smiled genially upon her; and, returning, sat down by his brother.

'By Jove, Nevil, you've my hearty congrats!' he said under his breath.

'Thanks, old chap.'

Nevil spoke without enthusiasm and glanced toward the other end of the table. But the elder men were discussing Sir George's cellar—an engrossing topic; and George the younger went on, still in the same confidential undertone: 'Hindu or no, she's a jewel of the first water. You don't get a sight of her sort in India. And perhaps it's as well, for the peace of the community! Alluring. That's the word. A woman all through as they still make 'em in the East; though we're losing the art this side, worse luck.'

Nevil—listening with amused indifference to the sort of comments one expected from George—sipped his port and thought of Phillippa Weston, who was none of these things.

But his brother's next words put indifference to flight.

'All the same, old man,' he went on with a twinkle of jocose saga-city, 'when it comes to that type, the purdah has its advantages, eh? No risk of complications——'

Nevil straightened himself with a jerk.

'Damn your impertinence! What the deuce do you mean?' he asked sharply under his breath, and was grateful for a shout of laughter from Broome.

'Oh, nothing, my dear chap, nothing.' George's tone was a meta-phorical pat on the shoulder. 'Can't you take a bit of chaff in the right spirit? You seem to have grown almighty touchy since your marriage. I'm a plain practical chap with a shrewd pair of eyes in my head—that's all.'

'Keep your shrewdness for your own affairs then.' Nevil's cooler tone had a touch of incision, and leaving his chair he sat down near Broome.

George, scowling across at him over the top of a lighted match, reflected sagely that a few years with the Regiment would have done old Nevil a power of good. As it was, he half suspected his brother of turning prig—most heartily hated word in the British language. But Nevil Sinclair was neither prig nor Bayard. He had the fastidiousness of his temperament—and its susceptibility. Did he err, his heart must be involved. It must be *the* woman, however transitory. For George the indefinite article sufficed: a radical distinction.

Yet, in a sense, the younger brother's puzzlement was justified. Six months of marriage and steady work had wrought imperceptible changes in Nevil Sinclair, as he himself was aware; though he scarcely realized yet how much was due to the girl-wife who swayed him by the very completeness of her submission, as only the true woman-spirit can. At this moment he was merely angry, and glad to be quit of George, who—being deserted—took his own small revenge.

The opening flourish of a Chopin polonaise suggested the possibil-ity of quiet talk under cover of 'Kit's fireworks'; and deliberately extinguishing his cigar he went in search of amusement more congen-ial than the dining-room could offer.

Phillippa, deep in shooting prospects with Jane, started and flushed a little at her lover's entrance. But George, incapable of finesse, had eyes only for the thing he sought.

'Jove! I'm in luck!' was his mental comment. For his sister-in-law sat alone on a settee near the grand-piano, over which Morna Broome leaned, absorbed and envious. Jane and Phillippa sat by the fire, and Aunt Julia had taken Lady Margaret to her own room.

George made straight for the sofa, where Lilamani lay back with eyes half closed, thankful for a brief respite from the need to 'make talk.' At his approach she looked up and smiled.

'I'm not disturbing you, am I?' he asked perfunctorily as he sat down. 'And you don't mind talking a little while Kit makes that unholy noise?'

'No,' she answered untruthfully, as in duty bound; and he was content.

For a space he talked platitudes, one arm laid along the sofa-back in casual brotherly fashion; while she murmured polite responses, seldom raising her eyes. Once during a softer passage in the music her lifted hand pleaded for silence; and he sat watching her, wondering whether, after all, he would have had Nevil's pluck when it came to the point. He began to believe he would. The longer he looked at her, the more firmly he believed it. The conviction did not disturb his placid affection for Phil. It enhanced the pleasure of sitting so close to this delicately alluring bit of femininity—that was all. It made him want to bring a light into her eyes, colour into her cheeks, to enforce some sort of recognition that she was talking to a man.

Renewed crashing of chords gave him his chance. He leaned nearer.

'Am I allowed to speak now—Lilamani?'

He paused before the name and pronounced it 'Lillamarny.' She winced and shook her head.

'Not say it that way, please.'

'What way, then? Teach me.'

'Lilamani.' She spoke the word with a dainty crispness the first syllable slightly stressed, the second 'a' almost a 'u.'

'It's a thundering pretty name, the way you say it,' was his masculine comment. 'And the meaning's prettier still. Nevil told us. If I can't pronounce it to please you, let me call you Jewel instead. Comes more natural to an Englishman, and they couldn't possibly have picked anything more appropriate.'

Something in the tone, rather than the words, called up the slow, veiled blush that had so charmed Nevil in early days. He entered at the moment with Broome; saw the blush, and noting his brother's attitude, made straight for the settee.

George greeted him with imperturbable complaisance.

'We've been making friends—Lilamani and I.'

'That's all right,' quoth Nevil dryly; and drawing up a chair, sat down beside his wife.

Talk languished; Christina's Polonaise crashed to its conclusion; and George, seeing that no more blushes would be his, sauntered over to the fire-place for consolation. But Phillippa, on his approach, became the more ostentatiously engrossed in Jane; and he, with a resigned movement of the shoulders, returned to the dining-room, to enjoy the smoke he had sacrificed, and await a probable game of Bridge.

His last glance was not toward the fire-place but toward Nevil's wife, whose eyes were upon her husband's face, mutely demanding was he satisfied with his Lilamani—now?

His answering smile reassured her; though, in his heart, he felt she had been over-successful in the wrong direction, and hoped for better results on the morrow.

TWO

'Heaven's own screen
Hides her soul's purest depth and loveliest glow;
Closely withheld, as all things most unseen—
The wave-bowered pearl, the heart-shaped seal of green
That flecks the snowdrop underneath the snow.'

—Rossetti

The morrow brought its own fresh ordeal to the new Lady Sinclair; added its own quota to the discovery, each day enforced more clearly, that married life with Nevil, the rising artist, was one thing, and married life with Sir Nevil Sinclair of Bramleigh Beeches, in the stronghold of his fathers, was very much another.

Tea-time found Lilamani in the large hall presiding at the gate-leg table over a bewildering array of Crown Derby teacups, and a purring silver urn that carried its banner of steam. More girlishly demure than ever she seemed, in dead-white dress and *sari* bordered with palest grey; more 'impossible' than ever also, in the opinion of the elders, who had made an honest effort to 'draw her out' by talking of India before the kettle arrived. Sir Robert, mildly pompous and impersonal, had enlarged on the climate and the sport; Lord Roscoe contributed a few polished and paralysing questions on India's premier Native State, while Lady Margaret and Aunt Julia embarked hopefully on the field of missionary endeavour. A barren field, in this case.

Not that Lilamani's answers were other than intelligent and polite. But these Western elders, inured by now to the airy self-assurance of their own young, felt checked and a little chilled by lowered lids and deferential murmurs; not realising that this was her idea of correct behaviour to the more venerable members of a husband's family.

The arrival of the kettle had been a welcome relief to all. But soon there would be other talk to make; fresh strangers to encounter. Nevil and Christina had driven out to meet the new-comers; rank Bohemians both; peculiarly distasteful to Jane. Morna and her father, after a short turn with Lilamani, had wandered on through the burnished glories of the beech-wood. George and Phil had gone for a ride. There had been a slight coolness between them all the morning, much of which George had contrived to spend in Lilamani's neighbourhood. But fresh air and exercise readjusted things; and on their return, the drive being empty, he had lifted his *fiancée* out of the saddle and kissed her soundly, on the lips.

'Oh—George!' she murmured, as he released her. But he had turned aside and was opening the front door.

It was George's way of making love. Little of tenderness in speech or tone; only an occasional kiss, half passionate, half shamefaced, when heart or senses were stirred. Phillippa did not altogether approve. But she wanted George—for several reasons; and one could not accept a man piecemeal.

It was not so easy to accept his instant gravitation to the 'harem child' on entering the hall. Mere masculine instinct, she assured herself; and bore Nevil a grudge for giving him a chance to gratify it. But he had not gratified it for many minutes before wheels and a stir outside announced Nevil and his friends.

Lilamani braced herself for renewed 'inspection' and her young vanity craved the more distinctive setting of mother-o'-pearl or almond-blossom *sari*; the golden gleam of armlets, belt and shoes. She wearied of this eternal white and grey. Its insipidity seemed to infect her soul; its——

'Lilamani—here is Miss de Winton.'

Nevil's voice roused her. She started; smiled obediently, and held out her hand. It was retained for a second or more while its owner regarded her leisurely out of long, level-lidded eyes.

'This is a great moment, Lady Sinclair,' said Leslie de Winton in a full contralto as leisurely as her gaze. 'I've been counting the days *and* the hours ever since the invite came. I've known this Nevil of yours'— she grasped his arm—'how many years is it, old boy?'

He shrugged and laughed. 'I'm weak at arithmetic! And I've lived a lifetime this summer.'

'Well—we'll say a lifetime then!' Her eyes seemed reluctant to leave his face. ' "We were boys together," like Mr. and Mrs. Alphonso Browne! And I couldn't induce myself to believe in Nevil's *wife* till I'd seen her in the flesh.'

Lilamani had no immediate answer at command. Something in the look and tone of this mere stranger—little more than Audrey's age—who laid hands on *her* man and called him 'old boy' fired her with a hot rush of anger. But she kept her gaze steady, lest hesitation be deemed shyness, and a delicate shade of sarcasm lurked in her question: 'Perhaps you are a little more able for believing it now?'

Miss de Winton, vaguely aware of something amiss, turned it off with a laugh. 'Why, yes. Very much so! But even now, I can't manage to believe in those pictures! The Nevil *I* know could never have achieved the amount let alone the unique subject.' Again her eyes dwelt upon him with their odd look of veiled power. 'It seems that I am here to meet a new Nevil as well as a new wife! But I beg your pardon, Noll'—this to Norris. 'It's your turn now. Once *I* get into the middle of the stage I'm rather apt to stay there unless some one kindly pushes me aside!'

Still unhurried, she moved on her way, shaking hands and talking in the strong, deliberate voice that was almost a drawl; while Lilamani, only half appeased, must endure the scrutiny of eyes the more embarrassing that they were masculine, prominent and boldly appreciative, under rough, irritable brows. But for Norris the drawing-room and the tea-table were unfamiliar mediums—'not being a placard-painter,' was his own explanation; and he had no platitudes at command.

Having covered his small hostess with confusion by a look that comprised her from caste-mark to shoe-buckle, he announced bluntly: 'Strikes me, Lady Sinclair, that you came over from India expressly to do this lucky husband of yours a double service. He's just the Fate-favoured type that would get all the plums dropped into his mouth, without any prelude of starving and agonizing such as we poor devils have to grind through first——'

'Well, you shan't starve and agonize under my roof, old chap!' Nevil interposed promptly, seeing that the speech was quite beyond his wife's power to answer.

He would fain have set her at ease by a tender word or two, a hand on her shoulder; but that he knew too well by this time how all her 'Hindu-ness' shrank from the lightest revealing of their hearts before others.

'Give this ill-used pair some tea, Lilamani!' was all he could say. 'Unless you'd prefer drinks and cigarettes in the studio, Norris?'

No. They voted for tea. But Miss de Winton smoked a cigarette with hers, and flicked her ash about the carpet, to Aunt Julia's amaze and Jane's unspeakable disgust.

The family dispersed more or less during the interlude and the moment tea-drinking was over Leslie de Winton rose.

'Now then, Nevil, I'm in a most egregious hurry to be convinced of the existence of these myths!'

'You look it!' said he, surveying with a smile her lazy length, that held the same kind of power as her eyes, 'You'll tear me into ribbons between you. But you're more than welcome——'

He motioned her to the door; and as they went forward, he lingered a moment to lean over his wife's chair.

'Aren't you coming too, Jewel of Delight?'

'Not now—please,' she answered, and her eyes clung to his for one appealing instant.

But as soon as he was gone, she lay back and closed them, simulating weariness as a cloak for vague trouble and bewilderment of soul. Weeks of monopoly had made the studio dear and sacred almost as her shrine. It was one thing to admit Christina, who was 'Nevil in a girl.' But to share it with strangers—the one, too openly intimate with him; the other too likely to persecute her with his eyes, in the fashion of M. Leseppes—was more than she would willingly endure. It began to dawn upon her that this trouble of the way men looked at you must be an inevitable phase of unveiled life: a phase that made her long for the cloistered shelter of the Inside as nothing else had done yet. Even George, brother and promised husband, was not above reproach.

And to-day—fresh perturbation on her lord's account. If it were *dastur* that the free women of England should behave with the husband of another as this bold-mannered one behaved with her's— Lilamani's, then, better a thousand times that wife should be shut away where she might not feel the poison-pricks of jealousy—fierce and primitive in this gentle creature even as her hate. But of what use to consider advantages? The unveiled life was of her own choosing; and must be accepted, good with ill.

At this point the insistent murmur of voices tangled her thread of thought. The room had fallen very still. All who remained were occupied with pen or book. Only those voices came from the fireside, where Jane and Aunt Julia discussed the recent misfortunes and follies of a poor relation, Clara by name. She lived, it seemed, at a place called Gunnersbury, where rooms were few and small; and servants either were not, or did little to earn their wages since this Clara appeared to have 'everything on her hands' from cooking to making the children's clothes, which she did badly enough, according to Jane. For there were children also in this abode of dinginess and small space. That one word enchained Lilamani's attention; and a vision of children, who were also relations, redeemed the sordid picture. One had been ill. So had Clara herself.

They spoke of the ill one as 'Nevil,' and Lilamani's heart contracted. It was her foolish thought that no living woman, save herself, could be mother of a man-child and call his name Nevil. But the fact, though disconcerting, quickened her sympathy for one so blest yet so ill-fated. She listened eagerly. Aunt Julia was speaking now.

'Of course, dear, one *knows* her capacity for muddling things almost amounts to genius. But then—these illnesses, with her income! And after all, she *is* poor dear Richard's widow——'

'Which means you've been sending her another cheque. Aunt Ju, you're incorrigible!'

Disapproval lurked in Jane's half-playful remonstrance and a hint of apology in Miss Sinclair's reply.

'Only five pounds, dear, to help her take the child to St. Leonards. But the money has melted; and they've never been. There were difficulties——'

'There always are. There always would be, with Clara, if she had a thousand a year!' This from Jane, with her touch of asperity. 'She's one of the patently unfit. And really, Aunt Ju, you make things worse by pauperizing her. She knows quite well that whenever a tight corner comes, a cheque will drop out of the sky. If she didn't, she might at least try to make *some* sort of provision for bad times like these.'

Lady Roscoe had never troubled herself to discover by a simple sum of arithmetic what manner of provision for emergencies could be achieved by a woman of gentle birth, doomed to feed, dress, and educate four children on a bare two hundred a year. Hers was the supreme handicap of the unimaginative: utter inability to see life through other eyes than her own.

Miss Sinclair, softer of heart and conscience, could only reiterate her unanswerable argument: 'After all, my dear, she *is* poor Richard's widow.'

And 'Richard' having been first cousin to Sir George—though only a degree less unfit than his wife—Jane could but acquiesce, and change the subject; which spoilt everything. Lilamani wanted to hear more, or be left in peace to think of this unknown 'Clara'; this woman of her husband's family, who lacked space and money, and even food, while she and Nevil were overburdened with useless servants, empty rooms and more than sufficient money to fulfil their needs. For Nevil had said little to her of his own inability to make ends meet. As head of the family, surely his duty was clear. If relations were in need or sickness, their place was at Bramleigh Beeches. That was her Eastern view. For in India organized charity is not. Each family group is more or less responsible for its own. Possibly Nevil had not heard, or did not realize. Children in the house—young children! Her woman's heart thrilled at the prospect. Rising quickly she slipped out of the room, and ran up to the Tower, that she might think things out in her shrine. But she reckoned without Nevil's quick ears and keen desire of her.

At the sound of her light step without, he opened the studio door.

'Come and join the private view, Lilamani,' said he. 'The pictures are as much yours as mine, And so I've told them!'

'However much you are telling it, they will never believe such foolishness!' she made answer, laughing; reluctance dispelled by his tribute.

'I'm not sure of *that*, Lady Sinclair,' quoth Norris, regarding, with quickened interest, her girlish outlines of face and figure. 'Personally, I'm inclined to score under the polite remark I achieved downstairs! This scene in particular, Sinclair, stamps you—places you even more than the rest.' He flung a declamatory hand towards the easel, where Nevil had just set up Sita in the Asoka Garden, with its grimly suggestive background of fiends vigilant, and its foreground of delicate beauty veiled and blurred with grief, as the face of the moon by passing clouds. 'No man of our school could have resisted such a chance—and the abduction gave you another—of making your thrill the wrong way round. Even a touch of bestiality wouldn't have been amiss. Degenerate or no, there's a certain chill down the spine producible by vigorous, remorseless handling of the hideous that leaves the more commonplace appeal to beauty miles behind.'

For a moment, Nevil considered the matter, and his canvas; then shook his head.

'I find more than enough of ugliness and terror in both scenes,' said he.

'Quite so. You're not Leseppes' "god-son" for nothing. But for all he's left his mark on your work, you've the reticence, the delicacy and mellow sanity of an older school. You're not afraid of simplicity; and it's clear you believe in beauty all along the line.'

'Yes, thank God, I do.' Nevil glanced involuntarily at his wife. 'I hope no school or movement or "ism" will ever tempt me into deifying the ugly and abnormal, even for the sake of your chill down the spine!'

Norris laughed. 'For ever and ever. Amen! Eh? Wait till you've seen Leslie's latest. But I doff my hat to the rising apostle of sanity! I can still admire work on your lines when—and only when—it bears the clear stamp of personal vision, in addition to such notable brushwork and force of colour. Yes, my dear chap, in spite of your confounded healthiness, I believe you'll do! But as I've leave to quarrel with a thing or two—look here——'

And securing the 'apostle of sanity' by the arm he launched into a tangle of minor technicalities that swept the talk far above Lilamani's head.

Leslie de Winton, noting this, drew her aside.

'Let them wrangle it out between them, Lady Sinclair,' said she. 'I want to hear something more about this magical Epic, that seems to have fired your husband as I've never seen him fired yet. One knew the name, of course; and Nevil has given us the bare bones of the story. What a big conglomerate thing it is! And what an uncomfortably high standard of wifehood it reveals. Thank heaven, *our* men don't set us on such heroic pedestals in these days! And I suppose even Indian ideals have come a shade nearer to earth in the last thousand years or so?'

Lilamani, half puzzled, half repelled, could only shake her head.

'I don't quite know your meaning about nearer to earth. Of course it is difficult, always, for those not heroine-made to climb to such a height. But Sita is still ideal for all true Indian wives to-day.'

'Poor misguided souls!' The Englishwoman's genuine dismay set Lilamani smiling in spite of herself.

'Not so misguided, nor so hardship as you think,' said she.

'Not hardship? My dear Lady Sinclair! To be condemned to worship a very fallible and human husband as god? *I* should say insult would be nearer the mark!'

The daughter of Rajputs frowned.

'It is not "condemned," nor insult,' she said, with touch of heat. 'It is by nature, by religion——'

'Then it's high time nature and religion tried a change of programme! Rare luck for you, isn't it, marrying into a saner and more reasonable state of things?'

'I? How you mean? No difference with me. I am still Hindu. You think by change of name and country the soul can change beliefs, ideals, as if like clothes.'

'I'm afraid I didn't think. But then—good Lord——' The incredible conclusion dawned on her. 'You don't mean to tell me that Nevil is— that if Nevil were to——'

'Please not say any more,' Lilamani broke in hurriedly, the hot blood surging into her face. 'It is not—I am not able for discussing so sacred subject . . . with strangers——'

To hide her confusion and check further speech she turned abruptly toward the window; and Leslie de Winton's sallow face changed colour. She was sorry to have trespassed on this quaint child's preserves: but irrepressible amusement narrowed her eyes. Nevil—most casual and unheroic of men, whom no one but herself had ever seemed to take quite seriously till now——!

He turned at the moment, caught her smiling, and inquired innocently: 'What's the joke?'

'*You* are!' she answered, stepping closer and lowering her voice. 'You'll soon be invisible to us earth-worms—the rate you're going up. A baronet; a budding R.A.; and now I find that mere marriage has exalted you into a "sacred subject!"'

'Oh, hang it, Les. Shut up.' Nevil frowned sharply and glanced at his wife's figure in the window. 'It's not me. You don't understand.'

Low as he spoke, Lilamani caught the words and the 'small name' that hurt her like a blow. How little it might imply she did not stay to consider. She hated its owner; and was racking her brain for a polite means of escape, when the leisurely voice remarked: 'Well, so long,

Nevil. It's good to be here again. I must go now and uncrumple my evening dress.'

To Lilamani it seemed a miracle wrought in her favour. It did not strike her that an exchange of glances had sufficed; and that Leslie had carried off the bewildered Norris by force, to explain 'the joke' in her own ribald fashion, outside. She only knew, with a lift of the heart, that they were gone. What matter how? She only stood waiting, with young intensity of expectation, for the beloved footstep, the beloved arm round her body.

And when these came, quietly, without speech, in the English fashion she had learnt to love, she turned swiftly and hid her burning face in the roughness of his coat.

He gave her a minute or so to recover herself, his left hand pressing her head against its shelter.

Then:

'You must make allowances, little one,' he said, 'if some of them *do* trample unawares on your holy ground. The sanctities are out of fashion here, nowadays. But Leslie's a good sort. She meant no harm.'

'Is she—cousin, that you call her by that private name?' came the muffled voice, shifting the issue in a manner so purely feminine that the man smiled and pressed her closer.

'No. She's no connection. But we're very good friends. She's bound to be here pretty often; and I want you to like her. She's a very clever artist—and quite a good sort really,' he repeated, feeling the movement of negation under his hand.

Her speech confirmed it.

'"Good sort" your Lilamani doesn't know. She is horrid woman. Profane woman. Not worthy for having a husband—or—or sons— ever!'

It was her supremest malediction, as Nevil knew by now.

'Poor Leslie!' said he, and his eyes grew soft with a passing memory. 'Worthy or not, the odds are against her having either—now.'

He did not feel bound to add that at one time she had openly aspired to become the future Lady Sinclair. Even with the dear head against his breast he had a momentary qualm in realizing that but for a timely separation, at a critical juncture, his house of marriage would have been builded upon sand and this pearl of womanhood would never have been his. Leslie, with her strong irregular features, lithe body, and hint of power in reserve, had fascinated him mentally, to the verge of obsession. She fascinated him still. But this flower of the East, this very woman compact of fire and dew, held every fraction of him prisoner in her softly-clinging hands.

'She mustn't be a hard-judging, narrow-minded Lilamani,' he reproved her in all gentleness. 'And she mustn't make foolishness about the "private name!" You didn't mind it with Audrey. She's no cousin either.'

'No. Yet not the same with her. I can't tell—I feel——' She lifted her head in the effort to crystallize vague yet unerring intuitions; and Broome's voice sounded at the door.

'You there, Nevil?'

Sinclair glanced at his wife.

'Yes—yes. Him I love!' she whispered, freeing herself from his arm.

'Come on, old man,' Nevil called out; adding, as the novelist entered: 'Here's an honour that you dreamt not of. Lady Sinclair loves you!'

'Oh, Nevil! I didn't mean—how trouble you are!' she cried, in a pretty flutter of embarrassment; and Broome, with genuine pleasure in his eyes:

'Don't spoil such a charming confession, my dear. I heartily return the compliment.'

Then, with one of those touches of the Southerner that so well became him, he lifted her hand to his lips.

'I came to say,' he went on, beaming at his astonished host, 'that Christina and Morna are having quite a concert in the drawing-room. My infant sings rather nicely. She's shy of performing after dinner, as yet. But I'd like you to hear her, if you've done with each other *pro tem.*'

Lady Sinclair crumpled her brow over that last.

'*Pro tem?* That is what Audrey was calling something in the food.'

Nevil burst out laughing. 'Proteids! Not half a bad shot! Poor old Audrey's teaching didn't leave much of a mark.'

'A girl to be reckoned with, though. Character enough for two!' Broome remarked with a twinkle, recalling the day of the storm. 'Heard anything of her since Antibes?'

'Yes. She's in Scotland with her people. We've asked her to look us up when she comes in this direction.'

He opened the door for his wife in speaking, and they went out.

THREE

'Yet we are one;—
One in the perfect sense of Eastern meaning:—
Gold and the bracelet, water and the wave.'

—Laurence Hope

Dinner that night was something less of an ordeal; though it would be long before this puzzling fashion of entertainment could be anything but distasteful to Lilamani Sinclair. Lord Roscoe seemed a shade less formidable; and in the drawing-room Jane made an honest effort at friendly talk with Nevil's wife. But not all that wife's devotion could impel her to genuine response. Wax in the hands of these she loved, Lilamani had yet her share of the fighting spirit and fierce pride of her race, that leaped in flame at every word or look from this condescendingly dutiful sister of her husband, in whose heart were poisoned arrows and a sharp sword. So the effort proved barren of result; and Jane, having done her duty, reverted to the faithful Phil.

Again there was music for the younger ones; Bridge for the elders; and clumsy attentions from George, whom she smiled upon sweetly as 'a brother.' But through it all she was acutely aware of Leslie de Winton's tall figure in its elaborately simple grey-green sheath; seldom far from Nevil's elbow. Some lightning instinct whispered that here was only the mask of friendship; and every time the deliberate gaze rested on her lord's face, or the deliberate voice 'took his name,' Lilamani's heart burned with a murderous resentment, for which no one present would have given her credit; least of all the husband, who believed he knew her by now. And there was trouble with Norris' eyes. Not such barefaced persecution as that of M. Leseppes; but sufficient to make this child of seclusion feel strangely unsheltered and defenceless, even under her husband's roof, shrine of all the sanctities to an Indian wife.

Altogether it was a time of puzzling complexities and strange discoveries, that interminable week-end; the forerunner of many such. That was the worst of it. Nevil had explained that, at least while shooting lasted, 'the clan' regarded the week-end at Bramleigh Beeches as its due; and little Lady Sinclair, with never a germ of social or sporting instinct in her composition, must needs adapt herself to a sacred form of ritual that seemed to take the place of religion in the West. There were moments of pure enjoyment with Christina and Morna, or Broome; moments of half-fearful pleasure with the over-appreciative George; and one blessed escape to tea with Helen Despard, she and Christina alone. Yet it was with unfeigned relief that she received the last handshake; the last kiss on her cheek.

They were gone—all gone! It was as if a ton-weight fell from her shoulders. Christina would return in a few days to say good-bye. In the meantime, tea in the studio, and Nevil all to herself for hours and hours! He too was relieved. She felt it in the air; though she did not divine that at least a part of his relief was due to the fact that she had not produced quite the effect he had hoped for. He made every allowance for difficulties no Englishman could fully understand. But he had sincerely hoped 'things would go better next time.'

As for her, she wanted to forget that next time would ever come. She also wanted to talk of Clara, whose story, in outline, she had drawn from Aunt Julia: a sordid, commonplace story of one of the world's poor things, foredoomed to go under in the struggle for life. Richard Sinclair, it seemed, had been an idle good-for-nothing. Truth compelled Aunt Julia to admit the damning fact; while loyalty prompted her to regret, in the same breath, that everyone noticed his unfortunate likeness to his mother! He had died—two years ago—leaving his second wife in genteel poverty, with a young stepson and four children of her own. A feckless creature, it seemed, always ailing; but devoted to the children; and the new niece's evident sympathy had gone far to win Aunt Julia's heart.

Now—tea being over, and she, crouched on her low stool, arms resting on his knees, while he smoked, the cherished plan found utterance. Had he heard? Had he realized? Those others that he had invited were well-provided as themselves. But this poor woman, widow of blood-relation, mother of sons, sick, in trouble . . . and they, with so many empty rooms——.

She broke off uncertainly, for Nevil had opened his eyes.

'My dear little wife—what *are* you driving at? D'you want 'em all *here?*'

Her smile, tremulously pitiful, was a lovely thing to see.

'I thought . . . only natural, like in India—when you knew there was trouble——'

'But there always *is* trouble in Clara's direction. I'm awfully sorry for her, poor soul; and I'd be glad to give her a helping hand, though hardly to the extent of turning Bramleigh Beeches into a *crèche*, overrun with unruly children——!'

Something in his tone brought her heart into her throat.

'Are you not caring very much—for children?' she asked, moving one hand nervously up and down his knee.

He covered it with his own. 'Of course I'm fond of children. Most decent men are. But Clara's are a harum-scarum lot. She has as little control over them as over anything else. And what would the great Mrs. Lunn say to such an invasion?'

The soft mouth took a line of decision: but Lilamani had to swallow before she could speak. The dimmest sense of disappointment in him—her idol, was hard to bear.

'The house is belonging for you, not for Mrs. Lunn,' she said, looking intently at the long fine hand on his knee. 'And—he is ill—that littlest one called by your name. Aunt Julia was sending money for a place called St. Leonards. But one cannot go without all. Oh, Nevil!' she looked up eagerly confident—'How easy to send money for all! You have so much——'

He looked deep into her eyes before replying. Her appealing beauty of soul and flesh moved him more, it is to be feared, than Clara's need.

'I haven't "so much." That's the difficulty. This great house with all its staff and hundreds of acres doesn't mean untold wealth rolling in to keep it going. It may sound queer to you, but I'm almost as hard put to it as Clara to make ends meet.'

'Oh Nevil—dear lord! But why then—have all these . . . wealthy ones . . . not in trouble?'

'That's a riddle not to be answered off-hand, little wife! It would take a deal of explaining; and I wanted if possible to shield you from all contact with the sordid struggle between ways and means. To you money is nothing more than a name; and I should prefer to keep it so

as long as may be. But you're such a stern moralist, you creature of
sweetness and light! so imbued with the logic of your race, that it
might save friction and misunderstanding if I make my position clear
once for all. Only you must have patience with dull talk and ugly
words!'

At that, she drew herself up radiantly elate. Here was privilege indeed! So rarely is an Indian wife admitted to a share in the masculine
side of her lord's existence; at least until she be mother as well.

'No need for patience. I am proud with all my soul that you are
wishing me to share. I know I am stupid for such things. But I will try
to understand.'

It was not so easy, strive as she might. For a quarter of an hour and
more his quiet voice flowed on, leaving a very mixed train of impressions in its wake. The mortgage bewildered her beyond measure.
She saw it as an actual bogey, to be propitiated by means of money
doled out at intervals; a bogey that he might be rid of in time if his
pictures 'caught on.' She understood his wish to try to keep things
going in the old way, for the sake of family honour, and that sentence
in his father's last letter. She began to understand also that there is no
family system in England, as in India; no great nexus of responsibility,
which obviates the need for workhouse and orphanage, since none of
the blood can look for support in vain.

But one discrepancy puzzled her; and when all was said, she drew
his attention to it, not without hesitancy.

'Lord of me—you are seeming to forget . . . there is my dowry also.
Not small. Though how much, you know better than I——'

'Your dowry? But my dear, it's your own, always and altogether.
Do you suppose I would use it to keep up the estate or help my poor
relations out of the ditch they have dug for themselves? I hope I'm man
enough to win through my own muddles, without coming down on
you.'

It took her a second or so to grasp his masculine and very British
point of view; then she challenged it straightway with her Asiatic
logic.

'Oh Nevil—dearest, what a foolishness! Forgive me for saying
that. But think only—can there be any of me altogether my own when
every part is belonging to my lord, for this life and all lives to come?'
Lightly touching head and feet, she indicated the completeness of his

dominion. 'All great things, real things—life and body and heart— you let me give without making this trouble of mine and thine. How then talk of holding back so small a thing, like money? That your Lila- mani will never understand if you explain up to night-time.'

'Then my Lilamani must accept it without understanding!' said he, drawing her close against him, till head touched head.

Still she shook her own with gentle obstinacy. 'It is foolishness between wife and husband, this pretending of thine and mine; especially when there is trouble.' Then her logic triumphed afresh. 'But Nevil—if mine, I can give where I please; even to relation of yours. For that you cannot refuse permission!'

He could not; and he gave it straightway, in the fashion she loved best.

'But look here, darling,' said he, when their lips were free for speech. 'Unless I keep some sort of check on you, you'll be flinging away the lot. So listen to me and be sensible. We'll send her a cheque between us—say twenty pounds. That will give them all a month at the sea and help square the doctor. Will that suit you, Lady Sinclair?'

She nodded, beaming, and clapping her hands without sound.

'That is beautiful! And after——? Can they not come here . . . ever?'

'Why, yes. For a visit. If you're so keen.'

'I want . . . oh, I want to hold that man-child . . . called of your name . . . in my arms,' she whispered, a thrill in her low voice. 'You said there must be family party for Christmas; and that is your feast for worship of children. Could it not be then?'

'M—yes. A bit of a crowd. But still—anything to please you. By the way, Ronald, the stepson—he's a goodlooking boy of twenty— wouldn't make half a bad model for Rama. I believe my father had some scheme about training him up as agent to take Thornbrook's place. We'll have him down one week-end and see.'

So the matter was settled, and the letter written; Lilamani leaning over her husband's shoulder while he filled in the magic paper that stood for twenty golden pounds, ten of them her own. Not until next morning was Nevil tripped up by the question—what would happen when these unconstitutional doings should reach the ears of Jane?

FOUR

'There is a bitter drop in the cup of the best love.'

—Nietzsche

It was a clear morning of sharp, white frost; the first of the year. Lilamani's spirit sprang out of sleep with a sense of being suddenly very much awake. The window of the large old-fashioned bedroom stood wide. Nevil had all the strong young Englishman's faith in fresh air. And through the opening his wife caught a glimpse of tree-tops dazzlingly arrayed. Even lying in bed she was conscious of a new nip in the air.

Curiosity at this rare sense of alertness tempted her to creep out of bed—very gently, so as not to disturb her lord. Slipping into her quilted dressing-gown, she stood looking down at him in a wrapt adoration, undimmed by the manifold disappointments and difficulties of this bewildering English fashion of life. And the five weeks that had elapsed since that first coming of the clan had held their full share of both for husband and wife.

Three more week-end parties, each bearing a strong family likeness to the first, had come and gone; and Nevil's confident hope that 'things would go better next time' had been scantily fulfilled. His own flexible nature had responded readily to the wholesome reaction from six months of secluded, unswerving dedication to the twin lodestars of his being—art and the woman. For the moment, at least, he was thoroughly enjoying his first taste of dispensing hospitality under his own roof, and naturally desirous that the woman of his heart should shine in the eyes of others even as in his own. This, in a limited measure, she did. Her cool, perfumed apartness and unmistakable high breeding gave to her beauty a distinctive quality that men were quick to approve; though the women, with one or two notable exceptions, were apt to label her 'insipid' or 'impossible': the last, an unconscious tribute to her clear-eyed insistence on essentials, which they believed themselves to have outgrown. Thus she still remained over-successful in the wrong direction and still shrank from strange human beings in the mass, especially at food-time. More than all, her own enforced prominence—so unbecoming in a young wife—distressed her soul and made her seeming shyness the harder to overcome.

It is difficult for the West to understand the Eastern woman's complete lack of social instinct; difficult also for a race inured to the arrogant pre-eminence of its youth to realize how slowly, yet how surely, she of the *purdah* comes to her own: and it did not occur to Nevil Sinclair that in these early days of marriage his young wife felt herself more or less in her novitiate, one who must walk humbly and possess herself in patience till the great consummation was hers. But the consummation came not: and once again the haunting fear crept in lest he regard her as a failure in respect of the supreme gift.

For the first few weeks his sympathy with her fish-out-of-water sense had been unfailing. But of late she had detected an occasional undernote of irritation; and could but decipher his moods by the light of her own lamp.

Only last night something had seemed to vex him; and on her venturing to ask what was amiss, he had answered with a touch of weariness: 'Oh, nothing, of any consequence. Things will right themselves in time.' Fervently she prayed that this steadfast conviction of his might be fulfilled, while yet remaining far from a clear understanding of all that fulfilment implied.

In her view one event alone would work the miracle without fail. And now, standing at the bedside, lost in worship of the beloved face—the vigorous brow, straight nose and tender mouth with its endearing touch of the woman-pain and bewilderment gave place to the rapturous certainty that some day, some day the son who should bear his name and nature would lie warm against her breast. And on that day things would right themselves once for all.

One hand lay uncovered on the pillow. Holding her breath, she touched it lightly with her lips; then sped to the window, dread of cold forgotten in the new wonder that met her gaze.

Out there, in the blue-grey dusk of dawn, the familiar garden lay translated. A world of enchantment—all crystal-white, pencilled and stippled with delicate shadows, grey and sepia and black. No leaf or grass-blade, twig or pine-needle but wore its fairy garb of frozen dew. Crisp brown beech-leaves were silver-edged, and a group of young birches reared plumes of diamond-dust against the pallor beyond.

A real, visible awakening of earth and sky had become almost an event in the procession of tearful days that was called November: and sudden longing seized her to escape, as a bird from its cage; to stand alone in the midst of that enchanted world at the moment when it would flash into many-coloured laughter at the kiss of the sun. A childish spirit of adventure stirred her pulses. She would go. They might think what they pleased: 'they' being Jane and George and Phil. For it was Saturday, and a select party of 'guns' had assembled for three days' pheasant-shooting.

It took no time to slip noiselessly into her clothes, crowning all with fur-lined cloak and hood, and a high, dainty pair of snow boots, the only form of boot she could endure to wear. A cup of tea, made in her shrine, fortified her against the cold. Then she flew down and out, unmindful of amazed glances from the second housemaid, who was shaking out the hall mat.

The garden slept in silver, softly still. But the moment of awakening was near. Once outside, the novelty of it all and the pure joy of freedom lured her on. She craved the wide spaces of the moor, the scrunch of frozen heather underfoot. A short cut up through the pine plantation soon brought her out into the open; eyes alight and blood astir with rapid movement. Stepping to the edge, she sat her down upon a rock overlooking the valley where Bramleigh nestled; grey church tower and groups of dull red cottages only half awake, their trailed pennons of smoke tilted southward by a light breath from the north. Plunged knee-deep in misty hollows, the pine woods on the farther rise stood dreaming, their sharp tops fretted upon a toneless sky, that only at its zenith achieved a hint of blue.

Still as any tree among them all sat the lone small figure in the purple cloak, while behind those dreaming woods the benign smile of morning grew wide and wider. Quietly, without pomp and flare of cloud-pageant, the God of Light slipped up over the edge of the world. Trillions of diamond-sparkles from furred ling and gorse flashed back the mild light of him. And it was day.

Lilamani sat on, yogi-fashion, letting that mild light baptize her also and chase away the greyness that had entered into her very soul.

Even on this wonder-morning of fairy raiment and keen sweet air she was aware of something lacking; of stirrings deep down in her primitive, passionate nature that found no response in this gentle dimplement of moor and field; these half-tones and blurred outlines; this pastoral, emotionless peace. Her Eastern soul craved colours more vivid, stronger lights and shadows, a Nature more fiercely, radiantly athrob with the pulse of life. The memory of a certain blazing Egyptian sunset—crimson-red as though the heart of heaven were laid bare—smote her almost with a pang. Here in England the heart of all things, and even of most humans, lay hid so deep, that at times she dared to wonder was it there at all.

Loyalty might refuse to admit the fact; but, in truth, the whole atmosphere of her husband's country—that she had so ardently desired to love for his sake—chilled and repressed her sensitive spirit, that had blossomed in the sunshine and close comradeship of Italy. There the essentials had been their bread and wine of life. Here non-essentials triumphed; and she, having small talent for these, began to feel herself a futile, ineffectual thing beside these vigorous Englishwomen who could carry guns, talk politics, literature, art, with fluent ease, and treat their men-folk with scant respect. Was it possible that he would ever feel the same——?

The desolating question produced a physical shiver; a reminder that in her absorption she had sat still too long. The warmth of walking had subsided. Hands and feet were bitter cold. Foolishness again! She ought not to have sat down at all. For the last few days there had been uncomfortable symptoms, and Nevil had feared she was 'in for a cold,' that distressing and unbecoming ailment which seemed almost as persistent a feature of English life as the rain. Now he would be vexed again; the more so because she had forgotten that breakfast was earlier on shooting days.

Luckless Lilamani! A fit of sneezing shook her. She ran across the open to regain her lost warmth; and on reaching the pine plantation entered a new realm of faery delicately aquiver with sun-smitten mist; the breathing of earth made visible, like her own, by the chill air. Bathed in it, the slender pine-stems showed almost black, their eastward rims painted clear golden, their shadows barring the ground, where moss-cushions gleamed like great emeralds dropped by Sita in her flight. And at intervals, through the stillness came the soft flutter and rush of a breakfast-hunting bird. Hard not to linger and worship afresh; but duty lent wings to her feet: and she sped on.

They were all in the dining-room when she entered—flushed, and a little short of breath. Jane had made tea and was dispensing it. Lord Roscoe stood over the fire, airing *The Times*. George and Phil were discussing the merits of a new gun she had given him. Young Ronald Sinclair and Captain Shadwell of George's regiment were helping themselves at the sideboard.

A polite murmur greeted her appearance, and Nevil shook his head at her without severity. 'Not a very wise Lilamani!' he whispered, as she slipped past him to take her rightful place.

Jane, resigning the tea-pot with reluctance, muttered pessimistically of pneumonia and advised ammoniated quinine.

'*Much* more sensible if you drove out to lunch with the guns instead of running about alone at unearthly hours,' she concluded sagely.

'Yes—perhaps,' murmured the gently persistent renegade with a half-smile at the characteristic remark. 'Sensible' was the keyword of Jane, even as health was the keyword of Audrey, and *dastur* of Mataji. But at thought of Mataji, her heart contracted strangely; and she forced herself to join in the general talk.

Breakfast over, there was bustle of departure, and a few seconds alone with Nevil in the dining-room. He was not vexed, it seemed. But if anything, a shade more tender than usual.

'Take good care of yourself, little girl,' he said, kissing her. 'Don't mope. And you might do worse than try that quinine!'

'Very well; if you wish,' she agreed meekly; conscious of burning eyeballs and rasping throat.

In the large hall Ronald Sinclair contrived a parting word with her. It was not his first visit, and she had a sisterly affection for the boy, strengthened by the fact that an occasional turn of the head and shoulders recalled her husband. Wasn't she coming out to lunch, and wasn't she well? he asked with frank, boyish dismay. How rotten! It would just spoil everything. But he dare say he'd get back early. 'I'm not much of a hand at shooting,' he added by way of excuse. 'And I'd far sooner have a quiet talk with you.'

'I would like it also,' she agreed, smiling, unaware of the vigilant eyes of Jane, who had already noted and resented her disturbing effect even upon the sound and satisfactory George. Now it was to be Ronald Sinclair. Really Nevil was a fool! Further proof of it had lately come to her ears. For the past few weeks she had been too busy organizing an Emigration League and shooting the pheasants of political friends to keep abreast of family news. But she had heard of Clara's windfall now: and finding Aunt Julia innocent, had come down, determined to impress on Nevil, for his own good, the fatal mistake of establishing that sort of precedent with poor relations; Clara, above all: a determination strengthened by Lilamani's evident predilection for Clara's stepson.

When they were gone a great silence fell; a great emptiness. No one to speak to; nothing to do, for the next five or six hours at least; unless Ronald returned soon after lunch. And she hoped he would. Since pheasant-shooting had become an obsession, there had been many such lonely days; and for the first time since her marriage there awoke dim longings for that life of the Inside, where the daily round did not hang entirely on the ways and whims of a man. In Italy there had been work and comradeship, and certain small duties which she had insisted on performing for her lord. But here——! Work was, for the time, in abeyance; and comradeship no less. In this unlovely craze for slaying beautiful birds by the score, she had no wish to share; and even the smallest duties were taken out of her hands by silent, ubiquitous servants, whom she had almost grown to hate.

To-day incipient illness darkened her despondent mood. The promise of the morning had not been fulfilled, without or within. Her cold was decidedly worse; and by now, the sky was overcast. A brisk wind from the west lashed the windows with fine rain. Lilamani sighed. There seemed no end to this English sky's capacity for tears. Having completed a long letter to Mrs. Despard, she lunched alone in her shrine; cooking the meal herself, as always on shooting days; let the tyrants belowstairs think what they would.

The lunch post brought two letters: a welcome interlude. One from her father; one from Audrey. But neither contained cheering news. Her father wrote that the chances of getting home next spring were far from certain. At best he could only hope for a flying visit; and she must not count too much on that. Audrey's was a belated answer to

Lilamani's invitation for Christmas; a week, at least. Disappointing here also. Audrey wrote with sincere regret. For Lilamani's sake she had forced herself to live down the dread of seeing these two as man and wife. But there had been illness at home, and much nursing; and now she herself had 'gone all to pieces.' The doctor prescribed a long rest if she hoped to be fit for India in the spring; and directly it was possible she would go straight out to Antibes. She would try for a night or two at Bramleigh on her way through——

Antibes! Antibes! Headland of blessed memories. Every nerve in Lilamani ached for the glowing warmth and colour of it all; the laughter of the sun upon that sapphire sea with its foam of diamonds; and his strong, warm kisses on her face when she lifted it to him shielding her eyes. Lying there on her couch by the rain-blurred window, half-thinking, half-dreaming, she fell into a light doze, from which Madgwick's knock roused her with a start.

Young Mr. Sinclair was in the drawing-room, said Madgwick, and sent to ask was her ladyship at leisure?

Yes. Her ladyship would come at once; though burning eyeballs and chilled limbs made her wish she had been left to sleep on.

His young concern at sight of her, his protective airs of budding manhood, were very engaging, slang or no. He was a tactless duffer to have disturbed her. A cold made you feel so rotten; and it was stunning of her to come down. Just like her sweetness! But, having come, would she please lie there—he dragged the Chesterfield half across the hearthrug—and not trouble about him any more than if he were the fender-stool! He sat down on it forthwith and produced a silver cigarette-case; her gift.

'Just one. You're not rigid about it, are you?'

'Oh, no.'

'And you don't want to hear how many brace we shot?'

'No—please.'

The delicate wrinkling of her nose emphasized her recoil from all thought of the beautiful slaughtered birds; and he drew her on instead to talk of her own country, its legends, ideals and beliefs.

From the first she had felt singularly at ease with this sympathetic young cousin, whom she treated frankly as a brother; there being small distinction in her own land between the two. In truth, she admitted to him a closer intimacy than George; first because of his youth, and second because, for all his frank admiration, he never troubled her with his eyes.

While they sat talking dusk drew on, peopling the great dim room with restless lights and shadows from the blazing wood fire, worshipped by Lilamani only a few degrees less than the sun. She was feeling soothed and rested; headache almost forgotten; when an unmistakable step sounded without and Lady Roscoe came briskly in.

'No lamps!' Her surprise was tinged with irritation. 'We expected to find tea all ready. Why on earth are you two moping in the dark?'

'Not moping,' Lilamani answered, a faint note of challenge in her tone. 'I had a headache. It was pleasant; and I forgot the tea. I am sorry. Please to ring, Ronald.'

He obeyed, and moved towards the door; anxious, boy-like, to escape 'ructions' that seemed to lurk in the militant tone of Cousin Jane. Directly the door closed on him, she spoke.

'He's not half a sportsman, that boy. A great mistake to have him always idling about the house. I shall tell Nevil. Quite easy to find some young fellow on the spot, who would come in now and again, and do just as well.'

Lilamani roused herself and sat upright.

'No. You are mistaking,' she said, with unwonted decision. 'Others would not suit, like Ronald. And we are so glad for chance to help. He—Nevil, is thinking to train him for land agent here, like his father wished.'

'Agent, is he? That's the first *I've* heard of it. Nevil seems remarkably solicitous for Clara and her contingent all of a sudden. Or is it *you* that are so keen, because she happens to have a good-looking stepson?'

The question was unworthy of Jane. But sport had been poor, and she was annoyed at finding no tea; or she might have refrained. The thrust glanced harmlessly aside.

'Yes. I am liking Ronald very much. But especially I am glad to help because of that smallest son—godson you call . . . of Nevil's name——'

Had Lady Roscoe been in another rank of life she would have sniffed. As it was, her smile had more than a hint of scepticism.

'That's all very well, my dear. Very charming in theory. But if Nevil is still such an infatuated fool that he will dash off twenty-pound cheques to order whenever one of Clara's chronically sick offspring needs a change——'

She broke off short, for Lilamani had sprung up and stood confronting her; anger smouldering in her eyes.

'That is unkindness and untruth! He—he is *not* like . . . what you say; and you shall not speak such rude words of him to me!'

Jane, though hardly less amazed than Balaam on a memorable occasion, was by no means nonplussed.

'Your wifely airs and graces are quite thrown away on me, child,' said she with her exasperating air of condescension. 'It strikes me the rudeness is on your side; and I shall say precisely what I please about my own brother. For it's true.'

'Not true!' Lilamani flashed back fiercely. 'It is simply . . . you cannot understand such big feeling. You said same thing before——'

'I? What d'you mean? I've never mentioned the subject.'

Lilamani, realizing her slip, went hot all over. 'What *do* you mean?' Jane persisted, angered at her silence. 'It's pure invention on your part. Just to make mischief, I suppose.'

'Not invention.' Lilamani's tone had grown suddenly cool and restrained. 'Only—being angry, I made mistake. I was forgetting——'

'What, pray?'

'I . . . cannot explain.'

'Very mysterious! Perhaps "won't" would be nearer the mark.'

At that Lilamani's head went up.

'You are right. Better to speak truth. I *will* not explain. That is all.'

Then—startled at her own temerity, she went swiftly out through the morning-room, avoiding the large hall.

Even as she went, Madgwick appeared.

'Lamps, please. And tea in the large hall,' said Jane.

Nevil crossed him in the doorway, and looked quickly round.

'Hullo! Where's Lilamani?'

Jane made an ungracious movement of the shoulders.

'Gone off in a fit of temper——'

'Temper? She?'

'Yes. Is it news to you that she has one? Is she always butter and honey with you?'

Nevil ignored the question.

'Ronald says that she's not at all well. What did you say to upset her?'

'Merely commented on your latest bit of folly about Clara, and she flew out at me furiously. I suppose one *may* express an opinion about you to your divinity, who seems peculiarly unwilling to bestow any of her butter and honey on *me*——'

'My dear Jane—that's all nonsense!'

'My dear Nevil, it's a fact. I've been as decent as I could to her for your sake; and at least she might be moderately pleasant in return. It can't be——' she eyed him with sudden keenness. 'You weren't mad enough to show her my first letter?'

'Oh, Lord, no!' He fairly flung out the denial thankful for the sheltering dusk.

'Then it's sheer whim, and you should give her a good talking to. One reads that Indian wives are paragons of obedience. But yours, under all her surface silkiness, seems no better than a spoilt child; and you, in your blind infatuation, are laying up a bad time for yourself——'

'Look here, Jane'—Nevil's voice had a touch of her own decision—'you don't understand Lilamani. Never will. I do: and there's an end of the matter. She's my wife——'

'She is also mistress of the dear old Place, worse luck, and the possible mother of future Sinclairs. Though I tell you frankly, it's my fervent hope that if children must come of this crazy marriage there may at least be no son——'

'For God's sake, keep your fervent hopes to yourself!' Nevil cried out sharply, white-hot anger in his eyes: and turning on his heel he went out, leaving her to put her own construction on his flash of wrath.

All things considered, it did not displease her. She took it for indication that her shaft had gone between the joints of his harness and touched the one weak spot in his seeming blind content. She was sorry to have hurt him. But, on the whole, he deserved it. Upon which righteous conclusion, she went in search of tea.

FIVE

'Weak souls are apt to lose themselves in others, whereas it is in others that the strong soul discovers itself.'

—Maeterlinck

It was Christmas Eve. The empty rooms and silent passages of Bramleigh Beeches were alive with footsteps and voices and the high clear music of children's laughter. All the pulses of the staid old house seemed athrob with the immemorial spirit of the day: that child-spirit of loving and giving that shines, like a star fallen on a dust-heap, through all the cynical indifference and vulgarization of our sophisticated age, even as it shone in the Bethlehem Manger near two thousand years ago. Lilamani's eager interest in all that concerned this 'Great Birthday and festival of children-worship' made her husband the more desirous to show her the traditional English Christmas at its best. Hence his readiness to invite Clara, that the child element might be supreme; as indeed it had been ever since the coming of the 'contingent.' Rather more so than Nevil cared about. But he had said little, and devoted himself strenuously to his first big, complex picture—the meeting between Rama and Sita in the hour of victory.

And now the days of fevered activity, of secret preparation, were at an end. In the morning-room a home-grown Christmas tree, bedecked to the last parcel, the last tinsel star, stood alone in the dusk awaiting its brief apotheosis on the morrow. Windows, doorways, and portraits of distinguished Sinclairs, bore their yearly burden of evergreens starred with the living scarlet of holly, the moonlike pallor of mistletoe. George had not failed to catch and kiss his alluring sister-in-law under the great bunch in the large hall with results that plunged the simple-minded soldier in amazement and dismay. She had thrust him fiercely from her, cheeks and eyes ablaze, rubbing the desecrated waxen lobe of her ear as though an insect had stung her: and it had needed much soothing and explaining from Nevil—who rejoiced not a little at his brother's discomfiture—to restore peace. Only in Phillippa's memory the pin-prick rankled. Not the kiss itself, but his desire of it; his exceeding readiness seemed to justify a fundamental doubt of her lover that at times threatened to wreck the 'sound and satisfactory' engagement altogether.

By now the clan was assembled in force; Sinclairs, by blood and marriage, sixteen in all. No outsider save Leslie de Winton; her advent the one bitter drop in Lilamani's present cup of content. Yesterday had brought Nevil's crowning surprise: Christina, home on a brief holiday at her brother's expense; an extravagance Jane herself could not cavil at. For promise of success was in the air. Even she could doubt it no longer. Cultivated London was manifestly impressed by the picture at the Goupil Gallery. Captious and contradictory critics concurred in recognizing that Sir Nevil Sinclair was no longer to be dismissed with the kid-glove applause due to a gifted and titled amateur, but dealt with faithfully as an artist very well worth watching. Better still, in Jane's regard, had been rumours of a purchaser; an art patron with a discerning eye for new talent and a long purse. A week ago rumour had crystallized into fact. Negotiations were in progress. Hence his wire to Christina.

And to-day, sitting alone in his studio, smoking the pipe of reflection while daylight ebbed, he found himself looking back upon the casual, aimless amateur of ten months ago as upon another Nevil Sinclair in another life. Ten months; an infinitesimal fraction of man's allotted time on earth; yet into them had been concentrated more of real living, feeling, thinking, and doing than he had known in the ten years that were as stepping-stones to his appointed goal. The surprise of it all smote him afresh in meditative moments like the present. Almost it seemed as if the instant he set eyes on the Arabian Nights Princess in her balcony, the current of destiny had changed its course. Through her and the love that was her genius, he had found, not merely himself, but a new world and new values. Yet now—when promise of achievement crowned the twofold joy of love and possession, the one shadow in his sunlight was just this small passionate woman who filled so great a space in his life.

It needed no word of complaint from her, no glaring social failure or open clash with Jane to convince him that her new rôle was as ill-suited to her as she to it. Six weeks of shooting and shooting-parties had tried her sorely and Ronald Sinclair's boyish devotion had cost her more than one jarring scene with Jane, though she had not grasped as yet the underlying implication.

He in his fashion had been tried by return visits to the 'needless ones.' But what would you? He was not the man to send her forth alone in quest of the British matron on her native hearthrug; and in the course of these dutiful peregrinations from tea-table to tea-table Nevil Sinclair had perceived more clearly than his wife that not even his own prestige as one of the county could reconcile Bramleigh to the fatal Hindu-ness of his girl-wife. For Bramleigh, being High Church to its kid-glove finger-tips, was disposed to be more zealous in the matter of correct genuflexions and the strict keeping of holy days than in fulfilling the law of love. The former is so much simpler and leaves such a gratifying after-glow of self-righteousness; while the unloved brother is too often unlovable to boot. At best Nevil foresaw kindness tempered with condescension such as the Rajput spirit of his Lilamani would not brook: nor his own Anglo-Saxon one either, if it came to that.

The only result, so far, had been a sparse crop of invitations to dinner; and once or twice, in a dutiful mood, he had suggested acceptance. Lilamani had looked pathetic and submissive; Nevil, thankful to spare her, when feasible, had refused. For himself, he was glad enough not to go. But, at this rate, what of the future, for her? In the summer there would be Helen Despard and, when possible, Christina. Outside these two, if she could not have him, it seemed that she preferred to be alone.

The modification of their own close comradeship had been no less unwelcome to him than to her; but his masculine nature saw it as inevitable, if he were rightly to fulfil himself as artist, landowner, and husband. The Italian conditions had a perfection and fitness all their own. They could be renewed; and should. But they were manifestly incompatible with the demands of the moment. Even when the shooting obsession gave place to a renewed zest for work, there was much in the complex picture now on hand in which she had no part. The crowded background, being new to him, brought fresh faculties into play; while his fastidious eye for grouping and the thematic use of colour made him untiring in regard to preliminary studies, the groundwork of all fine achievement.

At this time the week-end brought artist friends in place of 'guns.' With these Lilamani had seemed more at her ease; and Nevil himself had frankly enjoyed picking up the threads of his lapsed friendship with Leslie de Winton. Apart from the stimulant of talk with a fellow-worker on totally different lines, he found Leslie's comments, whether of blame or praise, singularly illuminating. Once or twice the two had sat up talking in the studio till near midnight; while Lilamani lay throbbingly awake with murder in her heart. Her complete silence, since that first protest, deceived her husband into the belief that she had accepted the friendship for what it was worth: and he enjoyed it accordingly while the mood for mental stimulant was upon him.

At this time he would have dearly liked a short spell in town. But to leave Lilamani was as yet unthinkable; and to take her there hardly less so. By way of experiment he had suggested spending two nights with Broome before Clara came; Mrs. Broome being away. He had baited the suggestion with the promise that on Sunday she should hear a service at the Abbey, and on Monday buy Christmas presents to her heart's content in a shop full of Indian arts and crafts. For in the 'gift-buying' phase of the Great Birthday, she could and would take her full share; investing it, in true Eastern fashion, with a sanctity rarely dreamed of by professing Christians; and Nevil had need of all his authority to save her from spending every penny she possessed.

As for that service, in the dim, richly-toned twilight of the Abbey, it surpassed her most exalted imaginings. Kneeling beside her husband at its close, in awe-smitten ecstasy, while sonorous organ music vibrated through all her sensitive frame, the innately religious heart of her cried out like Festus, 'Almost thou persuadest me to be a Christian.' Not to be at one with her husband in so great and vital a matter hurt her more keenly than he ever guessed; while yet the ancient wisdom of her race warned her that, if change so radical could be genuinely achieved, it must neither be forced nor hurried. And on that morning, in the hush that fell upon her soul when the music ceased, something within whispered that in due time the change would come—as come all great living changes—slowly, imperceptibly, like the opening of a flower.

Yes; the great church, the great shop were wonderful exceedingly; each in its own fashion. But London itself—a monstrous fog-blurred phantasmagoria of life and death, laughter and tears—that was another matter altogether. Driving from Waterloo Station through mean streets, grimed with past fogs and seen through the ochre veil of a present one, she had clung to her husband's arm as to a life-belt in mid-ocean, shrinking close against him, frightened, repelled. To her vivid fancy it seemed that they fared through some hideous fashion of Hell, through which lost souls in their hundreds surged aimlessly to and fro.

'Oh Nevil, is all this noise and ugliness your so great city?' she had ventured, after looking for improvement and finding none.

'Only one unsightly corner of it, at a very unbecoming time of year!' he had explained, smiling.

'And do people really live here, who have choice to live otherwheres?'

'Yes. Hundreds. Wait till you see Broome's house. London's not half so black as she looks at first sight, little wife.'

'Not——?' A sudden fear seized her. 'But you—would you ever——?'

'No—I've no such deadly designs!' he hastened to reassure her. 'Of course, I'd enjoy an occasional month or two in town. But I promised your father I would never keep you here long, or ask you to live here.'

Her sigh of relief spoke volumes.

'Ah, wise one! He knew how the wings of my soul would become crushed—broken in so nightmare a place.'

The two wonder-days that followed were days not readily to be forgotten.

None the less, on Monday she sped joyfully back to clean air and grey skies.

'Like a bird escaped from the snare of the fowler!' Nevil had said, laughing as he lifted her from the landau; while in his heart he relinquished forthwith the desired fortnight in town. He would devote himself instead to the completion of his big picture by the end of the year.

It was close on completion now; and, though far from faultless, he saw that it was good. Yet, as he sat smoking in the dusk, a shadow clouded the native serenity of his eyes and brow.

The past week had been a trying one. Neither Clara herself nor Clara's children were attractive specimens of their kind; and Sinclair was fastidious to a fault.

Mrs. Lunn wore her air of resigned martyrdom with ostentation. 'They childer,' she confided to her ally, Mr. Barnes, 'with their "can'ts" *an*' "won'ts" *an*' their everlastin' muddiness are a deal more trouble in the house than twenty normals. An' the way her ladyship fags after 'em, ill or well, gits me altogether.'

It 'got' her husband also, after another fashion. Almost he could forgive these undisciplined intruders on his peace, for the sake of the new Lilamani their presence brought to light. Her twofold joy in their mere youth, and in her own opportunity for service, was a lovely thing to see. All the true womanly charm of her—dimmed of late by vain strivings to be the thing she was not—shone out with fresh lustre when seen against the right background. But man, though reputed more reasonable than woman, is nothing if not—well, let us say human; and the sudden preoccupation of this new Lilamani in things other than himself gave Nevil Sinclair the first real twinge of jealousy he had known. In her zeal to give the overtaxed widow some measure of rest she spent herself without stint. For, as usual, Clara was ailing, even after her month at the sea; and within three days of their coming, Cissy, aged five, developed tonsils and a temperature, to Nevil's disgust.

Lilamani, armed with a confused jumble of Audrey's teaching and Mataji's primitive skill, begged leave to nurse the child: and Clara— amazed at this heaven-sent heathen cousin-in-law—murmured oh, no, she really mustn't; while devoutly hoping that she would. Nevil remonstrated in private. Lilamani looked pathetic; and won the day. Nevil, half angry, half adoring, had carried Ronald off to the studio and devoted himself to studies of Rama for the ordeal scene; while Lilamani did what she could for her fractious, disobedient charge.

Between Cissy and Christmas parcels and the privilege of bathing Baby Nevil every night, it had been a hard week. And though the spirit rejoiced in service, flesh rebelled. That first cold had led to a second, which left her curiously tired, with a small dry cough that broke her sleep and stirred vague apprehensions in her husband's heart. But Cissy revived; and Nevil welcomed the influx of the clan that would merge Clara's contingent in the general crowd.

More than all he welcomed Christina, whose love, and understanding of Lilamani came within measurable distance of his own. It was his hope that her tact and good temper might serve to mitigate friction with Jane. The latter had scarce been three hours in the house when some disparaging comment upon Clara had fired Lilamani to hot retort; and there had followed as near an approach to a scene as good breeding on both sides would permit. Nevil, for once, had spoken sharply to them both, and been at odds with himself ever since.

Discord, whether in sound, colour, or human relation, jarred the whole nature of the man; and it was this increasing antagonism between wife and sister that clouded his brow to-night; the more so since he was honest enough to recognize that Lilamani herself, though never the aggressor, was the more implacably hostile of the two. Jane's friendliness was a rough-cut jewel at best; and her not very gracious attempts to proffer it had been barren of result. Mercifully, she had never reverted to the letter; had in fact almost forgotten it; while every sentence lived poignantly in Lilamani's brain. If only she had trusted him and left those cruel words unread, it was at least conceivable that all might have gone well in time. Devoted as he was, he could not quite exonerate her from blame, though always he blamed Jane more for the writing of them and his own unthinking carelessness most of all.

Is it one of life's inimitable ironies, or proof conclusive that accident is not—this growth of tragedy from the chance-flung seed of careless unthinking acts? There were moments when it maddened Nevil Sinclair to contemplate all that those half-dozen lines left in his blotter had brought to birth; and to-night he bethought him of an appeal to his wife. Hitherto he had stood aside of set purpose. Even the name of Jane was tacitly avoided between them. But the season, with its insistence on peace and goodwill, seemed to pave the way for speech; and an innate strain of loyalty to the sister he could not love impelled him to do what lay in his power.

The odd thing was that he could by no means foresee the result. At least he knew where to find her at this time of evening: and rising, squared his shoulders as one resolved not to countenance defeat.

'Mine ear is full of the murmur of rocking cradles;
"For a single Cradle," says Nature, "I would give every
one of my graves——"'

—Roumanian Ballad

The door of the day-nursery stood ajar; his own day-nursery, the one room in the house where the spirit of his mother seemed still to linger. He had grudged it not a little to Dick's unruly offspring. But well he knew how she would have approved, both the act of fellow-kindness and her who had urged it—that fragile-sweet wife of his, who, for all her gentleness, seemed rather to set her impress on others than to take colour from the enveloping influences of the West!

As he neared the door a low crooning reached him; broken wordless music, and gurglings of baby laughter. He guessed her alone with the 'man-child called of his name,' whom she had longed to hold in her arms; and, promising himself a glimpse of her unseen, went forward lightly, without sound. A gentle push when he reached the door; and a long pause while he stood on the threshold scarce daring to breathe; the artist entranced, the man inly and deeply stirred.

At the far end of the great dim room she sat, in a mellow zone of light from the green-shaded lamp on the table at her side. A flannel apron shielded her silken daintiness; and on it lay the two-year-old boy in all his pristine rosiness and roundness, kicking out dimpled legs and stretching up eager hands to the glitter of gold and glass dangled above him just out of reach. Wrapt, entranced, Lilamani leaned over him, brow, cheek, and delicately aquiline nose outlined in light; the curve and tinting of her lifted arm a picture in itself. Released from strict mourning, she wore her night-sky *sari* of betrothal, and the great wood-fire woke quivering points of light in breast-girdle and armlets, rings and shining shoes.

A Madonna true to type, was the man's thought. Some day he would paint her thus, with the mother-worship in her eyes. And the child——?

A sudden pang smote him. Jane's voice proclaiming her fervent hope came to him, startlingly clear, across the intervening weeks. Jane, for whom he had come to speak, could find it in her heart to wish—to hope——. Now, as then, white-hot wrath flamed up in him. And yet——? Had he himself——?

'Oh Nevil—I did not hear——!'

An unconscious movement had betrayed him; and her low voice put questionings to flight.

'Sorry if I startled you,' he said, smiling. 'I may come in?'

'Dear lord—what need to ask?'

She glanced from him to the child, and the colour flooded her face: part shyness, part emotion. It was the first time he had sought her out in these regions. That unworthy twinge of jealousy forbade. Even to-night he would scarcely have come, but for Jane. Well, at least he owed her one unforgettable moment; and such return as he could make was very much at her service.

With an undersense of treading on holy ground, he went forward and stood beside his wife.

'A bonny little chap,' said he, looking down at the jubilant creature that rollicked on her arm. 'You'll miss him when he goes.'

She nodded; then glanced up at him, softly content. 'You were wanting me?'

'Am I ever doing anything else worth speaking of?' he asked with a sudden access of lover's ardour, that quickened every pulse in her body; and catching his hand that hung near, she pressed it to her lips. Even after nine months of marriage this was still almost her only spontaneous form of caress. There fell a silence. Two cinders clinked on to the hearth, and the small Nevil chuckled at some private joke of his own.

'I was meaning—did you want me for special reason?' she said.

'Well—yes. I'd like a talk in the studio before dinner.'

'I also. I will come.'

Deftly and quickly she slipped on the small night-things, untied her apron and, rising, stood before him with the other Nevil clinging about her neck, his petal-soft cheek against her own.

'Just one minute for putting him in bed,' said she.

'No—no!' in commanding tones from the embryo lord of creation, jigging up and down like a thing on wires; and she pressed him closer, her lips caressing his hair.

'Little Auntie says yes, O Princeling. And not to cry,' she told him, a hint of authority in her cooing tone that the child never heard in his mother's and instinctively obeyed.

Then she passed on to the night-nursery, with the rhythmical grace of movement that was hers, and the man stood looking after her with very mingled feelings at his heart. It annoyed him that he must needs dispel her mood of mother-tenderness with sententious talk of Jane. He wanted simply to make love to her, to enjoy their rare moment alone; wanted it still more when she sped back to him with flying draperies, and slipped a hand through his as they went.

Till the studio door closed upon them neither spoke. Then it was the woman, softly solicitous.

'Dearest, what now? Something troubling you? Difficult to say?'

And he, pressing the fingers he still held: 'Little witch! How did you know?'

'From your eyes; from your touch of hand,' she answered simply. 'True?'

'Yes, true. Better speak straight and be done. It's about Jane.'

Chin and brows went up ever so slightly, and the gleam that recalled her father lightened in her eyes.

'You are still vexed for that? I am sorry. But how to help being angry? She has no kind feeling when there is trouble. Her heart is little and dried up like a nut. Oh, forgive that I speak like that of your sister! But it is truth. Pity that we must talk of her at this so happy time.'

'A pity indeed. I own I shirked it, as you realized before I spoke. And yet—isn't this "so happy time" just the right moment, Lilamani? My dear little Hindu wife has been so eager to share the spirit of our Christmas festival; and the core of it is peace and goodwill. Could you choose a better time than this for trying to think more kindly of her?'

'I? Oh Nevil—it is *she*——!'

'Lilamani, ask yourself—is it *only* she?'

The blue eyes, that were her heaven, looked straightly, almost sternly into her own; a look that steeped the whole of her in one burning blush. Yet she returned it bravely while he went on: 'I know her manner is often brusque and disagreeable to the verge of rudeness, and yours never. She is hard, unimaginative, everything almost that you are not. But in her own queer fashion she did try, just at first, to be friendly with you, for my sake. Did *you* ever try to make a shadow of response?'

'No,' she answered very low, her voice steady as her gaze; and for the unadorned directness of that denial he admired her the more.

'Isn't the door of your heart bolted and barred against her?'

'Yes. How shall it be otherwise—ever?'

'But, my darling!' His dismay held a note of reproach 'You—the soul of tenderness—how can you be so implacably unforgiving?'

'In our belief there are things it is not good to forgive. Insult to great race of my father, and cruel wound to you, lord of my life. Only by chance was it that in my madness I did not go from you, leaving you without Sita for your so great pictures. Can inmost heart of me ever forget—ever forgive?'

The very quietness of her tone intensified its primitive fierceness of conviction. Before it, he stood speechless, half in amaze, half in admiration. Here was no pretty child to be coaxed into good behaviour; but a woman with all her woman's heart on fire of such strong love and hate as are the heritage of her emotional race.

Capturing one small clenched hand he drew her nearer. 'Not an easy task,' he said gently. 'But you have never tried. Won't you try now, Lilamani, for your lord's sake and for the sake of the Great Birthday we shall keep tomorrow?'

'Oh Nevil!' She drew a deep breath. 'Easy to make such promise with the lips. But how to keep? Loving and hating are not any more to be commanded than sun or sea.'

'No; but at least controlled,' said he of the West, using the key-word of his race. 'And you have to remember this, little wife, that although Jane may be harsh and prejudiced, the real trouble on your side springs from your having read a letter you were never meant to see——'

She started. 'You are still thinking I did wrong by that?'

'In a sense—yes. But it was a great temptation; and I blame myself more than all. I hardly realized then what a proud, fiery-hearted little woman I had to deal with. But unhappily, the thing's done. You know what Jane must never guess that you know; and it follows that you must either be more forgiving or be constantly misjudged by one who is already prejudiced, and who is, after all, my sister. I don't want things to come to such a pass that she shall feel herself unwelcome in my father's house; and this incessant friction hurts me even more than it hurts either of you. So you see, it is for my sake I ask you not to go on cherishing anger, but to give your own tender heart a chance. Will you try?'

For a long minute she stood silent and very still, but for the quickened rise and fall of her breast. Even now he did not feel sure of her answer, till she unveiled her eyes.

'King of me—I will try,' she said gravely; and the concession was a bigger one than he realized. 'I cannot promise for succeeding. But because your wish is like command to me, I will try.'

Then, with a swift, enchanting transition from Indian to English wife, she lifted her lips for the reward that was her due.

'Now—shall we have a quiet time here till dinner?' he asked, his arm still round her. 'Or have you a hundred more things to do?'

'Only to fill three small pair stockings in my shrine.'

'Santa Claus, masquerading in *sari* and spangles!' he said, 'Are the contents a sacred secret? Or may I come too?'

'Come too.'

But as he opened the door of her room, she flew past him with a little cry: 'Oh, I had forgot——!'

The lid of her sandalwood casket stood open, and she closed it swiftly as he came up. Never yet had he seen its contents; and knowing her a creature hedged about with reserves, had refrained from question. But the last few minutes had brought them very near together; and now, obeying his natural impulse, he spoke.

'Shall I ever be allowed to see the treasure hidden in your holy of holies, little wife? I have often wondered what it might be, and when you would think me worthy——'

'*You*? Oh, dearest—that was never my thought! It is only—— How to explain? Indian wife has always some private god for worship; not speaking his name to any, even to her husband. But now—I am trying also to be English wife. There comes no priest between us, as often in India. And—if you are really wishing——'

'I am wishing very much——' he said quietly; and she, with head reverently bowed, lifted the lid.

It has been said that to overhear the prayer of a man is to know him; and Nevil Sinclair, looking down upon the tiny blue image of Baby-hood, gold-crowned, with gilded lute and scroll, had a sense of over-hearing the most intimate prayer of his wife's heart. The primitive simplicity of it moved him beyond speech; and it was she who broke the silence, speaking softly with lowered eyes.

'That is Krishna. Him you have read with me in Bhagavad Gita. That colouring of blue—like sea and sky—is for symbol of infinite. Scroll is for symbol also, meaning the Gita; and lute because he was humbly born among cow-herds, by river Jumna, even like your Christ in that manger. For us he also is Holy child, Healer of World-disease, Shepherd and Lord. Indian mothers are calling this Baby-image their Gopâla, little cow-herd; and to him we pray always for desire of the heart——'

A pause. Her own heart's desire and secret fear trembled on the verge of utterance. Never in their most blessed moments of intimacy had she felt quite so near to him she worshipped; so certain that he would understand. Secure in that certainty, she found courage to speak on.

'To him I pray also for the coming—of that other, too long delayed. And though yet he is not seeming to hear, surely there will come pro-mise soon.' Her voice dropped a tone; and she spoke as one who con-soled him for lack of that which he needs must crave. 'Then you can no longer feel—I am useless wife——'

'Useless! You—my Sita, my main source of inspiration! What put such a notion into your head?'

'Nothing put. It is natural,' she answered quietly. 'I am—oh, so glad for the pictures. But they cannot always be. And then—what use for wife who cannot command servants, or shoot with gun, or make all kinds of talk for dinner-table, unless—by giving of that great gift——'

She could say no more. His arm was round her; his lips against her cheek.

'My darling, you must never think such foolishness again. And as for—the other—— All in good time. Why, you're still almost a child yourself——'

'I am *not*! I am woman!' she cried out with sudden vehemence; contradicting him flatly for the first time and half withdrawing herself from his clasp. And he, looking back on the past half-hour, knew that she spoke truth.

'You are. Very much so. I spoke thoughtlessly,' he admitted, smiling. 'But still—it's full early to be troubling your head about it. And if it's me you're concerned for, you may set your mind at rest——'

'You mean, you do not—you have never——?' His attempt at reassurance chilled her strangely. He seemed suddenly very far away. 'In all these months you have not thought—have not wished——?'

'Is that very dreadful of me?' he asked, drawing her closer; puzzled to know what was wrong. 'I suppose the truth is I've been so well content with my Sita Dévi and the splendid field of work she has opened up for me, that there has hardly been space for other wishes, other hope——'

'Nev-il! Nev-il! Are you there?'

The voice was Leslie de Winton's; and Sinclair felt the small shiver with which his wife released herself.

'Go now. They are wanting you,' she said hurriedly, as the call came again.

'Yes, yes—I'm coming,' he answered impatiently. Then, to her: 'No quiet time, after all, I'm afraid. But remember, little wife, you're not to brood about me. I'm in no hurry to share you with anyone; and quite content with things as they are.'

He was gone; and she stood alone beside the open casket, his final reassurance sounding ironically in her ears.

Nine months married, and neither thought nor desire of fatherhood had been his! That which was, for her, the sum and crown of marriage, was for him a mere side-issue. He was in no hurry for that greatest gift it was her one desire to give. With no Indian husband could it have been so. It was the first time she had compared him thus with one of her own race; had recognized with piercing clearness that on this supreme subject they must needs speak and think in different tongues, spiritually; be their hearts never so close entwined. True, the Hindu sees in his son not merely the torch of life passed on, but the prime factor in that complex transaction, the future welfare of his own soul. Yet even an English husband, for whom wife and son have less of spiritual significance, must surely crave the certainty of an heir to carry on his name; the more so when there are broad lands and an ancestral home, that must otherwise go elsewhere——.

At this point memory flashed a paralysing sentence through her brain—a sentence branded there six months ago, and lightly overlaid with happier things; 'A native mistress at Bramleigh Beeches! Half-caste sons to carry on the name of which we are so rightly proud——'

It was as though a scorpion had stung her. Could it be—that he, her King, shared, even in a small degree, his sister's racial recoil from mixed blood, even of the best? In the deep of his heart did he dread rather than desire the price of possession? It would be like him to feign jealousy of that other, sooner than let her guess——.

Dismay flowed over her like the waters of a cold and bitter sea. All strength seemed to go out of her. Outlines wavered. She swayed a little where she stood. And yet—she could not, she would not so much as harbour the thought. Loyalty forbade. None the less did she foreknow that the hideous thing would return again and yet again to torment her, whenever the way of life was hard or the wheels of being low.

Already it shadowed her joy in this great festival of children-worship. And as she closed the casket two teardrops splashed the Baby image of Him on whom all things are threaded 'as gems on a string': that Blessed One, too preoccupied, it seemed, with the troubles of the orthodox to heed the secret cry of her heart.

SEVEN

'Life is stronger than a single soul.'

—Herrick

Rain and wind; wind and rain; rattling at blurred casements, lashing and battering the patient trees.

Lilamani Sinclair, sick in body and soul, lay listening to the unwearied rush and patter of it in the premature dusk of a February afternoon; till it seemed as though the downpour beat upon her bared nerves, and the wind blew chill through her heart. Now and again the hard dry cough—born of that first cold and never quite dispelled—shook her unmercifully, and drove shafts of pain through her head. Otherwise she lay motionless, with closed eyes, acutely aware of alternating cadences in the storm without; while images and sensations drifted to and fro in her brain scarce coherently enough for thought.

Nominally, she was resting in obedience to doctor's orders, enforced by Nevil. But true rest implies peace of mind—a condition neither doctor nor husband could ensure: and true rest had been far from Nevil Sinclair's wife these many weeks. Morning and night she felt unaccountably tired—mind, body, and soul; unable to feel strongly about anything, even about the pictures, her one supreme link with the artist and the man. They were nearing an end now; the last one already on the easel; the private view for the first week in March. Rejoice though she might in this his great consummation, for her it meant a break beyond which she could see nothing plain, save that he must needs embark on others in which she would probably have no share. And she—with no life of the Inside, and small taste still for the mixed social life of the outside—how would it be with her then——? Unless—unless——?

But no beacon of promise gleamed in that direction. Nor could she hope and pray with the same whole-hearted fervour since the cruel instant of illumination in her shrine. Loyally though she strove against that haunting suspicion, the pain and dismay that had engendered it still acted like a bruise under the skin. How long ago it seemed, viewed across the grey stretch of half-hearted illness and yet more half-hearted convalescence that lay between!

Yet, pain or no, that Christmas fortnight showed like an oasis in the winter's uphill stretch of effort, that seemed to progress at the rate of three steps forward and two steps back: effort to play her part as Lady Sinclair, more especially at the dinner-table; effort to ignore sudden sharp attacks of nostalgia; to still the mother-longing with its attendant fear; to conquer her jealous hate of Leslie de Winton and the seemingly established antagonism of Jane. For Nevil's appeal had been over-long delayed; and though his wife religiously kept her word, such shy, tentative advances as she could bring herself to make had, as often as not, passed unregarded. Nor were matters made easier by a disturbing spell of friction between George and Phil, which Jane shrewdly guessed to be less unfounded than it seemed. That episode of the mistletoe had rather stimulated the man's admiration than otherwise. But, since Phillippa had her pride, and he his modern remnant of chivalry, Lilamani's name was tacitly avoided by both. Lady Roscoe did not doubt for a moment that the disturbance would fizzle out in time. Phillippa's reasonableness and George's good sense were surety for that. None the less she hardened her heart against the unconscious offender; and Lilamani's reluctant hand knocked, almost unheard, upon a closed door.

Happily, after Christmas, meetings had been less frequent. The obsession of the pheasant gave place to the obsession of the fox, and the three carried the light of their countenances elsewhere. But there seemed no evading the malice of the gods. Less of Jane brought more of Leslie de Winton, who infuriated Lilamani by an almost proprietary enthusiasm for a subject peculiarly her own. The intrusion of Janes and Phils, Uncle Bobs and Aunt Julias was as nothing to the renewal of an intimacy so clearly congenial to Nevil that his wife could only keep the door of her lips and suffer the more.

January and February had been months of strenuous work, interspersed with Bohemian week-ends that had brought Mrs. Lunn near to despair. But for Leslie weekends had not sufficed. While the Ordeal scene was in progress she had frankly begged leave to stay 'the clock round,' and her critical, conversational presence in the studio had made this—the crowning picture of the group—an ordeal indeed. Above all things Lilamani enjoyed the atmosphere of quiet while her husband worked. How could she lose herself in Sita and Sita's tragedy, as she loved to do, while the slow, strong voice jarred on her nerves, and the deliberate gaze brooded now on her, now on her lord? If the physical energy of her sister-in-law had made her feel ineffectual, how much more so did this artist woman's breadth and vigour of brain, that matched and challenged the brain of the man; that also, in some subtle fashion, made the things of the heart seem childish, the things of the spirit shadowy and unreal. Worse than all, the dread conviction grew in her that here was her lord's true mate of his own race. Did he not guess it now—yet, at any moment, there might come the knowledge that would wake him from his 'foolish passion outside control of judgment.' And then—then? An end of Lilamani. That was certain. She would not survive, by so much as five minutes, the death of his love.

So passionate a drama of jealousy and pain at work within; and without a smiling acquiescence that did not altogether deceive her husband. At the week's end he had apologized, half in jest, for the infliction, adding: 'I know you're not quite in tone with Leslie; but it's been a real help having her. I find her extraordinarily stimulating. Always did.'

And she—marvelling how he could stand so blindly on the threshold of knowledge: 'If help to your work, you must not trouble for me.'

'I must and I do,' he had answered gravely. 'Though you did have Ronald to balance things a bit!'

The words were ordinary enough to be scarce worth noting, save for the veil of constraint, new as it was unwelcome, that too often of late had hovered between them: so slight a thing, that natures less sensitive had hardly felt it. The trouble was that neither seemed able to brush it aside. Perhaps Lilamani had yet to learn that overmuch self-suppression, however heroic, is good neither for man nor wife, in the more equalized marriage of the West. She could and did hide from her husband her remittent attacks of home-sickness, her secret jealousies. But she could not altogether hide their effect upon her spirits; and at this time an underlying sense of discord jarred their daily life;

saddening her, irritating him. For in the last white-heat of inspiration the artist dominated the man; a passing dominion essential to true creative achievement.

Now it was he who would fain have recaptured the conditions of their life on Como; and behold a tired, listless Lilamani—at moments even a little fretful; her inner self seeming to keep *purdah* from her lord. Small wonder if he gravitated toward the only other woman in any degree able to supply his need. At this time all thoughts, all interests that did not concern the pictures were apt to be ruthlessly swept aside. Only deep down, even in the most strenuous hours at his easel, lurked the ache of anxiety about his wife's health.

Her first winter in his country without a climate had been a singularly unlucky one. A drenching November and open December had given place to bitter weeks of black frost with interludes of snow; and now February seemed determined to outvie March in the matter of gales. That early morning escapade, and the severe cold which followed it, had left seeds of chest trouble, unnoticed at the time. The excitement of Christmas, following upon over-much zeal in Clara's service, had culminated in a fresh chill. Pneumonia supervened; and slight though the attack was, she had never quite rallied. Doctor Ransome, fussy and good-hearted, if not a brilliant specimen of his kind, wrinkled his brow in growing puzzlement over this child of an alien race, who would have none of the stethoscope, obviously resented his questions, and in secret watered the evergreens under her window with his favourite tonic. His faith in that tonic was invincible as his faith in the British Constitution; and seeing it fail, he had muttered vaguely of hysteria and nervous depression, change of air and scene.

This morning he had spoken straightly to Sir Nevil in his wife's hearing, bidding him get her out of England as soon as might be, and keep her out of it till spring's smiling treachery was overpast. Lilamani's heart leapt at the words. She forgave the old man his questions and his chest bogey forthwith. But the worried frown on her husband's brow held her silent. Just at present, he had said, leaving England was impossible. He would see what could be done.

Now, while she lay listening to the swish and patter without, their talk came back to her, and a sudden conviction glowed in her like a star. India—India! There lay the one certain cure for mind, soul, and body. To her own home and people she could not go. But India was a great land and a wide. The mere sight and smell and feel of the country would instil new life into her veins. Only ten days now, and her father would be with them for three little weeks. Then—if they could all return together——! If Nevil would but allow——!

She started. His step was on the stair; his hand on the door. Now for courage to broach her daring request. The coincidence of inspiration and opportunity lit a spark of hope in her heart.

But at sight of his face it went out. The clear blue of his eyes had the veiled, tired look not uncommon after long hours at his easel; and the set of his brows bespoke irritation near the surface. Listlessness flowed over her again like a Dead Sea wave; and she waited for him to speak. He came close and stood looking down at her.

'Well, little wife, it strikes me you've been mooning up here quite long enough. Rested—are you?'

'Yes. A little.'

Disappointment lent an added weariness to her tone and he sighed.

'Only a little. What's come to your natural sparkle, Jewel of Delight? Sometimes I think you're overdoing the sofa business. Do, for my sake, try and pull yourself together instead of drifting limply like a bit of seaweed. You must know how it spoils everything to have you lying here day after day, a mere shadow of your true self. Here's the great end we've both been working for almost in sight and really sometimes it's hard to believe you care——'

'Oh Nevil—dear lord!' she broke in, her lips a-quiver. 'Your heart *must* know, how I am caring. Only some days there seems no life in me—for anything. You said once not ever to think—I am useless wife. But now——'

'Look here, Lilamani—I've told you that's all nonsense, and you must believe it. If you let yourself be hag-ridden by such foolish notions, you'll end in becoming worse than useless.'

'Oh, forgive! It is only—I am ill——'

He caught the appealing hands held out to him and knelt at her side.

'Yes. You *are* ill, in some vague mysterious way. I'm hanged if old Ransome seems to know what's wrong. Perhaps a specialist——'

She shrank into her cushions.

'No, no. Not any more doctor-people, please!'

'But, my dear, you must be reasonable. How can there be any peace of mind for me till we get you right? And your father—what will *he* say if he thinks I've married you only to kill you by inches——?'

'He is too wise to think any such thing. He will understand how it is difficult at first for Indian-born when all is so cold—so grey. Oh Nevil——' the concern in his eyes gave her courage to speak—'there is one thing that can make me a new Lilamani, better than all doctors and medicines. It is—when father is going back to India'—she caught her breath—'if—if we could only go too——'

'India—India?' he repeated the word in amazed iteration. The idea was more than a surprise. It was a shock. It recalled too vividly that one experience of the East which he had no desire to repeat. It also awakened a new fear. His grasp on her hands tightened.

'Lilamani, tell me truthfully—is home-sickness at the root of it all?'

He did not see that the question was a temptation hard to resist.

'If—if it is . . . then *can* we go?' she breathed, scarce able to hold eagerness in check. But the set of his lips gave answer before he spoke.

'My dear little wife, can you seriously ask that? Heaven knows it's hard to refuse you anything, especially at present. But just consider—with this great house on my hands—— I thought I made my position pretty clear to you before Christmas.'

'Yes—yes.' She bit her lip to steady it. 'Only I was hoping—money from that picture——'

'Most of it went to help clear the mortgage. The rest to meet Christmas expenses and the cost of starting our little exhibition.'

She hesitated; then spoke without looking up. 'But for such a thing as this—my own money——'

'You've been spending that too freely, as it is, on Clara's children—to say nothing of your own expenses. You don't realize what it costs to dress a Lilamani in mother-o'-pearl and night-sky *saris*, still less what it would cost to take her out to India——'

She sighed. 'Then—then father? He would so gladly——'

'My darling, you are tantalizing yourself to no purpose,' Nevil checked her with a touch of impatience. 'India's impossible—for a dozen reasons. You must just be plucky and accept the fact.'

'You mean—you do not wish——'

She could get no further. Tears streamed down her cheeks, and sobs shook the whole of her slight frame.

In a moment her husband's arms were round her, his lips on hers. 'My little one—my poor little one! Is it as bad as all that? Didn't you realize, when we married, that most probably—you would never see India again?'

'Y—yes.'

'And did you mind so terribly—then?'

'N—no.'

'Yet now—has England, and the whole life here, been such an utter failure?'

'No—no!' she clung to him, quivering. 'Only—I could not help for hoping. But—if *you* do not wish——'

'I wish above everything to get a well and happy Lilamani back again. I'm so hedged around at present. But the first minute it's possible we'll get you out of this.'

Her light fingers caressed the hair at the back of his neck.

'Perhaps—Egypt?'

'No. I think not. Give me time to turn things over in my mind, and I'll do the best I can.' He kissed her again with lingering tenderness. 'Now I'm going to dry your eyes, and carry you down to the studio. I've done with Rama for the present, and Broome's there waiting to lift you out of the flames.' Broome had volunteered his services as fire-god, to the delight of both. 'It's an ordeal by water that *my* Sita has to win through—eh?'

She laughed and nestled closer, while he dabbed her eyes with his own handkerchief.

'Your Sita is not worthy for going through fire. She is not enough heroine-made.'

'Quite enough to suit her husband! So she need not trouble her foolish head about that. Now then—ready?'

'Yes. But—will he have to hold me in arms again?'

'Once more. I haven't got all the lines right yet. You mustn't mind. He's as old as your father.'

'I am willing for anything to help your pictures. It is only . . . I don't like . . . other kind of arms.'

'No more do I. We're agreed on *that* point!' And he gathered her up in his own.

Outside the studio door she insisted upon being set down and Broome, looking keenly from one to the other, decided that a plain fact or two must be submitted to Sir Nevil Sinclair before they parted that night. Ronald had gone home after another dream-week in the paradise that held his Peri. But not until the Peri had been carried off to bed did the novelist get his chance.

Nevil, returning to finish the evening in the studio, found his friend standing squarely on the hearthrug; pipe between his teeth, smiling determination in his kindly eyes.

'Light up, my son, and don't use language if I touch you on the raw,' said he without preamble. 'Broome on the Responsibilities of the Married State may prove worth listening to.'

'Oh, Lord!' groaned the other, only half in joke. 'Responsibilities were never my strong point. How the deuce have I been shirking them now?'

Said Broome, shifting his pipe to the corner of his mouth: 'Thy question bewrayeth thee. It tacitly admits a prick of conscience. As for mine—the Puritanical thing will give me no peace till I've said my say.'

'Fire away, then.'

Nevil sank into a chair and opened his cigar-case with a leisured air of detachment less deceptive than he believed. The shock of that one word, India, and his wife's unusual paroxysm of grief, had so deeply perturbed him that he had no mind to speak of it even to Broome, unless in self-defence.

'Well?' he queried, looking up and throwing his match into the grate.

'*Is* it well, Nevil—there's my question? Is it well with that exquisite, porcelain wife of yours, who has sacrificed all that really counts for her on the altar of marriage, and has given you, not herself only, but'— he waved a hand round the studio walls—'a new kingdom? Have you asked yourself yet, point-blank, how it seems likely to work out, this unique experiment of translating a love-bird from the tropics into a British barn-door fowl?'

Nevil frowned. 'No. I've not,' he answered bluntly. 'First, because I've no use for a British barn-door fowl; second, because even the amount of adaptation that *is* essential must take time. Though I admit things don't look as promising as they might.'

'My impression exactly. The obvious dissonance with Lady Roscoe is more than unlucky. And how about the good folk of the neighbourhood?'

Nevil shook his head.

'I thought not. Between religion and the Island Pharisee business there's little hope, in the country, for a human product not measured in our own workshops and cut out to pattern. London's another matter. Fish of every shape and colour have a chance in her seething ocean of nationalities and types.'

'Yes. If the fish can live out of water. In London, I believe Lilamani would die outright.'

The older man brooded a moment over that statement. Then: 'Hasn't it struck you, Nevil,' said he, 'that the same process may possibly be going on here—at a reduced rate?'

Nevil Sinclair started and paled as if under a blow. 'Good God, Broome! you don't think——?'

Broome's hand closed firmly on his shoulder.

'Forgive me, old man. I didn't mean to give you such a shock. But I see now it's just as well I spoke. You've been blinding yourself to the obvious; metaphorically bidding everyone and everything stand aside till the last touch is laid on, the white fervour of inspiration spent. Oh, I know it all down to the ground, my dear chap. I've sinned in much the same fashion myself before the birth of every blessed book that bears my name. The Lord our God is a consuming fire, jealous of every impulse but the impulse to create—and all the rest of it. I don't deny we're bound to feel that way if the divine spark is alight inside; and our belongings too often pay the price. But yours is a very special case, Nevil. Your love-bird of the tropics is dependent on you for almost everything, in a way that no English girl would be; and . . . well . . . May I say what I think?'

Nevil nodded, without looking up; and, while Broome spoke on, the formation of a glowing cave between two blocks of coal photographed itself upon his brain.

'I think,' said the novelist with a quiet deliberation not devoid of feeling, 'that of late your wife has grown too light and too transparent even for a porcelain Princess. Dr. Ransome must know better than I can the state of her lungs. But it's my belief that in spite of a devotion to yourself that is little short of worship, she is eating her heart out, in secret, for the light and warmth and colour which are quite as essential to her health of mind and body as fresh air and cold water to yours. I may be wrong——'

Nevil looked up quickly, decision in his eyes.

'Quite the reverse, old man. You're most confoundedly right.'

He paused; shirking further speech; then went resolutely on. 'I suppose you saw that she seemed rather upset when I brought her down. Well—she had just told me, for the first time, that the one certain cure for her would be a spell of India. Seems she had a notion we might go out with her father. I can't tell you the shock it gave me to know the craving was there.'

Broome brought his teeth together with an audible click. 'And you refused?' he asked quietly.

'My dear chap, could I do anything else?' Unstrung by the recollection, he rose and paced the room. 'Look at my position. This exhibition just coming off. The estate on my hands and that millstone of a mortgage round my neck!'

'Quite so. Yet—on the other hand, there's your wife's health in a precarious condition. The trip she craves would be a certain cure; and the house difficulty's not insuperable. You could let for the summer.'

'At a month's notice! And—the deuce of it is I've not the smallest wish to leave the old Place just now. I never guessed what a grip it would get on me once I handled it myself. But that's beside the mark. The truth is'—he swung round sharply, hands plunged in pockets—'there's a bigger obstacle behind. I never meant to speak of it to a living soul. But you've such a confounded way with you——!'

For half a minute their eyes held silent conference. Then Broome spoke.

'Well—what is it now? Sit down, my son, and keep yourself in hand.'

Nevil obeyed to the letter; and it was Broome who paced the room with meditative deliberation, finally coming to a standstill before the first picture of the nine—Sita clinging to her lord, imploring devotion in her gaze.

When all was said that Nevil Sinclair could bring himself to say, of Egypt, of that nameless alienation, and the struggle to win free of its insidious taint, Broome came slowly back; laid an extinct pipe on the mantelpiece, and sat down opposite his friend.

'I see,' he said gravely. 'And—in a measure—I understand. Poor Lilamani! It's a serious complication. You're really afraid a repetition of that might wreck everything?'

'I'm hanged if I know. I can't picture such a thing. All I'm certain of is that—as yet, I shirk the risk, for both our sakes.'

Broome nodded feelingly. 'But the fact of her ill-health remains. If it can't be the East, it must be the South, and that speedily.'

'Yes. She has my promise.'

'Good man. As for the Beeches, a highly desirable "let"—for whose respectability I'll go bail—is sitting not ten feet from you at this moment.'

'By Jove, Broome! D'you mean it—honour bright?'

'As bright as you please! Name your terms.'

'Oh, as to that—a nominal sum——'

'Nonsense! I intend to pay a good fair rental. Since, by some queer accident I managed to catch the long ear of the public, I've been raking in more than one man has any right to possess.'

'Glad to hear it. As for me, I'd be thankful to hand over to you at any price, instead of to a stranger.'

'So I thought! And the sooner the better. Why not Antibes? Miss Hammond's there. Get her father to go too; and you add to the sweet influences of light and warmth the greater one of happy association.'

'Capital! We'll tell her to-morrow. I want to see her looking different before Sir Lakshman arrives——'

'M—yes. It would be advisable.'

Something in his tone made Sinclair eye him closely. 'What are you thinking now?'

'Merely wondering what *he* will say to it all. When fathers love as he and I do their intuitions become extraordinarily keen.'

'I don't know about saying. But if he really thought she was unhappy, I believe he'd be capable of knifing me straight.'

At that Broome's big laugh broke out. 'No fear, my dear boy! But melodramatics apart, I anticipate some plain speech between the two of you if she looks like this. In fact, the way things are going now, it strikes me you will soon have to consider seriously how far you are prepared to vindicate your great experiment by meeting sacrifice with sacrifice on a bigger scale than you have contemplated yet. It's the ultimate test; and in your complicated case, may prove a severer one than you realize.'

Nevil watched the roof of his glowing cavern crumble. Then he drew a long breath. 'I'm beginning to realize it now,' he said slowly; and the coals fell together with a soft crash.

Broome reached for his pipe. The artist rose, and going over to his unfinished picture stood before it lost in thought.

EIGHT

'Love leaps higher with her lambent flame
Than Art can pile the faggots.'

—E.B. Browning

The seventh of March in the year of grace 189– stands out as a red-letter day in the annals of the house of Sinclair. For on that day Sir Nevil—long tacitly written down failure and renegade from historic traditions—made triumphal entry into the kingdom of his choice. Not the type of kingdom precisely befitting a Sinclair. But, before the day was out, Jane, Lady Roscoe, could perceive that her brother stood on the threshold of a unique success. And success is the golden calf of the West; worshipped indiscriminately whether it spring from an inspired group of pictures or a patent hair-wash.

All practical arrangements for the private view had been made by Cuthbert Broome, that Sinclair might not be obliged to leave his wife, or bring her to town a moment sooner than need be. It was Broome also who offered house-room to Sir Lakshman, Martino, and Leseppes; Nevil and Lilamani feeling bound—sore against their will—to accept the dutiful invitation of Jane. On such an occasion, her brother's rightful place was in Grosvenor Square. Mr. Broome, whose unwarrantable offer to 'rent' the Beeches still rankled, was welcome to do all the rest. The which he did. A small gallery in Leicester Square had been chartered; Ramayana pamphlets printed, and invitation cards dispatched to a picked number of artists, art-critics, relations, and friends, bidding them to the said Gallery, where Sir Nevil and Lady Sinclair would be At Home, from three to five.

They were At Home there now. Eighty or so of London's social and intellectual *élite* sauntered, paused or sat about in groups; the low-toned murmur of talk merged in the subdued harmonies of an invisible string band. Those who had ears to hear discerned in the music—carefully chosen by Nevil himself—a subtle fitness to the epic drama present before their eyes: a drama that evolved from the heart of a nation not yet arrived at self-consciousness; and for near two thousand years has retained its power to mould the characters and ideals of a race still unpractical enough to set soul before body, heart before head.

Straight out of the thin, fugitive spring sunshine and keen wind, the unresting clamour of London streets, they had stepped, these complex men and women of the West, into an atmosphere charged with the idealism and the passion, the subtlety and barbaric simplicity of the ancient East. Individualists, egoists, products in varying degree of the modern competitive struggle for existence, they found themselves drawn into the core of India's greatest love-story, builded upon a twofold ideal of duty, fulfilled to the uttermost: of the Queen to her lord; of the King to his people. For although no magic of line and colour could portray the mutual recrimination, the spiritual tragedy of the aftermath, Lilamani had recounted it in the pamphlet, writ by herself, in her own quaintly characteristic English; desiring, above all, that none might miss the typical Eastern culmination, wherein every silent hour of Sita's undeserved banishment speaks, louder than words, the wife's acquiescence in her husband's will.

Along the western wall were ranged six full-size panel pictures, the more arresting for their simplicity, for the entire subordination of effective superfluities to one supreme idea—the proving, through ordeal upon ordeal, of a pure and noble soul.

One only, of all the six, held more than two figures; and in each—whatever its outstanding qualities of emotion, workmanship, colour—the eye rested inevitably on Sita's face. Sita regally arrayed, pleading for her rightful share in the fulfilling of the old King's vow: Sita (Princess no longer) in primitive coat of bark, stepping with subdued elation through Dandak forest; Rama, the path-finder, going before; Lakshman, soul of chivalry, following after. Sita, alone in the forest hut, amber-robed and lotus-crowned, awaiting the brothers' return; all her listening, longing soul in her eyes, while the stealthy ash-smeared figure creeps nearer through the dusk. Sita, terror-struck, yet fighting for dear life, in the ogre-king's embrace. Sita prostrate in the fiend-haunted garden, 'a pool with all her lilies dead': and at the last

Sita, revived in heart and hope, bestowing on the monkey-general her token of unsullied wifehood—the jewel that was her father's wedding-gift.

In these six scenes, linked together by Lilamani's printed record, one phase of the Epic stood revealed; while upon the eastern wall three larger and fuller canvases portrayed the culmination of Sita's proving after the defeat and death of Ravan. In these three scenes—poignant, terrible, triumphal—played out against the living background of Rama's victorious army, Nevil Sinclair proved himself master of the more complex grouping, the larger theme, while yet the queenly, appealing figure of Sita remained supreme. Here, too, the subdued colouring of the earlier pictures gave place to an appropriate effulgence of barbaric splendour, an orchestration of regal harmonies, red and purple and gold.

It was the first of these three—the meeting of husband and wife before two assembled hosts—that drew and held the *élite* of the art world among Sinclair's guests. Here, murmurs of criticism, or appreciation, died into the higher tribute of silence; and here again—for all the fine portrayal of Rama's mute denunciation and Lakshman's pain, the tense expectancy of waiting hosts—it was the figure of Sita, royally dight in crimson robe and wreath, that stirred heart and imagination and checked the futilities of speech. Unveiled for the first time,—proud yet visibly shrinking—she stood, one woman alone in a world of men, with eyes for none but Rama; and in those eyes the dawning of a tragic recognition that here was no kingly welcome, but insult such as no true Indian wife could endure and live.

'Believe it or not, *mon ami*, that one canvas alone would suffice.' It was the voice of Leseppes, low and confidential, in Sir Nevil Sinclair's ear; and grasping his arm, the great man drew him away from the charmed circle of silence. 'Did I not tell you—I, myself? I am not one that looks through tinted glasses. What I said in Cadenabbia— you remember? "You shall stir the blood even of those colossal Philistines, your own countrymen." See them now before that picture— even those that have all the dictionary of art in their finger-ends. Proof enough that you have moved something bigger than the brain. Your father-in-law is satisfied, h'n?'

'Yes. Oh yes.'

The restraint of the Englishman was strong upon Nevil in this his hour of atonement for the locust-eaten years; and the Frenchman as

much elate with his own perspicacity as his pupil's justification
thereof.

'*Bien!* How else? To me it seems that within this hundred feet or so
of space you have presented the very essence of that India to which
you owe your inspiration, together with your wife.'

And it was so. The critical eye of the Frenchman saw plainly that
here was no mere triumph of anecdotal art scorned by an impression-
istic age. Sinclair had imbibed the spirit of the Ramayana through the
spirit of his wife. In these his pictures, as in the Epic itself, the story,
with all its subtle analysis of motive, its barbaric opulence of colour,
served as background, merely, for the proving and revealing of a
woman's soul, triumphant in purity and renunciation: twin kernels of
the Hindu faith.

Not the pictures alone, nor the haunting minor music, but the
whole long room, was imbued with the glow and glamour of the East.
Costly rugs and hangings, quaintly carven chairs inlaid with ivory, on
the temporary dais where Lady Sinclair received her guests, had come
over from India with Sir Lakshman, that the harmony of the subject
and setting might be complete. By Lilamani's wish gold was everywhere the prevailing colour: and she herself—in the midst of sober
black coats and the half tones of early spring—flashed like a living ray
of sunlight: all gold, from veiled head to shining feet; save for the
aquamarines on her breast, and the gleam of sapphire and emerald in
the minutely-jewelled border of a *sari* the most regal she had ever
worn.

For the sake of Nevil and that dear father, from whose keen insight
little could be hid, she had made a last determined effort to shake off
the paralysing listlessness that clouded her clear spirit and hung like
a weight upon her limbs. In a measure will had triumphed. But the
strain and the supervening excitement had taken their toll of her; so
had three days in London, though no longer an ochreous nightmare
of lost souls.

To-day her heart veered between overwhelming shyness and
overwhelming pride. The unnatural brightness of her eyes, the dusky
glow in her cheeks, illumined her like a lamp. Yet Sir Lakshman,
listening courteously to Lord Roscoe's polished turns of phrase, found
eyes and mind wandering incessantly to the small regal figure in the
throne-like chair. For him, no passing illumination could gloss over
the fact that she was thinner. The fine lines of nostrils, nose, and brow

were just perceptibly sharpened, and purplish brown shadows ringed her eyes. Was she well? Was she happy? Or had this notable young
Englishman, with the acquisitive instinct of his race, taken all—devotion, inspiration, fame—and given little in return? To such questions
her lightly-closed lips would vouchsafe him no answer. That he knew.
In eleven months of marriage his child had become woman, and he
must needs accept the veil between. None the less, before returning to
India, he would make very sure——.

'It is remarkable—most remarkable, in a poem of that era, the
mingling of purely epic and barbaric qualities with an insight, a
psychological subtlety peculiarly modern——' Lord Roscoe's well-
bred voice at his ear reminded him that now was not the moment for
anxious brooding over the daughter of his heart.

For the moment she sat alone, glad of a brief respite even from the
friendly volubilities of Martino, who had gone off, on compulsion,
with two brother-artists to give his opinion on a disputed point. For
an hour and more she had endured an unceasing flow of small talk,
compliments, bewildering intellectualities and genuine enthusiasm
that set her head buzzing and left her hands uncomfortably cold.
Here, in this vast, seething London, always agape for some new thing,
was no sign of Bramleigh's nervous shrinking from the unorthodox,
the unusual. Artists, art-critics, minor planets of the social system, all
were eager for more than a passing word or two with the living Sita,
who, until quite lately had been 'a genuine *purdahnashin.*' Glad for
Nevil's sake, she had yet found this avalanche of appreciation a little
overpowering. It had left her small chance of talk with her real friends,
whose joy in Nevil's achievement almost equalled her own.

From her too-prominent seat of honour she sought them out in the
thinning crowd below. Broome on a centre seat, beaming alternately
at Morna and Christina, who talked eagerly across him. Clara, in the
flowing grey gown that was her own gift, nervously pleased and important, clinging to the arm of Rama, who obviously longed to escape. Lilamani did not guess how the longing concerned Sita and a
cup of tea; nor how Clara, in her foolish pride, had been chattering
of two sonnets discovered in her son's rooms, that also concerned Sita,
minus the cup of tea.

Nevil she spied with Leslie de Winton, in the group Martino had
joined, before the terrible scene of Sita's abduction; considered by

some of the younger men the finest thing in the room. Lady Roscoe, on the other hand, pronounced it repulsive and unnecessary; tried not to be aware of it, and failed altogether. Look where she might, uncomfortable sensations assailed her. The 'native element' jarred; and there was far too much primitive, unvarnished emotion in the air to suit her taste. It was more than satisfactory, of course, to feel that at last, by some mysterious accident, Nevil, the impossible, stood on the threshold of distinction. But satisfaction was marred by private worries; and the whole atmosphere of the place set her Philistine bristles on end. A set of vigorous hunting pictures would have been infinitely wholesomer and pleasanter, infinitely more in keeping with the name of Sinclair, than this theatrical farrago of abductions and ordeals by fire!

She had avoided the dais so far; but Lilamani caught sight of her now, in sober purple and ermine, standing with Phillippa near the Hanuman scene, deep in earnest talk that clearly did not concern the picture before them. Once or twice they glanced in the direction of George, who stood at the opposite end of the line, hands clasped behind him, gazing abstractedly at the upturned face of Sita pleading with her lord.

To Lilamani, George still seemed little more than a friendly big dog to be patted and smiled upon because he belonged to her husband; and George absorbed in a picture was a contradiction in terms. She amused herself now with speculating on the nature of his thoughts, that must surely have drifted miles away. It did not occur to her that he was absorbed in no picture, but in the face and figure of a woman rendered almost living by the magic of Nevil's brush.

Possibly her thought drew him, as thought will. Certainly he turned; and seeing her alone made straight for the dais.

'Great luck catching you like this even for a minute,' he said with his Sinclair directness. 'I thought I should never get a look in. I'm nobody to-day!'

'How nonsense!' She smiled indulgent reproof as at a child. 'You are just so much "George" as other days!'

'But you're not a bit the same Jewel. In that ripping frock you look more than ever like a Princess out of a fairytale. And I tell you, that first picture's a stunning portrait. I must get old Nevil to have it photographed for my benefit. Now—do come and have a cup of tea.'

'Very well.'

But as she rose, behold Jane confronting them, with the militant gleam in her eyes that Lord Roscoe had learned to respect.

'One minute, George. Phil's had enough of this. She wants to exchange some books before going home.'

George's scowl emphasized the likeness between brother and sister to a remarkable degree.

'And I'm one of the books she wants to exchange—eh?' he asked, with a gruff attempt at a laugh. 'Phil's quite capable of facing a librarian without an escort and I didn't suppose she'd be keen on mine to-day.'

'My dear boy, don't talk nonsense. Go and call a hansom. She'll be ready in a minute.'

'Oh well—if it's General Orders——! But I don't suppose she's in a mortal hurry; and I want to give Jewel some tea.'

'George——!' Lady Roscoe remonstrated sharply under her breath; then checked herself and stood on guard, while two cups of tea and two sandwiches were swallowed in comfortless haste.

Lilamani, puzzled beyond measure, was thankful when George put his cup down and gripped her hand.

'Sorry I'm obliged to run off like this; and a thousand congratulations on a stunning good show. I couldn't have believed old Nevil had it in him. But he's had all the luck going, this last year.'

His eyes lingered on her a moment in open defiance of Jane. Then he was gone: and, in the silence that fell, Lord Roscoe's even voice could still be heard drawing abstruse comparisons between Homer and his contemporary, Valmiki, hermit and singer, who enriched the national life of India by the story of Rama and his Queen.

Lilamani spoke first.

'Anything gone wrong—with George?'

'Yes. He's making a fool of himself all round. But we can't talk of that here.'

Lady Roscoe scrutinized her sister-in-law for a few seconds, and decided afresh that her dress was far too conspicuous for good taste; then she added in the tone of schooled friendliness Lilamani knew too well: 'You're beginning to look fagged, my dear. If you want to be fresh for the dinner to-night, and fit for travelling tomorrow, you'd better come straight home in the brougham with me. All the best people have gone. Kit can very well play hostess for Nevil's artist friends, and give you a chance to lie down before you dress. I know you're glorying in it all. But be sensible, for once, and come away with me.'

Command lurked beneath the conciliatory flow of words, and Lilamani—puzzled and a little reluctant—felt too tired to resist.

'I am quite ready for being sensible this once!' she said, forcing a smile. 'If he is really not needing me.'

'Come and ask him yourself.'

'Very well.' Crossing over to Sir Lakshman she touched his arm. 'I am going now, Father—for a little rest.'

'Very wise, my child. You look to need it,' he answered, laying a hand over hers and deliberately searching her face. 'We meet again soon—for this great dinner!'

And she passed on. The great dinner—given by Broome—was to be a private one at the Carlton; a gathering of choice spirits to give Nevil and his wife a hearty 'send off' and drink long life to the Ramayana Exhibition.

They found Nevil in the thick of an argument with Martino on the link between motive and art. He commended Jane's wisdom, while privately wondering at it. Lilamani wondered also; the more so that her over-sensitized nerves divined hostility in the air. But not until they reached the drawing-room door and she turned to escape did the true inwardness of Jane's manoeuvre come to light.

'Don't run away at once, Lil. I want a talk with you first,' said she; and Lilamani winced, as always, at the anglicized mutilation of her name.

'I came home for rest,' she objected, without her usual spirit.

'Well, I won't keep you long. But it's important. There's tea in there. One never gets any worth speaking of in a crowd like that.'

Clearly resistance was useless. When Jane meant to have her way she usually had it. Nor did she waste time in beating about the bush. An arm-chair and a cup of tea were the limit of her concessions to Lilamani's weakness.

Her speech was straight and plain.

'Of course it's about George. You asked what was wrong. But you must know as well as I do——'

Lilamani started and set down her cup.

'I? How do you mean?' she asked blankly, and Jane's vexation flashed out.

'My dear innocent! I suppose you're aware that he admires you?'

The frank statement fired Lilamani's cheeks. 'I know he is very kind—almost like real brother. Only sometimes he . . . he troubles me with his eyes. But if you are so bad of heart to think . . . because of that . . . he . . .'

'For goodness' sake, child, give *me* a chance to speak. George is a gentleman and a Sinclair. I'm not suspecting him of anything more serious than a passing fascination for a new type; and that's hard enough on Phil. But she's most reasonable; most sensible. And though Nevil says I "make friction," I'd have let things alone if George hadn't been fool enough, yesterday, to talk airily about running over to Antibes for Easter. Phil says she told him plainly that if he went their engagement would be at an end; and they've scarcely spoken since——'

'But Jane——! How to break so sacred a thing?'

Lady Roscoe waved aside the futile question.

'This isn't a treatise on racial customs. Still—you can take it from me that, in England, we've good sense enough to consider an unsuitable marriage much more disastrous than a broken engagement. But this one is not unsuitable; and it shan't be broken off if I can help it. Women may be over-plentiful. But not girls like Phil, *plus* five thousand a year.'

Lilamani did not quite see the connection of this last. The whole subject jarred her fastidious sense of reserve; and she could not be expected to perceive that it really was rather trying, for Jane, to find this insignificant Hindu child upsetting the whole of her sacred Family.

'I hope there will come no such trouble,' the Hindu child murmured, with a touch of constraint.

'Hoping's no use. I want facts. Has he mentioned this last bit of folly to you? Have you encouraged the idea? Perhaps—with your queer "sisterly" notions, you've been asking him to come——'

'I—oh, what *are* you saying? What shall I, who am wife, have to do with coming and going of—other men?' She rose abruptly; pulses hammering at her temples and in her throat. 'With us it is insult to make any such suggestion; and for—for other kinds of foolishness, how can *I* help——?'

'That's for you to answer. I know *I* could'—which was true enough. 'No right-minded woman fascinates men promiscuously without knowing it; and if you go on at this rate, there'll always be trouble.'

'At what rate?' Lilamani murmured blankly; and Jane, extinguishing her with a glance: 'Don't ask childish questions, but listen to me. It's not only George. There's Ronald writing sonnets to your eyebrows—or some such foolery—by way of being violently original. But Nevil's to blame for that. I'm only concerned for George. If he talks to you of coming out——'

'He will *not* talk,' Lilamani retorted with sudden anger. 'He is not like you think. Only friend. But now all that is spoilt, by your saying such things. I do not wish even to see him——'

'My dear Lil, do sit down. Heroics are futile and bad form.'

Jane spoke more placably, perceiving she had gone too far. But Lilamani shook her head.

'I am tired, and not wishing to hear any more. If you have more to speak you can tell it to Nevil——'

'Nevil, indeed! much use talking to Nevil to-day about mere human beings! He'll be hopelessly in the clouds.'

'Better that, than to be in such ugly kind of mud as you have pushed *me* in now.'

'What nonsense, my dear! That's just your Eastern trick of exaggeration. I'm a practical woman of the world; years older than you; and when I see things going wrong in the family all on your account, I have every right to speak. If you were not so spoilt and so unreasonable, you would take it in good part, and Nevil need not be bothered at all. But really you two haven't an ounce of commonsense between you!'

'For that I am glad and thankful from my inmost soul,' Lilamani made answer with heartfelt fervour of conviction; and was gone.

Alone in her room, she pressed cold fingers against her throbbing temples and flaming cheeks. Then flinging herself on the sofa, she lay chilled and rigid with burning head; her thoughts a chaotic mingling of Epic India, Nevil's triumph and her own renewed hatred of Jane. Foolish? Perhaps. But her health was far from normal. It had been a day of strain; and That Terrible's sacrilegious hand upon her sanctities seemed more than she could endure.

At the approach of Nevil's footstep she sat upright—waiting.

From the rhythm of it she pictured him bounding up, schoolboy fashion, three steps at a time; and his face, when the door opened, confirmed her vision. Dazzled by the day's triumph, he saw nothing, for the moment, but the radiant figure that throughout had been the lodestar of his eyes and mind.

'Rested already? Good!' was his cheerful greeting. Then he came quickly forward, closing the door.

'Oh, my Sita Dévi—it's been a supreme day! And I've come to lay all my laurels at the feet of the Queen. You won't allow me near you in public. Now I claim atonement to the full!'

Laughing, he knelt before her and bowed his head upon the hands that lay in her lap.

At the touch of them he started and looked up. 'Darling—you're ice-cold. And your cheeks are on fire. I thought Jane took you home to rest.'

'Yes. But first she was telling me cruel things—to me like insult— how I am making trouble in your family; breaking betrothal of George——'

'*You?* So that was at the bottom of her sisterly concern. I might have known! That engagement was of Jane's making. If anything goes wrong it's her look-out. You—indeed! Was she unkind?'

'No—no. Only she is not understanding how, for Hindu wife—oh Nevil! Rather would I go back in strictest *purdah*—even from menfolk of husband's family——'

A fit of coughing shook her; and he, tenderly masterful, laid her back among the cushions, covering her with a quilt.

'You stay there and shut your eyes *and* your mind!' he commanded, with a lightness he was far from feeling. 'Leave Jane and George to me; and don't give the matter another thought. That's *hukm*—d'you hear! I want you to be at your very best to-night. Sir Lakshman seems bothered about you as it is; and we don't want fresh trouble in that quarter—— Oh, confound it all!' he broke out desperately. 'She might have let you alone, to-day, of all days, that ought to have been one of unclouded happiness——'

'But King of me'—she clung to his hands—'I am happy in spite of all. Heart and spirit are singing in the air like birds. Only this stupid body, so strangely without life—like a flower faded and thrown in the dust.'

'A very brilliant and beautiful flower,' he said softly, and passed a slow, soothing hand over her from shoulder to ankles. 'It will never be thrown in the dust while I'm alive.'

Her lids fell almost before he had ceased speaking. Yet still he stood over her, watching intently.

With the swift approach of sleep the whole delicate face relaxed its tension. Lips drooped at the corners, shadows under the lashes seemed to darken; and the curve of the cheek was unmistakably less perfect than on the day he sketched it first: significant trifles to the eye of love.

A haunting remark of Broome's returned to trouble him. 'Of course I know you must wait. But the deuce of it is that you can't bargain with the ghostly sisters to "go slow" while an insignificant human completes an insignificant fragment of his life's work.'

Bargain or no—there remained a fundamental reliance on the Great Unseen, strangely intensified by eleven months of union with this Hindu wife of his: and leaning above her now the man's heart breathed a broken prayer that she might not slip away from him on the threshold of achievement.

Then he went softly out, bent on speaking his mind to Jane, with a directness that for once should outrival her own.

NINE

'O greying of my dawn, suspiring into rose: O grey veils of dusk,
that obscure the tender flushing of my dawn!'

—Fiona McLeod

At a small deal table, set across the oval window of her
third-floor bedroom, Audrey Hammond sat writing. It was the selfsame corner room where they had all drunk tea with Signor Martino
in the far-off beginning of things. And now—only four days ago, they
had been shocked and saddened by a letter from Broome announcing
his death. It transpired that sooner than miss Nevil's hour of triumph,
he had come straight from a sick-bed, in defiance of doctor and sister.
And within two weeks the most murderous month in the English
calendar had done its work.

To-day, on the deal table that had once been sticky with his paints,
Audrey Hammond's books and papers, and a photo or two, were set
out with mathematical neatness. Her hand moved steadily over the
ruled page. The lines of her intent face had been graven deeper by a
year's leave that had brought her little of holiday or enjoyment, much
of struggle and pain. She had believed the pain dead and buried, the
emotion that caused it atrophied by stern disregard of its existence,
until she met Sir Nevil Sinclair and his wife at Antibes Station a week
ago. The night or two at Bramleigh had not been achieved: and on that
day of arrival she had discovered, as do all who suffer, that though
love and pain be buried never so deep, they die hard—if they ever die
at all. For are they not twin seeds of the tree of life? And a seed, though
it come not to fruition, remains, for an incredible time, a vital spark
in darkness.

Three days from now, the s.s. *Arabia*, outward bound, was due to
leave Marseilles, with Sir Lakshman and Audrey Hammond on
board. Only three days. On the whole, Audrey would be glad when

they were over; still more glad to take up regular work again. She was at work now, completing an article on nerve crises for a semi-scientific magazine; her fair hair neatly coiled and brushed back as of old, a deep furrow of concentration between her brows. She wore a blue flannel dressing-gown and her bare feet were thrust into slippers. For it was early, very early: a dawn of lucent stillness was stealing over Golfe Juan after a night of sudden tempestuous wind and rain. A last lowering mass of storm-cloud low in the east threw all the bay into gloom. The near hills above Cannes loomed purple-violet. Yet, away in the north, day triumphed on far-off ice-fields and glimmering peaks.

But Audrey Hammond's eyes looked inward rather than outward. The storm had banished sleep and left her at the mercy of importunate thoughts: importunate, because—when not definitely in harness— they were apt to fall back upon those two; the sole human beings who had ever deeply and lastingly disturbed her equipoise, or, in her own phrase, knocked her off her centre.

Lilamani, wife and budding woman, was still for her 'the child' of an earlier day; lovable and gently intractable as ever behind her delicate, impenetrable veil of reserve. This last Audrey understood. She knew enough of the Hindu wife not to expect the sort of confidences that might have been bestowed upon her by an English girl-wife of nineteen. On the whole she was thankful to be spared. But she was not altogether happy about Lilamani; and she suspected that Sir Lakshman was not happy either.

More than once he had asked her searching questions about lungs and nerves; and Audrey, being honest by nature, had not quite succeeded in setting his heart at rest. As regards individual suitability and devotion the marriage was a manifest success; manifest enough to humble the pride of the girl who, in secret, had believed herself the more fitting mate for this man of her own race. But in Lilamani's case the secondary considerations of family and country counted for much. How had she fared with Lady Roscoe, and her large, yet, in a sense, narrow circle of sporting and political friends? What of the neighbours round Bramleigh, and her position as mistress of a great house?

Little could be gleaned from Lilamani. She grew restive under questioning, and Audrey drew her own conclusions. In the matter of her health, this doctor-woman had less need to rely on question. Her quick medical sense detected incipient lung trouble and nerves over-strung either from repression or strain; and conscience urged her to speak a word of warning to Nevil before the last day. No easy task, even for one who had scaled the steeps of stoicism. And yet another vital discovery made speech more difficult still.

Lilamani's shadowed eyes, slightly sharpened features, and her fainting fit on the night of arrival, indicated a hope that would prob-ably readjust altogether her state of body and mind. She wondered whether the child realized things yet; wondered still more what, pre-cisely, was Nevil's attitude toward this, the crux of intermarriage be-tween East and West. She approached Lilamani's husband discreetly, even in thought. Since she could not think of him dispassionately her scrupulous conscience bade her refrain from thinking of him at all. But on this particular point she had always held strong opinions common to the majority of her race. Her own feelings apart, this, the inevitable consequence, had been her main argument against the mar-riage: and, at the time of the engagement, it had seemed to her quite in keeping with Nevil, as she knew him, to snatch impetuously at the desire of his heart, without looking—or perhaps without choosing to look—the more complex issues frankly in the face.

But Nevil, as she knew him then, had seemed little like to develop so swiftly into the restrained and purposeful Nevil of to-day. The fact that a year of marriage had wrought more perceptible change in the man than in the girl-wife eleven years his junior was, for Audrey, the most unique and interesting factor in the whole situation. It had been natural to wonder what would be the effect on Lilamani of marriage with an Englishman and close contact with the ways of the West; and lo, it was he who had taken colour from her. His hyper-civilized brain and soul appeared to have acquired not inspiration only, but a new grip on all things, from contact with the elemental strength and pas-sion underlying her surface pliability. Would Nevil, man and artist, have so developed, so triumphantly found himself, after a year of mar-riage with her—Audrey? On that inadmissible question she sternly slammed the door; and fell back upon her former wonderings. Did the child realize——? And did he——?

One thing was certain. For all her devotion, she had something very much on her mind. Something that concerned her husband; and, in her present state, brooding was the worst of evils. She would be certain to exaggerate trifles, to distort simple facts. If only she would speak——! Invariably Audrey's thoughts came back full circle upon that paralysing 'if'——

And, unguessed by her, the same refrain was, at that very hour, disturbing the mind of Sir Lakshman Singh, who sat sipping his early cup of tea by the open French windows of his first-floor room. Far better even than Audrey Hammond did he understand and appreciate the wifely loyalties and reticences of his child. But he argued that her case was exceptional, that his own responsibility, in regard to the great experiment, privileged him to fuller assurance than he had yet received that she had not bought her heart's desire at too great a price. Finally, he knew that he could not leave her again indefinitely till his doubts had been set at rest. Not her reserve alone, but her manner of evading question, drove him to mistaken inferences, which might have been dispelled by more open speech.

This brief reunion, so ardently longed for, had proved singularly disappointing on the whole. He had spent ten days at Bramleigh and five in London; had spoken little and noted much that gave him food for anxious thought. In spite of immense satisfaction at her vital share in Nevil's success, and his frank recognition thereof, the father's heart—jealous for his child's happiness—foreknew the dangers inherent in overgenerous draughts of the headiest wine on earth; the fatal human tendency to lose sight of the giver in the gift. And when sons came to them—how would it fare with her then? Would the brave words spoken in the glow of desire hold good in face of concrete facts? Nevil was an excellent fellow and singularly wide-minded: not a doubt of it. Yet Sir Lakshman wondered very much.

But when all was said the one imperative anxiety overshadowed every other—her health. Too well he knew the heavy toll paid by his race for the doubtful privilege of culture; the tale of promising young lives cut short by the treacherous grey winters of the West. Her small dry cough and smiling listlessness pierced his heart. They worried Miss Hammond too. That was plain. Something more radical was needed than two or three months on the Continent. A winter in India might very well work wonders. She need not come to Hyderabad. He would mention it to Nevil. If need were, he would insist.

Soothed by the prospect of definite action, he emptied his teacup and lit a cigarette. Most certainly he must find or make opportunity for a frank talk with his son-in-law before the day was out.

Lilamani came down looking a shade more fragile than usual. She had slept badly, she said, on account of the storm; and Sir Lakshman had a moment of quite unreasoning annoyance as he glanced from her dusky pallor and shadowed eyes to her husband's clear-skinned, virile face. Health has, at times, a knack of appearing unsympathetic, even when it is not. For, though Sir Lakshman did not guess it, Nevil's secret anxiety matched his own.

In the middle of breakfast he was called down to the telephone. An artist cousin of Martino's, passing through Nice, begged him to come over for the day. He accepted; and returning to Sir Lakshman's sitting-room, announced his intention and his train. The Indian mentally relegated his straight talk to the after-dinner hour; a propitious hour, when the dinner is likely to be a good one; and the faintest possible shadow clouded Lilamani's face. Her wakeful night had culminated in a decision; and she too must wait till evening for a chance of speech.

'You don't mind my running away, do you, dear?' Nevil asked later, when they had a moment alone. 'If you lie down this morning, you may get back some of the sleep you lost. And you've no lack of good company for this afternoon. I don't doubt Sir Lakshman's blessing me for giving him a clear field!'

'Yes. That is possible!' she answered lightly, though her smile had the shadow of constraint that had troubled him for a week or more.

Questions as to what was wrong produced the invariable answer: 'Not anything,' and immediate change of subject. Some fanciful bogey no doubt; and he had decided not to worry her till sea and sunshine had more nearly wrought their perfect work. 'Go for a drive out Esterelle way, you two,' he suggested.

'Yes. That I would like—better than all.'

But the lost sleep was not recaptured: and when Sir Lakshman unwittingly echoed Nevil's suggestion—in the hope of a confidential talk, that should determine the tone of to-night's arraignment—she baffled him by including Audrey in the plan. It was not the first time she had eluded him thus, since coming to Antibes; and whether she did it of set purpose he could never tell. For once he attempted protest.

'I was not meaning Miss Hammond. Do you want her specially to-day?'

Her grave smile hinted at reproach. 'Not more than other days. Only—think how unkind, Father mine, leaving her in the cold. And she would so much enjoy to come.'

She did enjoy it; more than Sir Lakshman, who left conversation mainly to the women, and carried on a vigorous argument with Nevil in his own mind.

After tea Lilamani slipped quietly away without a word to either: and, as sunset drew on, Sir Lakshman wandered out alone to the rocky headland, raging inwardly against the invisible. Something that debarred him from heart to heart communion with his Jewel of Delight. The very name he so loved seemed a mockery now, in view of her pale cheeks and trouble-haunted eyes. Enforced repression, and a sense of being baffled at every turn, stirred the primitive passions that burn beneath the surface impassivity of the Rajput, and wrought him to a mood of mind ill-befitting the delicate task of approaching an Englishman on the subject of his wife.

But mere movement and the nameless influences of the hour were not without effect; and he decided to make the round of the Cap before going back to his room, where he hoped to find a vanished Lilamani awaiting him in the dusk. He had intended that she should share his stroll, and enjoy with him, as of old, the evening pageantry of sea and sky. But the Gods were against him every way; and their glory manifest in the heavens mocked him rather than consoled. He walked on, bathed in it, while the chill wind of doubt blew through his heart. Could it be that he had done wrong in granting her the thing she craved? If so, well—it was conceivable that he might forgive himself; but never the man who had tempted him to her undoing.

He had reached the Cap now. Fretted and caressed by the darkening waters, it lay before him empty of the usual sunset strollers, who were over at Cannes waging a Lenten Battle of Flowers. No threat tonight of coming storm. The wind was sinking with the sun, and all the west one still, clear lake of gold barred with flakes and strands of dusky purple cloud. Deeper purple still, the carven headland of the Esterelles brooded darkly between a bronze-green sea and a molten sky. Beautiful past question: yet without her vivid, peculiar joy in it all, mere beauty seemed to lack significance.

Suddenly Sir Lakshman stood still. He was not alone after all.

Some distance ahead of him, under the lee of a myrtle bush, sat a dark figure, huddled together, as if the head rested on the hands. But the arms were not visible. Their owner was cloaked and hooded. The father's heart quickened, as he moved a step or two nearer. Then he knew. She had come out after all; and had preferred to come alone. A trifling detail; yet it hurt the man as she had never hurt him yet.

At the sound of his step she sprang up so swiftly that he hurried forward, half-fearing she would evade him even now.

'Lilamani—my child!' he cried, slipping an arm round her. 'What has come over you that you should run away like this, deserting your old father when so few days are left for being together? Why shut the door of your heart against me—unless that you are unhappy——?'

'No—not that, Father mine. Only some foolishness through not being well. But you must please believe—whatever comes, your Lilamani is happy—happy——'

And by way of confirming her statement she fell sobbing on his breast.

For a few minutes he soothed her without speech. But the doubt and trouble that seethed in him could no longer be repressed.

'A strange fashion of happiness, Light of my Life. I know you would not speak lies to me. Yet neither will you speak all the truth. You would not even drive alone with me to-day, when I so greatly wished——'

'To-morrow, dearest—to-morrow,' she assured him, choking back her sobs. 'We will ride on the sea, like old times. You and I only. Nevil will understand. Then we shall talk more freely of—of some things——'

'And why not to-night?' he asked, increasingly bewildered.

She shook her head without lifting it. 'Please not ask. Please understand.'

The old childish formula smote him, and he held her closer.

'Take me back now,' she pleaded; and still supporting her, he led her along the path. 'Not any more Lilamani-talk,' she commanded, smiling. But the doors being once opened the trouble of his mind must out.

'Do you imagine one moment I shall make criticism or discussion of your husband,' said he, quietly disregarding her behest. 'Am I not Hindu also, and you the daughter of my begetting? But I cannot return to India, seeing you in this state, and knowing my child of the sun must again endure that grey cold of English autumn and winter, so fatal for our race.' He felt the small irrepressible shiver and went rapidly, on:

'No daughter of Rajputs will cry out for trifles. But, from my own heart, I know it is telling on you more than you will confess. So much was changed by the sudden death of Sir George. That I understand. Also success and many friends will make Nevil more inclined for living in England than before. But I shall suggest that he must bring you to India, where he can make further study of Eastern subjects on the spot——'

'No, *not* say that,' she broke in with such decision that he came to a standstill and looked searchingly in her face.

'Lilamani—what is your reason? More mysteries? Or is it possible—you do not wish——?'

'Oh, Father—Father!' In the mingled reproach and longing of that cry from her heart, he had all the answer he desired. But she added swiftly, lest he take self-justification for consent. 'We have spoken of that already; and he says not possible. Too far. Too much money, I think—*he* does not wish——'

'Leave all to me, child. There is duty of husband to wife, as of wife to her lord; more especially in the West. Leave it to me.'

His decision outmatched her own; and she, between secret longing and innate instinct of submission to the masculine note of command, said no more.

TEN

'A man's whole victory over Fate begins with a question.'

—Percival Gibbons

Except as regards the *menu*, dinner that night, in Sir Laksh-man's former sitting-room, could not be reckoned a notable success. To Audrey it recalled an earlier dinner, after the storm, when she had counted the moments till she could escape. But to-night she was less concerned for herself than for 'the child,' whose eyes suggested tincture of belladonna; the more so that two dusky patches of carmine burned in her cheeks.

How much did she know of her father's intent? A few words from him before dinner had apprised Audrey of his wish to secure half an hour with Nevil alone. Lilamani would no doubt retire early, and he would regard it as a favour if she left at the same time. The man was clearly too intent upon his purpose to leave anything to chance; and Audrey, as was natural, fell to wondering what he meant to say, and how Nevil would receive it, when she ought to have been coining talk.

Of the four, Nevil only was not obsessed by the sense of something impending. Yet even he gleaned a hint of it from his wife's face, and the fact that she wore her mother-o'-pearl *sari*. He had not seen it for more than a week; and his eyes were not so 'deaf for the language of colour' as they had been a year ago. He knew now that she never wore that *sari* in deeply-troubled or despondent moods, and took its reappearance for a sign that the mercury was rising within. No doubt she had dismissed the hidden worry that hung between them like a veil; and he was glad.

But, Lilamani apart, his natural serenity was clouded by much talk with Carlo Martino of the dead Andrea, who, in spite of mortal frailty, had seemed always too vividly, too passionately alive to go down into the Great Silence, even for a space.

Though caring little for money, and rarely speaking of it, he had, it seemed, left more behind him than a distinguished name. But no form of will had transpired, beyond a half-sheet of foolscap, folded and sealed, bequeathing two incomparable sea-pieces 'to Sir Nevil and Lady Sinclair (Lilamani) for grateful remembrance of one summer, not-to-be-forgotten, on Lake Como.' Nevil Sinclair had felt no shame of the tears that ached behind his eyeballs when he looked upon that half-sheet of paper, henceforth to be counted among his most priceless possessions.

To-night the voices of the living were lost in the clarion call of that dead friend who had bidden him cease from making glow-worms with his eternal cigarette, and from choking with earth that 'spark from the fire of God,' which had since leapt up triumphantly in flame. To-night his art, and all it stood for, shone full in his eyes as when one looks toward the rising sun; while against the radiance of it men and women moved as silhouetted shadows. But for this, he had surely lifted before now the veil, woven of worshipful, fanciful tremors, that had shut him out of late from the inmost sanctuary of his wife's heart.

Thus it befell that the thoughts of all were more active than their tongues; and soon after coffee had been served, Lilamani rose to go. She was tired, not having recaptured that lost sleep, she explained vaguely to whom it might concern. Then she kissed her father with a heart so full of her husband that she missed the meaning pressure of his hand. In passing Nevil, her eyes said: 'Come, I have something to say'; and he nodded a smiling assurance. He himself had much to say of Martino; and decided to join her when he had finished his cigar. A stroll in the moonlight, if she were not too tired, would suit his mood.

Audrey went out with her, smiling to think how little Nevil guessed at collusion; and at Lilamani's door they stopped.

'Am I to come in?' Audrey asked. Her voice had a gentler note than of old.

'Not to-night, please, dear Audrey. I have reason.'

She lifted her face to be kissed with so childlike a gesture, that Audrey, guessing the 'reason,' felt a queer contraction of heart.

'You will never get back lost sleep or lost health, my dear,' she said, kissing the flushed cheek, 'if you bury your troubles and brood over them. There's been one in your eyes all this week.'

'Not trouble.'

'Well, then—something else. Can't you tell Audrey? You said once I stood in place of Mataji——'

For a second or two Lilamani confronted those quiet questioning eyes. Then a hot blush submerged her even to the temples.

'I believe you know quite well, without any telling,' said she, studying the tip of her gold-embroidered shoe.

'I believe I do,' Audrey answered gravely. 'And—is that all?'

'That is all—for now.' And Audrey kissed her again.

'He doesn't know. She is afraid to tell him,' was the older woman's thought as she went slowly down to the central hall. 'And he——? I wonder——!'

His wife was wondering also, as she stood alone on the threshold of her open French window, watching a tawny golden moon disentangle herself leisurely from the last of the tree-tops, and dissolve as leisurely from orange-golden to the amber glow that puts the stars to shame. She had been wondering now for a week and more without arriving at any definite conclusion, save that, for her father's sake, she could put off speaking no longer. Absorbed in her own anguish of uncertainty—her unreasoning self-torment over the unavoidable, intensified by ill-health—she had not realized, till to-night, how wrong it was to keep silence when half a dozen words might set her father's mind at rest.

And he—her lord—himself the giver——?

That there could be any shadow of doubt on such a matter, was to her Eastern heart a calamity almost beyond endurance: her crowning punishment at the hands of her outraged Gods. Joy in the knowledge that at last the great consummation was hers, had been strangled at birth by the old serpent suspicion—scotched, not killed—that, in the deep of his heart, her husband might be hoping to evade the full price of possession; the stigma of passing on the Sinclair title and estates to a son who had not pure English blood in his veins. Not unnatural; that she must needs admit. Pride of race was an instinct she could very well understand. Yet, in such a case her heart cried out that he had no right—no right——

A dry sob shook her; and covering her face she sank into a low chair, set always near the threshold.

Before they left Bramleigh she had known how it was with her. But at that moment the fulfilling of her first gift had absorbed him to the exclusion of all else. Better wait, her heart had whispered, and tell him after—at Antibes, where all things would speak to him of those early days when father, family, country had weighed as feathers in the scale against his great love and desire of her.

But, alas, waiting gave time for thought; and thought bred a host of fears that grew and whispered and distorted themselves with a fiendish versatility; speaking always in the voice of That Terrible, whose unforgettable sentence was the germ whence they had sprung. Had this great hope of motherhood come sooner, no doubt she had accepted it more simply and sanely. But now, ill-health and strain and long brooding on the one idea inclined her to see all things a little out of their true proportion, till at moments she wondered if she would ever find courage to speak at all. Well she knew that, if her fears were grounded, not all his chivalrous tenderness and reticence could blind her to truth. From such knowledge he could not shield her—he could not! One look into his eyes would suffice. And if—if——!

Sooner death for herself and her gift, than that he should not deem it the crown of all, was her desperate thought. With a shuddering sigh she let fall her hands. Oh, when—when would he come? His eyes had said he understood and with each moment of waiting courage waned.

Her room adjoined their dining-room, and the steady murmur of voices through the wall recalled that earlier day, when her fate had hung in the balance. Suddenly the voices grew louder. Was her father, in sheer love for her, making fresh trouble on her account, just when she had that to tell which might be deemed the greater trouble than all?

A torment of restlessness took hold of her. She rose and paced the room, every sensitive nerve of doubt and suspense strained almost to breaking-point. Then she stood still again upon the threshold, and saw how the moonlight seemed magically to be drinking up the shadows along the wide path to the sea. The brooding calm of it all drew her with the potency of a command. Again, as on that still morning of frost, sudden longing seized her to be out there alone in the heart of silence. Surely there, if anywhere, peace and courage would revisit her soul. At least she would escape from those distracting voices that might go on for another hour.

When nerves and imagination are overwrought, impulse seems the voice of inspiration. The garden called her. She would go. Already she was fastening her cloak with unsteady fingers, thankful for the mere relief of movement after the nervous tension of waiting.

Outside in the passage she started and stood still. Through the sitting-room door the voices sounded clearer; Nevil's raised this time in manifest remonstrance. Again, as on that night at Cadenabbia, all thought of right or wrong was blotted out by the imperative need to know; and again came punishment, sharp as the stroke of a sword.

'My dear sir, I'd infinitely rather not,' she heard Nevil say, with a touch of impatience. 'I don't think you quite realize what a big sacrifice you ask of me. Last year, as I've explained, my position was utterly different. But now—with so many new interests opening up, to lease Bramleigh Beeches and practically live abroad——!'

Lilamani heard no more. She had no business to hear. His anger at Como, came suddenly back to her. And clapping both hands over her ears, she sped like a thing pursued, down the shallow staircase, through the empty public dining-room, out into the night——

And the two in the sitting-room, guessing nothing of danger to her they loved, from tension of waiting and nerves at strain, continued to weigh her fate in the balance, even as they had done a year ago, in that very room, on a moonlit night of March.

Nevil's wish to join her, after a brief concession to politeness, had been increased by a vague sense of disturbance, almost of antagonism, in the air. Too well he knew that Sir Lakshman had cause for anxiety; nor did he look to part from him without rendering some account of his stewardship. But to-night, between thoughts of Martino, desire of his wife, and an inspiriting review of his exhibition in *Le Temps*, by Leseppes, he was not in the mood. Moreover, he had all the Englishman's distaste for interposition, however legitimate, between man and wife.

But as he rose Sir Lakshman put out a detaining hand.

'You will spare me another fifteen minutes, Nevil. There is a matter, not yet freely spoken of between us, that has been on my mind all day.'

Politely repressing a sigh, Nevil sat down again and prepared to light a cigarette. 'Very well, sir; if it won't take too long. Lilamani's waiting up for me, and she's tired.'

'That I know too well. And it is because of that—because every day she is seeming a little more tired—that I must ask you plainly, before leaving—is your heart satisfied about her? Mine is not.'

Nevil frowned thoughtfully at his empty coffee-cup, recalling his talk with Broome. This man had twice the right to speak; and yet . . . Nevil felt perversely restive under the Indian's look and tone.

'She is in a very poor state of health,' he answered with studied quietness, 'or we should not be here. Are you implying anything else?'

'No need to waste time in implying. My child's welfare and happiness are more than my own. I am troubled—uncertain about many things; and only straight talk will serve.'

Nevil inclined his head. 'You shall have straight answers, I promise you. About her health I am as worried as yourself. It's the one grave drawback——'

'And you think to make it right by a few months on the Mediterranean?' the other put in quickly. 'That is where you mistake. I know that specialist of London said no lung trouble yet. But unless there is great care, great improvement of health—I tell you, Nevil, it will come. It is your country's backhanded fashion of encouragement to pioneers of our race, especially when very young and over-early developed. Being myself responsible for permitting this marriage, how shall my conscience not feel disturbed in seeing her thus? No criticism of you is in my thought, you understand. And yet—you cannot know as I do——'

'I know quite enough to make me confoundedly anxious,' Nevil declared with a touch of heat. 'You did permit the marriage, thank God; and for her sake I've left England and my Place at a moment when I particularly wanted to be on the spot. What more would you have me do? You must consider that I am an Englishman, with peculiarly strong ties binding me to the country——'

'That I do consider. I also consider that you are husband of a woman outside the ordinary. Though her father, I think I have right in saying there are not too many of her quality in India or otherwheres. For love of you, she is facing many difficulties. Is it good to make them greater than must be? When we spoke of such things in this same room one year ago, you said, from your own impulse, that difficulty of climate need not count, because you would be willing to live chiefly abroad. But now——'

He turned out his hands, Eastern fashion; and Nevil Sinclair leaned suddenly forward, a spark of fire in his eyes.

'You infer that I have gone back on my word, sir?'

'My dear Nevil, I infer no such thing. But in justification of myself I repeat only what you said.'

'Yes. I did say it. And I meant it. But how on earth could I foresee such big changes in so short time? Then I was an amateur artist; a cosmopolitan Bohemian, with no taste for loafing at home, and no very urgent duties to keep me there. Now my duties are obvious and imperative: my father's place to fill as best I can, and a big, heavily-mortgaged estate to keep going, as far as possible on the old lines. What's more, I have grown to love the Place in a way I never thought possible. As for my work, I'm an amateur no longer, but an acknowledged artist—of promise—if no more——'

Sir Lakshman raised his hand. 'Consider one moment, Nevil, in speaking of that last. It has been my pleasure and pride to see that no one is more ready to acknowledge how much of your so rapid success is owing to Lilamani herself. Ask your own heart then—does it square with your British sense of fair play, that you reap all benefit of these changes you speak of, while she must pay all the price?'

'Of course not. Surely you know me better than that.'

'So I was imagining,' the other answered with his grave smile. 'And in such a case you will listen fairly to what I shall say. A couple of months here will not make Lilamani fit for facing your English autumn and winter again so soon and your friend Broome, if willing for a longer lease, can surely be trusted to look after your interests as if they were his own. Why not, then, leave your estates in his care—I do not say for always; but for a term of years, that you may be more free——'

'My dear sir,' Nevil broke in sharply, 'I'd infinitely rather not. I don't think you quite realize what a big sacrifice you ask of me. Last year, as I've explained, my position was utterly different. But, now—with so many new interests opening up—to lease Bramleigh Beeches and practically live abroad——!'

'Not even for the sake of bringing greater health and happiness to that wife who has made, for love of you, a sacrifice bigger than you—not being Eastern—can ever understand?' Sir Lakshman drove home each word of his plea with a quiet, forcible distinctness, that did not fail of its effect. Nevil Sinclair extinguished his cigarette stump, and for several minutes considered the pattern of the carpet with profound attention. The Indian, determined to gain his point, found encouragement even in such negative acquiescence.

'No harm, but rather benefit to your art,' he went on, exchanging the forcible note to one of persuasion, 'from some years spent in other lands than England. And since you have done so well with Eastern subjects, you will be the more able to combine closer study for yourself with the light and warmth that are so needful for this child of the sun you have taken to wife. Better than all, give her a year in India, Nevil——'

Lilamani's husband looked up quickly. 'No, not that, sir. Not India—yet.'

From the moment Sir Lakshman began to speak he had known it was impending. Yet the actual word came as a shock. So also did his abrupt refusal to the man who had believed victory in sight.

'And why not India?' he asked, up in arms at once for his own country. 'Surely——'

'Please don't think me unkind or unreasonable, sir, or take my refusal amiss. I can't explain myself. But you must accept my word for it that India's out of the question.'

As if to clinch the matter he rose, braced his shoulders, and going over to the open door stood there in a long silence, while the opposing forces of passion and ambition, pride of possession and worshipful devotion to her through whom he had found himself, clashed within him mightily, yet without sound. Gazing abstractedly down the pearl-grey path of radiance that ended in the ghostly glimmer of the Mediterranean, he noted, with vague interest, a dusky speck that moved from one pool of shadow to another, far away, down by the balustrade where the rocks fell sheer to the sea. That this moving speck concerned him, even remotely, he did not dream. Unthinkingly he saw it vanish into the last of the shadows; and straightway forgot it altogether.

Sir Lakshman, wondering and waiting in a pained suspense, never removed his gaze from the significant-looking figure in the doorway. If not India—what of the first proposition, unanswered so far?

The question was almost on his lips when Nevil Sinclair turned abruptly and spoke.

'You're right, sir. Absolutely right. For the present, at all events, Bramleigh Beeches must stand back. There are difficulties, of course. It's a matter that can't be fixed up in five minutes. But I shall not change my mind. So you can set yours at rest.'

Sir Lakshman let out a breath of relief. 'The Gods be praised! I have not believed in you without good reason, Nevil. And I am the more thankful for your decision because—not through any word from her—I have a thought that more than her health is concerned.'

Nevil nodded. 'Yes—yes. I admit things have been difficult—for us both, in many ways. Surface things that time will set right; but still—— With me, as you are aware, her nationality simply doesn't count. She's herself, and God knows a man need ask no more of her. But I can't make others see with my eyes all in a moment——'

He broke off with a start. For the door opened suddenly and Audrey stood before them; a little pale, a little out of breath.

'Lilamani's not here?' she asked.

'No,' from both men at once, and Sir Lakshman sprang to his feet.

'I looked in on her to say good night,' Audrey went on. 'But her room was empty. D'you think—would she go out into the garden alone, at this time of night?'

'Why d'you ask that?' It was Nevil who spoke.

'Only because I saw someone in a cloak pass along the verandah about ten minutes ago. I thought no more of it till I found her gone. But I know she has something very much on her mind; and she has such fanciful notions about things—the moonlight and the sea——' Poor Audrey floundered sadly out of her depth. 'At any rate—we might ask the waiters. It's possible——'

'Yes, indeed, it *is* possible. And other things—worse things, are possible as she is to-night.'

Sir Lakshman, knowing the women of his race, spoke with a strange vehemence quite unlike himself.

'Go, Nevil, go!' He gripped his son-in-law by the arm. 'Bring her safe back with you, or—by God——'

Nevil did not wait to hear the rest. He strode out, slamming the door. That speck moving from shadow to shadow came suddenly back to him; and remembrance of a certain night on Como laid an icy clutch upon his heart.

Audrey followed him out, leaving the distracted father alone. Hearing her footsteps, Nevil turned and confronted her.

'Something very much on her mind you said?'

'I thought so.'

'Did she tell you what it was?'

'Not exactly. There was no need. I understood.' A pause: then, for Lilamani's sake, Audrey found courage to add with deliberate, unmistakable significance: 'Nevil—can't you guess?'

Look and tone enlightened him.

'That? Good God!' he exclaimed under his breath—and was gone.

Audrey stood still for many minutes looking at the empty space where he had been, wondering what that fervent expletive might bode for Lilamani's 'great gift.'

ELEVEN

'O very woman, god at once and child,
What ails thee to desire of me once more
The assurance that thou hadst in heart before?
For all this wild, sweet waste of sweet, vain breath
Thou knowest, I know thou hast given me
        Life, not Death.'

—Swinburne

And out there in full moonlight, while the two men talked, the dusky speck, seen of Nevil, moved restlessly to and fro in the open sandy space, where no balustrade intervenes between sheer rocks and the sea.

Not even night and silence could baptize the soul of Lilamani Sinclair with the dew of peace. Fleeing from her overwrought self, imprisoned within four walls, she found only that self, and none other, here at the edge of all things. None other: that was the horror of it. But there came another; a ghostly presence, unseen, yet acutely felt, close to her shoulder, whispering insistently at her ear. And the voice was the voice of Jane. One half of her mind knew it for a product of nerves and imagination; the other half shivered, at the chill nearness of it, like a naked soul in the winds between the worlds.

And through all these importunate unrealities of sight and sound, Nevil's voice, with its note of remonstrance, sounded clearer than all. 'You don't quite realize what a big sacrifice you ask of me.' 'Give up Bramleigh Beeches and practically live abroad——'

Oh, it was impossible, past thinking. How could that dear father—always so wise—make fresh trouble on her account, when already she had made too much in this great English family? Nevil had told her nothing about his own bearding of Jane, save that she need not distress herself over George, who could be trusted not to fling away five thousand a year *plus* a woman who loved him. His parting with her had been awkward and constrained; Jane's, frigidly polite; and her own secret wish had been that she might see neither of them again. They had rubbed the bloom off everything with their 'muddy thoughts.' For that last encounter with Lady Roscoe, striking sharp on her joy in Nevil's triumph—and she peculiarly unfit for emotional strain—had produced upon her an effect out of all proportion to the cause; dashing her rudely to earth, just when her wings had begun to flutter afresh; obscuring the worth of her first great gift in renewed sense of her own unfitness, not for wifehood, but for Lady Sinclairhood and all it involved. Better for him by far, whispered the malign voice at her ear, had he married his true English mate—Leslie de Winton, who would have fulfilled the needs of his art and of his great house no less; and—bitterest 'and'—would have given him sons of his own blood to carry on his distinguished name.

Yet of his own heart and will he had chosen her—Lilamani; perhaps without thought of sons or of great names. And now—when she told him, would he be glad in his inmost heart? Or would he——?

Oh, what foolishness to torment herself thus for more than a week! And yet—better uncertainty than a certainty she could scarce endure, and live. Had she been capable of pouring out her heart to Audrey, much had been spared her. But she was not so made; and it is written that passionate love has a danger for natures over-sensitive and re-served, unknown to the more volatile and expansive. Yet had her sole lapse from self-imposed silence—one shower of tears unexplained, one cry from her heart—wrought this gravest complication of all.

Instinctively her Eastern womanhood rebelled against the idea that her lord should change his way of life in any degree on her account. And her father—himself a Hindu—what possessed him to suggest such madness? Too well her heart knew the answer—love, sheer love, hard pressed by secret fears. For a week or more, whenever his eyes rested upon her, she had seen that love in them suffering dumbly, and yet had not found courage for speech. Oh, coward, and self-thinking, to spoil that dear father's last week with her, through fear of her own pain.

And in two small days he would be gone. The great sea, that brood-ed and murmured below among the rocks, would turn traitor, even like the moon to-night, and take him from her. If only they two might go also—they three, her heart whispered shyly, as she turned her steps seaward and stood upon a grey slab of rock, gazing out across that mysterious other-world which casts so strange a spell over dwellers on land.

Softly still and dark, the wide waters slept beneath the stars, save where moon-butterflies, in their thousands, made a shimmering path of light. The eternal wonder and glory of it was new every morning, every evening. Yet to-night, for the first time, she hated it, almost, that it divided her irrevocably from the dear, deserted Motherland; that India where no doubt could ever be how husband would receive such news as she had to tell.

A verse from the English psalm-book she loved, spoke the cry of her heart: 'Oh, that I had the wings—the wings of a dove——!' And with evil intent that voice at her ear whispered of strong unclouded sunlight, the still lakes and feathered palm-fronds of her own Hyderabad. The temple-bell, the familiar street cries and scents, assailed her with poignant vividness. And through it all, as through a brilliant veil, she saw the chill grey skies of her husband's land; the great house, the ubiquitous servants, the 'needless ones' for ever at her gates! By some fiendish freak of her distraught imagination, Nevil seemed purposely to obliterate himself from the picture——.

What did it mean? What madness had come upon her? Pressing her hands to her temples she stood so, striving for self-mastery. And lo, another voice—a voice of temptation, from the great sea itself. 'Here is rest. Here forgetfulness,' murmured the lazy breakers that lapped against her rock. Like Eve in the old, old legend, this daughter of lake and plain seemed to have hid a wave of the sea in her blood. And now, wave called to wave, with alluring insistence.

A little foam upon the water; and the sea, that incomparable, insatiable lover, would take into his deep heart the dream that was her body, while the dream that was her soul passed on——

Startled, she stepped back a space; and the wonder grew and strengthened in her—was this no temptation, but inspiration rather, pointing the way, not so much to rest from her strange weariness, as to freedom for him—her god among men? No passionate impulse now—as on that night by the waters of Como: but the innate desire of her storm-tossed heart to win happiness for him at any cost to herself. Would not Sita, model of wifehood, have done no less? Sooner than shadow of stain on her lord's name, or shadow of trouble on his heart—an end of Lilamani——.

True, that night on Como he had been angered, desperate, hurt. Yet now—how different! Then—she had much still to give. Now, it seemed she had given all that he had need of—from her; all that she and none else could have given. Must she then pass on; leaving that other—(a red-hot shaft of jealousy here)—to give him those things which were beyond her power——?

How should she tell? How think clearly when thoughts and voices buzzed in her brain like angry bees——!

Stepping again to the rock's edge, she stood looking down into the waiting depths—stone still, as one who listens for a signal.

But there came no signal: only the alluring whisper of the sea.

With a despairing gesture she flung out her arms; swayed a little backward; then forward——

'Lilamani—Lilamani—where *are* you?'

The call reached her just in time. Almost miraculously she regained her balance, and stood rigid, scarcely able to believe her ears.

The desperate note in her husband's voice stilled every tremor, every doubt. It was the signal. The gods did not demand this twofold sacrifice at her hands.

'Lilamani!'

The call came again, appreciably nearer.

'Come to me. I am here,' she called back; a ring of triumph in her clear tones.

Two minutes later he sprang, a flying shadow, out of the massed shadows behind. . . .

For almost an eternity, it seemed to her, they stood, locked together; his pulses hammering, his breath coming in short gasps from the speed of his race. The terror of that night on Como had been his, increased fourfold by his lightning-flash of knowledge: and now that he held her warm and living in his arms, emotion struck too deep for any word of love, or of thanksgiving. He did not even kiss her. It was enough that he held her, almost crushed her against him, forgetful for once of her fragility. The pain of that mute, passionate embrace was pure balm to her heart; and when at last he spoke, his voice had an under-note of sternness more thrilling than a caress.

'I believe—I was only just in time?'

'Yes.' The word was a breath merely.

'You really would——?'

'Oh-h, not say it!' She shuddered; and he gripped her closer. But the note of sternness deepened.

'Lilamani, when I left Como last year, you swore to me, by—the most sacred of all things, that this madness should never come back. How—dare—you break your promise?'

'Oh Nevil! I promised—for then. Not thinking beyond. But now—so different. I am no more needed for Sita; no more making sister of you seem like murderer. I am only making too much trouble in your family, your home. And to-night—passing the door, I stopped—I heard——'

'*What?*'

'You were saying—true enough, how can you give up Bramleigh Beeches and be living abroad, because of me. Much too big sacrifice——'

'Think a moment, little wife. Did I say "too big?"'

'N-no. You said "what a big——" But, dear lord, it was madness of my father to speak such a thing. It is not possible—not right—that for one small woman such great sacrifice shall be made.'

'Not even when that small woman'—his lips were close to her ear—'is to be the mother of my son?'

At that word, heard for the first time, she drew a soft breath of rapture.

'How—how did you know?'

'From something Audrey said—I guessed.'

'And—you are wishing—that son, truthfully, in your heart?'

'I am wishing him truthfully, with all my heart.'

A long pause, filled with the whisper of the sea; tempter no longer, but prophet of peace. Then she—taking courage in both hands, determined to know all: 'Nevil, have I been hurting my soul with pain and doubt for nothing? Did you wish him—just so much—from the first?'

Freeing a hand, he pressed her head against his shoulder.

'Lilamani—if there is to be an end of doubt and pain between us, you must have the truth,' he said quietly. 'I did not wish him—just so much—from the first. For some time I simply put away the thought.

I had you. That was enough. Then—when we got home to the Beeches, I began to realize—well, how much I was my father's son, after
all. It was a bad minute for me, little wife; and it came just when things
were so discouragingly difficult. You remember?'

'How shall I forget?' she spoke quietly as he; all her quivering
sensibilities held in leash. 'And you were wishing—no children?'

'Not that. Never that. I thought—if we had daughters——'

'O-oh!' Her low sound of dismay was Eastern to the core. 'And
since when—were you feeling different?'

'Since Christmas Eve. When I saw you that night, worshipping that
other Nevil, who was no son of mine, a rage of jealousy flamed up in
me; and I knew—not quite then, but afterwards—that no narrow prejudice of race could come between me and the need to see you so, with
a son who should be yours and mine.'

'You are not wishing him daughter now?' she murmured in an ecstasy of content.

'No indeed. Shall I tell you just how I see him?'

'Please tell.'

'You have given me a new spirit of understanding in so many
things, my Sita Dévi; and in this one above all. Six months ago I confess I shrank from the idea of a son handicapped by the stigma of
mixed blood. But now—*you* being his mother—I refuse to admit the
stigma. I see him as one who will have the strength of his handicap,
as one doubly endowed with the best that two great races can give—
the spirituality of the East, the power and virility of the West; one
whose destiny it may be to draw these mighty opposites nearer together by his own intimate love and understanding of both. Is it a good
vision you have given me, beloved?'

She drew in a deep breath.

'Glorious past telling. But it is not I that gave. It is your own so big
heart, and——'

'Hush—listen again. There is more—— You remember I told you
once India was impossible for us?'

'Yes?'

He heard the thrill of eagerness in that whispered question; and had
a fleeting instant of hesitation before committing himself irrevocably
to the inspired impulse of a moment. Then he burnt his boats.

'Well—I had no right to say that. Nothing but my own selfishness stands in the way of our going out there—later on. Next time your father comes home we *will* go out with him—we three. For your sake, and for the sake of all your inspiring love has given me, I promise never again to grudge India her share in the heart of my son.'

And she, laying both hands upon him, looked up at last—her face a beatific vision, in the full light of the moon.

'Husband of me—you are ready for doing all this, only because of—your Sita Dévi?'

'Only because of my Sita Dévi,' he made answer gravely. 'But I also ask a promise in return. Never—while you live—must you let to-night's madness conquer you again.'

'No—no. I promise for always in the name—of him that shall come after.'

And stooping, he sealed that promise with his lips.

Suddenly, the wonder of it all, the incredible change in heart and hope and outlook, swept over her with the force of a breaking wave.

'Oh, I am not deserving!' she cried out, half pushing herself from him. 'All these things you will do, only for your little wife; and I—I thought, I feared—oh, I have been a wicked, doubting Lilamani, this long time. But now—now——'

Swiftly she hid her face against him; and once more, as on the day of betrothal, the deeps of his manhood were stirred by her passionate murmur: 'Live for ever, my lord and my king——!'

EXPLANATORY NOTES

In preparing these Notes I am particularly indebted to the following sources: Jan Knappert, *Hindu Mythology: An Encyclopedia of Myth and Legend* (New Delhi: HarperCollins, 1992); Ivor Lewis, *Sahibs, Nabobs and Boxwallahs* (1991; Delhi: Oxford University Press, 1999); K.M. Sen, *Hinduism* (1961; Harmondsworth, Penguin, 1981); Stanley Wolpert, *A New History of India*, 2nd ed. (New York and Oxford: Oxford University Press, 1982); Henry Yule and A.C. Burnell, *Hobson-Jobson: The Anglo-Indian Dictionary* (1886; London: Wordsworth, 1996); and such reference works as the *New Oxford English Dictionary* (2nd ed., 1989) and *The Oxford Companion to English Literature*, ed. Margaret Drabble (2nd ed., 1985).

EPIGRAPHS

p. 1   *To hold by leaving . . .*: from 'Out of the House of Childhood,' published in Part 4 of *Towards Democracy* (4 parts, 1883–1902); Edward Carpenter (1844–1929), English poet, prose writer, and social reformer. Diver's transcription is inaccurate; the lines should read:

> To take by leaving, to hold by letting go.
>
> . . .
>
> Leaving and again leaving, and ever leaving go of the
>   surfaces of objects,
> So taking the heart of them with us,
> This is the law.

p. 2   *There is a collaboration loftier . . .*: quotation unidentified; Maurice Maeterlinck (1862–1949), Belgian poet and playwright. He was awarded the Nobel Prize for Literature in 1911.

BOOK ONE: THE SEED

CHAPTER ONE

p. 5   I s*tay my haste . . .*: John Burroughs (1837–1921), popular nature writer. The lines are from the poem 'Waiting.' The poem is included in the Preface to *The Light of Day* (1900), vol 11 of

Burroughs *Collected Works*, and has been widely anthologized. The third line of the stanza correctly reads 'I stand amid the eternal ways.'

p. 5   *Cap d'Antibes Hotel*: the Hotel du Cap is the most famous of the hotels on the Cap d'Antibes, a magnificent, isolated peninsula between Cannes and Nice on the French Cote d'Azur, or Riviera. Jules Verne wrote *20,000 Leagues under the Sea* (1869) here.

p. 5   *Riviera*: the southern, Mediterranean coast of the Alpes Maritimes Département, stretching from Cannes to the Italian border; also known as the Côte d'Azur.

p. 6   *The Princess from the Arabian Nights*: a reference to *The Arabian Nights* or *The Thousand and One Nights*, a collection of tales from Indian, Persian and Arabic sources. The most celebrated English translation is that by Sir Richard Burton (1885–1888).

p. 6   *Peri*: from Persian mythology, originally a malevolent superhuman character, but later a beautiful, graceful, good fairy or angel.

p. 7   *lived and moved and had her being*: Acts 17:28. The King James Bible reads: 'For in him we live, and move, and have our being; as certain also of your own poets have said, For we are also his offspring.'

p. 7   *'music and pictures must needs come. But woe unto him through whom they come'*: see Luke 17:1. The King James Bible reads: 'Then said he unto the disciples, It is impossible but that offences will come: but woe unto him, through whom they come!'

p. 7   *the first man child she had gotten from the Lord*: see Genesis 4:1. The King James Bible reads: 'And Adam knew Eve his wife; and she conceived, and bare Cain, and said, I have gotten a man from the LORD.'

p. 7   *understanded of*: the phrase appears in the *Book of Common Prayer*: 'A tongue not understanded of the people.'

p. 8   *General Election*: held at regular intervals to elect members to the House of Commons, and thus to choose the next government. Until the 1911 Parliament Act (when a five-year limit was introduced), elections had to be held within a period of seven years from the first meeting of a new parliament. The date of the General Election referred to is not made clear. The action of the novel certainly takes place in the 1890s; Nevil's sister, Christina, is described as a 'nineteenth-century rebel, less easily quenched than her of the eighties,' and Nevil's exhibition takes place on '[t]he seventh of March in the year of grace 189–'. Two General

Elections were held in Britain in the 1890s: the 1892 election returned a Liberal government under Gladstone, while the Conservatives were returned to power in 1895 with the Marquis of Salisbury as Prime Minister. The novel contains a number of anachronistic references that suggest a later date, including Nevil's reference to 'the savage wars of peace,' from Kipling's poem 'The White Man's Burden' (1899), and the references to Cornelia Sorabji's *Between the Twilights* (1908).

p. 8   *Hyderabad*: founded in 1586 by Mohammed Quli, fifth Sultan of the Qutb Shahi Dynasty of Golconda, the city has a rich architectural and cultural history. Today Hyderabad is the capital of the state of Andra Pradesh.

p. 8   *zenana*: a part of a house in which women and girls are secluded.

p. 9   *the Woman Question*: refers to the debate during the Victorian period in Britain about the nature and role of women in society. Central to the Woman Question was the campaign for female suffrage (i.e. the right to vote), eventually granted in 1918, and the agitation to allow married women to own and handle their own property, which was secured by the Married Women's Property Acts, 1870–1908.

p. 9   *a picture on the line*: a picture in an exhibition (hung so that its centre is about on the level of the eye).

p. 9   *the savage wars of peace*: the line is from the third stanza of Rudyard Kipling's (1865–1936) poem 'The White Man's Burden' (1899):

> Take up the White Man's burden—
>   The savage wars of peace—
> Full fill the mouth of Famine
>   And bid the sickness cease;

p. 10   *Minerva*: the Roman goddess of wisdom.

p. 10   *Apology for Idlers*: an essay by Robert Louis Stevenson (1850–1894), published in 1876.

p. 10   *Quartier Latin*: in Paris; since the Middle Ages this riverside quarter has been dominated by the Sorbonne, France's most famous university. The area, which acquired its name from the early Latin-speaking students, has long been associated with artists and intellectuals, and known for its bohemian way of life.

p. 11   *high caste*: according to the Hindu caste system (*varna*), Hindus are born into one of the four main castes: Brahmin (priests and teachers); Kshatriya (rulers and warriors); Vaishya (merchants and traders); and Shudra (workers and peasants). The untouchables (Harijans; Dalits) were outside this four-tier system. Sir Lakshman Singh, a Rajput, would belong to the Kshatriya, or warrior, caste.

p. 12   *purdah*: the seclusion of women from the sight of men and strangers.

p. 12   *units*: people.

p. 13   *Au revoir*: (French) goodbye.

p. 13   *earnest*: pledge.

CHAPTER TWO

p. 14   *The new hath come . . .*: Sarojini Naidu (1879–1949), Indian poet and freedom fighter. The lines are from the poem 'Past and Future' (lines 1 and 7–9), included in *The Golden Threshold* (1896).

p. 14   *impasse*: (French) figuratively, a fix, a position from which escape is difficult.

p. 15   *Rajput fighters*: (or 'king's sons') Hindu warriors of the Kshatriya caste, from Rajasthan (Rajputana) and elsewhere. Rajput fighters provided the strongest opposition to the Muslim conquest of the subcontinent in the 12th century, and, though forced out of one desert fortress after another, never completely surrendered.

p. 15   *recruited*: recuperated.

p. 16   *dost*: does.

p. 16   *Durga the Ten-handed*: in Hindu mythology, this fierce form of the Mother Goddess is a symbol of shakti or divine power. The yellow-faced Durga rides a lion, and is depicted as beautiful and ferocious at the same time, ten-armed and holding a symbol of the power of the gods in each hand. Other forms of the goddess are Devi, Kali, Parvati, and Uma.

p. 17   *Cornelia Sorabji*: (1866–1954) Indian lawyer and author. The first woman to graduate from Bombay University and to pass the Bachelor of Civil Law examination at Oxford University, though, because of her gender, she was not admitted to the degree. Denied entry to the British Bar (which did not admit women until 1922), and therefore unable to practise law in India, Sorabji devoted herself to improving the lot of Hindu *purdahnashins* (see p. 51 *Purdahnashin*). Sorabjji was a prolific writer. As well as her memoir, *India Calling* (1934), she wrote biographies of her parents and her sister, and several works of fiction and non-fiction including *Love and Life Behind the Purdah* (1901), *The Purdahnashin* (1917), and *India Recalled* (1936). Sorabji was a strong supporter of British rule in India, and an outspoken critic of Indian nationalism.

p. 17 'Wise Man, Truth Named' . . . : Chapter 7 of Cornelia Sorabji's *Between the Twilights: Being Studies of Indian Women By One of Themselves* (1908).

p. 17 *a tithe*: a tenth.

p. 17 'God! By what sign shall we know him? . . .': a largely accurate quotation from Cornelia Sorabji's 'The Wise Man, "Truth named"'.

p. 17 'And the Wise Man says also . . . : from Cornelia Sorabji's 'The Wise Man, "Truth Named"'. The passage Lilamani paraphrases reads:

> the windows of the soul get dimmed and the flame gives no light. Is that the fault of the flame? Clean the windows of the soul; such work is allowed to man, such only, not his to create Light, *that* was and is from Eternity. (Cornelia Sorabji, *Between the Twilights*, London and New York: Harper and Brothers, 1908, p. 76.)

p. 18 *Mataji*: the word is glossed by Maud Diver as 'Honoured Mother.'

p. 19 *the Esterelles*: the Massif de l'Esterel stretches for twenty-four miles along the coast from La Napoule to St-Raphaël.

p. 20 *shawm*: a medieval musical instrument of the oboe class.

p. 20 *nocturne in a minor key*: a musical composition of dreamy character; the minor key lends it a sad or melancholy mood.

p. 21 *Indian ink*: a black pigment consisting of lampblack, made into a paste with gum, dried, and sold in sticks. It was brought to Europe from China, via India, in the seventeenth century.

p. 21 *Yogi*: a devotee of the philosophy of yoga, a Hindu ascetic.

p. 22 *champak and neem*: also called the temple tree, champak is a small species of magnolia which bears highly scented creamy-white flowers which are used for puja (worship); the sacred neem tree, or margosa, grows throughout India. Both trees are believed to have medicinal qualities.

p. 22 *the sacred tulsi*: a basil plant sacred to Vishnu, frequently placed in Hindu temples or domestic shrines.

p. 22 *quinine*: widely used to treat malaria and cholera in the nineteenth century.

p. 22 *a fetish*: an object worshipped for its inherent magical powers.

p. 22 *dastur*: custom or tradition.

CHAPTER THREE

p. 23 I find, under the bows of love and hate . . .: from 'To the Rose upon the Rood of Time,' lines 10–12, first published in *The*

Countess Kathleen and Various Legends and Lyrics (1892); W.B. Yeats (1865–1939), Irish poet, playwright and nationalist.

p. 23   *an article of Audrey's faith*: the Articles of Faith (or Religion) are for Christian theology what fundamental principles are for a science. The 39 Articles of Religion of the Church of England are set out in the *Book of Common Prayer*.

p. 23   *their own Book of Books*: the Bible.

p. 23   *whether ye eat or drink, ye shall do it unto the Lord*: 1 Corinthians 10:31. The King James Bible reads: 'Whether therefore ye eat, or drink, or whatsoever ye do, do all to the glory of God.'

p. 24   *discussed their dinner—in both senses*: i.e. debated and digested.

p. 25   *Hebraic Germans*: German Jews.

p. 25   *Nice*: a city on the French Riviera.

p. 25   *noisettes de veau*: (French) a dish containing prime veal.

p. 25   *mahl-stick*: (also maulstick) a stick with a pad on the end, used by painters to steady their brush hand.

p. 25   *'Life but a coin, to be staked in the pastime, whose playing is more than the transfer of being'*: from 'The Song of the Sword' (1892) by W.E. Henley (1849–1903), English poet and editor, published work by Thomas Hardy, Rudyard Kipling, Robert Louis Stevenson, W.B. Yeats, Henry James, and H.G. Wells. The poem is dedicated to Rudyard Kipling;

> Life but a coin
> To be staked in the pastime
> Whose playing is more
> Than the transfer of being;

p. 26   *a ton of best Wallsend*: coal of a certain quality or size, originally dug at Wallsend (i.e. the end of the Roman wall) in Northumberland, north-east England.

p. 26   *clave to*: stuck to.

p. 26   *Serimamide*: an opera by the Italian composer Gioacchino Rossini (1792–1868), first performed in 1823.

p. 26   *Cannes, Nice, and Monte Carlo*: In 1860 Cannes was included in the newly-formed Alpes-Maritimes Departement. Cannes' transition from a small fishing village into a major resort town began in 1834 when Lord Henry Brougham and Vaux, Lord Chancellor of England, decided to have a home built there. Nice, see p. 25 *Nice*. Situated 20km from Nice on the Cote d'Azur between Cap d'Ail and Menton, and just a few kilometres from the Italian Riviera, Monte Carlo is the capital of Monaco, an independent sovereign state located between the foot of the Southern Alps and the Mediterranean.

p. 27   *yclept*: called or named (archaic).

p. 27   *'pompadour coiffeur'*: hair dressed by rolling it back from the forehead over a cushion, named after the Marquise de Pompadour (1721–1764).

p. 27   *Mentone*: situated in the extreme south-east of France in the Alpes-Maritimes Departement, Menton, along with the town of Roquebrune, was given to France by the Prince of Monaco in 1861.

p. 27   *a 'system'*: a method devised by a gambler for determining the placing of his bets.

p. 27   *Patience*: a card game for one person.

CHAPTER FOUR

p. 30   *Les rencontres ici-bas sont souvent preparés de loin*: (French) 'Meetings here are often arranged from afar,' quotation unidentified; Pierre de Coulevain (pseudonym of Jeanne Philomène Laperche Fernand-Lafargue, 1853–1927).

p. 31   *the red caste mark on her brow*: a symbol on the forehead denoting a person's caste.

p. 31   *Alma Tadema*: Sir Laurence Alma Tadema (1836–1912), known for his painting of exotic subjects.

p. 31   *joie de vivre*: (French) joy of living, exuberance.

p. 31   *Bella*: (Italian) beautiful woman.

p. 31   *francs*: the main unit of currency in France from 1795 to 2002.

p. 32   *tamasha*: an entertainment, show, or fuss.

p. 33   *from a guttersnipe to an archbishop*: guttersnipe, a street urchin from a slum area; archbishop, a metropolitan bishop who superintends the bishops in his province as well as exercising Episcopal authority in his own diocese. In other words, from the bottom to the top of the social scale.

p. 33   *mazurka*: the music, in triple time, for a lively Polish dance of the same name.

p. 34   *valse*: (waltz) a German dance, in triple time.

p. 34   *nautch-girl*: professional dancing girls.

p. 36   *'the Inside'*: the zenana or women's quarter.

p. 36   *'bachelor-girl'*: a young unmarried woman who supports herself.

p. 37   *to the top of their bent*: to the utmost or the limit of their capacity; from Shakespeare's *Hamlet*: 'They fool me to the top of my bent' (3.2.373).

p. 37   *If modern India produced more of his type we should hear little of nothing of political unrest*: for a detailed account of the political unrest of the time see, for example, R.C. Majumdar,

History of the Freedom Movement, 3 vols (Calcutta: K.L. Mukhopadhyay, 1963).

CHAPTER FIVE

p. 38   *A spindle of hazel-wood had I* . . .: unidentified.

p. 38   *a Turkish Djimjim*: a high-quality flatweave rug or throw-rug, similar to a kilim.

p. 38   *Alpes Maritimes*: the mountain range is situated in the Department (06) of the same name, in the south-east corner of France, on the Mediterranean coast, with the Italian border to the east.

p. 39   *houri*: one of the voluptuously beautiful young women who, according to the Koran, reside in the Muslim paradise.

p. 39   *bellissima*: (Italian) very beautiful woman.

p. 40   *'Chut!'*: an expression of impatience.

p. 40   *bene*: (Italian) good, well, or, as in this case, okay.

p. 41   *mio*: (Italian) mine; a term of endearment.

p. 41   *'Leave father and mother, leave all—and follow me'*: paraphrased from the Gospels; see, for example, Matthew 19.

p. 41   *'more honoured in the breach than in observance'*: from Shakespeare's *Hamlet*, 1.4.18.

p. 41   *cloke*: cloak.

p. 41   *Ebbene*: (Italian) well.

p. 42   *'it is mystery that he chases finally, not beauty or love or any success'*: unidentified.

p. 43   *serge*: a strong twilled fabric.

p. 45   *the spirit, that bloweth where it listeth*: John 3:8. The King James Bible reads 'The wind bloweth where it listeth, and thou hearest the sound thereof, but canst not tell whence it cometh, and whither it goeth: so is every one that is born of the Spirit.'

p. 49   *Much Ado about Nothing* . . .: an allusion to Shakespeare's play; Nevil's reflection, 'Queer creatures women—even the soundest,' calls to mind Benedick's misogyny in *Much Ado about Nothing*.

CHAPTER SIX

p. 50   *Drive nature out with a fork;—she comes running back*: from Horace's *Epistles*, 1.10.24; Horace (Quintus Horatius Flaccus, 65–68 BC), Latin poet. An alternative translation would be: 'You may drive out nature with a pitchfork, yet she'll be constantly running back.'

p. 50   *the blue goddess Durga*: the Hindu goddess also know as Parvati, Uma, Kali, Devi, Sati; with her consort, Siva, and their sons, Ganesh and Kartikeya, she represents family unity.

p. 51   *Purdahnashin*: a woman who observes the rules of purdah, or the seclusion of women from the sight of men and strangers.

p. 52   'Wisdom and Destiny': (La Sagesse et la destinée, 1898) an es-
        say by Maurice Maeterlinck.

p. 53   Browning or Maeterlinck or Miss Sorabji: Robert Browning
        (1812–1889), English poet and husband of Elizabeth Barrett
        Browning; Maurice Maeterlinck, see p. 2; Cornelia Sorabji, see
        p. 17.

p. 53   Consistency is the bugbear of small minds: see Ralph Waldo
        Emerson (1803–1882), 'Self-Reliance', in the first series of Es-
        says (1841): 'A foolish consistency is the hobgoblin of little minds,
        adored by little statesmen and philosophers and divines.'

p. 54   Miss Sorabji's book: Between the Twilights: Being Studies of Ind-
        ian Women By One of Themselves (1908). As the events of the
        novel are set in the 1890s (see p. 8 General Election) Lilamani's
        references to this book are anachronistic. See also p. 17 'Wise
        Man, Truth Named'; p. 17 'God! By what sign shall we know
        him? . . .'.

p. 54   distrait: (French) distracted, absent-minded.

p. 54   with the brand snatched from the burning: Zechariah 3:2. The
        King James Bible reads: 'And the LORD said unto Satan, The
        LORD rebuke thee, O Satan; even the LORD that hath chosen
        Jerusalem rebuke thee: is not this a brand plucked out of the
        fire?'

p. 55   rated: berated.

p. 56   zubberdust: the word is glossed by Maud Diver as 'Tyrannical.'
        In The Dream Prevails (1938; London: John Murray, 1939), the
        fourth volume of a loosely-connected quartet of novels, of which
        Lilamani is the first, Diver glosses the word as 'High-handed'
        (p. 25).

p. 56   the retort discourteous: and the retort courteous; an allusion to
        Shakespeare's As You Like It: 'He sent me word if I said his
        beard was not cut well, he was in the mind it was. This is called
        the Retort Courteous' (5.4.69–71).

p. 57   tête-à-tête: (French) private or confidential conversation.

p. 59   a white witch: a witch of good disposition, who uses magic for
        beneficial purposes.

p. 59   sal volatile: smelling-salts; ammonium carbonate, or a solution
        of it in alcohol and/or ammonia in water used to counteract feel-
        ings of faintness.

p. 60   'fares': fare-paying passengers.

CHAPTER SEVEN

p. 61   There stood one with a heart in her hands . . .: quotation un-
        identified; Maurice Henry Hewlett (1861–1923), English novel-
        ist, poet, and essayist.

p. 62   *rated herself roundly*: berated.

p. 65   *carbons and proteids*: compounds now usually known collectively as proteins.

p. 66   *bromide*: a salt of hydrobromic acid (HBr), used as a sedative.

p. 66   *When man comes in at the window . . . anent Poverty and Love*: the common version of the proverb concerning poverty and love is: 'When poverty comes in at the door, love flies out of the window.'

p. 67   *the laws of Manu*: this encyclopaedic Hindu text provides a guide to the way life should be lived, in public and private, in all the stages of life, by both untouchables and priests, and men and women. In short the work is about dharma (or duty).

CHAPTER EIGHT

p. 69   *Love, the great volcano, flings . . .*: from 'The Woods of Westermain,' lines 166–69; George Meredith (1828–1909), English novelist and poet.

p. 72   *Corsica*: a Mediterranean island belonging to France.

p. 73   *crescent-topped outline of a spurious Moorish archway*: after being adapted as an emblem by the Turkish sultans, the crescent became a recognised symbol of the Muslim religion; Moorish refers to the style of architecture produced by the Moors in North Africa and in Spain (during the 8th–15th centuries).

p. 73   *hazards*: chances.

p. 73   *the god out of the machine*: (deus ex machina) providential interposition or divine interference; a power of some sort that arrives just in time to solve a difficulty.

p. 74   *somewhen*: at some time, sometime or other; common in the nineteenth century.

p. 75   *the sword of Damocles*: used as a simile to indicate imminent danger which could fall on one at any time. It has its origin in the story of Damocles, who, having extolled the happiness of the tyrant King Dionysius of Syracuse, was treated by him to a rich banquet, but with a sword suspended over his head by a single hair, to impress upon him the perilous nature of the happiness of the rich and powerful.

p. 76   *the immaculate elder brother in the parable*: Luke 15:11–32, commonly referred to as the parable of the prodigal son, the parable of the father and his two sons is the longest one in the Gospels. In the parable, the father forgives and welcomes home his errant younger son, while the faithful elder son resents the reception afforded to his brother for whom his father kills the 'fatted calf.'

p. 77   *alternations*: alternatives.

CHAPTER NINE

p. 78   *O little more, and how much it is! . . .*: from Robert Browning's 'By the Fireside' (1855), stanza 39.

p. 78   *Heavy-laden*: Matthew 11:28. The King James Bible reads: 'Come unto me, all ye that labour and are heavy laden, and I will give you rest.'

p. 80   *Anglo-Indians*: members of the British community in India as opposed to members of the mixed-race community who were then known as Eurasians.

p. 81   *tussore silk*: (also tusser) a fawn-coloured silk from wild Indian silkworms.

p. 81   *'How brave and wise of you to cross "the black water!"'*: a reference to the belief that orthodox Hindus who cross the black water (the sea) lose caste.

p. 82   *Sapristi!*: (a corruption of the French sacristi) a mild oath; an exclamation of astonishment or exasperation.

p. 82   *amico mio*: (Italian) my friend.

p. 82   *The last infirmity of the true artist*: an allusion to John Milton's (1608–1674) 'Lycidas.' The relevant lines read:

> Fame is the spur that the clear spirit doth raise
> (That last infirmity of Noble mind)
> To scorn delights, and live laborious dayes;

p. 82   *petits fours*: (French) small, fancy biscuits.

p. 83   *'mother and eldest daughter'*: Britain and India.

p. 83   *Bengal agitators or inflammatory news-writers*: for a detailed account of the political climate of the time, see, for example, R.C. Majumdar, *History of the Freedom Movement*, 3 vols (Calcutta: K.L. Mukhopadhyay, 1963).

p. 84   *Even in your own Book . . .*: St Paul, 1 Corinthians 14:8. The King James Bible reads: 'For if the trumpet give an uncertain sound, who shall prepare himself to the battle?'

CHAPTER TEN

p. 89   *O sun of heaven, above the worldly sea . . .*: from *Tristram of Lyonesse*, Part One, 'The Sailing of the Swallow,' an untitled song sung by Tristram; Algeron Charles Swinburne (1837–1909), English poet, dramatist, and novelist.

p. 91   *scherzo, with variations*: a lively and light-hearted movement occupying the second or third place in a symphony or sonata.

p. 91 *Voyez donc, Messieurs . . .*: (French) 'Look, Messieurs, turn around quickly!' . . . 'It's coming like a hurricane.'

p. 92 *Attendez bien*: (French) listen well, pay attention.

p. 92 *monsieur*: (French) mister, sir, gentleman.

p. 92 *louis*: a French gold coin replaced in 1795 by the 20-franc piece.

p. 92 *'les messieurs Anglais'*: (French) the English gentlemen.

p. 98 *kummerbund*: (cummerbund) a waistband or sash (Hindi).

p. 99 *You know our Bible legend? . . .*: Genesis 9:13. The King James Bible reads: 'I do set my bow in the cloud, and it shall be for a token of a covenant between me and the earth.'

p. 99 *Love and faith can move mountains*: 1 Corinthians 13:2. The King James Bible reads: 'And though I have the gift of prophecy, and understand all mysteries, and all knowledge; and though I have all faith, so that I could remove mountains, and have not charity, I am nothing.'

CHAPTER ELEVEN

p. 101 *C'est un ordre des dieux qui jamais ne se rompe . . .*: (French)

> 'It's a rule of the gods that is never broken,
> That they sell us dearly the great things they make.'
> quotation unidentified; Victor Hugo (1802–1885), a leading figure in the Romantic movement in France.

p. 101 *saturate*: saturated.

p. 102 *'lords of creation'*: males.

p. 103 *who came not*: see Alfred, Lord Tennyson (1809–1892), 'Mariana' (1830):

> She only said, 'My life is dreary,
> He cometh not,' she said;
> She said, 'I am aweary, aweary;
> I would that I were dead!'

The poem, inspired by Shakespeare's Mariana of 'the moated grange' in *Measure for Measure*, describes a woman waiting hopelessly for her lover.

p. 104 *The Spinners of Destiny*: in Greek mythology, the three Fates, the three goddesses supposed to determine the course of human life: Lachesis, Clotho, and Atropos, or Past, Present, and Future.

p. 106 *Kama, godling of the arrows*: the god of love in the *Puranas*.

p. 108 *those lines about East and West, that the two may not meet*: the lines are from Rudyard Kipling's (1865–1936) poem 'The Ballad of East and West' (1889). The famous opening lines of the poem are:

> *Oh East is East and West is West, and never the twain shall meet.*
> *Till Earth and Sky stand presently at God's great Judgment Seat;*
> *But there is neither East nor West, Border, nor Breed, nor Birth,*
> *When two strong men stand face to face, though they come from the ends of the earth!*

p. 108 *Mai Lakshmi, goddess of Fortune*: daughter of Brahma-Prajapati and wife of Vishnu; other forms of the goddess are Radha and Sita.

p. 108 *'to her triumph or her undoing'*: unidentified.

p. 110 *suttee*: an Anglicized spelling of the Sanskrit *sati*, meaning a faithful or virtuous wife. The Anglo-Indian application of the word is used to describe both a Hindu widow immolated on her husband's funeral pyre (as intended here) and the act of immolation. The practice was most common among Brahmins, particularly from Rajputana and Bengal. The custom was outlawed in British India by Lord Bentinck's administration in 1829. In the nineteenth century Indian opposition to the practise was led by Raja Ram Mohan Roy.

CHAPTER TWELVE

p. 111 *He which observes the wind shall hardly sow . . .*: from 'The Night of Foreboding'; Francis Thompson (1859–1907), English poet. See also Ecclesiastes 11:4. The King James Bible reads: 'He that observeth the wind shall not sow; and he that regardeth the clouds shall not reap.'

p. 112 *ayah*: an Indian servant, a nanny, nurse-maid, house-maid, or lady's maid.

p. 113 *kismet*: destiny or fate; one's portion or lot.

p. 113 *Bond Street suits*: Bond Street, in London's W1 district, was and is home to some of London's most fashionable and expensive 'haute couture' shops, including many Royal Warrant holders (suppliers to the Royal family).

p. 115 *mésalliance*: an unsuitable marriage, often to one of a lower social rank, but here to one of a different race.

p. 116 *The wife being spiritually higher than her husband . . .*: see p. 150 *And woman stands. . . .*

p. 117 *half-breed, which Nature herself is said to abhor*: ancient wisdom has it that 'Nature abhors a vacuum' (which phrase appears on p. 131).

p. 118   *Kazi*: a civil judge (in Moslem law) with the power to conduct marriages. The proverb is used by Rudyard Kipling as an epigraph to his story 'Miss Youghal's Sais' (1887).

p. 119   *Roman taking of veil*: as in Roman Catholic; to become a nun.

CHAPTER THIRTEEN

p. 121   *'Take each man's censure, but reserve thy judgment'*: the words are spoken by Polonius in *Hamlet*, 1.3.69; William Shakespeare (1564–1616), English dramatist and poet; (censure = opinion).

p. 122   *pumps*: light shoes.

p. 122   *I'd give a hostage to fortune*: see Francis Bacon (1561–1626), *Essays* (1597–1625), 'Of Marriage and Single Life': 'He that hath wife and children hath given hostages to fortune; for they are impediments to great enterprises, either of virtue or mischief.'

p. 123   *burnt-offering*: a sacrifice offered to a deity by burning; here, total submission.

p. 125   *'A Daniel come to judgment!'*: the words are spoken by Shylock in the trial scene in Shakespeare's *The Merchant of Venice*, 4.1.220.

p. 126   *Park Lane*: Park Lane, which runs between Marble Arch and Hyde Park Corner on the eastern side of Hyde Park, was and is one of the most prestigious addresses in London's 'West End'.

p. 127   *Oxford shoes*: a style of low-heeled shoe laced over the instep.

p. 127   *Zenana schools*: or Zenana missions, took (often Christian missionary) education to women in the zenanas (see p. 8 *zenana*). The work was necessarily conducted by women.

p. 128   *Cagnes, La Tourelle, Gorge du Loup*: Cagnes, situated on the coast between the Cap d'Antibes and Nice, was made famous by such painters as Cezanne, Renoir, and Modigliani; La Tourelle is inland of Cagnes on the route to the Gorge du Loup.

CHAPTER FOURTEEN

p. 129   *We are children of splendour and flame . . .*: (Sir) William Watson (1858–1935), English poet. The lines are from the poem 'Ode to May' (lines 37–8).

p. 129   *Dantesque*: resembling the work of the Italian poet Dante Aligheri (1265–1321); sublime, austere.

p. 129   *Grand Corniche*: or high road that links the mountain villages of the Côte d'Azur, was built by Napoleon.

p. 129   *the world, the flesh, and the devil*: from the Litany, or General Supplication, contained in the *Book of Common Prayer* of the Church of England: 'From fornication, and all other deadly sins;

and from all the deceits of the world, the flesh, and the devil, *Good Lord, deliver us.*'

p. 129 *orris-root and patchouli*: the fried root of the Iris, smelling of violets and used in perfumery; a perfume derived from the dried branches of a labiate shrub.

p. 130 *Faites vos jeux, messieurs, Faites vos jeux!*: (French) the croupiers call to place bets; 'Make your bets, gentlemen, Make your bets!'

p. 130 *the fool who said in his heart 'There is no God'*: Psalms 14:1. The King James Bible reads: 'The fool hath said in his heart, There is no God. They are corrupt, they have done abominable works, there is none that doeth good.' See also Psalms 53:1. The King James Bible reads: 'The fool hath said in his heart, There is no God. Corrupt are they, and have done abominable iniquity: there is none that doeth good.'

p. 130 *Hotel de Paris*: one of the grand hotels of the era, built in 1864, and situated in the Place du Casino in the centre of Monte Carlo.

p. 130 *gendarmerie*: (French) here a police station; also the French police force.

p. 130 *chocolat and patisserie*: (French) hot chocolate and pastry or fancy cake.

p. 131 *Pension*: (French) a boarding-house.

p. 131 *déjeuner*: (French) lunch.

p. 133 *Ultima Thule*: the extreme limit, their northernmost destination.

p. 133 *Grasse*: in the Alpes-Maritimes Department inland from Cannes. Grasse is the perfume centre of France.

p. 133 *Valescure*: inland from the Cap Esterel.

CHAPTER FIFTEEN

p. 134 *O king, thy kingdom who from thee can wrest?* . . .: the closing lines from 'Dammayante to Nala in the Hour of Exile,' lines 24–8, published in *The Golden Threshold* (London 1896; Hyderabad 1905); Sarojini Naidu, see p. 14 *The new hath come. . . .*

p. 136 *Gospel of John*: the last and most spiritual of the four Gospels (Matthew, Mark, Luke, John).

p. 136 *St. Paul's dissertations on wifely submission and womanly modesty*: see 1 Corinthians 7 and 1 Corinthians 11.

p. 136 *Sarasvati, Goddess of Wisdom*: and goddess of the arts (literature, poetry, song, music); she also takes the form of Vak, the goddess of eloquence. Her husband is Brahma the Creator.

p. 136 *Sita, the ideal woman of Hindu legend, and heroine of India's great Epic the Ramayana*: an incarnation of the goddess Lakshmi, the pure and faithful Sita is a model for all Indian women. Her story is told in the *Ramayana*, a poem of about 50,000 lines, composed by Valmiki, probably in the third century. It is divided into seven books, each dealing with an episode in the life of Rama, son of King Dasharatha, and his brothers Lakshmana, Bharata and Shatrughana.

p. 136   *India's two great Epics*: Mahabharata and Ramayana.

p. 136   *Sita Dévi*: Sita, see p. 136 *Sita* . . .; Devi, the word for a goddess.

p. 137   *house of cards*: cards built up into a house or castle, hence a flimsy or precarious structure or scheme.

p. 144   *Lake Como*: in Italy's Lombardy region, north of Milan.

p. 144   *Cadenabbia*: a hamlet on the shore of Lake Como.

BOOK TWO: THE BLOSSOMING

CHAPTER ONE

p. 149   *And now my cheek is warm against thy cheek . . .*: unidentified.

p. 149   *the well-grate with its plain oak mantel*: invented in the late nineteenth century a 'well-grate' is a type of fire that burns on the hearth, with combustion being aided by an air-chamber below; the mantel is a shelf or other ornamental structure above and around the fireplace.

p. 149   *a Punjab phulkari*: a flower embroidered cloth.

p. 149   *the sacred three—Rama, Sita, and the devoted Lakshman—setting out, in 'coats of bark,' for their fourteen years of banishment*: see the second book of the *Ramayana*, the Ayodhya Kanda, or Book of Ayodhya. On the eve of Rama's coronation as Yuvaraja, his stepmother, Kaikeyi, demanded the two boons King Dasartha had once promised her for saving his life. Her two wishes were that Rama, dressed in deerskin and tree-bark, should spend fourteen years in Dandaka forest, and that her son, Bharata, should be crowned instead of Rama. The king, bound by his oath, could not refuse. On hearing of Rama's fate, first Sita, his wife, then his brother, Lakshman, insist on accompanying him. See also Lilamani's account in the novel, p. 163ff.

p. 149   *lotahs*: small, traditionally brass, pots used for holding drinking water.

p. 149   *There is no likeness of Him whose name is great glory. Deathless they become who, in heart and mind, know him as heart-dwelling*: from the *Upanishads*, which have dominated Indian philosophy, religion and life for over 3000 years. See *The Principal*

Upanisads, ed. S. Radhakrishnan (New Delhi: HarperCollins India, pp. 736–7).

p. 149   *Bhagavad Gita*: or *Gita* is 'The Song of God,' and is part of the great epic, *Mahabharata*. The poem (with 606 verses arranged into 18 cantos), which recounts a dialogue between the great warrior Arjuna, and his charioteer, the divine Krishna, takes place on the battlefield of Kurukshetra. Krishna's advice to Arjuna, who is reluctant to begin a battle that will pit his Pandava camp against their cousins in the Kaurava camp, and result in slaughter on a massive scale, is that he must do his duty as a warrior. Krishna goes on to discuss the problems of dharma or right action.

p. 150   *a Paquin 'creation'*: a dress designed and made by Paquin. The House of Paquin was founded in Paris in 1891 by Monsieur and Madame Insidore Paquin. Madame Paquin is considered to be the first major female couturier. She went on to open establishments in London, Madrid and Buenos Aires.

p. 150   *bewrayed*: a conscious archaism; exposed.

p. 150   *He that is greatest among you let him be your servant*: Matthew 23:11. The King James Bible reads: 'But he that is greatest among you shall be your servant.'

p. 150   *And woman stands . . .*: the duties and position of a Hindu wife are set out in the *Laws of Manu*.

p. 150   *the talent he bade her hide under a bushel*: a reference to the parable of the talents; see Matthew 25:14–30.

p. 151   *pillau*: a dish of boiled rice, usually with meat, fish or fowl, and spices and raisins. Popular with Anglo-Indians.

p. 151   *chupattis*: small, flat, thin cakes of unleavened bread.

p. 153   *sevenfold circling of the sacred fire*: the Hindu equivalent of Christian wedding vows.

p. 153   *Milan*: the principal city of Italy's central, northern Lombardy region.

p. 154   *choga*: a long-sleeved garment worn by Afghans.

p. 154   *Como*: the principal town on Lake Como.

p. 154   *Shiva or his sacred bull*: (or Siva) one of the three great gods brought together in the Hindu triad: Brahma, Vishnu, and Shiva. Shiva personifies both the destructive and creative forces of the universe. His sacred bull is Nandi, a symbol of dharma and the guardian of all four-footed animals.

p. 154   *Tremezzo*: a town on the shore of Lake Como.

p. 155   *'Light of Asia'*: *'or the Great Renunciation'* (1879), a poem by
Sir Edwin Arnold (1832–1904) depicting the life of Gautama
Buddha.

p. 155   *the great Prince's 'pleasure-home'*: 'Prince Siddartha's pleasure-
home' in Book 4 of Arnold's *Light of Asia*; the home of the
Prince before his enlightenment.

p. 156   *fondants*: sweetmeats common in France.

p. 157   *My heart, my heart is like a singing-bird . . .*: from 'A Birthday'
(1861), lines 1–8, by Christina Rossetti (1830–1894), English
poet and younger sister of Dante Gabriel Rossetti

CHAPTER TWO

p. 160   *My heart in me was held at restless rest, . . .*: from Swinburne's
Tristram of Lyonesse, Part Six, 'Joyous Gard.'

p. 161   *vesta*: a wax-stemmed, or a short-stemmed wooden match, named
after the Roman goddess of hearth and household.

p. 164   *hideous giantess, sister of Ravan*: the Rakshasi, Surpahakha.

p. 164   *That Terrible*: Ravan, or Ravana.

p. 164   *Brahman*: or Brahma, the Creator, the Supreme Being, the first
of the Hindu triad: Brahma, Vishnu, Shiva.

p. 165   *Hanuman*: commander-in-chief of the monkey people. The son
of Pavana, a wind god, he is of divine origin and has superhuman powers; he is a faithful servant to Rama in his war against
Ravana.

p. 165   *Asoka garden*: a park near Ravana's palace in the kingdom of
Lanka.

p. 166   *Universal witness, Fire, . . .*: the ritual of fire, where Sita proves
to Rama that she is without sin, is found in the Yuddha Kanda,
also known as the Lanka Kanda or the Book of War. The longest
and most popular book of the *Ramayana*, the Yuddha Kanda
records the defeat of Ravana, the recovery of Sita, the return to
Ayodhya and the coronation of Rama.

p. 166   *Lord of Fire*: Agni.

p. 167   *Uttra Kanda*: (Uttara Kanda) the least of the seven sections of
Valmiki's *Ramayana*. Uttara means later or subsequent, and the
events narrated here are those which follow the coronation of
Rama and Sita, the happy moment where many versions of the
epic end. In the Uttara Kanda Rama abandons the pregnant Sita,
who descends into the embrace of Mother Earth.

CHAPTER THREE

p. 169   *Oh laisse frapper à la porte . . .*: (French) Emile Verhaeren (1855–
1916), poet, dramatist, and leading Belgian symbolist; the lines

are from the poem 'Oh! laisse frapper à la porte.' The lines should read:

> Oh ! laisse frapper à la porte
> La main qui passe avec ses doigts futiles;
> Notre heure est si unique, et le reste qu'importe;
> Le reste avec ses doigt futiles.
>   . . .
> L'instant est si rare de lumière première,
> Dans notre coeur, au fond de nous;

An approximate translation would be:

> Oh! let knock on the door,
> The hand which passes with its futile fingers;
> Our hour is so unique, and the rest which imports;
> The rest with its futile finger.
>   . . .
> It's a special moment, of first light,
> In our hearts, in our souls

p. 169 *Buon riposo*: (Italian) rest well.

p. 170 *sole genie of his lamp*: probably a reference to the story of 'Aladdin and his Magic Lamp' in *The Arabian Nights*.

p. 171 *a stone of stumbling*: a stumbling block; see Romans 11:9. The King James Bible reads: 'And David saith, Let their table be made a snare, and a trap, and a stumbling block, and a recompence unto them.'

p. 174 *My love is like a red, red rose . . .*: from 'My Love is like a Red Red Rose' (1794) by the Scottish poet Robert Burns (1759–1796).

CHAPTER FOUR

p. 176 *Oh, I would be to thee . . .*: quotation unidentified; Stephen Phillips (1864–1915), English poet and actor.

p. 176 *the Dolomites*: a mountain region marked by stark mountains and cliffs now in North Italy. Until the Second World War it was part of the South Tirolia region of Austria.

p. 177 *Inglese*: (Italian) English.

p. 177 *exigeant*: exacting.

p. 177 *Vishnu the Preserver*: as the preserver, Vishnu is one of the three great gods brought together in the Hindu triad: Brahma, Vishnu, and Shiva. His avatars include Rama and Krishna.

p. 177 *the Baby-God Krishna*: the eighth incarnation of Vishnu, the modern deity Krishna is perhaps the most popular of all the deities in Hindu mythology.

p. 177 *holland coat*: a coat made of Holland cloth, a linen fabric.

p. 179   *your zeal for the honour of our house*: see John 2:17. The King James Bible reads: 'And his disciples remembered that it was written, The zeal of thine house hath eaten me up.'

CHAPTER FIVE

p. 186   *Her strength with weakness is overlaid, . . .*: from 'A Helpmeet for Him,' by Christina Rossetti. Diver mistakenly gives the source of this epigraph as '"True Woman"—C. Rossetti'. 'True Woman' is actually a sequence of three sonnets composed by Dante Gabriel Rossetti.

p. 186   *guerdon*: archaism, reward or recompense.

p. 189   *though that there Miss Juliet was a 'taking piece, and pretty much up to the balcony-trick'*: a reference to Shakespeare's *Romeo and Juliet*.

p. 189   *British Bass*: a pale ale brewed in England since 1777; pale ales brewed for the Indian Empire were known as India Pale Ale (IPA).

p. 189   *scholard*: a variant spelling of scholar.

p. 190   *moving like Agag*: walking like a cat.

p. 191   *Lucerne*: situated on the Ruess River at the north-western end of Lake Lucerne in Switzerland.

CHAPTER SIX

p. 193   *Life struck sharp on death makes awful lightning*: the text is from *Aurora Leigh* (1857), an 11,000-line life-story of a woman writer, described by Browning as a 'novel in verse'; Elizabeth Barrett Browning (1806–1861), English poet and wife of Robert Browning.

p. 193   *Cherton*: not a real location; within the novel, Cherton and Bramleigh Beeches are probably in Surrey.

p. 193   *a fly*: a light vehicle on hire, drawn by a horse.

p. 193   *brougham*: a one-horse closed carriage, with two or four wheels, intended to carry two or four persons, named after Lord Brougham (1778–1868).

p. 193   *landau and the greys*: a four-wheeled horse-drawn carriage with a folding top, here pulled by a team of grey-coated horses.

p. 194   *a dozen sightless windows*: the closed curtains signal that there has been a death in the family. In Victorian Britain curtains were closed, clocks stopped and all mirrors in the house covered during the period of mourning. Family members and also servants in the house wore black clothes, and black-edged paper and envelopes were used for all correspondence.

p. 197   *'dirty shekels'*: a slang term for money; shekels were the unit of currency used by the ancient Hebrews.

p. 200   *Dust thou art——*: Genesis 3:19. The King James Bible reads: 'In the sweat of thy face shalt thou eat bread, till thou return unto the ground; for out of it wast thou taken: for dust thou art, and unto dust shalt thou return.'

CHAPTER SEVEN

p. 201   *A man's foes shall be they of his own household*: Matthew 10:36.

p. 202   *Home Counties*: the counties nearest to London: Surrey, Kent, Essex, and formerly Middlesex; sometimes with the addition of Hertfordshire, Buckinghamshire, Berkshire, and occasionally Sussex.

p. 205   *pince-nez*: a pair of glasses with a spring which clips over the nose.

p. 205   *a goodly heritage*: the phrase appears twice in the King James Bible (Jeremiah 3:19; Psalms 16:6).

p. 206   *Romanists*: Roman Catholics.

CHAPTER EIGHT

p. 213   *in two little rooms my heart divides, . . .*: quotation unidentified; Heinrich Heine (1797–1856), German poet. Though Maud Diver attributes the passage to Heine, it is not characteristic of his work.

p. 213   *Lugano*: situated on Lake Ceresio, it is the most important town in Southern Switzerland, providing a bridge between Mediterranean Europe and Northern Europe.

p. 214   *the Alpha and Omega*: the first and last letters of the Greek alphabet; the phrase means 'the beginning and the end', and was originally applied to God.

p. 215   *Menaggio*: situated on the western shore of Lake Como at the point where the road bordering the western shore of the lake and the road leading through the Val Menaggio to Lugano in Switzerland meet.

p. 219   *Abbey*: Westminster Abbey; started in about 1045 by King Edward I, it houses the tombs of monarchs, and has been the setting for every coronation since 1066. Neither a cathedral nor a parish church, Westminster Abbey is a 'royal peculiar' under the jurisdiction of a Dean and Chapter, subject only to the Sovereign.

p. 219   *a stately Largo by Beethoven*: a Largo is slow piece of music; Beethoven (1770–1827), the German composer.

CHAPTER NINE

p. 222   *Naught is done that has not seeds in it*: quotation unidentified; Morley Roberts (1857–1942), minor novelist and man of letters.

p. 222   *myrmidons*: in Greek mythology, a tribe of warriors that accompanied Achilles to Troy; a member of a band of ruffians under a daring leader.

p. 223   *Brindisi*: a natural port on Italy's south east coast, centrally located in the Mediterranean and close to the ports of the Middle East and North Africa.

p. 223   *Goupil Gallery*: the Goupil Gallery had branches in several countries, selling paintings, engravings and reproductions throughout the world.

p. 223   *Cairo*: situated on the banks of the River Nile, it is the largest city in the Middle East and Africa and lies at the centre of all routes leading to and from the continents of Asia, Africa and Europe.

BOOK THREE: THE FRUIT

CHAPTER ONE

p. 233   *Whom does love concern beyond the beloved and the lover? . . .*: E.M. Forster (1879–1970), English novelist. The lines are from *Howard's End* (1910), the opening paragraph of Chapter 20. The passage correctly reads 'Whom does Love concern beyond the beloved and the lover? Yet his impact deluges a hundred shores.'

p. 233   *cheval glass*: a full-length mirror swung on a frame.

p. 237   *land-agent*: a steward or manager of landed property.

p. 237   *bags, coverts, and meets*: bags, the contents of a game-bag, i.e. the quantity of game killed during a single outing; coverts, places of concealment for the shooters; meets, gatherings, in this case shooting-parties.

p. 237   *'Not at Home'*: the arrangement signalling that one is not prepared to receive callers (see p. 300 *At Home*).

p. 237   *shibboleth*: a word used as a test for detecting foreigners.

p. 237   *Vedantic times*: contemporary with the *Vedas*. The *Vedas*, which represent the first stage of Hindu mythology as we know it today, were composed in the second millennium BC.

p. 238   *goleshes*: usually galoshes or goloshes; over-shoes, usually made of rubber, worn to protect ordinary shoes from wet or dirt.

p. 242   *the morsel of ice at her heart*: a reference to 'The Snow Queen,' a fairy tale by the Danish writer Hans Christian Andersen (1805–1875).

p. 243   *regnant*: ruling.

p. 245   *Bayard*: a self-confident fool.

p. 245   *a Chopin polonaise*: a polonaise is the music which accompanies a slow dance of Polish origin, or any music which follows its peculiar triple rhythm; Chopin (1810–1849), the Polish composer and pianist.

CHAPTER TWO

p. 248   *Heaven's own screen . . .*: from 'Herself,' the first of the three 'True Woman' sonnets, sonnet 56 in the 'House of Life' sequence; Dante Gabriel Rossetti (1828–1882), English poet and painter and brother of Christina Rossetti.

p. 249   *'We were boys together'*: the quotation appears to be taken from the opening line of the poem 'We Were Boys Together,' by the American journalist and poet George Pope Morris (1802–1864).

p. 252   *Gunnersbury*: a London district (W3/W4).

p. 252   *St. Leonards*: St Leonards-on-Sea, a seaside town in East Sussex, on England's south coast. St Leonards was a fashionable and popular resort during the Victorian period.

p. 254   *For ever and ever. Amen*: commonly said at the end of a Christian prayer.

p. 255   *R.A.*: initials after a name used to denote a member of the Royal Academy.

p. 257   *Pro tem*: from the Latin *pro tempore*; for the time, temporarily.

CHAPTER THREE

p. 258   *Yet we are one; . . .*: quotation unidentified; Laurence Hope (pseudonym of Adela Florence Nicolson, 1865–1904), Anglo-Indian poet. Married to Colonel Nicolson of the Bengal Army, she poisoned herself after his death.

CHAPTER FOUR

p. 263   *There is a bitter drop in the cup of the best love*: quotation unidentified; although Diver suggests Friedrich Nietzsche (1844–1900), the German philosopher, poet, and classical philologist, is the author of this epigraph, the self-pity that marks the passage is not characteristic.

p. 264   *her novitiate*: the probationary period of a novice before she takes her religious vows.

p. 265   *ling*: a name used in the North of England for various ericaceous plants, now more commonly called heather.

p. 268   *Emigration League*: during the late nineteenth century Emigration Societies (or Leagues) were formed in various parts of the United Kingdom by guilds, charitable organizations, and various religious groups, to assist those wishing to emigrate to the colonies.

p. 269   *fender-stool*: a long footstool, usually positioned near to a fender (a frame placed around a fire to contain falling coals).

p. 271   *Balaam*: a reference to the biblical story of Balaam and his donkey; see Numbers 22. Balaam is amazed when his donkey speaks to him.

CHAPTER FIVE

p. 273   *Weak souls are apt to lose themselves in others, . . .*: quotation unidentified.

p. 275   *High Church*: a section of the Church of England that exalts the authority of the episcopate and priesthood and the saving grace of the sacraments, and the various rituals that distinguish the Church of England from the Calvinistic churches of the Continent, and the Protestant Nonconformist churches in England.

p. 275   *correct genuflexions*: bending the knee in worship in the approved manner.

p. 275   *holy days*: religious festivals.

p. 276   *cried out like Festus, 'Almost thou persuadest me to be a Christian'*: Acts 26: 28. The words are those of King Agrippa, not the nobleman, Festus, as Diver suggests. The King James Bible reads: 'Then Agrippa said unto Paul, Almost thou persuadest me to be a Christian.'

p. 276   *Waterloo Station*: opened in 1848 and known as 'Waterloo Bridge' station until October 1882. Trains for Surrey and Hampshire depart from Waterloo Station.

CHAPTER SIX

p. 280   *Mine ear is full of the murmer of rocking cradles; . . .*: unidentified.

p. 280   *day-nursery*: a nursery where children are cared for during the day as opposed to where they sleep at night.

p. 385   *river Jumna*: (or Yamuna) a river of Northern India which rises in the Himalayas and flows through Fyzabad, Delhi, and Agra, before joining the river Ganges at Allahabad.

CHAPTER SEVEN

p. 288   *Life is stronger than a single soul*: quotation unidentified; Robert Herrick (1591–1674), English poet and clergyman.

p. 295   *'Thy question bewrayeth thee'*: an allusion to Matthew 24:73. The King James Bible reads: 'And after a while came unto him they that stood by, and said to Peter, Surely thou also art one of them; for thy speech bewrayeth thee.'

p. 296   *the Island Pharisee business*: probably an anachronistic reference to *The Island Pharisees* (1904) by John Galsworthy (1867–1933); the book, concerned with an English gentleman who has spent a long period abroad, is a satire on the pharisaical egoism of England's ruling classes.

p. 296   *The Lord our god is a consuming fire*: Deuteronomy 4:24. The King James Bible reads: 'For the LORD thy God is a consuming fire, even a jealous God.'

CHAPTER EIGHT

p. 300   *Love leaps higher with her lambent flame . . .*: the lines are from Elizabeth Barrett Browning's *Aurora Leigh*, and correctly read 'And Love strikes higher with his lambent flame / Than Art can pile the faggots.'

p. 300   *golden calf of the West*: a reference to the story of Moses and the golden calf; see Exodus 32. The golden calf is used proverbially with reference to the 'worship' of wealth.

p. 300   *Grosvenor Square*: bordered by Mayfair and Park Lane in London's fashionable and expensive W1 district.

p. 300   *Leicester Square*: in London's WC2 in the heart of the theatre district.

p. 300   *At Home*: an indication that one is available to receive visitors (see p. 237 *'Not at Home'*). An 'At Home' is generally held in the late afternoon, and is so called because of the invitation which notifies the recipients that the lady (or gentleman) who sends it will be at home on a particular day and time, and would be glad to see them. The phrase is still current, albeit now somewhat dated and ironic.

p. 302   *dight*: archaism, dressed (as in decked).

p. 303   *the locust-eaten years*: probably a reference to the lean years in the story of Joseph and the seven lean years; see Genesis 41. Locust years are years of poverty or hardship.

p. 306   *a hansom*: a light two-wheeled horse-drawn cab with the driver's seat raised behind.

p. 306 *General Orders*: orders issued by the commander-in-chief of the forces.

p. 306 *Homer and his contemporary, Valmiki*: Homer, the author of the early Greek epics *The Iliad* and *The Odyssey*; Valmiki, the poet who composed the epic Sanskrit poem *Ramayana*, probably in the third century AD.

p. 307 *the Carlton*: located in London's central area of Victoria and fashionable Belgravia.

p. 310 *hukm*: [hukum, hookum] an order or command.

p. 311 *Heart and spirit are singing in the air like birds*: an allusion to the opening line of Christina Rossetti's 'A Birthday': 'My heart is like a singing bird.'

p. 311 *the ghostly sisters*: the three Fates; see p. 104 *Spinners of Destiny*.

CHAPTER NINE

p. 312 *O greying of my dawn, . . .*: Fiona McLeod (pseudonym of William Sharp, 1855–1905), Scottish poet and novelist. The lines are from 'Grey and Rose,' in *The Silence of Amor*. Written in 1895, 'The Silence of Amor' was publihsed in *From the Hills of Dream* (1896) and later, separately, in book form in America in 1902. The quoted lines correctly read: 'O greying of my dawn suspiring into rose: O grey veils of dusk that obscure the tender flushing of my rose-lit dawn!'

p. 312 *s.s. Arabia*: built by Caird & Co. of Greenock, and launched in 1897. She entered P&O's India service on 12 March 1898, the last single screw steamer in that service. The Arabia was torpedoed and sank on 6 November 1916, approximately 112 miles (180 km) southwest of Cape Matapan.

p. 313 *Golfe Juan*: on the Cote d'Azur, or French Riviera, between Juan les Pins and Vallauris. It is famous as the place where Napoleon disembarked in order to reconquer France on 1 March 1815 following his escape from Elba, and the point of departure for his march to Paris and the '100 days' before his defeat at Waterloo.

p. 317 *a Lenten Battle of Flowers*: a parade, which takes place during the Lenten carnival, in which ladies on the floats throw flowers to the onlookers, who throw them back. A more famous Battle of Flowers takes place along the Promenade des Anglais in Nice.

CHAPTER TEN

p. 320 *A man's whole victory over Fate begins with a question*: quotation unidentified; Percival Gibbons unidentified.

p. 321 *belladonna*: an alkaloid prepared from the roots and leaves of the deadly nightshade plant; apart from its various medicinal uses, belladonna was also used as a cosmetic by women to dilate their pupils.

p. 322 *scotched, not killed*: an allusion to Shakespeare's *Macbeth*: 'We have scotched the snake, not killed it' (3.2.13).

p. 324 *Le Temps*: French daily newspaper, became *Le Monde* on 19 December 1944.

CHAPTER ELEVEN

p. 330 *O very woman, god at once and child, . . .*: the passage is from Swinburne's *Tristram of Lyonesse*, Part Six, 'Joyous Gard.'

p. 332 '*Oh, that I had the wings—the wings of a dove——!*': Psalms 55:6. The King James Bible reads: 'And I said, Oh that I had wings like a dove! for then would I fly away, and be at rest.'